Praise for Bri…

"A propulsive … minds us of the perils … books, and the duty we all have to stand up for the freedoms we hold dear."

—Kristin Harmel, *New York Times* bestselling author

"This novel is a timely reminder that the burning or banning of books is the first step in an escalating war on freedom of thought and expression that can have devastating consequences. . . . An entertaining and riveting read."

—Kim van Alkemade, *New York Times* bestselling author of *Orphan #8* and *Bachelor Girl*

"In her excellent debut novel, Brianna Labuskes writes lovingly of the power of books, libraries, and friendship to sustain us in difficult times, while also offering a stark, unmistakably relevant warning about the dangers of censorship. Fans of historical fiction featuring courageous women will savor *The Librarian of Burned Books*."

—Jennifer Chiaverini, author of *Resistance Women*

"As Labuskes weaves perspectives together, she not only highlights the pain of censorship, suppression, and dehumanization but also issues a stark reminder that history repeats itself."

—*Booklist* (starred review)

"Terrific research buttresses strong writing that will keep readers riveted."

—*Library Journal*

"A thoroughly engrossing page-turner that proves how powerful words and ideas can be, no matter the era. Filled with intrigue and secrets, this timely novel follows three women from Berlin to Paris to New York City to right past wrongs using books as their weapon of choice."

—Elise Hooper, author of *Angels of the Pacific*

The Lost Book of Bonn

"Equal parts riveting and heart wrenching, this is a story of fighting back, of doing what's right. Brianna Labuskes has done it again with another powerful book about books that historical fiction fans will adore."

—Madeline Martin, *New York Times* bestselling author

"A poignant tale of courage and sacrifice in the face of great evil . . . Both enlightening and heartrending, this book is impossible to put down!"

—Sara Ackerman, *USA Today* bestselling author of *The Codebreaker's Secret*

"Self-righteousness, self-loathing, and self-recrimination surface throughout the narrative, along with dawning self-awareness, forgiveness, and redemption . . . The power of books to connect different people together strongly resonates throughout. Highly recommended."

—*Historical Novel Society*

The BOXCAR LIBRARIAN

ALSO BY BRIANNA LABUSKES

The Lost Book of Bonn

The Librarian of Burned Books

The Lies You Wrote

A Familiar Sight

What Can't Be Seen

See It End

Her Final Words

Black Rock Bay

Girls of Glass

It Ends with Her

The BOXCAR LIBRARIAN

A NOVEL

BRIANNA LABUSKES

wm

WILLIAM MORROW

An Imprint of HarperCollins*Publishers*

This book is a work of fiction. References to real people, events, establishments, organizations, or locales are intended only to provide a sense of authenticity, and are used fictitiously. All other characters, and all incidents and dialogue, are drawn from the author's imagination and are not to be construed as real.

FIRST EDITION

Interior text design by Diahann Sturge-Campbell

Illustration of a Boxcar of a cargo train © patrimonio designs/Stock.Adobe.com

Library of Congress Cataloging-in-Publication Data has been applied for.

ISBN 978-0-06-337630-4
ISBN 978-0-06-342756-3 (simultaneous hardcover edition)

24 25 26 27 28 LBC 5 4 3 2 1

To anyone who has ever called Montana home

Hearts starve as well as bodies:
Give us Bread, but give us Roses

—James Oppenheim,
"Bread and Roses," 1911

The BOXCAR LIBRARIAN

CHAPTER ONE

Millie

Washington, DC
1936

Millie Lang could hear the girls gossiping through the thin walls of the boardinghouse.

They were talking about her.

She tried to tune them out as she used up the last bit of her cherry lipstick. It was a luxury that she shouldn't have splurged on but sometimes when the entire world was dreary and terrible, a pop of red could save the day.

Millie kissed a handkerchief and then smoothed down the fashionable bob she was still getting used to. Desperate for a paycheck, she'd cut off her long, thick braid right after she'd left her ranch in Texas in order to compete for jobs in the city.

It turned out a hairstyle couldn't hide the stink of a life of mucking out stalls and slipping in cow dung.

Not in Dallas—where she'd first landed—and not here in DC, either.

The girls in the room next to hers giggled as if they could hear her thoughts, and Millie shook herself out of her mood.

There were plenty of people in the country who had worse things to deal with right now than snide remarks and cold shoulders. Maybe Millie had naively dreamed of making friends at Mrs. Crenshaw's boardinghouse, but mostly she was just thankful for a roof over her head. Even if said roof leaked with the slightest hint of rain.

Millie beat the other girls to the kitchen, though not the landlady who had likely been there since 5 a.m.

"Good morning," she said softly, always too aware that as a tall Texan, people expected her to boom out greetings and obscenities alike.

Mrs. Crenshaw grunted something approximating a hello in return, and then went back to her behemoth of a stove. Millie tucked into the slice of toast and creamed eggs without any further pleasantries. The widow who ran the boardinghouse was neither welcoming nor rude. Millie was just another boarder in a long string of them that let her keep a roof over her *own* head.

The other girls filled in around Millie, chattering on about their plans for the evening. Never once had they asked Millie if she were free, and she tried not to mind.

They were all luckier than a lot of folks and if she had to keep repeating that every few minutes to get through these mornings, then that was a small price to pay for keeping the right attitude.

When Millie stepped out of the boardinghouse, she turned, as she always did, to try to catch sight of the gleaming white dome of the Capitol. Laundry lines full of undershirts and unmentionables crisscrossed the garden court, blocking the view for now, but the dome was there, a promise that there were people working to try to make Americans' lives easier.

At least, that's what she told herself.

Barefoot, dirt-crusted children of various ages played jacks in front of the house across from Mrs. Crenshaw's, their mother darning clothes on the back porch. Millie hopscotched through the remnants of a board drawn several days ago, wobbling dramatically to make the children laugh and the mother shoot her a wan smile.

They hadn't traded names despite the fact that they saw each other most days. A lot of people simply didn't have space in their lives for one more thing to remember.

Mrs. Crenshaw's was one of dozens of slim brick town houses behind the Capitol. Some of the people who Millie worked with had deemed the area a slum, but Millie had trouble seeing it that way. Of course, the neighborhood smelled of human waste and garbage, beer and vomit, but that was the natural consequence when the privies were in the streets and families were packed into too-small rooms because they couldn't afford anything else.

The people, though, they all helped each other. Maybe Millie didn't know the name of the mother who darned clothes across the courtyard, but if Millie asked her for her last eggs, the woman would give them to her.

She waved toward the old men who'd taken up their daily posts on the stoops just at the edge of the neighborhood before it gave way to federal buildings, and then she had to sidestep the grocer who tried to entice her into buying an apple. It was a dance they did every day—the man knew Millie sent all her extra pennies back home to Texas where her aunt and uncle were still raising six boys through years of devastating dust storms—but it was his way of saying hello and she mostly appreciated it.

Then came the job boards. A large group of loud men jostled for position just ahead of her on the sidewalk, where they waited every day.

Each morning, someone would hang a list of positions that needed to be filled, and anyone who was unemployed in the area lined up for the handful of opportunities. Some people camped out overnight just so they could get the first shot at the job.

There were never enough for everyone who needed the work.

Millie scanned the crowd for a checkered hat, and found it on the outskirts. She hated any day she spotted the thing—it meant Phil likely wouldn't get work that day, because she should be gone by now. But Millie also loved the few minutes she got to talk with the one person she considered a friend in the city.

She bumped an elbow into Phil's side. "A little too much fun last night?"

Phil—or Philomena by birth, though she would never go by that while job-hunting—rolled her eyes. "The boys were sick and Lilly has colic. So, whatever the opposite of too much fun is, that's what we had."

Millie had met Phil in the shared courtyard of their buildings three days after Millie had moved to Washington. They could only ever chat briefly in passing because Phil had three younger siblings she helped provide for by dressing as a man for the better paying jobs. Still, Millie had recognized a rare kindred spirit in her.

"I'm sorry." If Millie had any extra money at all beyond the couple cents she'd used to splurge on that lipstick, she would have gladly handed it over. Instead, all she had to offer was a book. She pulled it out now and watched Phil's entire face brighten.

For Phil, who never let herself splurge on anything including lipstick, one book could make her entire month. Millie always hunted for any that had been discarded at work or in cheap library sales or even on the top of trash bins, though she never mentioned that part. She'd only ever been able to bring a few, but each one had felt like a gift *to* Millie instead of from her.

"*The Secret Garden*," Millie offered.

Phil paged through it. "'Is the Spring coming? What is it like?' 'It is the sun shining on the rain and the rain falling on the sunshine . . .'"

The words tugged at Millie. The past few years had felt like a never-ending winter, and while none of them could truly see the spring yet, there were signs that it might be coming.

"This is for you," Phil said, shoving a newspaper under Millie's arm. Millie knew it would be open to the advertisements for housing because Phil hated the gossiping girls more than Millie did. Millie couldn't afford anything better, not with how she sent most of her paycheck home. It was the least she could do after her aunt June and uncle Matthew had taken her in as a child, but it often meant eating a handful of pickles for lunch and potato soup for dinner, always wondering if she was one emergency away from sleeping beneath someone's overhang instead of in a sometimes-warm bed.

Phil winked at her. "And now it's time to make my own luck."

Then she was gone, ducking under the arms of the larger men pushing and shoving to get closer to the job board.

Millie was still smiling as she caught the streetcar toward the old theater that housed her little department of the Works Progress Administration.

The Federal One Project was the Roosevelt administration's answer of what to do with America's white-collar workers—the artists and actors and authors and historians—who were just as unemployed as the rest of the country. Out of it had been born local theater initiatives, Living Newspapers, murals on post office walls, and best of all, at least in Millie's opinion, the Federal Writers' Project (FWP).

In the beginning, there had been lofty goals that the FWP could spark an American Renaissance in literature. In reality, that simply wasn't a practical way to employ the sheer number of writers who needed relief.

So the American Guide Series—Baedeker-like travel books for each state—was born.

Introducing America to Americans was the tagline used most around the office. So many people were like Millie and had never ventured outside the town in which they grew up. The guides weren't just meant for road trippers, but also for anyone who wanted to learn about the rest of the country in a way they hadn't ever been able to before.

People had ideas about the places they didn't know or understand, and they were all eager to assume the worst rumors they'd heard, especially these days. The guides helped show what it was really like out there, to replace scary shadows with names and faces, landmarks and landscapes.

Their existence—and that of the FWP—also meant Millie had a job. She wasn't sure what would have happened to her without the program.

Aunt June and Uncle Matthew had been so generous to take her in and feed her, but about a week after they'd survived a dust storm so biblically vengeful it was given its own name, Millie had overheard a discussion she probably shouldn't have. June had suggested to Matthew that she should simply walk into the dust-laden wasteland so there would be one less mouth to feed.

Millie had left the next day, headed to Dallas. Looking back seven months later, she couldn't imagine what had given her the courage to do so. If she had to guess, it had probably simply been ignorance of how bad it could be on her own.

Dallas had quickly enlightened her.

She generally thought of herself as resourceful, but she wasn't sure that she would have made it another week in the city if she hadn't seen the Federal Writers' Project advertised on a sign in the window of a shoe store.

The program had seemed too good to be true.

It hadn't taken her long to realize that maybe it was.

But she had a fresh start in DC, and she didn't want to waste it.

The streetcar stopped not far from the Old Auditorium—the

converted theater that was acting as the headquarters for the Federal One Project. Millie took one last gulp of fresh air before she entered the stifling building. DC had been built on a swamp, and the Old Auditorium didn't let them go a day without remembering that.

She was already damp by the time she took her seat on the old stage. Millie was used to heat, but not this air that suffocated a person with each breath.

Discreetly, she dabbed at her forehead, and then she reached for the packet of pages waiting for her on the desk.

What she liked most about her new editorial position at the FWP headquarters was that she got to read travel essays from all the states rather than just Texas. Millie enjoyed the thrill of being transported across the country and then back again on any given day as she searched for misspellings and grammatical errors in the guides.

Today's pages were from Louisiana, a state that was known to be troublesome to edit. Not because of the content, but because the state director was the wife of a friend of a senator and had grand visions of being the hostess of a poets' studio. She had such little interest in the guides, she'd originally forbidden her staff from working on them in hopes they would instead create the next great *Walden*.

The woman might have been removed from the position, but her legacy lived on in the purple prose that was known to slip through into the essays.

Still, Millie always liked working on Louisiana. It had been the state just next door to her own—and it was one she'd never been to or even thought of before.

Curiosity had died in the years after the crash, when survival had been constantly front of mind. But like the spring in *The*

Secret Garden, curiosity was in the air once more. There wasn't quite room for it yet—as Millie had thought just that morning about learning the name of her neighbor. It was slowly returning, though.

And that was important, Millie was beginning to realize. When someone was curious about the world, about both their neighbors and strangers who they shared a country with, it countered the hate that could brew from ignorance and fear.

Also, it was simply fun to learn about so many different people with lives that were so different from her own. Millie had made friends with a maid in Massachusetts, a boxer in Chicago, a fisherman in New Orleans.

As someone who had never had anyone other than family to care about, it was almost exhilarating. The town Millie had grown up in hadn't had any children her age, her cousins were too young to be companions; in Dallas Millie had made a fuss about a too-friendly supervisor and then had been ostracized for doing so; and in DC everyone was too busy to socialize.

Maybe it was a bit sad Millie found connection in these pages that passed over her desk day in and day out, the ones telling stories of people who rode horses in rodeos and rode waves off the coast of California, who skied mountain passes in Denver and performed acrobatics on the wings of airplanes in North Carolina.

But it was more than she'd ever had before.

"If you look at a map you will see that Louisiana resembles a boot with its frayed toe dipping into the Gulf of Mexico."

Millie smiled. You couldn't remove a poet's heart from their body. Or their writing.

She went to make a note in the margins and then cursed when the nib of her pen snapped.

The FWP had to keep their supplies in a closet buried deep in the back of the theater to discourage casual visitors from getting light fingers.

Millie wound her way through the dark hallways of the Old Auditorium, wrinkling her nose at the pungent mildew that grew stronger the deeper she went into the theater.

When she got to the closet, she paused, hand on the knob.

There was someone inside.

She considered knocking—not wanting to startle whoever it was.

But then she heard "No."

It wasn't a calm rebuke or even an angry one.

It was a plea, laced with panic.

Millie yanked open the door.

All she could see was a man's broad back and then high heels and long legs. The man was gripping the woman's thigh tightly and had the other hand pushing her head into the wall.

He shifted then, and Millie caught sight of his profile, recognizing him immediately.

Foxwood Hastings, the son of a powerful senator who was trying to cut all the funding to the Federal Writers' Project.

There was talk that Foxwood would make a play for the White House one day.

The woman's eyes were wide and wet, her mascara smeared on her cheeks.

Millie thought about her boardinghouse, which wasn't perfect, but gave her some semblance of security. She thought about the money she sent back to Texas that meant all six of her cousins could eat that week. She thought about Phil dressed in workman's clothes just on the hope of getting a few bucks that day. She thought about creamed egg on toast and pickles for lunch and that last tiny bit of lipstick that she'd already chewed off on her way over.

She thought of pink slips and job boards, and what would happen if she did exactly what she wanted to do.

Then she did it anyway.

Millie curled her hand into a perfect fist, hauled her arm back, and then let it fly directly into the face of a man who could, unequivocally and completely, ruin her life.

CHAPTER TWO

Alice

Missoula, Montana
1924

Montana was going to kill Alice Monroe.

She'd heard that all her life, so many times that she'd started to believe it.

Alice had been born in a blizzard and had survived because her aunt was used to delivering breeched calves. When she'd been five, Alice had been playing on the banks of the Blackfoot River and slipped. The rapids pulled her under, the water nearly devouring her. A fly fisherman had been in the right place at the right time, and still had nearly been too late.

At twelve, the wildfire smoke from the plains had filled her lungs. Her chest had gone impossibly tight as her lips turned as blue as the glacial ice in the mountains. She didn't know how she'd survived that one, though she'd heard stories of her father scooping her in his arms and running, full speed, through town toward the doctor's house.

Montana had already taken her mother. And no woman Alice knew was stronger than Mary Monroe.

Montana was going to kill Alice one of these days, but not today. Today, Murdoch MacTavish was going to kill her.

"You carried them out?" Mac asked, his voice flat as he stared at the apple crates full of books stacked neatly on the library's steps.

Murdoch MacTavish—Mac to everyone including his mother—was her father's right hand. One time, Alice had asked what Mac's position actually was, and her father had waved as if to encompass everything. In practice, that often meant shadowing Alice to make sure she didn't do more than lift a finger to turn pages in a book.

A lot of his time was also spent smuggling hooch in from Canada. Federal Prohibition might have been passed only four years ago, but Montana had been "dry" since 1918. She had a feeling her father had been thriving in the six years since, especially because she'd yet to meet a person who had trouble finding liquor in Missoula. There were speakeasies and "soda shops" and gentlemen's clubs on every corner.

"You should have waited for me, Miss Monroe," Mac said. His tone was deferential, but his eyes screamed in betrayal. She was making his life so much harder. Her father would blame Mac for allowing Alice's little rebellions, and for that she did feel guilty.

Still, she could carry a couple damn apple crates to the sidewalk.

"I'll certainly let you load them up," Alice said brightly, pretending to wipe at her brow. In the more frustrating moments, she reminded herself that the overprotectiveness instituted by her father, and then carried out by all his various minions, came from a place of love. Despite what the doctors told him, Clark Monroe had become convinced any level of exertion beyond an empty-handed stroll along the Blackfoot was too much for Alice. And she was only allowed that if she promised not to get too close to the water.

Fall in once at five years old and get deemed a slip-risk the rest of your life. At nineteen, the restraints were starting to chafe.

Mac stacked three crates on top of each other and lifted them with hardly a grunt. Alice sighed as his muscles bunched and pressed against his simple white shirt, his golden curls falling over his eyes. The sweat-slicked skin at the nape of his neck glistened and Alice fought the silly urge to press her mouth there to taste the salt.

Alice startled when someone called her name, and she prayed her end-of-summer sun-kissed skin would hide the blush that was inevitably working its way over her cheekbones.

"I found *Treasure Island* just in time," Mrs. Joseph cried in triumph. She was old—one of the original six women who'd founded the Missoula Library out of their ladies' reading group back in 1882—but she moved with the agility of the native Montanan that she was.

"Oh, thank you. Nathaniel will be beside himself." The book was one of their more popular volumes; every boy within town limits had checked it out at least once. Part of Alice balked at the idea of bringing it with her to the mining towns on the outskirts of Missoula, but those children needed a little laughter in their lives, too. Maybe more so than the children in the city.

Mac, loaded down with three more crates, waited for her to put the novel on top, but she shook her head and held on to it. She wanted to hand deliver this one herself.

"I saw you're taking the new Agatha Christie," Mrs. Joseph said. "Dawn will appreciate that one."

Alice grinned. *The Secret Adversary* wasn't actually new—it had been published two years earlier in 1922. But for Montana standards the book might as well be fresh off the presses.

Mrs. Joseph was right, too. Dawn Chatham, a young bride from New York with an innocent face and a macabre imagination, had become enamored with Mrs. Christie's work after reading the author's debut, *The Mysterious Affair at Styles.*

As she did with most of the books the library ordered, Alice had read *The Secret Adversary* before shelving it, and the dedication had hit her in the chest.

"To all those who lead monotonous lives in the hope that they may experience at second hand the delights and dangers of adventure."

The sentiment felt mean, a little cutting, even, given that Mrs. Christie herself experienced plenty of thrills and delights. Yet Alice's world had reshaped itself around the notion. Alice could imagine the same was true for many of Mrs. Christie's readers, Dawn Chatham included.

Life in the mining towns surrounding Missoula was difficult, at best. Montana wasn't going to kill those residents because they were too tough, but the land certainly did try. The settlements were made up mostly of men, especially the more rudimentary camps deep in the northern woods. But there were a few that hosted wives and children, too.

As one of Missoula's three librarians, Alice tried to bring a little secondhand delight and adventure to all of them when she could.

"Don't you worry about closing up tonight," Mrs. Joseph said, her expression mischievous, her eyes darting between Mac and Alice.

"We won't be any later than usual, God and roads willing." Alice was fairly certain her infatuation with Mac was the worst-kept secret in Missoula and had been since she was a girl. Her father had hired Mac when the boy was just fourteen and had employed him for the past six years as a secretary, an enforcer, a driver and everything in between. When Alice had come up with the idea of delivering library books to the mining camps surrounding Missoula, he'd become her chauffeur, as well.

Alice both lived for and dreaded the two days a month they made the trips. She got to spend time with him, but was also painfully reminded that he would never view her as anything but the fragile daughter of the employer he worshipped.

Mac pulled away from the curb and started down Higgins Avenue, and Alice waved to several people out and about doing their shopping. As the mayor's daughter and one of the town's librarians, she recognized most of the city's residents even if she didn't know all their names. Community was important out here. Even though Missoulians on the whole had fairly comfortable lifestyles, they never took for granted that they lived at the mercy of nature. Isolation was death in the Western territories.

After Mac took the road that ran along the Blackfoot River, he nodded to the book in her lap.

"Is that a special one?" he asked, in that lilting way of his that was such a contrast to his big frame. His parents were from Scotland, like so many others who'd settled in Missoula. He didn't have their accent, but that magical cadence had been baked into his speech patterns. She could listen to him talk for hours, though he was, unfortunately, a man of few words.

Alice smiled down at the novel, her fingers tracing the title. "This one is for Nathaniel Davey. He finished *The Wonderful Wizard of Oz* a little while back and was so disappointed when I didn't have anything as fun on our last trip."

"I haven't read it either," Mac admitted, like it was a confession.

"Well, you can't read this one now," she teased, tapping *Treasure Island.* "It will be on loan for the next month."

"What about the other one?" he asked. "The one with the wizard?"

"You would like it," Alice promised. "It's all about courage and heart and finding your way home. It's one of our most popular books, though, so you'll likely have to wait your turn if you want to check it out."

"Is it a children's book?"

Alice didn't rush to reassure him it wasn't. He was proud, like so many of her neighbors. That trait had been the hardest thing to overcome as a librarian. Not acquiring books, not the social work expected of her, not even smiling at patrons who didn't deserve to be smiled at. No, it was chipping through that pride, which too often kept people from checking books out at all for fear they wouldn't understand them.

"They're written in a way that's accessible for children, but that any age group can appreciate," she said. "The best children's books are the ones that trust young readers with big ideas. And those will resonate with us, even when we're past the point of thinking we need to be taught lessons."

"What kind of big ideas?" he asked.

She swallowed. "Love."

His brows rose and she rushed to continue. "Familial love. Friendship, a sense of self and finding a place in the world."

"Your father gave me that, you know," he said. "A place in the world."

Alice's stomach clenched. Her father would forever be the third person in the space between them. No matter how much Alice sometimes daydreamed about throwing caution to the wind and climbing into Mac's lap—right there, in the Ford—that fact stopped her. Even if a miracle occurred, and it turned out Mac would actually welcome the weight of her on his thighs, Alice would wonder if it was just as a favor to her father. Or if Mac thought it was the obvious step to marry into the family so he could be the son her father had really wanted.

She hummed some noncommittal sound and returned her attention to the river. They were deep in the dog days of August. Winter awaited them, but it was hard to imagine now with how the heat baked the earth.

Even though the summer weather could be uncomfortable in

its own right, Alice liked to store up the sun when she could so she had an excess to help her get through the dark, cold days that were to come.

They pulled away from the Blackfoot eventually, and began the long climb toward the largest mining town within driving distance. The roads were rough and rutted, and when it rained or snowed they became nearly impossible to navigate. But at least they existed.

Alice loved the moment they crested the top of the hill and Garnet came into view. The town had been built in a valley and so was cradled by the side of the mountain. The main street, boasting a mercantile, a hotel, three saloons, a blacksmith, and other shops, wound its way toward them.

In truth, Garnet was a ghost of the town it once had been during the gold rush days of the last century. The earth went bare, a fire razed half the buildings, people fled. But Garnet still stood. For her, it had become a symbol of resilience.

The children—currently numbering ten—had learned to recognize the sound of the automobile engine. They probably came running for any visitor, but Alice liked to think they were especially excited for the haul she brought with her.

She didn't like to credit the penny candy Mac made sure to stock up on for their enthusiasm. It was the books the children liked most, no one could convince her otherwise.

They gathered around the Ford now, greedy and grubby hands banging on the doors as Mac drifted to a stop. He hollered at them to move, but there was a fondness to his smile that the children could spot. Boys and girls who grew up in towns like this learned early to recognize real anger when they saw it.

Alice laughed as she greeted them, and toppled slightly when one of the younger boys hugged her around her knees. Mac's hand steadied her immediately, his palm hot against her lower back. She shifted away. No matter what the men in her life thought, she wasn't actually made of glass.

The chaos eventually subsided, the children knowing by now they couldn't just rush in and grab for the books. They formed a polite line behind the Ford as Mac opened the trunk.

Idly, Alice scanned the heads, and realized one was missing. She lifted her attention to some of the adults who'd gathered around, hanging back for now, but nearly as eager as their young ones.

She found Nathaniel's mother, Jane, easily.

"Is Nathaniel all right?" Alice asked after they'd exchanged greetings. Nathaniel was Jane's oldest boy, but he was also the oldest of all the children in Garnet. As such, he often wore the serious expression of someone wise beyond his years, his shoulders heavy with too much responsibility.

Since the age of the children in Garnet skewed so young—and they were all forced to attend class together with the one teacher—Nathaniel had lost interest in school. He said he didn't need it, he said as soon as he was old enough he'd find work with a mining company. And that would be far too soon. Alice had ached for him as she all but watched the raw and pure joy of childhood in his eyes dimmed by the realities of this life.

So Nathaniel had become her secret project.

Alice knew better than to try to argue with him outright. But the trip following that conversation, she'd brought him a special book, one that only older boys could read. One he didn't have to share with the little children.

The Call of the Wild had yet to fail her.

"He's pouting," Jane said now on a sigh, one of her babies hanging off her skirt, thumb in his mouth. "We're leaving."

"Oh." Alice wanted to say *You can't.* She had been making headway with Nathaniel. But, of course, that would have been a ludicrous reaction. Instead, she asked, "To where?"

"Toward Butte," Jane said. "Nowhere as fancy as the city, but in that direction."

"Oh," Alice said again, off-kilter. Families came and went in towns like these. She'd seen plenty of that in the two years since she'd started coming out here. But she had a feeling Nathaniel would put his next book down and then never pick one up again if there wasn't someone in his life encouraging him to read. "Is he here?"

Jane jerked her head toward the trees. "Too stubborn, like his father."

Impulsively, Alice hugged Jane. "Good luck."

"Thank you, Miss Monroe," Jane said. "We don't say it enough."

Alice shook her head. This was part of her duty as a librarian, she didn't need gratitude. "It's my pleasure."

Mac was still handing out the books, making sure to keep track of who borrowed what. The adults were swooping in now that the children had been satisfied. Dawn was already sitting on the ground with her Agatha Christie cracked open, not even able to wait to get back to her cabin.

Alice smiled at the group, and then made her way toward the trees.

"I hear you're going on an adventure," Alice said when she found Nathaniel.

"Screw the adventure," Nathaniel all but spat. Maybe she should chide him for his language, but that would be a silly hill to die on.

"Would Buck say 'screw the adventure'?" Alice asked, knowing how much Nathaniel had loved the main dog character in *The Call of the Wild*. "Or Dorothy?"

"Buck wouldn't say anything, he's a dog," Nathaniel said, a little slyly. And that's why he was one of her favorites. "And Dorothy was trying to get home, not trying to find an adventure."

"Sometimes the adventure finds us," Alice said. "And along the way you might find your home."

Nathaniel pursed his lips. He was too polite to roll his eyes, but she knew he wanted to. Instead, he stared at the ground, and whispered, "I don't think they'll have any books there."

Oh.

"Well, you'll have this one," Alice said, holding out *Treasure Island*, now more glad than ever that Mrs. Joseph had been able to find it in the returns pile.

Nathaniel's eyes flew from the novel to her face, then back again, like he was hungry for the gift but knew too much about disappointment to get his hopes up. "I won't be able to return it."

"It's yours now." Alice would replace the library copy with a new one, of course. She couldn't do it as often as she liked—her father realized that she would spend his vast fortune on books if he let her—but she could get away with buying one or two every once in a while.

"I don't have to share?" he asked, finally taking it. He met her eyes, his own wide and wondrous. "It's mine?"

Alice loved and hated how much joy it gave him, because it was such a small gesture. She thought of a passage from the next book she had been planning on bringing him—*The Adventures of Huckleberry Finn.*

"It was only a little thing to do, and no trouble; and it's the little things that smooths people's roads the most."

"You don't have to share," she promised him. "Though you might want to when you make friends in your new town."

"Thank you," he said, his attention locked on the gift. Alice hugged him, lingering for just a second longer than she would have otherwise. She wondered what would become of him. Of course, he probably would end up in the mines, especially in Butte. Alice shivered at the thought. She had talked to miners before, and they all wore the haunted expression of those who went deeper into the land than any one man should.

She just hoped that for Nathaniel, the stories would accompany him into the darkness, that they would offer him escape when he needed it most.

An old library book was a small price to pay for that.

Alice couldn't shake the grim mood that settled over her as Mac drove to the two other mining towns that were close to Missoula. By the time they were headed back home, it was all she could think about.

"You have something on your mind," Mac said, a comment more than a question. That was one of her favorite things about the quiet man—he opened the door but never shoved anyone through.

"It was only a little thing to do, and no trouble . . ."

"These books mean so much to them," Alice said. The sun had settled in around the tops of the trees, painting everything golden. Not even the dust kicked up from the dry road could detract from the beauty of the land she adored and feared and claimed as her own no matter what.

"You're doing a good thing, Miss Monroe," Mac said, as if she'd been fishing for compliments.

She shrugged it off, along with the use of her surname. Alice had conceded that was a battle she was never going to win. "But we only help the three settlements around Missoula. There are so many more people out there who don't have any kind of relief from . . ." She trailed off.

Alice knew she was lucky to have been born into her family. That even when she complained about long winters and wildfire smoke and the fact that any kind of rare book took years to arrive in Missoula, she was insulated from the sharpest edges of living out here. Mac hadn't been—at least not until he'd turned fourteen. She had no interest in insulting his childhood.

But he just nodded and said quietly, "I would have loved the books, too."

That ache slipped into her chest again.

"I just wish there was more that I could do," Alice said.

"It's not your responsibility, though. Other towns could help out the same way we do," Mac offered. But they both knew Alice was unique. Most people didn't have access to their father's car and their father's bodyguard. She kept up steady correspondence with the librarians in Butte and Helena, both of whom had explicitly told her they didn't have the resources to expand their borrowing system to the logging and mining camps.

"They can't," she said, and he glanced at her.

"You're scheming," he said, a smile in his voice even though it didn't make it into his expression. He knew her so well. In fact, he was probably the best friend she ever had. And she wanted him to kiss her. And she resented him in many ways. It was a strange relationship. "I can't drive you all over the state every day of the week, Miss Monroe."

"No, of course not, that wouldn't be efficient," she answered absently. If she wanted to make a real difference in Montanans' lives, it would have to be on a larger scale than one librarian driving around in a beat-up Ford. She'd read about buses-turned-bookmobiles traveling to isolated places, but even that didn't seem like enough to accomplish what she wanted.

Alice came back to herself when Mac laughed—such a rare sound that it felt like a gift every time she provoked it.

"Yes, that's the problem with that plan," Mac murmured. "Efficiency."

You would do it if I asked, Alice thought helplessly. Then she corrected herself. *You would do it if my father asked.*

"Maybe the problem is that you would get very bored of me very quickly," she said.

He glanced over at her long enough that he steered into a rut, jolting them both slightly. "I think that would be impossible, Miss Monroe."

As much as the sentiment warmed her, Alice almost wished he wouldn't say things like that. It gave her hope that she shouldn't be allowed to have.

"You'll come up with something," Mac continued with an intensity that drew her eyes back to him. He looked so convinced of that simple fact. "You always do."

She couldn't think of anything she had done that would have warranted that conviction.

Alice had led a sheltered life. She'd only become a librarian because she loved books and would have died of boredom otherwise, not because she needed the work. She couldn't keep Nathanial from the mines; she would have been terrified to run for state or federal office like Congresswoman Rankin had done; she wasn't even sure she would have been able to live like Dawn and Jane, out there in the towns, raising their families away from most creature comforts.

She hated being treated like glass, but what had she done in her life to convince anyone that she was made of tougher stuff?

This, a voice whispered. Whatever *this* turned out to be.

Maybe she couldn't be as strong as the people who lived out in those towns, but she could certainly help make their lives easier.

Of course, it was a little thing to do, but sometimes those little things mattered the most.

THE TRAIN WHISTLE woke Alice.

Everyone who had been born in Missoula learned to sleep through it when they were babies and that carried into adulthood.

But when Alice was at her most worried, or most thoughtful, or most restless, it always seemed to cut through her dreams. As if it knew she wanted company—or perhaps it was the train that wanted someone to notice it.

The steel monster roared along the north side of town, heading west, chasing the night as dawn stalked along behind it.

Alice crept out of bed and then down the hallway toward the bench that sat beneath a large window overlooking the Clark Fork River. She tucked herself into the corner, pulling her knees up to her chest and wrapping her arms around her legs. The glass was cool against her forehead as she stared down at the dark water, the current catching and swirling the moonlight to its satisfaction.

She sat there thinking about books and mining camps and children who wore the grim resignation of adults until the whistle cut through the night once more.

Alice straightened.

The train's voice was no more than a feeble cry now, but that didn't matter.

She could hear the idea that it carried as clear as a shout.

CHAPTER THREE

Colette

Hell Raisin' Gulch, Montana
1914

Colette Durand was taught to love stories by her father. He didn't look like he would cherish books above any other earthly possession. Claude Durand was a miner, assigned by birth and poor circumstance. They lived in the West, so he pulled copper from the earth. They lived in Montana, so he did so for the Anaconda Copper Mining Company.

When Colette had been little she'd thought him a giant, with shoulders made for sitting and hands that could tear metal from rock. Small children cried when they came upon him unexpectedly, something that had made him more upset than he'd admit to anyone but Colette. Men eyed him with a combination of jealousy and admiration, while women brought him dinner that Colette ate only when forced.

No one who saw him trudging home from a sixteen-hour shift underground would guess he could recite most of Shakespeare's plays from memory; no one who saw him bathed in the red-gold light of a union-led firebombing would guess he'd passed on his reverence of storytelling to the feral little daughter who seemed to run free in their ramshackle mining town.

No one other than Colette knew how tedious it could be listening to the Bard's works for the one thousandth time while having to pretend the genius of Mr. Shakespeare was unparalleled.

"Tell me a tale," Colette begged now. She and Papa were headed toward Seeley Lake, a day's ride north of their home in Hell Raisin' Gulch. They went on a camping trip there every summer.

"Our story starts with a shipwreck," Papa said without missing a beat.

Colette groaned. "Not Shakespeare again."

The flies were biting; their lunch stop had been hours ago and the summer heat had yet to break. Sometimes it felt like Colette had spent the entirety of her fourteen years on earth listening to Shakespeare and now she wanted to be entertained, not put to sleep. "He's boring."

"Câlisse," Papa muttered. When he swore, he sometimes slipped back into his native Quebecois. "Blasphemy, child."

That was almost fair. Colette could acknowledge that Shakespeare wasn't boring. But hearing his plays fifteen to twenty times a year *was.*

"If you know it so well, you tell it," Papa commanded.

Colette thought about fighting him. But Papa had a hard life. He had lost his son only a few years earlier to an accident in the mines, and his wife several years before that to tuberculosis.

After Henri had died—in an accident that had come about due to negligence rather than happenstance—Papa had thrown himself into organizing the workers in Hell Raisin' Gulch into a semblance of a union. That wasn't easy in Montana, not when the Company owned everything, including Papa.

Colette had known who was king around these parts since the moment she'd understood power.

And that moment had come three days after her eleventh birthday.

That had been the first time the men had shown up at their tiny house—the one Papa was forced to rent from the Company.

The men had come at night and they'd left Papa bleeding on the kitchen floor. They hadn't broken any bones because a troublesome worker was still a worker. But he'd been left bruised and battered all over.

Plenty of the miners had stopped listening to Papa after that. Mothers started crossing the street with their children when they saw Colette and Papa walking around town. The Company had made their point. They hadn't even had to go after every worker who talked about unionizing.

They'd just had to go after the right one.

Papa hadn't stopped then and now, three years later, he'd rebuilt up a following—even if it was a quieter one than in times past.

His message wasn't a hard sell. He wanted safety measures installed in the mines, he wanted fair wages that aligned with the profits reaped by the Company, he wanted to put a stop to the predatory practices that kept workers shackled to one place for life.

But the men he was trying to get to march into battle beside him were beaten down and dependent on their bosses. The lives of their families were at stake, and it was difficult to ask them to risk it all to stand up to the dragon.

So, Papa had a hard life.

Colette could have bickered with him about Shakespeare until Papa chose another tale to tell. He'd memorized plenty—he liked to keep his fellow workers entertained in the mines when he could.

She wanted to make one thing easy for Papa, though.

"The story doesn't start with a shipwreck, it starts at the duke's palace," Colette said, because even though he liked to tell it a certain way, that was not how the play had been written.

"Oh, my apologies, Monsieur Shakespeare," Papa said grandly. "Do go on."

And so for the rest of the ride to Seeley Lake, Colette recited the plot to *The Twelfth Night*, while Papa interjected with quotes that he had memorized long ago.

"Am I telling the story or are you?" Colette asked laughing as they started to set up camp. They didn't stay on the banks of Seeley, but rather had found a small pond just to the west of it where they had yet to see another human soul.

There were Indians in the woods, Colette knew. Papa always reminded her that the two of them were sleeping on ground that belonged to the tribes not too long ago.

In Colette's limited experience, white people out here mostly acted two ways about the Indians. They either thought an attack was coming at any second, to the point of hysteria, or they thought of the Indians as a relic of a bygone era.

Papa, who loved nature, Washington Irving, and also good stories, turned them into tragic romantic figures who spoke only in poetic stanzas and, inexplicably, Quebecois.

Everyone should speak Quebecois, Papa had said grumpily when she asked why the warrior in his story had just said "tabarnak."

Colette didn't know enough about the world to know where she or the Indians fit into it, but she thought probably none of the white men around her were right. Even Mr. Irving, one of the best-known defenders of the tribes.

"Why do you love Shakespeare so much?" Colette asked when they were settled with their fishing poles. It was early evening in summer, and the sky stayed bluebell blue well past dinnertime.

Papa plucked at his lower lip as he did when he was deep in thought, and she realized only then that she had never asked him that before.

"You can't love language and not love Shakespeare," Papa said. "All that glitters isn't gold; and all the world's a stage; brevity is the soul of wit; and you should always wear your heart on your sleeve."

It sounded like a poem, yet Colette knew it wasn't. "Those are all from different plays."

"But they're all phrases created by the Bard," Papa said. He slid her a look. "Do you truly find him boring?"

"No," she said, a little sheepishly. "I like listening to them more than I like reading them, though."

"They're meant to be watched and heard," Papa said, before pausing. He didn't speak again for a few minutes, but that was Papa. He tried not to talk carelessly. Ever. "Do you know what I like most?"

"What?"

"He wrote them for the common people," Papa said. "He was born during the plague. Do you remember what that was?"

Colette rolled her eyes at the impromptu history test. "A lot of England died."

Papa boomed out a laugh. "Well, that's not untrue. He wrote many of his plays as his countrymen died around him. His theater closed, his son died. It wasn't an easy life that he had. Yet he wrote on, and he wrote on for the commoners."

"Like us?" Colette asked.

"Like us," Papa said, swiping his big bear paw over her head. "And those commoners, they got to watch his plays, plays they understood, ones that they could laugh at and jeer at. They were used to taking punches and instead for a few hours got to be in on the joke. They got to forget for just a little while that people they loved had died, that they didn't know where their next meal was coming from."

She looked around at the lake, and thought about all they were escaping. It wasn't just the men who came at night or the

Company, which sent them after Papa in the first place. It was sixteen-hour shifts in yawning darkness, it was then getting a paycheck that was in the negative anyway. It was hoping your children could escape and also knowing they wouldn't. It was coal-blackened skin in the winter and smoke-coated lungs in the summer.

People deserved to have an existence made up of more than their worst moments. They deserved to laugh and jeer and have fun. Because what was life otherwise?

Colette sucked in a breath. She could give Papa so little. But she could give him this. "Our play starts in Athens."

"'Though she be but little, she is fierce,'" Papa murmured without missing a beat.

"Am I telling it or you?" Colette asked, with fake sternness. Papa waved his hand to get her to go ahead, and she grinned. "Enter Theseus . . ."

CHAPTER FOUR

Millie

Washington, DC
1936

Millie shook out her stinging hand. She'd broken bones before and didn't think she had this time—a good thing considering she'd surely be handed a pink slip once Foxwood Hastings stopped trying to collect the blood pouring from his nose.

The nose Millie had so efficiently realigned.

Millie considered simply making a run for it. The Old Auditorium's hallways would inevitably trip up a visitor who wasn't familiar with the layout. Hastings couldn't have gotten a good look at his attacker—what were the chances he'd be able to pick her out of a lineup?

But before Millie could decide what to do, the click of heels interrupted their frozen tableau.

"What's all this, then?" Katherine Kellock asked, and Millie stopped worrying about job boards and started worrying about the police. Katherine was one of the highest-ranking executives within the Federal Writers' Project, and one of the highest-ranking women within *any* of Roosevelt's New Deal programs.

She was not one to tolerate any foolishness in the department that she oversaw.

Millie silently cursed a blue streak, words she hadn't even

realized she'd picked up from ranch hands ricocheting against the inside of her skull.

She couldn't go crawling back to Texas. She couldn't be the one extra mouth to feed that sent her aunt walking out into the nothingness.

What was more, her family had started to rely on the money she was sending home every month. Her cousins' bellies were no longer swollen with hunger.

And she'd risked not only her own life but theirs when she'd made a fist.

Katherine's lips pinched as she took in the sight of the three of them. She was brilliant and brutal, exacting and clever. It took only a fraction of the intelligence she possessed to understand what had transpired. "Mr. Hastings, we expect any visitor to show every respect to our liaisons as they would to President Roosevelt himself."

Hastings wasn't listening. Instead he'd spent the time in which Katherine had assessed the situation to go from dazed pain to pure rage. "My father—"

Whatever Hastings Junior was going to say about the powerful Senator Hastings was cut off when a short, bald man hurried up to their little group.

"Ah, good. Mr. Rogers, could you help Miss Weber call herself a cab home for the day?" Katherine waved toward the secretary, who had lost all the color in her face. Then Katherine turned to Millie. "Miss Lang, if you could wait for me in my office? And Mr. Hastings, please, I will see you out myself. You can tell me about that new bill your father just introduced to cut all our funding."

For one moment, Millie thought Hastings would demand to watch her get fired—or arrested. But Katherine took his arm, and steered him away with the grace and fortitude of a general directing her troops.

Millie stared at their retreating backs and wondered if she'd been given a respite or a reprieve.

Knowing her luck, it was the former. Maybe she could get Katherine to reassign her, just like with what had happened in Dallas.

But how many times were people like her given three chances to start over?

She blinked back against the tears that threatened to spill over.

Millie hated to cry. Her cousins had always teased her mercilessly anytime she'd shown weakness, and she hadn't been able to complain to Aunt June, who wore her stoicism like a badge of honor.

If any situation deserved tears, though, it was this one.

"Thank you," the secretary whispered, breaking through the frenzied whirring of Millie's mind.

And Millie was reminded that, no, there were other situations that deserved tears far more than her own.

This wasn't the secretary's fault, and even now with a stomach clenched into an impossible knot of dread, Millie couldn't regret punching that man who'd pinned this woman to the wall so viciously. "You're welcome."

The secretary gave her a small smile, and then hurried off behind Mr. Rogers.

Millie, meanwhile, headed toward where she knew Katherine's office was, picking her way around some old props and costume chests as she made her way there. The walls inside were decorated with the Works Progress Administration propaganda posters that were so ubiquitous these days, their You Can Do It slogans splashed over colorful cutouts of faceless people toiling over farmland and roads and fire towers.

But the ones behind Katherine's desk all featured the Federal One Project and its various iterations.

They were similar to the ones that had caught Millie's attention back in Dallas. She hadn't eaten anything beyond a handful of peanuts in three days—she'd thought she might be seeing things.

A project just for writers?

She'd heard about the murals, though. How the government was sending artists to towns across the country to paint on buildings. Uncle Matthew had grumbled about it, and her aunt had reminded him that ranchers were helped by the New Deal and didn't artists have to eat, too?

Millie had needed to eat. And she'd always been good at reading.

So, she'd walked into the WPA office and applied, even though her cheeks had been bright red with the mortification of calling herself a writer.

As she waited for Katherine, she tried not to think about those days before she'd been hired. They didn't make much money in this position despite what naysayers like Senator Hastings said, but it was enough that she didn't have to live in a broken-down automobile in a shantytown at the edge of the city.

"Well, Miss Lang, you've had an adventurous afternoon," Katherine Kellock said as she swooped into the office, her arms loaded down with files. Katherine was not only the well-respected tours editor of the guides, she was also the one who'd come up with the idea of producing such volumes in the first place.

She eyed Millie sternly now. "That was a very foolish thing you did back there."

Millie's chin went up, and she realized only then how ready she was to fight. Not Katherine, but the world.

"The method not the motive, Miss Lang," Katherine said, settling into her chair. "Mr. Hastings is calling for your head on a pike as we speak."

"Are you going to give it to him?" Millie dared to ask.

"Not quite," Katherine said. "You know we're a constant target for Roosevelt's congressional enemies, though, and Senator Hastings seems to be leading the charge there. This certainly won't help."

The FWP—and the Federal One Project as a whole—was often deemed frivolous by anti–New Deal Republicans and the conservative press. Bringing any sort of negative attention to the programs was the last thing she wanted to do.

"I know," she said, and it came out meek. It was why she was expecting to be told to pack her things and leave. And she wouldn't blame Katherine for doing so.

"Do you know what I did before I became the tours editor?" Katherine asked.

Millie searched for a way the question could be a trap and couldn't find anything. "You visited field offices across the country."

The American Guide Series had set up branches in nearly every county in the United States, which was how the project could employ so many writers. Katherine, as one of the masterminds of the guides, had played a crucial role in those first few months of getting them all up and running.

"I did indeed," Katherine said, before tossing Millie a file with neat lettering across the front.

Missoula, Montana.

"I need a new editor for the Missoula branch of the Montana guide."

Millie tried to force the words to make sense and couldn't. Part of her had hoped Katherine would reassign her, but she had thought that a foolish impossibility. "What?"

"I have been hearing good things about your work, and I think you're the right person for the job," Katherine said.

Millie stared at the folder. “But I don’t know anything about Montana. I’m from Texas.”

The beauty of the American Guides was that they were written by people who knew the state the best—from its warts to its soul, from the tourist spots to the places only locals visited.

Katherine Kellock did not suffer fools and now she was looking at Millie like she was the biggest one around. “How did Texas work out for you, dear?”

The answer, of course, was not well. After turning down her supervisor’s advances, she had been deemed a *hellcat*, unfit for work by said supervisor.

Less than a week later, Millie had been reassigned to Washington, DC, a common tactic to hide the troublemakers in the FWP.

And then, apparently, if they caused trouble again, they were shipped to Montana.

“Miss Lang,” Katherine said softly, seriously, as if Millie hadn’t fully grasped just how much trouble she was in. “It’s this or a pink slip.”

Millie swallowed against the sudden pressure in her throat. She didn’t want to make any baseless accusations, but all she could think was that this was Katherine setting her up to fail, all the while taking an entire field office with her.

That thought stopped her, and she glanced up to study Katherine’s face.

These guides were going to be Katherine Kellock’s legacy. She clearly wanted to save Millie’s hide, but she wouldn’t do so at the expense of her pride and joy. So why would she risk entrusting an entire branch to an employee who already had two strikes against her?

“You’re not telling me something,” Millie realized, her big mouth moving before her common sense could even get its pants on.

This was her problem—well, one of them. Millie was too curious for her own good. She was always prying when she should just sit down and be quiet. It drove most people in her life mad, but Katherine didn't get angry. Instead, she looked pleased with Millie.

"There's something strange happening in Missoula," Katherine said carefully. "At the first deadline, the staff submitted a box of blank interview forms to the editor in Helena, along with some essays that were apparently incomprehensible."

That *was* strange. The FWP existed to help writers survive the hard times, but the only requirement for getting into the program was to swear the pauper's oath that declared oneself destitute. That meant the range of talent at each branch varied wildly. There were novelists who would certainly go on to be remembered as the voice of their generation; there were poets and playwrights; laid-off lifelong journalists; and even hobbyists who actually had a knack for storytelling. For each of those gems, though, there were the archaeologists who had no other options; the academics and accountants; the clerks who might know how to work a typewriter and the schoolteachers who probably didn't.

In practice, that meant everyone at FWP headquarters had realistic expectations about the quality of writing that would be turned in. For the essays to be deemed incomprehensible, they would have to be actual gibberish.

"Did the staff have an explanation?" Millie asked.

"That there must have been a mix-up in Helena," Katherine said, sounding a bit exasperated at that. "Everyone on the Missoula staff has sworn that they sent extensive interviews and high-quality essays."

"You don't believe them?"

"Mr. Joseph Sutter is the editor in Helena. He's a professor at the University of Montana," Katherine said. "And he is convincingly livid about the whole affair and wants everyone at the Missoula office dismissed."

"Over one missed deadline?" There was exacting and then there was unreasonable.

"He has high standards, to be sure."

Millie tried to read between the lines. "You want to give the Missoula staff another chance?"

"It's a small staff and I've met with most of them in person, in my previous position," Katherine said. "I don't know what happened, but I don't believe they simply shirked their duties."

That was a generous assessment from someone who was all the way across the country from the situation. But she wouldn't have expected anything less from Katherine, who'd so championed the idea of introducing Americans to their neighbors in the first place.

"Which is why I want to send someone I trust to give me a fair evaluation of what is happening," Katherine continued. "I want someone on the ground, I'm tired of hearing from both sides over the telephone."

"You . . ." The word came out a squeak and Millie tried again. "You trust me?"

Millie could hardly believe that. Katherine was the most polished, intelligent, and well-traveled woman Millie had ever met in her life. She could have picked anyone to do this, and here she was giving Millie a chance because she . . . believed in her?

"That was an impressive demonstration downstairs," Katherine said. "Hastings wants his pound of flesh of course, which means we have to hide you until this storm blows over."

"Of course," Millie repeated weakly.

"It also means you're the perfect person for this position."

"You need someone to go around punching the staff?" Millie guessed, only half joking.

Katherine laughed. "No, I need someone with a little fire who can withstand political pressure."

That was not what Millie had been expecting. They were talking about Missoula, Montana, not Washington, DC. "Political pressure?"

Katherine drummed her fingers on the desk. "There's a chance you'll get to the office and find it full of a bunch of people who were up against a tight deadline and were so overwhelmed that they sent blank interview forms in the hopes of buying themselves time. You might even find a staff who was hoping they could twiddle their thumbs and blame their lack of progress on a mishap."

"You don't think that's what's happening," Millie said, and Katherine shook her head.

"A handful of very rich men known as the Copper Kings own everything in Montana," Katherine said. "Everything. Including the politicians and newspapers and churches. You name it. I'm curious about potential"—she paused, searching for the right word—"machinations."

"Machinations," Millie drawled, duly impressed by the gravity of the situation. In Texas, oil had been king, so she wasn't exactly unfamiliar with the concept.

"I'm curious," Katherine said, again delicately, "if perhaps these gentlemen hired someone to make sure nothing was written about them in the guides that would hurt their reputations."

Millie leaned forward, both nervous and intrigued. "You think this was sabotage?"

Katherine kept her expression carefully neutral at the word, even though Millie had thrown it out between them like a grenade.

"I think that's far more likely than incompetence from what I know of the staff," Katherine said.

Millie wondered if she was biting off more than she could chew.

"And Millie? I can hold Sutter off through one more deadline," Katherine said. "But if the staff doesn't produce something usable by then, we'll have no choice but to get rid of everyone." She paused, and then just in case the stakes hadn't been clear, added, "That would include you."

Millie nodded. "Of course."

Her choice might be Montana or a pink slip, but in the Depression, there really was no choice at all.

CHAPTER FIVE

Alice

Missoula, Montana
1924

Trains," Alice said as she entered the breakfast room the morning after her epiphany.

Mayor Clark Monroe barely looked up from his papers. "Hmm."

Clark Monroe had been named after the river that ran through town. Missoula was in his blood, and he'd devoted his life to the city. But he hated Montana, blaming the state for taking his wife far too early. Once upon a time, he'd thought about heading to the East Coast, but the doctors had said the fresh, open air in the West would do Alice wonders.

That was all Clark Monroe had needed to hear. If there was any chance that a move could trigger Alice's asthma, Clark would veto it.

It was one decision that epitomized a lifetime with her father—he was fanatical about her safety yet he didn't much care about who she was or what she loved.

"If the Rutherford Mining Company agrees to it, I could repurpose one of their boxcars as a library." Alice had been turning the idea over all night as she stared at her ceiling unable to go back to sleep. The solution was perfect.

The Copper Kings who all but owned Montana had long ago built a network of rails to serve their logging and mining camps.

Why try to reinvent the wheel when those men had already figured out a way to connect all the isolated towns scattered between Missoula and Butte?

She would need the approval from their local mine owner, Mr. Logan Rutherford, along with some financial help outfitting the boxcar into a library. But, all in all, it seemed like a simple, elegant solution to a desperate need.

"Hmm," her father hummed again. She should have known better than to bring up the topic when he was already deep in the papers. He was preoccupied with the political maneuverings in the state to the point of obsession.

Now that she thought about it, it was probably best he didn't know anything about her plans. Sometimes people in Missoula assumed that she had her father's support in whatever she was doing for reasons that were unclear to her. But who was she to correct them?

At the end of the day, it was better to ask forgiveness than permission.

"I'm off, have a lovely day, Father," she said, pushing away from the table.

He glanced up briefly, looking a tad suspicious that she had cut off a conversation midway through, but also looking like he didn't care enough to figure out what she was plotting. She knew his ways well—he'd probably heard "library," which meant whatever she was up to couldn't be all that dangerous. He was Missoula's mayor, but he also had his fingers in many of the businesses, banks, and illegal activities that ran through the town. Clark was a busy man. He didn't have time to worry about frivolous matters.

"Trains, it's just genius," she praised herself as she skipped down the steps of the porch. The streetcar was set to arrive at any minute, but Alice wanted the walk.

She regretted it immediately when a sleek green Packard turned the corner in front of her. For a brief moment, she considered slinking back into the shadows to hide. In the end, she refused to let Sidney Walker dictate her actions.

"Miss Monroe, you're out and about early," Sidney called, slowing to a crawl so he could keep time beside her. His thick, dark hair was pushed back as if someone had run a hand through it recently—and she guessed it hadn't been his own. Not with the way his shirt was scandalously draped open, revealing a patch of hair on his chest that drew her attention against her better judgment. His eyes were hooded from lack of sleep and it didn't quite take much intelligence to guess where he'd been.

Once upon a time, Sidney Walker had been Missoula's golden boy, the heir to the Walker fortune, a Harvard man set to take over his father's business.

Then he'd left to fight the Great War.

If it had been anyone else, Alice would have said that was what had changed him. But he didn't act like other soldiers Alice had encountered, the ones who were hollowed-out versions of themselves even now, six years after the fighting had ended.

Sidney Walker didn't have ghosts in his eyes. He had simply gone the way of many wealthy young men who had the world at their fingertips. Where once he'd only been a touch spoiled, now he was rotten.

"And I assume you're out and about *late*?"

"Of course." He smirked, leaning his forearm on the open window as he kept pace beside her. "Would you like to hear about it?"

"Would you like to hear about my morning?" Alice snapped.

"God, no. Unless you'd like to come tell me about it in bed. I'll be asleep in seconds with your help."

Alice blushed, though the heat in her cheeks wasn't just embarrassment. Sidney Walker was good at pushing everyone's buttons, and she hated it. She hated it most because she had never been able to come up with any retorts that were as clever as the ones he delivered so effortlessly.

"It's time to move along, Mr. Walker." The voice startled both Alice and Sidney, though Alice shouldn't have been surprised by this particular knight riding in on horseback.

Sidney stared at Mac for a moment, looking like he was going to refuse. Why, Alice didn't know. It wasn't as if he *liked* talking to her. He was simply being pesky because he could and he knew she flustered easily.

Sidney met her eyes. "Don't you ever get tired of that?"

Then the Packard's engine roared and in the next breath, Sidney was gone, tearing down the empty streets toward the bed he'd taunted her with.

Alice gritted her teeth, annoyed that her morning had been derailed by both of these men. And annoyed that Sidney had a point, even though she would never admit it. "You didn't have to do that. I can handle him."

Mac was staring at the cloud of dust Sidney had left in his wake. "You shouldn't have to."

"Well, he's gone now, so . . . goodbye," Alice said, overloud. A demand instead of a pleasantry.

Mac finally looked down at her, his eyes crinkled in amusement at her attempts to dismiss him.

"Does he bother you often?" he asked.

Alice rolled her eyes and started toward Mr. Rutherford's office once more. She had a Boxcar Library to create, she didn't have time for Mac's overprotectiveness. "You would know if he did."

It came out bitter, but Mac was used to that.

It was also the truth. Sidney Walker wouldn't hesitate to tease her if she ended up in his path somehow—they attended the same events every now and then—but he didn't seek her out. She'd been a mere girl when he'd left for the war. When he'd come back, she'd taken pains to avoid that caustic attitude and sharp tongue, and he'd let her.

She'd overheard more than one conversation where he'd called her a stick-in-the-mud, and she'd spoken loudly enough on a handful of occasions to make it clear she believed him a no-good cad.

Missoula might be small, but they certainly kept different enough hours to manage seeing each other only once or twice every few months.

Mac relaxed at her reminder that he knew far too much about her life, which only irritated her more.

Alice supposed it was a good way to go into this particular day—ready for a fight.

"Don't you have more important things to do with your time?" Alice asked when he fell into step beside her, wishing the world was slightly shifted to the left. If only Mac wanted to walk with her on a pretty summer morning because he wanted her company, she would have been thrilled at his presence.

"Your father says you're scheming," Mac said.

"Oh, figured that out, did he?" Alice asked. Even though she was still annoyed, she let her arm brush against Mac's, enjoying the brief moment of contact for the false gold it was.

"Is this about the books for the logging towns?" he asked, sounding far more fond than stern.

"Yes, you can run back and tell my father I'm in no sort of trouble at all."

"That sentence was more complicated than it needed to be," Mac said slowly. "Which usually means you're trying to pull one over on me."

She was reminded that she could never get anything by him—he'd been her best friend for half of her life now. It was why it wasn't fair to hoist her own romantic aspirations onto him.

"You know my wicked ways so well, Murdoch MacTavish," Alice said with a teasing wink.

He burned bright red. "Not well enough to read your mind. Go on, tell me what you're planning."

Alice was too excited to play games. "Imagine this, Mac. A Boxcar Library."

His brows shot up. "On the mining trains?"

She grinned at his tone. He was impressed.

The trains that connected the camps were often used to transport lumber to the mines to be used as support beams as the workers dug deep into the earth. Most of the train was set up to carry those logs, but they always had extra cars for the conductor and crew, a kitchen and its chef, and a few passenger cars to move men between camps as needed. Hooking up an extra passenger-type boxcar would be about as difficult and onerous as blinking. "Yes, exactly."

Mac stopped, and it took her a second to realize. He was just standing there, staring at her, his mouth slightly agape. The early morning light caught the burnished gold in his hair, making him look almost cherubic. If baby angels could be hulking giants of men. She loved the contrast—his sweet face that made her love him; his body that made her want to touch and explore and do other wanton things that her father would murder her for even thinking.

"What?" Alice asked, touching her own hair in an absent, self-conscious gesture. She knew she looked fine, as she had dressed for respectability so people would take her plan seriously today.

In terms of looks, Alice had never thought she was anything to write home about. She had a passably pretty, sweetheart face that had been a gift from her mother; while she'd gotten her dark brown hair and hazel eyes from her father. Her pale skin burned like the rest of the Scots and Scandinavians who had settled in Missoula. When growing up, she'd been teased for being shaped like a boy, and had long ago given up the notion that she was a late bloomer. There was no way that Mac had suddenly been rendered mute, struck so by her beauty.

Mac shook himself out of whatever had caught him off guard. "You are brilliant. You could take over for your father, you know."

Alice wrinkled her nose. "Not that I would want to."

Clark Monroe engaged in enough dubious business practices that Alice often had to reconcile how much she loved him with how much she worried he was bound for eternal damnation.

That didn't even begin to cover his involvement in politics. He'd likely put some state lawmakers into seats they didn't deserve simply because they would play nice with him. Any destruction they wrought in those positions could be traced back to her father.

Alice had no desire to carry on that legacy.

She turned and started walking once more. "I do appreciate what he does for the town, don't misunderstand me. But if you don't get killed by bootleggers or the government men, it will be a miracle."

Mac's lips twitched. "I'm sure I have no idea what you're talking about."

"Sure, and neither does Sal," Alice drawled, dropping the name of the man who ran Missoula's most popular speakeasy. If it could even be called that—everyone knew where it was and you didn't even need a special password to get in.

"What do you have to get done to make this happen?" Mac asked, avoiding the topic. She didn't think Mac liked the unsavory aspects of his position, but he did them just as he would do anything her father asked. He viewed Mayor Monroe as his savior, as the best man he knew, even.

It was their biggest point of disagreement, ironically enough.

"I need to set up a book drive," Alice said.

They would require hundreds of books if they really wanted to make this project beneficial to the miners and lumberjacks. She would be able to convince her father to contribute as his charity effort for the month, but that probably wouldn't cover it all. Some of the books could be redistributed from the Missoula Library's catalog. But Alice had no interest in depleting resources that were already stretched thin.

What they needed to do was appeal to the community. There were plenty of people in Missoula who had overflowing bookshelves. They would be happy to donate if Alice framed it in the right light.

If Alice held a drive, though, it would be considered a town event—and anything like that had to get the unofficial nod of approval from Julia Walker, Sidney's mother and the self-proclaimed matron of Missoula's social scene. The rule was unwritten, of course, but without Julia's buy-in, the drive would be doomed from the start.

"So, you'll be talking to Mrs. Walker," Mac said.

"Yes, she's second on my list," Alice confirmed, pleased he'd followed along.

"Who's first?"

Alice stopped and waved to the sign above their heads. "Mr. Rutherford."

"You're not going to Anaconda?"

The Anaconda Copper Mining Company—known all across the state simply as the Company—had more resources, more trains, more camps. But the Company had a death grip on Montana and its people. They picked politicians who voted on legislation that would benefit big businesses and hurt workers; they owned the newspapers so that none of their misdeeds made it into headlines; they paid preachers to extol the virtues of tireless work; they viciously squashed any efforts by their workers to better their lives; there were even rumors they'd murdered union organizers along the way. They kept their workers in debt, forcing them to purchase their own equipment, to buy goods only in Company stores at marked-up prices and to live in Company houses with exorbitant rent.

While none of the owners had clean hands, Anaconda's were bloody more often than not. Alice wanted to avoid working with them if at all possible.

Mac seemed to read the answer on her face, because he simply nodded. "Is there anything else you need to do?"

"While I'm busy getting ahead of myself, I should hire a librarian," Alice said.

"What are you looking for?"

"I suppose the post should go to a man." Alice wished she could offer the job to a woman, as it was a secure position that would pay decently when taking into consideration that quarters would be included. But she would be nervous sending an unchaperoned lady out to those lumber and mining camps where the men might not have seen a woman in months. "Beyond that, I would want someone who comes in with an open mind."

"I don't think you can put that in the listing," Mac pointed out.

"No, but I'll be able to tell." She had no desire to hire someone who would mock or belittle the workers he was serving. The whole point of the Boxcar Library was to bring relief and entertainment, not lectures on literacy or sermons on what books were appropriate to read.

"Would you like me to place the ad?" Mac asked. He held up his hands when Alice narrowed her eyes, knowing that she didn't appreciate her father—which Mac was by extension—stepping in to solve all her problems. "I want to help. You're doing a good thing, Miss Monroe. That's all."

Pride battled with efficiency until the former whimpered off in defeat. She wanted to get this project moving as soon as possible and that meant delegating. "I would appreciate that, thank you. Perhaps place it in some magazines as well as the newspaper."

Mac saluted. "I would say good luck, but you don't need it."

As she watched him trot back in the direction of the house, her heart sighed and she told it to be quiet.

She didn't have time for love, anyway.

She had a library to build.

CHAPTER SIX

Colette

Butte, Montana
1917

They found notes on the dead miners, desperate letters written to loved ones, some with the acknowledgment that these were their last words. Some with the hope that they'd be rescued.

A total of 168 men perished in the Speculator Mine disaster after a foreman accidentally ignited oil-soaked insulation deep in the bowels of the earth. Most of the workers died from suffocation after the fire burned away all the available underground oxygen.

A few had been saved. Most hadn't.

Colette tried to imagine a worse death and couldn't.

"It could have been us," an angry voice came from the kitchen.

Colette closed her eyes and rested her head against the wall. She was sitting on the stairs, in the shadows so the union men who'd come knocking on their door once the disaster hit the headlines wouldn't see her.

At seventeen, she had the right to be part of these conversations. But just this once she didn't want to interrupt them.

"I know," Papa said, calm and reasonable. Even when everyone around him burned too bright, he kept himself under control. "What do you think I've been trying to do all these years, Jonesy?"

"So we're just going to sit here, our thumbs shoved up our asses?"

"I have a daughter in this house, watch your language," Papa said, his tone going taut for the first time. Colette rolled her eyes. As if Papa hadn't cursed a blue streak just three days ago when he'd hammered his finger instead of the nail. His swears were far prettier than Jonesy's but no less vulgar in intention.

Jonesy grumbled, but she thought there might be an apology in there.

In the meantime, one of the other men chimed in something Colette couldn't hear. There had to be a half dozen miners standing around their kitchen, pretending to be inconspicuous. Any Company man walking by would easily spot this for what it was.

But for once the Anaconda Copper Mining Company probably had other things on their mind than a secret union meeting.

"Frank Little will be there," someone offered.

"That doesn't mean we should go, too," Papa pointed out. Everyone in that room knew Papa wanted to storm the city with as many men as he could muster, but he liked to talk through it rationally and debate the points.

"It means we have the country's eyes on us," one of the men said, which Colette thought was the best point they'd made yet. "It's a moment we can't sit out."

At that, Papa broke. "We'll have a vote. Show of hands: we join the strikers."

Colette guessed every arm went up. That was mostly confirmed when less than ten seconds later, Papa said, "Then we'll leave before the first shift."

Papa had never kept Colette sheltered from his organizing work, so there had been no question about whether she would go with the men to Butte. They arrived a month after the Speculator Mine disaster, three weeks into a general strike that had brought out not just the miners but also most of the tradesmen in the area. The electricians, blacksmiths, and boilermakers all joined in marching the picket line.

Normally, she would best describe Butte as practical. Just like most mining towns were.

There were a few commercial streets, with advertisements plastered all over the brick walls; there were a few mansions reserved for the Copper Kings and their families, who would rather be anywhere but Butte, Montana. The smokestacks loomed over them all, a reminder of the importance and power the Company held in their lives.

Now, though, the city was alive, buzzing. Men were out in force, no longer simply marching like automatons to their shifts.

"Stay close," Papa directed. The handful of men who'd come with them from Gulch nodded, even though the command had been issued to Colette.

Colette barely heard him, her attention caught on a woman standing on a soapbox, addressing a small crowd.

She was dressed in all black with a widow's veil. Her voice was strong, carrying all the way to Colette, who drifted closer.

"'*Tell Margaret I bought the ring. I have it in my pocket here . . .*'

"'*Give Jamie an extra hug tonight from me. I'll be there to do it myself tomorrow, I promise. And you know I never break my promises.*'"

Colette's hand flew to her mouth as she realized what was happening.

The woman was reading the notes, the ones they'd found on the dead miners when they'd finally been able to clear away the rubble.

"'*We're not going to make it, my love. Not everyone here knows that, but we were in the deepest section when the rocks fell. And who cares about a few dozen miners, dying underground. It's what we do every day, isn't it? They'll replace us tomorrow, with machines they wouldn't even have to pretend to pay if they could. No, I'm sorry, I don't want my last words to you to be bitter. I want you to remember me during that first snowstorm we spent together. I told you I loved you and you told me the cold had addled my brain. I said if that's the case, I'm sure glad I live in Montana because I wouldn't want it any other way. Mama liked to say Montana was a slice of heaven, I hope she was right. I hope it's always cold there.*'"

Colette had hated the Company since the moment she'd learned about it, of course. She was a miner's daughter who'd lost her brother to the mines. She knew they were evil, because everyone whispered they were—only a brave few would dare say it out loud, but by the campfire and over a pint, all the miners were in agreement.

But it had been a vague sort of hate, the kind reserved for rivers that flooded and destroyed a year's worth of crops or God when he seemed particularly callous or the world for allowing greedy men to take and take and take.

In this moment, the hatred solidified into something sharp and jagged and tangible.

She didn't even know the name of this miner, and yet she'd go to battle for him right now.

Everyone has their own story. That had been what Papa had told her when she wondered why scabs undermined their fellow workers' efforts. It might have been Papa's way of offering grace to cowards and rats, but it was also true here. The 168 men who'd died down there all had a story, just like Colette had one.

And their stories mattered just as much as the Copper Kings who ruled this state.

This miner was right, he would be replaced easily.

Colette would remember him, though.

She would keep his story.

COLETTE LOST TRACK of Papa. She supposed she shouldn't be surprised. Butte was a madhouse let loose.

Men on horseback tore through town, carrying messages back and forth from the different industries; children only a few years away from the mines themselves abandoned their signs and were playing games in between the legs of their parents; merchants brought their wares directly onto the streets to sell; lookie-loos took bets outside tavern doors; and the workers marched.

Colette might be on her own, but she wasn't alone. She was caught up in the tide of bodies, the furious energy that connected all of them.

She stopped at the sight of a girl about her age standing on a soapbox, holding the crowd's attention easily. The girl was tall and slim as a willow reed and had a booming voice that came with authority she had no right to possess.

"'We hold these truths to be self-evident, that all men are created equal,'" the girl cried out. "'That they are endowed by their Creator with certain unalienable rights, that among these are Life, Liberty and the pursuit of Happiness.'"

The crowd roared its approval. After all, did the Company allow any of those? Their lives were spent working double shifts, eating breakfast and dinner, and sleeping. Their liberty had been taken by the first rental of equipment from the Company and then kept every day with each new debt. Happiness was merely a fleeting concept around here, found in moments but not in an entirely lived life.

Colette was happy, even if it felt childish to think that on a day like this. But she attributed that to Papa, who had given her his dinner whenever they hadn't had enough; who had made sure she knew how to read; had made sure she knew how to hunt if she ever had to feed herself; who had soothed every fear she had with logic and conversation when so many others in his position would have shrugged her off due to sheer exhaustion.

He had also taught her that just because she was lucky enough to lead a mostly happy life that didn't mean she didn't owe it to others to fight to make theirs better.

The girl finished reciting the opening salvo of the Declaration of Independence and was replaced by an older gentleman who warned the crowd to be on the lookout for Pinkerton agents as they were now infamous strikebreakers.

"They can't be all that bad, though, can they?" a young boy next to Colette asked his friend. "They hunt outlaws, don't they? Like Jesse James and Butch Cassidy and even the Sundance Kid. When I grow up I want to be an agent."

The boy's friend rolled his eyes so hard Colette heard it in his voice. "Only you would want to be the agent who caught them instead of wanting to be the outlaws."

The first boy shoved at his friend. The friend shoved back and then a girl a few years younger than Colette grabbed them both by the ears.

"Two things can be true," the girl lectured in the voice of an older sister. "Pinkerton agents are dirty scum strikebreakers and neither of you should want to be outlaws who go out in a hail of bullets with the rest of your friends dead at your feet."

"Better than being a Pinkerton scab," the second boy muttered. They both got an extra shake from the girl who then turned them loose.

Once they ran off into the crowd, the girl met Colette's eyes and shook her head. They shared a smile as the girl muttered, "Brothers."

Colette tried to hold her amused expression but something must have shown in her face because the girl's smile dropped. She reached out and squeezed Colette's arm, looking much older than she really was.

"I'm sorry," was all she said, before she, too, melted back into the press of bodies.

Colette was lucky, she knew. She was lucky.

But her chest ached and it wasn't just from the fleeting memory of Henri. The shared laugh, the quick sympathy, the universal recognition between girls who'd had plenty of experience with silly boys of all ages.

That was what having a friend was like.

She loved Papa, their small family meant everything to her. But growing up in a town like Hell Raisin' Gulch meant she hadn't had much opportunity to make friends. There had always been a few children around her age growing up, but they came and went with the seasons. The children of the families who'd stayed were all a little older or a little younger or all boys when all she really wanted was a girl to talk to.

It was a foolish, unnecessary desire, though, and it couldn't hold a candle to what the families of the miners who'd died in the disaster were going through. So she shook off the thought, checked the town's clock tower, and decided to make her way back to the hotel. Papa might start getting concerned if she stayed out too long.

"Stop him."

Colette didn't even pause to think when she heard the command from behind her. She turned, stuck out her foot, and winced as the weight of a grown man running at full speed met the resistance of her leg.

It was enough to send the man sprawling, and Colette quickly glanced to his pursuers. If they worked for the Company, she'd just inadvertently helped them track down their prey. But the three men looked just like her neighbors, with grimy hands and worn-thin shirts and boots that had clearly seen wear outside an office.

She assessed the man on the ground who was trying and failing to regain his feet. He wore an outfit similar to his pursuers, but it was brand-new, with a few strategic scuffs on his boots.

Not a single speck of dust had settled on him.

A Company spy.

Papa worried about them infiltrating his meetings. It wasn't just men from Gulch who attended, but a wide array of interested parties, including Wobblies representing the radical—in Papa's estimation—Industrial Workers of the World.

By the way Papa spoke of the spies, though, Colette would have thought they'd be smarter than this one appeared.

"Thanks, sweetheart," the pursuers' ringleader said.

She swung around to glare at him—she wasn't anyone's sweetheart. She'd just taken down their man for them—but her thoughts stuttered to a halt when she got a look at him.

He was beautiful, though she doubted he'd like to be described as such. His thick red hair fell over his forehead in a shock of careless curls; his shoulders were wide and his hips narrow and he wore his shirt unbuttoned in a way that made her flush with heat.

His smirk grew as she stared at him with what she was sure was open admiration.

"You saved the day," he said as his compatriots hauled the likely spy to his feet.

The ringleader stepped closer, took her hand and bowed over

it, his eyes locked on hers the whole time. His lips brushed her knuckles.

Something pulled tight in her belly and all she could manage was to blink at him, dumbfounded.

He straightened, winked, and then sauntered off behind the others.

And Colette never even got his name.

THEY STAYED IN Butte for two weeks and Colette never saw the man again.

She saw plenty of other men who came in and out of their hotel room. Everyone was chipping in for the visiting strikers' stay, but there wasn't much to go around, not even in these times when war profits were booming, lining the pockets of all their bosses.

By the end of July, the Gulch miners had run out of funds.

Colette packed slowly, awash with helplessness.

The Company had decided to leave the Metal Mine Workers' Union alone. Instead, it had gone after the allies, the ones who had joined the fight on behalf of the copper miners in hopes the strike would increase worker power across the board. The Company had convinced its peers to acquiesce to most of the demands from the electricians, the blacksmiths, and the boilermakers, leaving the metalworkers isolated, once more a mere human to an unbeatable Goliath.

"Gains are gains," Papa had said, but even he had gritted his teeth at the betrayal. He wouldn't judge those men, it wasn't in his nature.

But it was in Colette's.

She held on to the anger all the way home and in the days that followed.

She tended to it, just as she tended to the stories she'd heard while in Butte, refusing to forget even a single one.

Soft people didn't last in Montana, she'd heard that time and again. She'd liked the soft bits in herself, though. The hope, the optimism, the way she would turn her face up to the sun at the first sign of spring.

The anger was starting to eat away at those soft parts.

The last was swallowed completely one week after they returned from Butte.

Frank Little, a man renowned for his organizing efforts all around the country, had joined the metalworkers in Butte to help bring attention to the cause.

On August 1, he was pulled from his bed, beaten, tied to a car's bumper, and dragged down a road. For the finale, they hanged him from a railroad trestle.

The same could have so easily happened to Papa, and Colette nearly had to excuse herself to go retch in the bushes at the thought.

"How could they do that to someone?" she asked Papa quietly as they both stared at the headline.

For once, Papa didn't have a life lesson or a pithy passage from Shakespeare.

But Colette did.

"'If you prick us do we not bleed? If you poison us do we not die?'" she quoted, thinking of just what she would do if that had been Papa swinging from that railroad trestle. "'If you wrong us, shall we not revenge?'"

CHAPTER SEVEN

Millie

Missoula, Montana
1936

America passed Millie by.

She knew firsthand that the middle of the country had been decimated by dust bowls and poor agricultural techniques—according to the government men who came to lecture them about ranching—but right now all it looked was pretty.

And with each mile they flew closer to Missoula, the knot in Millie's chest pulled tighter.

Millie was no stranger to worry, she didn't think a single person in the country was. But this felt like leaping off a cliff hoping a net would miraculously appear before the ground did.

She would not fail this assignment. She would save the Missoula staff from destitution, she would save her own derriere, and she would show Katherine that her faith had not been misplaced.

A nasty voice in her head that sounded a lot like the girls at the boardinghouse whispered she would crash on the rocks. She was simple and plain and really only good at making breakfast for ranch hands and feeding chickens.

Millie shut that voice down. So what if she was all those things? That didn't mean she couldn't also do this.

What she needed to do here was to be prepared. Millie had been helping edit these guides for nearly a year now, and she knew what went into them. Still, she shuffled through the papers in the folder Katherine had given her, reading each of the detailed briefings carefully so she didn't miss a single thing.

The rules and regulations from Washington were strict. They needed to be because the books in the American Guide Series were all meant to be set up in the same way: general information, notable cities, and then itineraries for tourists.

The first section was the place writers could really stretch their skills.

That was where the essays lived, the ones about each state's history, its culture, its agriculture and industry, its flora and fauna, and its school systems and folklore. They were written by the FWP workers who scoured the state, county by county, knocking on doors and peeking into pubs; crashing breakfasts at diners and picnics at lakes; attending festivals and dances and rodeos and pageants; talking to folks at parades and beauty shops and funeral homes.

All of that was done in service of finding the voices, the voices of the people who made the country what it was. Farmers and ranchers got a spotlight, but so did former slaves and women and migrants and Hollywood starlets and schoolchildren.

They plucked at each thread that created the tapestry of the United States and made sure everyone else could see just how important the individual was to the whole.

When done well, the section could become the heartbeat of the guide, the *America* that was being introduced to Americans.

That was an ideology that did in fact live and breathe beyond the propaganda poster. Mr. Alsberg—the head of the FWP—preached it at every meeting, his speeches becoming all the more urgent in the past month since the Spanish Civil War had started.

They all could see that fascism was a rolling tide that had reached America's shores. The Ku Klux Klan's membership rolls were bursting at the seams; desperate Americans were blaming anyone "with a hard to spell last name" for the fact that they didn't have jobs; and prominent men like Henry Ford routinely spewed hateful anti-Jewish tirades while praising Adolf Hitler's grand ideas.

The American Guide Series was the counterargument to all of that. The FWP showed that a country could be strong because of its diversity, not in spite of it.

The second part of the guide was all logistics—the details it would be difficult to gather, but were essential to making the books successful.

That gave way to the third section. If the essays were the heartbeat, here was the backbone. The tours were what made the guides actual guides.

The routes weren't meant to be just points on a map, either. The best ones that Millie had seen during her time at FWP headquarters had been infused with local color. They talked about haunted houses and ghosts that supposedly wandered over battlefields; they uncovered out-of-the-way swimming holes and that on-the-side-of-the-highway saloon with a guitarist who could melt your bones; they had quirky notes on roadside attractions, like the Teapot Dome Service Station and Lucy the Elephant and the Big Duck and Paul Bunyan statues. Even sofa-cushion travelers could feel like they were actually experiencing the wonders, oddities, and warts of each state.

The last page in her packet was a simple list with only four names.

Sarah Marner
Oscar Dalton
Thomas Lyon
Sidney Walker

One of them might be in the pocket of the Copper Kings. One of them might be doing the dirty work for some politician who didn't want the New Deal to succeed. One of them might just want to cause havoc over some personal vendetta.

But first and foremost, this was Millie's staff.

They were her last chance.

But that also meant that she, apparently, was theirs.

If Millie had been expecting a Western town of myth and legend, with ramshackle facades and drunks stumbling out every swinging door on Main Street, she would have been disappointed with Missoula.

In fact, with its birch-lined sidewalks and picturesque Victorian houses, it almost reminded Millie of the quieter neighborhoods in Washington, DC.

It wasn't even cold.

Granted, it was August, but Millie wouldn't have been surprised to have disembarked the train and stepped directly into snow from what she'd heard about the state.

Maybe this assignment wouldn't be as punishing as she'd feared.

When she reached the FWP office, her optimism died a swift death. She stamped the mud from her boots, though it was habit more than anything else that had her doing so. She doubted a little dirt would hurt the place much.

Water bubbles, yellow at the edges, added an unwelcome depth to the garish floral wallpaper; something that looked suspiciously like mold seemed to be proliferating in the corners of the room; Millie spotted no less than four mice holes in the walls; and a collection of school supplies sat in a pile in the far corner. A radio crackled in the background, mostly static with disjointed lyrics that somehow created a haunted atmosphere.

She knew that Katherine strongly suspected sabotage, but perhaps the answer to the Missoula mystery was simpler than that. Maybe this office just lacked proper resources. Everyone thought the New Deal programs were simply handed as much money as could be printed, but that wasn't the case. Especially with programs so far down the ladder as the Federal Writers' Project.

"Excuse me." Millie rapped on the desk manned by a voluptuous young woman in a low-cut blouse. Her red-slicked lips and Bette Davis eyes made her look like she'd walked off an airman's pinup page.

"You take a wrong turn at the Mississippi, sugar?" Bette Davis asked.

"Oh, uh, no," Millie said, smoothing a hand down her blouse, hoping her nerves weren't as easy to read as she suspected they were. "Is this the building for the American Guide Series?"

"It sure is," Bette Davis said. She smelled of Juicy Fruit and too much Chanel and grinned at Millie like this was a big joke. "But if you want to pretend you got lost and catch that train back to Washington, we promise not to tell anyone."

Millie was thrown a bit but tried not to show it. "Well, I suppose you already know, but I'm Miss Lang."

"All the way from the WPA headquarters, come to whip our lazy rear ends into shape," Bette Davis said, and Millie raised her brows at the sudden acidity in her voice.

"All the way from the WPA headquarters to help make this guide into the best it can be," Millie corrected with forced cheer that grated on her own ears. The twang in her voice got more noticeable the more nervous she got, and right then it was thicker than Aunt June's bacon.

Bette Davis popped a bubble in Millie's face and then went back to flipping through her magazine.

"Right." These were her people. Her last chance, their last chance. Whatever the issue was here, she wasn't going to overcome it without their help.

She shifted her attention to the room.

In the far corner, a man sat curled over a typewriter with an unlit cigarette clenched between his teeth. He wore a fedora that he kept tipped back enough so Millie could see his face with all its sharp angles and shadows, and he looked to be about a year or two older than her own twenty-four.

"Oscar Dalton," he said when he realized she was looking, and for some reason that made her finally remember where she knew the name from.

He must be *the* Oscar Dalton, the king of those pulpy noirs with covers that featured women in various states of undress. He seemed to have a book published every few months, and they flew off the shelves of drugstores across the country.

She'd never picked up a copy of any of them, so she couldn't attest to the quality of his writing, but it was hard to imagine a staff with such a prolific crime author on it turning in incomprehensible drivel. "Did you actually write all those novels?"

His amused half smirk told her the question had been as inelegant as she'd feared—but also that he wouldn't hold it against her.

"Yes, but only a quarter of them are any good," he said.

"Surely, at least half," Millie said, unable to help her own smile.

"I'll give you forty percent and that's it."

"Well, you have plenty of enthusiastic readers," she said.

His brows rose. "But not you."

"Apparently, my foot and mouth are too well acquainted this morning," Millie said, and she swore he almost laughed outright then. That was a good sign. His welcome was already friendlier than ones she'd received in both Dallas and DC. "You'll have to point me in the direction of the very worst of them."

"Not the best?"

"I'm to be your editor, I need to know all your bad habits, don't I?" she asked.

"Shall we leave you two alone?" Bette Davis interrupted, blinking those wide, too-innocent eyes.

Oscar threw her an indulgent but chiding look, while Millie cleared her throat, the confidence she'd gained from the interaction disappearing as quick as that.

The man sharing the desk with Oscar saved them all by standing. This one had an academic air about him—his dark hair was neatly combed, and he wore thin spectacles and a shirt that buttoned tight against his neck.

The cartographer, Millie guessed before he confirmed it.

"I'm Professor Lyon," he said stiffly, looking like he wanted to hold out his hand, but was forced to acknowledge they were too far apart to make that anything but awkward.

"Tommy," Bette Davis chimed in.

Professor Lyon pushed his spectacles up even though they hadn't slipped. "Thomas, if you must."

"We don't stand on formalities around here," Oscar said, not looking up.

"Well, and you can call me Millie, of course."

"Thanks, sweetheart," Bette Davis said dryly, her mouth lifting in a half smile. "We would have anyway, but nice to know you're not too hung up on proprieties. They wouldn't serve you well. I'm Flo, by the way."

Millie blinked at her. "You're not on my list."

"That's because her name is Sarah," Oscar said, still typing. "Flo is her le nom de scène for when she leaves us behind for Hollywood."

Sarah Marner. Secretary. Typist. But that would be a waste if that was all she was used for. Even after a few minutes, Millie could tell she would thrive conducting the interviews that were crucial to creating the guides. She was quick and clever and friendly, despite the obvious edges to her personality. Those would help also. Talking to hundreds of strangers for weeks on end was not for the faint of heart.

"We're missing one," Millie said, mostly to herself.

Sidney Walker, the photographer.

"Oh, Sidney keeps his own hours," Flo said, going back to the magazine she was flipping through. "He's a rascal like that."

"A rascal?" Millie asked, unimpressed. She may have been sent to Missoula because she was a *hellcat* but there was a difference between sticking up for what was right and slacking off.

"This isn't a teasing matter," Professor Lyon said in the gentlest reprimand Millie had ever heard. For the first time since Millie had walked in Flo seemed contrite, a splash of pink breaking through her face powder. She glanced at Millie as if she'd forgotten she was there. Or, at least, had forgotten who she was. "I didn't mean that. Don't . . ."

The professor cleared his throat, obviously gearing up to help her backpedal. "Sidney—"

"Should my ears be burning?" a voice cut in.

Millie turned, coming face-to-face with a man in his late thirties wearing a white button-down shirt tucked into loose tan trousers. Around his neck, he'd tied a silk cravat the exact color of his pale green eyes. His black hair was just going silver at the temples, and a thin mustache lined his upper lip.

He looked as cosmopolitan as anyone who could be found in Flo's magazine.

"Oh, hello. I'm—" Millie started.

"Millicent Lang," Sidney Walker drawled, shifting closer. "Here to clean shop."

Flo had been equally as bitter, but Sidney's words dripped with a disdain that felt personal. Perhaps because she was a woman and she would be his supervisor. There were plenty of men in the FWP and the WPA as a whole who balked at the idea of women in government.

But she also wondered if this attitude was meant to put her on the defense. If someone was nervous that they were about to be uncovered as the saboteur, wouldn't they choose to either hide or bluster their way through it?

Millie narrowed her eyes, feeling steady for the first time since she'd boarded the train in DC.

And she realized in that moment this characteristic was why Katherine had sent her out to the middle of nowhere. When things got hard, Millie stopped fretting, and she addressed the situation head-on. She wasn't sure why she could get so nervous having a polite conversation, while this kind of interaction—or facing down a violent, rich man—had her spine stiffening into steel, but she wasn't going to second-guess it, either.

"What do you think should happen when an office such as this sends in a boxful of blank interview forms and essays full of gibberish to the state headquarters?" Millie asked. Someone sucked in a breath behind her, and she would put money on it being the professor.

Sidney's mouth pursed, but he said nothing.

"You think you should just be allowed to do whatever you want without consequences?" Millie asked, hardly able to believe the words were coming out of her mouth. "You know what would happen if I left the gate open back at the ranch and all the steers wandered off?"

He raised his brows, and in that gesture, she heard all the cruel jabs she'd dodged in the past year about her background.

She let it fuel her.

"I won't let anyone jeopardize a project that gives voice to Americans who have been voiceless for the entirety of this country's existence," she said. "So, if that does mean culling the herd, so be it. But I would hope we can find a way to work together to make sure that's not necessary."

Sidney studied her for a long moment. Then as he went to walk by her, he stopped and whispered, "While you're up on that high horse, you might want to look around and consider just what and who was here before 'the entirety of this country's existence.'"

Then he continued on toward the back of the room before she could react. She blinked after him, not ready to unravel what he'd meant, half scared that he might have made a good point.

Her eyes flicked to the other three. Oscar had his head down, but his fingers didn't seem to be moving as quickly. Flo was shamelessly watching, while Professor Lyon was trying *not* to shamelessly watch.

Millie didn't like how this had started at all. She wasn't yet sure what was going on here. She wasn't going to be as quick as Katherine to rule out incompetence or mismanagement. Maybe one of these people was a rat, in place to serve an anti–New Deal politician who wanted the guides to fail or a powerful business who wanted to protect its own reputation.

But right now, she had to think about the fact that they only had until the next deadline to turn this ship around. She needed these people to work hard for her. They would only do that if she inspired them to follow where she led.

They needed to trust her.

It wouldn't happen overnight, but she could set the right tone now.

"I'd like to set some matters straight," Millie said. "Yes, I am the new editor for the guide, but I'm not your enemy. I'm not sure what the political temperature is here in Montana, but there are plenty in Washington who want us to fail."

"There's plenty here, too," Flo chimed in, and Millie nodded in acknowledgment.

"Those people, they look at the Writers' Project and see only fat that can be trimmed, only excess that should be spent on concrete and agriculture and their own pet projects," Millie said. "What we're doing here is important, though. Not only with the guides, but with our existence. Literature, theater, music—they remind us that good times have happened once and they'll happen again. They let us laugh and cry and find a connection to each other. Art is what keeps us human even while starvation and desperation try to make animals of the best of us."

Montana or a pink slip. That had become her own personal mantra, but now she needed to make it theirs, as well.

"Our critics, they don't see that or they pretend not to. They want us to fail, because it benefits them. They want *you* to fail. So you can resent me for existing," Millie said, almost out of breath from her impromptu speech. "Or you can start proving them wrong."

In the silence that followed, Flo snapped her bubble gum and Sidney Walker offered up a sarcastic golf clap.

Oscar Dalton typed on.

CHAPTER EIGHT

Alice

Missoula, Montana
1924

Alice sold Mr. Rutherford on the Boxcar Library before their coffees cooled enough to drink.

He had been wary at first, but Alice didn't let him get a word in.

"Think of how you'll be praised for looking after the welfare of your workers," she said, laying it on thick, despite the fact that Mr. Rutherford didn't exactly require Machiavellian techniques to be convinced. Even if he didn't completely buy into her argument, Alice's surname carried a lot of weight in Missoula. She wasn't afraid to use that to her advantage.

She left his office with the promise that, as long as she and the community could provide the books, he would revamp one of his boxcars and outfit living quarters within it for a librarian, as well as offer a—meager—stipend.

Julia Walker would not be as easy to manipulate.

Alice went in search of the woman and found her coming out of the Missoula Mercantile, the shopping center that might as well be the heartbeat of the town.

"Mrs. Walker, how lovely to see you," Alice said, pleased she didn't have to launch a search effort but a little disquieted that she hadn't had more time to prepare herself. Julia Walker was a force.

"Hmm," Julia hummed dubiously, eyeing Alice as if looking for flaws. It seemed every time they met, Julia felt the need to lament the lack of a mother in Alice's life. That had taken the form of anything from a sly comment on an out-of-date hairstyle to leaving bookmarked furniture magazines in the Monroes' drawing room. Today, though, Alice was certain her dress—a black, polka-dotted number with both a tasteful hemline and a high-cut neck—and updo were beyond reproach. "Darling, your shoes."

Damn. They had been Alice's one concession to comfort. But Alice could turn this into a win. "They are a bit old, aren't they? I was just about to stop by the mercantile for a new pair. Perhaps you can direct me? You have such an impeccable eye for fashion."

"The mercantile. For shoes." Julia's mouth pinched. "I suppose it will do for now. Shall we?"

She offered her arm, and Alice gladly took it. They strolled in the direction of the store.

"How lucky it was running into you," Alice said brightly. "I wanted your advice on a project I'm working on."

The best way to approach Julia was to seek wisdom rather than straight-out approval.

"For the library?" Julia asked, inclining her head to the Darcy sisters, in the manner of someone who knew how much higher on the social ladder she was than them.

"In a way, yes," Alice said, sending Christine and Lilly a little wave of her own. "Mr. Rutherford has agreed to create and partially fund a Boxcar Library on one of his logging trains, and I'd like to do a community drive to bring in books to stock it."

Julia stuttered to a stop in perhaps the least graceful move Alice had ever seen her make. "Excuse me?"

Since their arms were linked, Alice stumbled awkwardly. "Well, the library will be able to offer up some stock, and I'll of course donate from my personal collection, but we'll need hundreds of—"

"No," Julia said, cutting off Alice's rambling with that one sharp word. "What is this about a library for Mr. Rutherford's workers?"

"Oh." The concept seemed self-explanatory to her, but perhaps it hadn't been. "I got the idea because . . . well, you know I take books out to the camps."

"To the children," Julia said deliberately. There was something off about this interaction. Like they were having two separate conversations, the intensity of both drastically different.

"Yes, but also for the adults."

"For the men?" Julia repeated, as if she were slow. But Julia Walker was one of the smartest women Alice knew.

"And the women," Alice said.

"You take books to the workers?" Julia asked again. "And now Mr. Rutherford is creating an entire library for them?"

Alice wanted to say *she* was creating it for them, but she just nodded instead.

"Oh dear," Julia murmured. And then she changed course entirely, pulling Alice along with her. She didn't say anything more until they were settled in the parlor of the Walkers' Victorian mansion a few blocks away from the mercantile.

"Miss Monroe," Julia started after the hostess duties had been seen to and the tea poured. It was the first thing she'd said to Alice since the sidewalk. "Have you ever read *The Jungle* by Upton Sinclair?"

"Of course." What librarian hadn't?

Julia studied her face, searching for something she clearly didn't find. She stood and crossed the room, firmly shutting the door before heading toward the wall-length bookshelf behind Alice.

After a moment of searching, she plucked a novel from the

shelves, flipping through the pages as she returned to her seat. "'The rich people not only had all the money, they had all the chance to get more; they had all the knowledge and the power, and so the poor man was down, and he had to stay down.'"

While Alice had read the book, she hadn't memorized it. Still, that passage seemed to fit with the themes. "Yes, that sounds right."

Julia stared at her again, her eyes narrowed as if Alice was pulling some kind of trick on her. But it was Alice who remained in the dark, reeling and confused about what was happening.

When Alice didn't do whatever Julia had been expecting, the woman flipped through some more pages. "'The great corporation which employed you lied to you, and lied to the whole country—from top to bottom it was nothing but one gigantic lie.'"

"Well, he certainly had a point of view," Alice tried, not sure what else to say to this impromptu book club.

"Oh, this is my favorite, perhaps," Julia said, holding one finger up. "'Because the majority of human beings are not yet human beings at all, but simply machines for the creating of wealth for others.'"

"That is . . . ," Alice started carefully. "Quite the condemnation of the state of factory workers."

Julia snapped the book shut and pinned Alice with a curious gaze. "Just factory workers, dear?"

"And other workers, I suppose."

"Such as lumberjacks and miners?" Julia prompted.

And everything finally clicked into place. "Oh."

"You want to take books like these to the workers out there and fill their heads with so much nonsense?" Julia asked. "Alice, you silly child. Books are not simply books. I would think you, of all people, would realize that."

"Of course I know that," Alice said, her cheeks too hot, her palms clammy now.

"You've read the headlines," Julia continued, ruthless. "How many miners died in that strike against the Rutherford Company?"

"Three." Alice had been horrified by the news and had followed the headlines quite closely.

"From one strike," Julia said. "How many have died over the past ten, fifteen years? Dozens. Or are you forgetting the Anaconda Road Massacre? That only happened four years ago, dear, you were old enough to hear about it then."

She had. Only one miner had been killed, but sixteen others had been gravely injured.

"If you think taking books out there is a brilliant idea, you simply don't understand the reality of what it's like in those camps. It's a powder keg, Alice." Julia waved the book in Alice's face. "You don't think this is a spark?"

Alice swallowed against a sudden rush of tears. She wouldn't cry in front of Julia Walker no matter how small she might feel. "I was just thinking they'd like some . . . entertainment."

It sounded so, so foolish now.

"Entertainment." Julia looked Alice up and down. "Do you like that pretty dress you're wearing? Do you like the limousine parked in your garage? Do you like the way merchants offer you wares on credit and the ability to buy all those outrageously expensive books that serve no purpose?"

Alice flinched.

She had spent that morning judging Sidney Walker for the way he lived his life, but weren't they similar? Julia wasn't wrong—Alice had been born to wealth, and while she did work, that meager paycheck hardly covered her expenses.

She didn't live extravagantly, and she could make do if it all disappeared tomorrow, but she knew she didn't have the same experiences as most of her neighbors.

So many in Montana were struggling.

People had streamed into the state ten years ago, chasing a promise that, with hard work, their lives could be happy and prosperous here.

Then the Great War started, bringing riches they could hardly imagine. The wood, the grain, the work. Everything in high demand.

Then the Great War ended, and what was good for the world and humanity was bad for Montana.

The drought when it came was written off as a onetime catastrophe. This, after all, was the land they'd planted hope in, deep like roots that couldn't be extracted.

The dust and locusts and fires came next, in the wake of the drought. Because when the land was thirsty everything burned.

Cars drove through town on a weekly basis, cardboard hanging off their bumpers.

TWENTY MILES FROM WATER, FORTY MILES FROM WOOD. WE'RE LEAVING DRY MONTANA, AND WE'RE LEAVING HER FOR GOOD!

Julia wasn't wrong. Their circumstances in which so many people lived had all the makings of a powder keg.

"Do you know what happens when men get ideas?" Julia asked. "When they start believing the propaganda in these books?"

"It's not propaganda," Alice protested, finding her tongue after too many minutes of letting it sit clumsily in her mouth. "Knowledge is not propaganda."

"No. Knowledge is power," Julia snapped. "And when you give it to workers they may actually wield it."

Alice pictured Nathaniel Davey, his hopeful but wary expression. She pictured Dawn with her Agatha Christie. She pictured the big, burly men who shoved calloused hands in their pockets as if they would ruin the books with a bit of tough skin. And she thought about how it hadn't been the workers who held the guns during those strikes. All they'd held were picket signs. "Books don't get people killed, Mrs. Walker. They might hold up a mirror to . . . to the . . . the sordid underbelly of wealth, but they don't pull any triggers nor tie any nooses."

"Oh, how little of the world you know," Julia said, all condescension. Now that she realized Alice would not be persuaded, the fire had died out of her. Ice had crept in its place, and Alice couldn't underestimate that.

"I suppose I can't expect your support for the community drive," Alice said, standing. She already knew the answer.

"I wouldn't count on there being a library to stock after I visit Mr. Rutherford," Julia said coolly.

Rage flushed through Alice's body, searing and intense. "You wouldn't."

Julia shrugged. "I care about people's lives, even if you don't."

Alice nearly gasped as if Julia had slapped her.

"No, you care about your bank account," Alice said, and then stormed past Julia.

Alice blinked quickly as she flew into the hallway, her vision blurred with angry tears, but not so much that she didn't see Sidney Walker leaning there against the opposite wall, looking every inch the lazy, spoiled American aristocrat he was.

She had never hated someone more than she did in that moment.

"Get out of my way," Alice spat, even though he wasn't blocking the door.

His eyebrows shot up, but he straightened and gave a bow toward the front hall, waving her forward.

She went to sail by him, but froze when his fingers wrapped gently around her wrist.

"Are you going to let her stop you?" Sidney asked quietly.

The door—he must have cracked it open to eavesdrop on the conversation without her or Julia noticing.

"No," Alice said. And, though she trembled inside, added, "I won't let you stop me, either."

Sidney just grinned, though his eyes remained hard and unamused. "Good."

CHAPTER NINE

Millie

Missoula, Montana
1936

It took approximately one minute for Millie to realize that Professor Lyon would be her best ally. Oscar Dalton appeared unaffected and uninterested in her presence, Flo seemed like she enjoyed drama more than she cared about helping Millie. Sidney Walker was not even in the race.

"Howdy," Millie said, leaning against the corner of Professor Lyon's desk. He pushed his glasses up in a nervous gesture, but his expression was open and curious. "I believe winter is going to be a problem at some point. Can you recommend what routes we should prioritize for the tours section?"

"Of course, yes, of course," he stuttered out. "I can show you now, if you'd like. I have the ones we used before."

As Millie pulled over a chair, she tried to figure out a way to probe for more information.

She wasn't actually sure where to start. Katherine had picked Millie because she'd needed to ship her somewhere and Millie had a little grit to her personality. That was the extent of her talents, though.

She had never launched an investigation into anything before—she didn't even read mysteries like Oscar Dalton's that might help her decide the best way to start crossing people off her suspect list.

Figuring out a possible motive seemed like a good idea, but she guessed in this case the motive was money. And everyone could use a payout these days.

That hardly narrowed anything down.

What she should probably be on the lookout for was odd or suspicious behavior—someone with a guilty conscience slipping through any mask they might attempt to put on.

If Professor Lyon was wearing a mask it was a very earnest one.

He took her through the options for tours, though agreed they should start with the northern routes as the snow would make some of the roads unpassable sooner than someone from warmer climates might think.

"What are our transportation options?" Millie asked. All the cars she'd seen on the way over from the train station had looked far sturdier than the ones that trundled around the city streets of DC, and she hoped that would be the case with the office's options, as well.

Professor Lyon glanced toward the back of the room where Sidney worked on his camera equipment. "We have a French-made mountain climber that we have access to."

That seemed a strange way of putting it. "What do you mean?"

"It's mine," Sidney called out.

"Ah." That was less than ideal. She didn't want to owe Sidney anything, especially if he was the one—

She cut herself off. She didn't want to let herself go down that route too early.

Assumptions were dangerous, as were first impressions that stuck around too long.

But all she was doing now was collecting information. No one could blame her for that.

"My chariot is at your service," Sidney assured her.

"All right, that's that then," Millie said, because there didn't seem to be any other option. And with what she thought she knew of the northern part of the state, they would absolutely need something called a French mountain climber even if she couldn't picture exactly what that was. "How familiar are you with these routes, Professor?"

"We just drove them last month," he said, and for the first time she sensed anger in his voice. "So very."

Millie hid her expression by digging for a pencil out of her bag—she wanted to believe him. But then where was all the work?

By the time she straightened, Professor Lyon was smoothing out a frown. The pinched V of his eyebrows gave away his displeasure.

"We've conducted dozens of interviews with people all over the county," he said, and she could tell he was making an effort to keep his voice steady.

As tactfully as she could, she asked, "Are there any copies?"

"Not of most of it," Professor Lyon said, and cleared his throat again. "We had been under the impression that if there were edits that needed to be made, Mr. Sutter would send back the originals, marked up."

"And yet Mr. Sutter and his staff say they received nothing usable." She studied the precise, buttoned-up man in front of her and decided to simply ask, "What do you think happened?"

The professor's eyes flicked to Flo as if seeking reassurance. She lifted one shoulder in a gesture that clearly read, *Up to you.*

"The staff in Helena lost our work and found it easier to blame us instead of taking responsibility," Professor Lyon said. "That's all we can figure."

And Helena had been insistent Missoula had made the mistake.

Millie wondered if they would ever get to the bottom of what happened with both sides pointing fingers.

"It's the only explanation that makes sense," Professor Lyon reiterated when she didn't say anything.

"Then all we can do is move forward," Millie said, because pressing the point with Sidney, Oscar, and Flo all watching them intently was not the right move in this moment. "What will be the most challenging tour for us to organize?"

"Glacier National Park," the professor said, running a finger along his map. "There will be an itinerary for the surrounding area, but Helena wants an entire section on the park itself."

While they'd been talking, Sidney had drifted closer. "This all looks good, but we got nothing out of these three towns the last time we did these routes. We should skip them this time around."

He absently tapped on tiny names Millie had to squint to decipher. The fact she couldn't read them at a glance meant that he was likely right. But the whole point of the guides was to offer interesting itineraries, not just direct visitors to every popular place in the state.

The professor craned his neck to see. "Condon. Elmo. Finley Point."

Two of the towns were located around Flathead Lake, the other a little farther south.

"You're right," the professor said without a hint of suspicion. "It would be worthwhile to spend more time in Polson and Big Fork, instead. I felt like we cut those days short last time."

"Silver linings to duplicating work, I suppose," Sidney said, before wandering back to his desk.

Millie committed the three towns' names to memory—she didn't want to overthink everything anyone on the staff did, but offering that kind of opinion seemed noteworthy at the very least. She glanced at the professor. "You truly don't think they're worth keeping in as stops?"

"Not with our abbreviated timeline," the professor said, easily, cheerfully almost. It seemed he liked this work. "We had more time in the summer, and Sidney's mostly right, we didn't find much interesting to report there."

"Mostly?"

"There was a bookmobile initiative I found intriguing in . . . Shoot." The professor nudged his glasses up. "Somewhere in that area. I was even able to get a photograph from a local resident of the librarian and all the books. Suppose that's lost now, and I can't imagine there'd be any copies."

"You don't think it's worth returning to check?" This didn't sound like it had anything to do with the sabotage, but a bookmobile project would be lovely to include in a guide funded by a project to employ the nation's writers. She was sure that was why the professor had found it worth noting, as well.

"No, not if it means you can spend more time elsewhere," Professor Lyon said.

"All right," Millie said. "How many of us will the mountain climber fit?"

The easiest thing to do would be to just take everyone. She could observe them better that way, and more boots on the ground wouldn't hurt.

"Four comfortably," Professor Lyon said, with a little grimace of acknowledgment that it wasn't the preferred answer.

Which meant someone had to stay behind.

Millie had to go, that much was obvious. And as much as she might dislike spending that much time with someone as combative as Sidney Walker, they couldn't visit a national park without their photographer. Their best writer needed to come, which left either Flo or the professor as the odd man out.

Professor Lyon cleared his throat and pushed his glasses up. "I am quite good at creating the routes, but, if we're being bluntly honest here, I am not the best person on the road. I not only get quite sick, but I struggle to get people to open up. Flo would be the much better pick."

"Don't sell yourself short, honey," Flo offered, but none of them looked like they were going to fight him too hard on the assessment.

"All right," Millie said. Out of the four staffers, she was the least suspicious of the professor, though she wouldn't be able to say why if pressed. Still, she was glad if one person had to get left behind it was him. "We'll leave a week from tomorrow. That will give us enough time to gather supplies."

And give her enough time to learn more about what she was working with here.

"I'll need to catch up on some basics about the state before we leave," she said, standing. "Is there a library someone could direct me toward?"

"Yes, of course," Professor Lyon said. "There are also university books I can bring for you. They might be more specific than what we have at the public library in town."

Flo chimed in, "The librarian here is a wonder, though. She'll magic up anything you wouldn't even think to look for." For some reason, Flo was staring at Sidney. "Miss Alice Monroe is her name."

Something loud dropped behind them.

"Dammit," Sidney cursed. A second later, he stormed past all of them out of the office.

"You shouldn't provoke him like that," the professor chided.

Flo smiled, a cat who had gotten the exact reaction she'd wanted. "Sidney always puts on a show when Miss Monroe's name gets brought up."

"Oh," Millie said, always too curious for her own good. "Do they have a history?"

"Not that we know of," Flo said as she crossed to them. She leaned her weight against Professor Lyon's shoulder, and the good professor went a delightful shade of pink. A secret there, too, maybe. But an open one. "That's what makes it so delicious."

And in that moment, Millie realized if she was going to get any information from someone in the office, it would be Flo.

"Will you walk me to the library?" Millie asked.

"Right now?"

"Yes," Millie said, with one more glance around. "Unless you need me here."

"I'll update our itinerary," the professor said.

"Thank you."

Flo tucked her arm through Millie's—clearly the type to have never met a stranger—and tugged her out the door.

"How did everything in the office work before I got here?" Millie asked. The staff were being asked to cover a substantial amount of the state with only a few people. And there had been no one overseeing it as the field office editor. All of this really might just be an overwhelmed staff needing extra help.

"We all went up north for the interviews," Flo said. "I would say Oscar, Tommy, and I talked to a couple dozen people each."

That seemed about right to Millie.

"I went through and flagged the interesting ones, and then Oscar and Tommy divided them up and then wrote the essays off them," Flo said. "I don't pretend I can actually write, though I'll lie three ways from Sunday if you report I said that."

Millie laughed. "Why the Federal Writers' Project, then?"

"We didn't have a theater program come to town," Flo said with a shrug. "And it was either that or . . ."

"Or," Millie agreed. Sometimes that *or* looked like selling your body to strangers, sometimes it looked like selling your body to a husband who could feed you with one hand and beat you with the other.

People could say what they wanted about the New Deal; Millie knew it had its critics. But the project had in a substantial way changed the fates of a lot of women.

"Who was the last person to handle the box of essays?" Millie asked.

"I suppose me," Flo said, sounding like she was realizing it for the first time. "I got the box ready to ship one night, but it was too late to go to the post office. I left it on my desk and then sent it off the next morning."

So someone could have come in and swapped out the materials in that time. "Who has a key to the office?"

"Just the four of us on the FWP staff," Flo said, and then shot Millie a look. "I know what you think. But I know those men in there. They wouldn't have ruined weeks' worth of work for any reason."

And you? Millie thought but didn't say. The Hollywood mention had been a blink-and-you-miss-it reference, but what if someone had offered Flo enough money to make it to California and all she'd had to do was replace a couple essays with blank paper?

"Neither would I, by the way," Flo added, probably reading Millie's question all over her face. "Like we said, all we can figure is that Helena made a mistake that it doesn't want to own up to. And no one is sending some big DC editor there to oversee their work."

Millie actually laughed at being called a "big DC editor," but stifled it when Flo sent her a curious glance. "I think it sounds like you all have been trying to do too much and I needed a place to, well, to put it bluntly, be forgotten. That's all there is."

"I wasn't born yesterday, peaches," Flo said dryly. "Anywho, here you are."

Flo gestured to a small brick building in front of them and then, before Millie could even thank her, turned on her heels and walked away.

Millie stared at her retreating back, until she disappeared around a corner.

Then she started up the stairs toward the woman whose mere name had caused Millie's prime suspect to storm out of the office like a child.

If Alice Monroe could provoke that kind of reaction in Sidney Walker, Millie couldn't wait to meet her.

CHAPTER TEN

Colette

Hell Raisin' Gulch, Montana
1918

The strike in Butte that followed the Speculator Mine disaster was officially called off in December, six months after it had started. Colette hadn't mentioned the event again, but she'd started collecting articles about it.

She didn't trust any of the reports from the big newspapers, but Papa subscribed to a niche union tabloid that had sent a reporter to cover the entirety of the strike.

There had been no gains made for the metalworkers.

Before the Butte strike, Colette had only attended Papa's underground union meetings when there was nothing else to do. Now, she went to every one.

Colette wasn't worried about her own future. When they'd returned from Butte, she'd secured an apprenticeship with the librarian, who had been impressed that the feral Durand girl actually knew about books.

Papa had taught her that she should never just fight because of her own life, though. She had to want to fight for the lives of her neighbors and every worker across the state. Across the country even.

If everyone she knew was meant to dig their own grave, shouldn't she have a say in trying to make the time they spent doing it just a little more bearable for them?

Papa would be headed to the meeting straight from work, so Colette left the house on her own, making sure to keep to the shadows.

The meeting was at a rancher's house just outside of Gulch, and the single light burning in the window beckoned her forward.

George Campbell, the rancher's son, leaned against the wall right next to the cellar doors, smoking a cigarette, looking very surly and young.

He blew out a ring of smoke, and eyed her. Everyone in Gulch had known each other since birth, and everyone in Gulch knew Claude Durand's daughter had a right to be at whatever meeting she wanted to attend.

Sometimes these appointed "guard dogs"—in place to flush out any spies in disguise—liked to flex their power on her because she was a girl.

After a few tense seconds, George shrugged one shoulder and waved her through.

"We tried a peaceful strike, now we need to arm ourselves," one man was saying as she slid into a spot next to Papa.

"They'll call us instigators," Tim O'Reilly countered. She'd always liked him. He used to slip her caramels when he came to Papa's meetings. "We'll be dead in the streets."

"Just like Frank Little, huh?" the original man said. "It's the same results either way. We might as well take a few of them bastards with us."

"We won't even get a chance to pull a trigger before they put us down like the animals they think we are," Tim's friend Roger said.

The man bared his teeth. "Then they'll learn just how painful an animal's bite can be."

Someone who had been standing in the shadows shifted, and Colette nearly gasped. It had been more than six months since she'd seen the man, but she would recognize him anywhere.

There, standing in the Campbells' basement, was the ringleader from Butte. The one who'd caught the Company spy that day they'd first arrived at the strike.

Her cheeks flushed when they locked eyes across the room.

Surely, he wouldn't remember her.

"We could carry guns or we could carry roses," he said, his attention drifting past her. "They'll call us animals even if we say please and thank you and follow every rule they've ever laid out for us."

Colette swayed toward him, and then chided herself for being silly.

"They'll call us animals, they'll call us machine parts, they'll call us dispensable and disposable," he continued. "Because if we're not all that? If we're human just like them? Then they would have to acknowledge how despicable their behavior is toward us. And they can't live with that."

He met her eyes, and everything around her stilled. He wouldn't remember her, not from a three-second encounter on the street six months earlier. He'd likely met hundreds, if not thousands, of people since then.

"You say they won't like the way we resist? Good, they're not meant to," he said, turning his attention back to the room at large. "The Company has never worried about what we think of their behavior, have they? When they force you to buy your supplies only from the Company store at marked-up prices, does that not make them monstrous? When they crowd you in elevators so tight you can't fill your lungs with air enough to breathe, does that not make them animals themselves? When they leave you to die because your body is no longer of use to them, does that not make them less than human? If they wanted civility, they should have worried about their own."

Applause boomed off the cellar walls; Colette's hands stung from how hard her palms slapped together. She glanced at Papa. "Do you know who he is?"

"Finn Benson, a Wobblie from Chicago," Papa said. His voice dropped when he used the slang name for Industrial Workers of the World agents. Even here, in the presence of one, they were dangerous to talk about. What with them being considered radicals.

"That all being said, that doesn't necessarily mean we should arm ourselves," Finn continued. "It means we should have a clear-eyed debate instead of one filled with emotion and bitterness, however justified it might be."

Some of the men who had been cheering him on seconds earlier quieted at that. They had expected him to pick a side—likely with the ones who were hollering for guns.

Finn shifted his attention to Papa. "Mr. Durand. Everyone here has told me that it is you who knows the fight best. What do you recommend?"

And with that, Finn sat down, ceding the floor to a Montanan.

Colette slid her glance to Papa, who was busy trying not to look too startled.

"'Now, for our consciences, the arms are fair when the intent of bearing them is just,'" Papa said, and Colette silently sourced the passage to *Henry IV, Part One*.

Colette loved the way her father thought, but it too often led to him being swayed by literary grandeur that should never be applied to real-life decisions. He was not king of England, nor were these men gathered here soldiers ready to march into war. Not every worthy fight was worth losing the same casualties over as a battle. If that were the case, there would be no one left at the end of any disagreement, just smoke and ash and death.

"Ah, but the Bard never took up a sword," Finn Benson pointed out, earning himself a point in her father's favor with his ability to identify the quote.

"Yes, but our pen is controlled by our enemy's hands," Papa countered, though she could tell he was pleased by the intellectual back-and-forth.

"Not necessarily," Finn said.

"What are you thinking?"

"I have a friend with a printing press," Finn said. "We can get our side of the story out, focusing on local miners here in Gulch." When no one said anything, Finn continued, "Come on. We can either write our own headlines, or be in them as a body count."

Papa thought for a long minute and then nodded, once. Decided.

The rest of the room erupted into noise, and Papa strode over to Finn, his palm held out toward the man.

Finn took it and grinned as they shook.

And that's when his eyes flicked over to Colette once more.

He wouldn't remember her, he couldn't possibly . . .

But. He winked. Right before he turned away, he winked at her.

As if everything that had just happened had all been a script, and she the only one who could see the author's hand at work.

She carried the heady feeling of being in on the secret the rest of the night.

It was only when she finally lay down in bed that she realized the wink had likely been part of the script, as well.

Colette had thought she'd known what life was like for the miners. But her worldview shifted after the mine disaster. Once she started attending the union meetings, she couldn't understand how everyone didn't walk around with their blood on fire.

She found herself trying to recruit the boys who avoided Papa's eyes because they knew they should fight and wouldn't. For whatever reason.

"Do you not find it outrageous you have to now man a drill meant for two people by yourself?" Colette asked Leon Banzhaff. They'd grown up together, though she wouldn't call them friends. His family was German—an unpopular predicament these days—and mostly kept to themselves. But he came in every week to the tiny lending library where she had her apprenticeship, and she knew he was well-read, clever, and intelligent. "And all so the Company can reap more profits and pay fewer men. Do you know how much more dangerous that makes the work?"

"Of course I do," he said softly. They were walking out to the field where the latest medicine show had set up on its way through western Montana.

Dr. Roman Stanley's Snake Oil Liniment.

The "doctor" had come into town last night with six covered wagons loaded down and bursting at the seams. That usually got everyone in the Gulch excited, because it meant more than a show that was just a dry recitation of all the miracle cures some tonic could offer up.

Their guess had, so far, been proven accurate. A magician was set to open the show, sawing his assistant in half as his finale. And if Roman Stanley's poster was to be believed, that was just the first of many jaw-dropping acts planned for the day.

But first they had to sit through the doctor's spiel—which she always rationalized as the price they paid for an afternoon of entertainment. Dr. Stanley was on the second half of his monologue now, pitching all the ways his potion could bring the dead back to life. Or near enough, listening to him sell it.

Some good people would be swindled out of their hard-earned money today, but that would happen whether she attended or not.

The air hinted at spring, and the field was muddy with snowmelt. Children giggled, and girls gossiped, and the ranchers traded notes on their summer cattle drives. Someone had set up a popcorn machine and so everything smelled of butter and salt instead of the usual manure, and Colette knew she should just enjoy this rare treat but she couldn't ever shut her mouth these days.

"Let's get a good spot," Leon said, hand at the small of her back.

"Leon," Colette said even as she let him direct her to the front seats.

He huffed out a breath and glanced around. "We can't talk about that stuff here."

"Leon—"

"No." Leon cut her off. It was the harshest she'd ever heard the gentle boy sound. "My aunt and uncle lost their three boys to the war, and no one cares because they were fighting for the Germans. But now they can't work, they can't afford the food they barely want to eat anyway. My mother is trying to take in more sewing, but we live day to day as it is and we're trying to figure out a way to help them. So, no. I'm not about to risk my family's lives to stand out on the street for six months while accomplishing nothing."

"But—"

"No," Leon nearly shouted now, drawing a few glances. "It must be nice to have the luxury of taking the moral high ground. The rest of us just have to muck around down here to survive, while you judge us for it."

Dismay slipped in beneath Colette's righteous indignation. "I'm so—"

Leon didn't wait for her to finish, he simply turned and walked away.

"That was, perhaps, not the best recruitment effort I've ever witnessed."

Colette spun to find Finn Benson lounging against one of the rails set up to cordon off the crowd from the performers.

Briefly, she closed her eyes and willed the ground to open up beneath her feet. When it stayed stubbornly solid, she sighed and met his amused gaze.

"It was my first time," Colette said, and then blushed without knowing why when he quirked a brow at her.

"You know the first time I tried to recruit someone to the cause, I got punched in the jaw for my efforts," Finn said, his smile delightfully crooked. "So, you bested me at least."

"A low bar, it sounds like," Colette shot back.

"It does get easier," Finn said, shifting so that she could come stand next to him.

She took the spot, her arm brushing his. Her whole body tingled at the contact.

"Does it get less frustrating?" she asked. Because she saw Leon's point, she did. Colette knew where her next meal was coming from, and so she could afford to take a stance she thought everyone should naturally take. What would she do if Papa was sick and the only way to get him care was to keep her head down and lick the Company's boot when they said so?

She would do anything for Papa, including that.

"The Butte protest didn't help our cause any," Finn said, pulling an apple from his pocket. He sliced into it and offered her the first bite.

The tangy sweetness was blessedly cool against her tongue and she cherished the gift, even though the gesture had only been a careless politeness.

"I saw you there," she admitted, because a tiny, tiny part of her wanted to test if he remembered her. Even if she knew he wouldn't.

The side of his mouth twitched up. "I know. You saved the day."

Pleasure as sweet as the apple slice bloomed within her, and she stared at the ground lest her expression give away something it shouldn't.

"Was that man a spy?" she asked, watching him from the corner of her eye.

Finn's expression immediately sobered. "Yes, the rat. You get rid of one, three more take its place. The Company doesn't even have to pay them well, it's a job for desperate men."

"How did you figure out he was a spy?" Colette asked, curious but hesitant to sound too naive. They seemed so dangerous and romantic to her—not the rats, but the men who flushed them out. Like Finn Benson.

Papa mentioned that in bigger cities the spies ran rampant—sneaking into union meetings for every industry. But Colette had never been able to think of them as anything other than a story, a boogeyman to keep everyone honest. It was hard to even imagine anyone would think their meetings in Hell Raisin' Gulch were worth the cloak-and-daggers.

"He had a camera hidden in his hat," Finn said.

"Never say so."

"Most of the spies aren't any good, like I said." Finn offered her another slice of the apple and then finished the last bit off. "But the ones called in from the Pinkerton agency, they're the ones you have to watch out for."

"I heard about them in Butte," Colette said, pleased to know something without having to be told about it.

"Ever since Pinkerton was founded, they've been going after

unions," Finn said. "Did you hear about that incident down in Colorado? Four years ago, now."

Colette shook her head.

"There were miners striking down there. Coal, not copper," Finn added, like it mattered. Neither was easy. "They were set up in a camp, for the strike. Pinkerton agents went in with the National Guard. More than twenty were killed, including women and children."

"But why?" Colette asked, stunned that she could still be stunned. Was there nowhere that workers were safe from the threat of death?

"People can give you reasons, I guess. You know what I've learned in life, though?" Finn gestured toward where Dr. Stanley stood on the covered wagon's steps, an impromptu stage. The man had been busy extolling the virtues of his tonic that was surely just water. He clearly had the rest of the crowd in the palm of his hand. "It all comes down to money. It's never more complicated than that."

"TABARNAK," PAPA SAID as he slammed the door behind whoever had come calling.

Colette marked her page in *Dracula*, and looked up. "What's wrong?"

"An accident at the mines," Papa said. "I don't know the details, but it sounds like a cave-in. I warned them, I told the foreman it didn't look stable, but did they listen?"

He shoved his hat on and stomped into the kitchen for his bag.

Colette stood and followed him, clutching at the book. She licked her lips. "Dead?"

"Just two," he said, and then laughed, though there was no humor in it at all. "'Just.' Listen to me. But, *just two* is still a miracle.

One of the men pushed two others out of the way before the wall collapsed on him."

"Who?" Colette forced the word out, already shivering. She knew everyone in town. It was never a stranger.

"Just a kid," Papa said, brushing past her to head toward the door. Colette couldn't move.

"Who?" she asked again, but this time she knew.

She closed her eyes dreading the answer.

The rest of us just have to muck around down here to survive, while you judge us for it.

"Leon," her father said, right before storming out of the house. "Leon Banzhaff."

CHAPTER ELEVEN

Millie

Missoula, Montana
1936

Millie hadn't had a hometown library.

She liked the idea of one, of the librarian getting to know just what kind of books she liked, of being able to lose hours in the stacks away from the responsibilities of real life.

But she'd grown up on her aunt and uncle's ranch, which was a good four miles outside of a tiny watering hole of a town. Millie had never been bored. They worked long hours keeping the animals fed and watered and the land taken care of. Even in the evenings, there were so many people in the house, they'd learned to entertain themselves. Millie and her six cousins would tell each other stories, or make up plays to be performed for the indulgent audience of adults. The older children gleefully recited ghost stories to try to scare the young ones. Her uncle had a collection of westerns that he'd let Millie borrow when she was old enough. Her aunt even had some classics scattered over the bookshelves to go along with the Bible, which was her primary reading material.

None of that came close to the pure luxury of an actual library. All these books at her fingertips, it was almost overwhelming.

"Good afternoon."

Millie turned toward the desk situated just to the side of the entryway, realizing just then that she'd been standing there silently for far too long. She truly hadn't expected something so expansive in Missoula, Montana. But she was starting to understand her ideas of what the Western territories would be like were out of line with what they were.

Introducing America to Americans, indeed.

The woman who'd called out a greeting was watching her with the patient expression of someone who'd done her fair share of gawping at books in her life.

She was tiny, though most women looked short from Millie's height. She also had a delicate build that gave her a somewhat fragile air. Her mahogany hair was pulled back in a neat braid that accentuated wide-set whiskey-gold eyes and a pretty face. Judging by the lines on it that made it interesting, Millie guessed she was a year or two past her thirtieth birthday.

"You wouldn't perhaps be Miss Lang of the Federal Writers' Project, would you?"

"Is Missoula so small you all recognize the strangers by name?" Millie asked, though made sure her tone was light.

"Something like that," she said with a smile. "I'm Alice. Alice Monroe."

So, this *was* the woman who had sent Sidney into a tailspin.

"Ah well, I was sent to find you," Millie said, and Alice's face lit up. "But you must call me Millie."

"How can I help you, Millie?" Alice asked.

Millie leaned on the desk and glanced back over the stacks. She sighed, knowing she had to be responsible. "I suppose I should get books for work."

"Oh, I think we can sneak a few in for pleasure." Alice winked and rounded the desk. "You'll be looking for books about Montana's history and other local knowledge?"

Of course this woman was three steps ahead of her. "Yes, precisely."

"Come with me." Without even once stopping to consult a catalog, Alice moved through the shelves, pulling books seemingly at random.

"I must tell you, I have been thrilled ever since the Federal One Project was announced," Alice said, walking briskly enough that Millie didn't even have to alter her stride for the woman's shorter legs. "Are you a writer? Or are you one of those who got lumped in with the rest?"

Are you a writer? That had been the second question the WPA agent had asked her when she'd gone to sign up for the program, the first being if she was actually destitute.

Her aunt had taken Millie's education seriously, which had helped Millie develop an eye for grammar, spelling, and logistical mistakes—a talent that had been praised highly during her time in Washington. She'd never published anything original, though, and wasn't sure she ever wanted to. Making up narratives, creating characters from a blank page, didn't appeal to her.

What did was telling real people's stories. Back on the ranch in Texas, when she'd been younger, she would put out a bulletin every week, featuring one of her cousins or her aunt and uncle or a passing ranch hand back when they'd been able to afford the help. It would include updates about who went to town or if an animal had an adventurous week from a birth or from getting stuck in the mud. It had even had a ranking of her aunt's meals—which was where Millie had learned to be diplomatic in her reviews.

That instinct to talk to people, to find out what made them tick and what they cared about—that was what Millie had liked about the guides project. That and a paycheck, of course. But in a perfect world she would enjoy doing this work no matter what her circumstances.

"I think . . . I'm a journalist," Millie said slowly. It was the first time she'd said that out loud to anyone, and the aftertaste sat strange on her tongue. But then she couldn't stop the smile that followed. "Yes. Or maybe. Eventually."

"It sounds like you are now," Alice said. "Isn't your job to go talk to Montanans? To ask them about their lives? That's precisely what journalists do, even if you're not writing a news article from the interviews."

Alice was right. Millie wouldn't be chasing a story about murder or corruption or scandal. But there was a certain skill to interviewing people, in getting them to talk and share parts of themselves that others would find interesting. It was a place to start, at least.

"I suppose, yes," Millie said, still hesitant to claim it out loud for some reason.

Alice paused, and searched her face.

"Well, we need journalists like you, that's for certain. For a very long time, newspapers in Montana have been owned by the Company," Alice said, before resuming her whirlwind flight though the stacks.

Millie trailed behind her. "'The Company'?"

"Oh, how silly," Alice said, without glancing back. "I suppose it is a bit strange that we all know which company we're referring to. You just don't realize it's odd until you're talking to someone who's not from here."

"And that company is . . . ?" Millie prodded, and Alice laughed.

"Sorry. The Anaconda Copper Mining Company. It's the largest, most powerful mining company in the state. Actually, in the world, I believe," Alice said. She began walking again, but this time it was a meandering thing. "They own . . . everything. Have you ever heard the phrase 'copper collar'?"

Millie shook her head.

"We wear the copper collar in this state," Alice said, bitterness laced into her voice. "The Company all but runs Montana. And in the twenties, they started buying up the newspapers."

"The newspapers?" Millie repeated, dumbly.

"All of them," Alice said, then shook her head. "The major ones. They could report on news, but nothing that went against the Company."

Alice slid her a look. "If they were the villain of a book, and you the editor, you might tell the author they went a bit heavy-handed on the evil."

Millie barked out a laugh. She'd done her fair share of editing overwrought prose during the past year.

"I know this guide project is meant to help visitors who are coming *to* Montana," Alice said, heading back to the front desk now. "But I think it will be . . . a revelation for Montanans, as well. Believing that they can tell their stories and that someone will care."

"They don't think anyone does?" Millie asked, her heart-strings well and properly tugged, as she assumed had been Alice's intent.

Alice shook her head. "The politicians are in the Company's pockets, the newspapers only print sanitized versions of any story, the businessmen only care about their own wealth. Any community work is largely dependent on the generosity of the very men who want to keep those communities poor and uneducated so they can have cheap workers. It's been too long since anyone really listened to the people who live in this state."

In that moment, Alice reminded Millie of Katherine Kellock.

"Now, let's get you signed up for a library card," Alice said before Millie could think of a profound enough response to meet the moment. "Where are you staying?"

"At a boardinghouse off Higgins Avenue." Another thing arranged by Katherine's brilliant yet overworked secretary.

"That's perfect," Alice said. "Mrs. Cross has a lovely attic room that gives you some privacy."

After they went through the formalities of the paperwork, Alice separated a pair of books into one pile and dumped the rest in another.

"These are your work books," Alice said, her palm flat on the larger stack. "History, geography, a few diaries of early pioneers, some journals on Lewis and Clark." She shot Millie an aggrieved look. "You will hear about them. Constantly."

Millie laughed. "I take it perhaps too much."

"Yes. Although, you may feel some kinship with them," Alice noted, and she sounded almost wistful. That nosy urge reared its head again, but Millie quieted it as Alice continued, "They were creating their own version of the guides, I suppose."

Millie tapped the two books Alice had left out of the first stack. "And these?"

"These are for you," Alice said, sliding them over the desk so Millie could get a better look at the titles.

Ten Days in a Mad-House.

Around the World in Seventy-Two Days.

"Nellie Bly," Alice said. "She was an investigative journalist who broke all kinds of boundaries."

Millie touched a finger to the name on the cover as she met the flinty gaze of a black-and-white Nellie. Then she looked up into the kind eyes of Alice Monroe.

It's been too long since anyone really listened to them, Alice had said of the people of her state.

But didn't that ring true for Millie, as well? Her aunt and uncle had saved her from an orphanage, and they'd welcomed her into their family with generous hearts. They'd never given her time, though, not beyond the necessities. Then after the crash, all anyone had cared about was survival.

Millie hadn't made any friends in Dallas, since she'd been there such a short amount of time. And then the same went for DC. Everyone was too busy to listen to Millie.

Alice, though. Alice had heard her.

"You're a good librarian," was all Millie could think to say.

Some complicated tangle of emotion flickered in and then out of Alice's expression.

"Some days," Alice teased with a wink. "You've just caught me on a good one."

Millie laughed because she was supposed to, but she studied Alice's face wondering what was beneath the mask she'd so effortlessly slipped in place.

CHAPTER TWELVE

Alice

Missoula, Montana
1924

War had been declared in Missoula.

It was a polite war, as Alice's opposing general was Mrs. Julia Walker, known both for her manners as a hostess and for her impeccable grace while delivering even the most cutting rebukes.

But it was war nonetheless.

Mr. Rutherford was now dodging Alice's visits; the editor of the *Missoulian* refused to meet her eyes when she asked about writing an editorial in favor of the Boxcar Library; and Alice had been disinvited—with extreme politeness—from three separate charity events over the past week.

Her father refused to intervene, especially after she'd explained why Julia had launched the campaign against her.

"She's not wrong, Alice," Clark said, from behind his paper. "It's already so hard to find good workers these days. And now you want to put ideas in their heads?"

He'd gone on to talk about costs and revenue and the poor Copper Kings who were only making a fraction of what they used to since the war had ended and shouldn't the workers just be grateful they had jobs? They'd even won several big concessions over the past few years so he didn't know what they were complaining about.

At some point, he lost track of the start of the conversation and she was unable to pull him back to it. That had been the end of the subject, no matter how many more gasping, indignant arguments Alice had tried to make.

For once in her life, though, Alice had a cause worth fighting for and she wasn't about to give up after a little adversity.

She had never felt strongly about anything before. She liked books and she liked bringing them to the camp families near town. But anytime the roads became too muddy, she gave up without trying to figure out a way around the problem. She liked Mac and his quiet smile, but she was too scared to tell him that. She liked her mostly peaceful, comfortable life, and hated the restrictions her father put on her "for her own good." But she never bucked his rules, never tried to give Mac the slip or sneak out to play in the river at night just for the hell of it.

Maybe this fight had been hers for only a handful of days, but it burned brighter in her chest than anything ever had. And losing this war—which she had to admit was what was happening—made her reckless.

She couldn't shake the memory of Sidney Walker leaning against the wall outside his mother's drawing room.

Good, he'd said when she'd assured him she wasn't going to give up the fight.

He might now be someone she couldn't respect or even stand to be around, but once upon a time he had been decent. And for whatever reason, he wanted her to succeed.

That was enough to get her to at least try to ask him to intervene.

The only problem was that whole mutually agreed on avoidance was working against her at the moment. Whenever she walked into a store it seemed that he'd walked out only a minute or two earlier. She couldn't simply drop by the mansion, as

Julia would surely have her turned away. And they had no close friends in common for her to call upon for help.

Alice decided that all this called for radical measures. She knew, through the roaring gossip mill in Missoula, that Sidney spent his nights at the poker tables in Lolo, a tiny town south of Missoula. If she was going to get him to talk to her, she would have to meet him on his territory.

She wasn't about to borrow the Ford to get there, though. Alice was feeling brave, not suicidal.

That left Sidney's car.

"Sweetheart, why aren't you in bed?" her father called from his study when she tried to sneak past him.

Alice made a face at the darkened hallway in front of her. She should have gone out through the kitchen she realized now. The problem with never breaking rules before was that she'd never learned the best way to do it.

"I'm just getting some fresh air on the porch," Alice said, making sure to step into the light. If she tried to stay in the shadows, her father would assume she was trying to hide something. He squinted at her and then pointed to a cashmere throw tossed on his leather chair.

"Take that for the chill," he said. "And don't stay out there too long."

"I won't," Alice said, praying that the failing eyesight he refused to acknowledge would keep him from seeing the tremor in her hands. When he simply went back to his books, she breathed a sigh of relief.

The nice thing about never having broken the rules before was that he would never suspect her of doing so now.

If a lifetime of good behavior meant that she might win this war against Julia, then all those years had been worth it.

The Packard was easy to spot—ostentatious and huge as it

was. Montanans tended to eschew the luxury cars that everyone on the East Coast fought over. Mac drove Alice around in a practical Ford, after all, which cost $300 to the Packard's $4,000.

Sidney enjoyed riding around in style, though, like the American aristocrat he was.

The impossibly shiny automobile was parked outside Mo's Soda Shoppe. A young boy Alice recognized as Jonas Kline sat on the running board, likely "guarding" it for a couple pennies' reward. No one in Missoula would dare touch Sidney's car, not with the threat of his father—a man with money older than the country—coming for their necks. But they got passers-through just as much as any Western town that stood in the way of the coast.

Alice bribed Jonas with a nickel, and the promise that she would make sure nothing happened to Mr. Walker's car. Then she climbed in the back. The jump seats were tucked up against the driver's bench, so Alice simply sat on the roomy floor, cocooned by the shadows.

She only had a ten-minute wait before Sidney slid behind the wheel and swiped at the ignition switch, muttering about flighty children as he did. Sometimes men with cars such as these didn't actually know how to use them properly, but Sidney handled the choke and throttle with ease, pulling out into the street. Alice exhaled quietly, the sound swallowed up by the purr of the engine.

Sidney hadn't once glanced in the back seat.

Alice didn't want to risk him throwing her out on the side of the street, so she waited until they'd cleared Missoula's city limits and were well on the way south to Lolo. The road was bumpy, and for all the swanky automobile innovations that seemed to pop up by the day, Alice still preferred the seat of a horse to this ride.

Finally, when the dark became oppressive, Alice pulled down one of the jump seats, reached through the partition opening, and tapped Sidney on the shoulder. "Hello."

While Alice had been braced—literally and figuratively—for a reaction, the one she got was even more intense than she could have ever predicted.

Sidney yelled, the car swerved, he cursed, the car skidded, he gritted out another yell from behind closed teeth, the wheel jerked wildly beneath his hands. Alice slid off the jump seat to sprawl on the floor in such an undignified manner she was just glad it was dark enough to keep her modesty. And that by then they'd slowed so much she didn't hit her head on anything.

When the car finally stuttered to a complete stop, Alice didn't move, just stared at the ceiling, the rush of the past thirty seconds singing in her blood.

She giggled.

She couldn't have stopped it if she'd tried, and she didn't actually find anything funny. But she made a sound that came out like laughter, and any hope that Sidney wouldn't blow his top at her was lost.

The front door of the Packard slammed open and then in the next breath, Sidney was there. The headlights illuminated only half his face, so he looked like a vengeful demon from Bible stories come to drag her to hell.

He did drag her from the floor out onto the rutted road, though his hands were surprisingly gentle. She'd already winced, expecting a bruising grip, and yet he just lifted her as if she weighed nothing. As if she were precious.

Then he dumped her to her feet, and crowded her in against the side of the car.

"What were you thinking?" His eyes were wild, almost like a spooked animal. And perhaps that's what he was.

She held up her hands just as she would with a horse that had the same darting gaze and sweat-slicked neck. "I'm sorry. I didn't mean to scare you."

Sidney stared at her for a long moment and then took off walking away from the Packard. "She didn't mean to—"

Alice knew better than to follow. He paced back toward the car, stared at her, and then walked off again. On his next pass he stopped.

"Do you think that was funny?" Sidney asked.

"No," Alice said, quietly, honestly. Something was happening here she didn't quite understand. This wasn't just Sidney angry at her scheming or annoyed at being startled.

This was more serious than that.

"Don't ever surprise me like that," he said now, his voice rough as gravel. His hands shook and when he saw her staring, he shoved them in his pockets. "I could have hurt you."

I could have hurt you. By driving the car off the road? Or something worse?

Sidney didn't have ghosts in his eyes. He wasn't a hollowed-out version of himself. He didn't flinch at loud noises. She had never once seen him locked in memories so traumatic that he forgot where he was.

He wasn't affected by the war.

He wasn't.

He was arrogant and hedonistic and lazy and . . .

Alice wanted to smack herself.

She had read enough poetry from the war to know it hadn't been some triumphant campaign of glory, but rather hell.

In Flanders fields the poppies blow
Between the crosses, row on row . . .

How could she have empathy for everyone except for a man who had spent months in trenches with shells dropping all around him? How naive could she have been that she could look at a man who was reckless, who drank to the point of oblivion enough times that even Alice had heard about it, who rolled into town looking freshly bedded on any given night, and not think it might have to do with his time overseas?

How could she have been so blind?

The only answer she had was that Sidney could get under her skin like no one else. When he'd first come back, he'd said outrageous things to her, clearly designed to get her to react. That must have been how he'd protected himself, though, from having to talk about anything difficult or painful. How easy it was to shove people away. Then he'd never have to worry about them doing it to him when he wasn't the perfect golden boy any longer.

She wasn't self-centered enough to think she could have offered him friendship—she had been young when he'd returned from war—but she could have offered him understanding at any point over the past five years and simply hadn't.

"All right," she said. "I'm sorry."

She wanted to touch Sidney, to bring him back to here and now. But she didn't dare.

Sidney stared at her for a long time, though she wasn't sure he was seeing her. Then he shook his head, rolled his shoulders, and, in an instant, became Sidney Walker, American aristocrat once more. The change was so swift, so startling Alice almost gasped.

But there was his smirk, his amused eyes. Even his posture had changed into something less threatening.

And, in that moment, she couldn't believe she had never seen it for the mask that it was.

"You just couldn't resist being bad once in your life, eh?" Sidney asked, his voice smooth and normal once more.

Alice hadn't earned the right to question him about what had just happened. Instead, she said, "I need your help."

He raised his brows and gestured toward the listing Packard. "Well then, my white steed awaits."

Lolo couldn't quite be called a town.

Alice had never actually been anywhere close to it—her father would have rushed to save her and then killed her himself as soon as he got her home. Even though he supplied half the establishments in Lolo with liquor and his men frequented the rest.

If Alice had been asked to draw what she imagined it would be like, though, she would have nailed it. There were a couple ramshackle houses, all with lights and music pouring out of them along with overloud men and scantily dressed women. The biggest of the establishments had a crooked, fire-hewn sign proclaiming itself a tavern. A half dozen cars were parked in the yard, but none as nice as the Packard.

"You really want me to go inside with you?" Alice asked Sidney, pretending the idea of it didn't make her tremble in the passenger seat.

"You're the one who wanted to come," Sidney pointed out. It was, of course, logical, but if she were being honest, Alice had been expecting him to drive them both right back to Missoula. She would have used the time to convince him to help her with the Boxcar Library fight and then he would have dropped her off around the corner from her house.

That's what Mac would have done. That's what anyone in her life would have done.

Before she could hint to any of that, he was out of the Packard and rounding the engine that might as well be a mile long.

"Won't someone steal this?" she asked as he helped her out, his hands gentle against her waist to steady her on the uneven ground. Alice was glad she'd at least worn a somewhat presentable dress and hadn't yet taken out her hair for the night.

"No," Sidney said, cocksure and dismissive. She wondered if it was more than just the fact that he was the Walker heir that kept the bandits and thieves at bay.

He wasn't a tall man, and his frame ran toward slim. But she'd seen the barely leashed violence in his eyes not too long ago now. Perhaps the rough men knew to stay away from him.

Sidney winked at her. "You'll be safe. I promise. Just don't count cards or make a pass at anyone's lady."

Alice blushed furiously. "Excuse me—"

"You've a wicked side, Alice Monroe, don't deny it now," Sidney talked over her. He skipped up the steps of the porch so he could hold the door open.

The light from inside spilled out, and she got her first good look of him of the night. Not touched by starlight or the harsh yellow beams from the Packard.

He wore a loose but clearly bespoke white summer suit, paired with a bottle-green tie that she knew matched the exact color of his eyes even if she couldn't see them at this distance. His black hair was slicked back with pomade—his hat probably lost in a ditch somewhere between here and Missoula. He had a rounder, softer face than what some would demand to be called handsome, especially out here, where rugged angles drew the eye for most girls. But he was beautiful, so beautiful she couldn't look away from him.

She had never had that thought about Sidney Walker before. And she realized now how much the revelation on the road had mattered.

He raised his brows under her scrutiny, but didn't prod her

into either moving or delivering a confession. He probably thought she was frozen, too scared to go inside.

Alice was, of course. But that had nothing to do with her hesitation.

A long time ago, she'd learned courage was a thing you could fake. And so she took a deep breath and walked into the tavern.

Sidney was right behind her, a hand on the small of her back.

Cheers greeted them. So did hoots and hollers and some choice names tossed in Sidney's direction. "Sonofabitch" was the most common one she could pick out.

Unlike some speakeasies, this place was no more fancy on the inside than the out. But it didn't matter. The room was packed, the music loud, the laughter even louder. It smelled like piss and smoke and burned meat, sweat and perfume.

At the gaming tables in the back, a cowboy leaped to his feet and dragged his neighbor into a brawl. The three couples on the impromptu dance floor only stopped long enough to step around the men, who were now horizontal.

The piano man picked up the pace of the fight, adding a rousing melody to the shenanigans.

A few women with dresses so low that a wrong move would expose their entire breasts sauntered around the room, looking for company.

A native man sat at the end of the bar, telling a hunting story to four or five white men who were all busy trying not to look impressed.

Three elk heads hung above the bar, and the man behind it already had glasses out for Sidney.

"Your favorite," the bartender said with a wink as Sidney directed Alice onto a stool. The man didn't spare her a glance and in the next moment, he was off to serve the next customer.

"You ever have a shot?" Sidney asked. He didn't take the

other vacant seat, but rather crowded into her space, blocking her partly from the room.

Alice barely heard the question, her attention kept getting pulled in every direction. The gunslinger in the corner reading *War and Peace*; the nervous poker player who had sweated through his undershirt; the pole right by the door with placards pointing in all directions, one proclaiming that Sydney, Australia, was 8,073 miles "thattaway."

"Hmm," Alice hummed.

Sidney laughed, and the sound finally drew her back to him.

He was too close.

From here, she could see the gold flecks in his eyes, the scattering of freckles across his nose that she was sure he would deny that he had.

His cologne wrapped around her, earthy and subtle. His thigh was warm against the inside of her knee, and she realized she was all but cradling his hips with her legs.

Alice tried to shift back but there was nowhere to go.

"Just one," Sidney said, nudging a glass into her hand. The liquor was clear. Moonshine. Or bathtub gin. It wouldn't be good.

She'd had plenty of wine in her life, nothing excessive but at social functions she allowed herself a glass. Her father kept his library stocked with scotch, Prohibition be damned. She'd sipped at a finger or two of it before.

But that wouldn't be anything like this.

She thought of gilded cages and birds with clipped wings and took the drink in one swallow.

It burned all the way down.

At first, she thought she'd managed it, but then she started coughing and couldn't stop. Sidney laughed so hard, he bent slightly forward, bringing him even closer to her.

For some reason, she didn't hear it as mocking anymore.

"One and done for you, Alice Monroe," Sidney said, taking his second.

She tried to protest that she could handle more, but she couldn't get the words out of her charred throat.

"So why did you decide to test the strength of my heart tonight?" Sidney asked, waving away a refill.

Alice almost didn't want to talk about it. She wanted to enjoy her one night of rebellion.

"The Boxcar Library," Alice said, because she was responsible. "Your mother seems to be winning our little battle. Do you have any advice?"

"No," he said carelessly. He wasn't looking at her any longer, and it was only then that she realized she'd had his full attention for the first ten minutes they'd been in the tavern. Now his eyes were on the gaming tables. "Don't get in trouble."

And then he was gone, so quickly that Alice felt unbalanced into the space he'd left behind. She put a hand on the bar to steady herself, watching in disbelief as he wound his way through the chaotic room, toward the back. A few people stopped him for handshakes, others threw curses at his back, and he moved, unmolested through it all.

He took a seat at the blackjack table, and immediately a pretty saloon girl with long strawberry-red hair and curves that would spill out of a man's palms sat herself in his lap.

"Lucky Penny," someone murmured behind her. And then, "He's gonna fleece them all."

"Rich bastard doesn't even need the money."

Sidney laughed and settled a hand at Lucky Penny's hip. Alice had a feeling she could strip naked and do the Charleston on top of the bar and he wouldn't even look up at her.

He no longer looked so beautiful in this light. She wasn't sure why she'd ever thought he was anything but a rascal, a good-for-nothing layabout, who probably was fine from the war.

Alice bit her lip and tried to make herself invisible. She could count on one hand the number of ladies in the tavern who weren't there to work. It felt like only a matter of time before someone approached her.

No one did, though. Somehow, miraculously. After ten minutes, Alice's shoulders relaxed. After twenty, she accepted another shot from the bartender.

A bang sounded outside: a pistol, Alice was fairly certain. But the man at the piano played on, a kid with a banjo joining in now, the twang of it tugging at something in her chest she hadn't realized was there.

When Alice got home, she might be skinned alive. If her father had decided to check on her even once, the jig was up.

If this was her last hurrah, she was going to make it count.

She swung back to the bartender and tapped the wood with her flat palm. "One more, good sir."

He wasn't the moral type or the type who cared if she was overserved. He filled her glass up to the top so that the sides were sticky when she lifted it to her mouth.

This time, it didn't burn going down.

A big man had settled in beside her, one of those quiet ranching types. He was minding his own business, but had kind eyes.

"Do you know how to dance?" Alice asked him, leaning her elbow coquettishly on the bar, and recovering beautifully when it slipped enough for her head to almost follow behind.

His kind eyes smiled at her, even as his mouth remained in a stubborn line. "I can manage."

"Time to go."

Alice took a second to realize it hadn't been the man who'd

said that, but Sidney Walker. Finally, coming to collect his unwanted baggage.

"No, it's time for dancing," Alice protested, proud that the words didn't slur together. She patted Sidney's hand. "You can go back to ignoring me. My new friend here wants to take me for a spin."

"I'm sure he does," Sidney gritted out.

The rancher held up his palms. "She asked me."

"Yes, and that's what's saving you a broken hand," Sidney murmured.

The mechanics of what happened next weren't all too clear, but somehow Alice ended up back in the passenger side of the Packard. Sidney gunned the engine in a way he hadn't the entire drive out.

"You weren't very nice to my new friend," Alice said, leaning her forearms against the windowsill, enjoying the cool air on her cheeks.

"Believe me, I was very nice to him," Sidney said, with that strange edge to his voice. "He was about to take advantage of a lady."

"You're speaking of me?" Alice said, insulted on behalf of the rancher who had seemed nothing but lovely.

Sidney just shook his head. "I told you not to get in trouble."

"And then you proceeded to ignore me," Alice said, going back to watching the silhouettes of the mountains in the distance. They looked like ink drawings now, not the giants that they were.

"Such a child," Sidney muttered.

Alice straightened. She was getting really tired of being called that. "I am not."

"You think you would have made it one minute in that place if you hadn't come in with me?"

"No," Alice admitted. She had known, in her heart, the reason why no one had approached her. "I didn't think you would take me."

Maybe she liked her gilded cage more than she realized.

Or maybe birds with clipped wings were terrified when they were allowed to fly.

Sidney Walker was the first person in her life to even let her try.

"I'm not a hero, Alice Monroe," Sidney finally said, just when they could see Missoula's lights in the distance. "You can't expect me to act like one."

A hero would have turned around the minute he realized he had an unexpected passenger, and that passenger was Alice.

"I don't think you're anything close to a hero," Alice said.

"Are you sure about that?" he asked softly, and Alice flushed with mortification as she remembered that moment on the steps when he'd opened the door and she'd thought him beautiful.

Not just on the outside.

Then, when he'd realized he'd won her over, he'd left her, had made sure she saw him at the gaming tables with a woman in his lap, whispering in his ear.

Alice couldn't say she was sure what his motive had been, she really didn't know what to think of Sidney Walker anymore.

But part of her wondered if that had all been part of his show.

He pulled the Packard to a stop a full block before her house, and she was silently grateful for the thoughtfulness. She was feeling quite petulant about everything else, though, so she didn't thank him.

When her fingers curled around the door handle, he reached out, brushed a thumb against her wrist. In the next second a wad of banknotes was pressed into her palm.

"To get you started," Sidney said. "You don't need a community drive if you already have the funds to buy the books."

Alice stared at him in disbelief, she knew well the weight of money in her hand. He hadn't just fleeced those men, he'd taken their shirts off their backs, and then some.

Or even worse, he was donating his own savings and not his winnings.

"I'll remind Rutherford he has a spine," Sidney continued. "And that while my mother might be the social matron of Missoula, I'm the heir to the actual business. You'll have your Boxcar Library."

She stared at him, a thousand questions running through her head.

Why are you helping? Why did you pretend to dismiss me at the saloon? Why didn't you do this a week ago?

All she could force out was, "Why?"

She didn't think he would answer. Then finally, he said simply, "Because once upon a time, I needed books, too."

CHAPTER THIRTEEN

Colette

Hell Raisin' Gulch, Montana
1920

It felt like Colette read about Finn Benson more in the union newspapers than she saw him in real life. Because of that, she'd started picturing him as a warrior, a radical, and, most importantly, a man with a good heart who fought for justice.

So, when he came to the Durand house for dinner—which he did every few weeks when he passed through Gulch—sometimes she felt starstruck.

Though she would rather cut out her own tongue than admit it to anyone.

Papa could tell. All three of them would stay up late on the porch, drinking now-illegal liquor, playing cards or swapping stories, and then Papa would finally yawn and stretch and see himself inside.

Finn never stayed very long after that; he wasn't going to ever test Papa's patience. But they always had a half hour or so at the end of the night to talk to each other, just the two of them.

"Where do you want to go when you leave here?" he asked her now. He was on his way to San Francisco—a rare jaunt out of state—which meant she might not see him for a while.

Wherever you go, she thought.

"What do you mean?" she said. "I'm not leaving."

She would eventually take over at the library, she knew that much. Gulch was home.

"Surely you don't plan to stay here your whole life," Finn said, watching her closely. "You could do so much for the movement in larger cities."

That was a point she hadn't considered. But she would never leave Papa. "My father—"

"Your father wants you to have a better life than he did," Finn cut in. "He would be thrilled to see you fighting the good fight."

Colette was lucky to be surrounded by men who encouraged her to launch herself into the big, wide world, but she couldn't help but think Finn was being somewhat—irritatingly—naive here.

"With who, Finn?" she asked. She never snapped at him, and she wouldn't even say she was now. But there was a bitterness to her voice she didn't bother hiding. "Not everywhere is Montana. Do you think I could simply get an apartment in Chicago as a young, unmarried woman?"

"There must be boardinghouses . . . ," he offered weakly after a pause.

"Maybe there are." Colette didn't know, if she were being honest. Perhaps it was easier being a woman in a place like Chicago than she imagined, but it was disheartening that he believed she could simply dash off to a big city, alone and nearly penniless, and somehow thrive. It showed just how little men—even the good ones—thought about the reality of a woman's life.

"Men are free to be brave and courageous, and as you say, fight the good fight," Colette said, not even sure where the anger was coming from. "And then history books and newspapers write about them as if they were the only ones who are free and brave and courageous. Yet a thousand barriers exist for me to overcome to even join the war, let alone lead it. Barriers you cannot even conceive of because you started well beyond them."

He huffed out an annoyed breath. "I know plenty of organizers who are women."

"Do you?" Colette asked softly. "Or do you know a handful and think it is a lot because you expect there to be none?"

Finn rocked back on his heels, but didn't say anything.

Colette knew this was a radical way to think, but . . . weren't they radicals? Didn't they strive at the edge of progress hoping for better lives for anyone who struggled?

Except maybe the rest of the movement was like Finn. Colette herself had only thought about the differences between men and women because she loved books and worked in a library.

Surely, she'd reasoned so many years ago, women were as gifted when it came to storytelling as men. And yet they only had a handful of books on the shelves.

"What do the mothers do with their children when they're attending union meetings?" Colette asked. "What do the women who have husbands who won't let them take a night off cooking do? What do young women who aren't let outside without a chaperone do? Do you really think they are all less courageous or less intelligent than you and your merry band of men because you don't have to figure those things out?"

She saw the answer on his face. "Of course you do."

"Don't put words in my mouth, Colette," Finn said, sounding angry at her for perhaps the first time. "You've told yourself a story of the world, but you haven't even experienced hardly any of it beyond Hell Raisin' Gulch."

"I have enough experience to see when someone is being a jackass," Colette said, standing. "I'd like you to go."

He stared at her for a long moment before putting his glass down gently on the rail.

In a quick stride, he crossed the porch and cupped her cheek. "I can't remove the barriers for every woman, but I would try for you. If you wanted."

Without waiting for a response, he turned and skipped down the steps of the porch.

When she shifted, it was to find Papa leaning against the doorjamb, an inscrutable expression on his face.

"Did you hear everything?" she asked.

"Only when your voices started to rise," Papa said, with no remorse. That was fair. Papa would never let her fend for herself if a man was yelling at her.

"What do you make of it?" she asked, because she trusted him more than anyone in the world.

He stared off in the direction that Finn had disappeared, and didn't say anything for a while.

"I think I might have been like him once upon a time," Papa finally said. "There is a fire that burns in young men that feels honorable and just and righteous. It was only with age that I recognized it for what it was."

"And what was it?"

"Pride mixed with arrogance," Papa admitted. "I'm not saying it's right, but I've seen enough young men up on their horses to remember how I used to think I was put in that saddle by God himself."

"So, I should forgive him his carelessness?" Colette asked, the ghost of his hand against her skin still lingering.

"You know something else I've learned with age?" Papa asked, waggling his thick eyebrows. "Not to tell a lady what to do."

Two WEEKS AFTER her confrontation with Finn, Colette heard a thump outside. When she went to check on the source, she nearly tripped over Finn on the ground.

"What are you—"

She cut herself off with a little cry as she knelt before him.

His face had been pulverized. There was no other way to put it.

He couldn't open one of his eyes, and he was holding his arm in the ginger manner that was a sure sign it was broken.

"Papa," she yelled, without taking her attention off Finn, who was trying to grin at her. He couldn't quite manage it with his split and bleeding lip. Her hands hovered near his body, but she didn't want to touch him for fear of hurting him by accident.

Papa cursed when he saw the state of Finn. "Let's get him inside."

They lifted him together, even though Colette froze when Finn grimaced so hard he swayed between them.

"If he passes out, I'll catch him," Papa said, and Colette gritted her teeth. She wasn't some weak-willed maiden. She could handle this.

Colette regripped his arm and ignored the groan she elicited. Together she and Papa managed to get him to the relative comfort of the sofa.

"Go find a good steak," Papa said. "And something from the pharmacist."

Colette followed his directions in a blur, procuring both the meat and the morphine.

Papa slapped the former on Finn's face and administered the latter. He'd tended plenty of people who'd come out of the mines in worse shape.

"I'll sit with him," Colette told Papa after he'd done all he could do to make Finn comfortable. "You have to be up in only a few hours."

Papa hesitated, but he knew she was right. He kissed her forehead. "Don't hesitate to wake me if he catches a fever or some such."

She nodded and then dragged Papa's heavy wooden chair over to the sofa, so she could see Finn's battered face in the candlelight. With a shaking hand, she pushed the strands of hair off his forehead.

He blinked up at her, his eyes struggling to focus. "Colette?"

"What happened?" she whispered.

"The Pinkerton men," he said, and she was almost surprised he'd been able to form an answer. He wouldn't be lucid for much longer. "There was a union meeting in . . ."

Finn trailed off, thinking. Then he shook his head. "Not sure. Butte?"

"That would make sense," Colette murmured. He couldn't have traveled far like this.

"There was an undercover detective there," Finn said. "He followed me back to the hotel. Told me to stay out of town. The rest, as you say, is history."

He tried to wave at himself, and then ended up in a wincing coughing fit.

"Shh," Colette soothed. "Just rest."

"Me and my merry band of men should just get out of Montana," Finn said, and she only remembered then that she'd been cross with him on his last visit. "Where does that come from? 'Merry band of men'?"

"A book called *The Merry Adventures of Robin Hood*," Colette said. "Based on a mythological outlaw in England. Actually, you would like it; I can't believe you haven't read it."

"Not all of us have time to read libraries full of books for fun," Finn murmured. "Why would I like it?"

"It's about a mischievous man who steals from the rich and gives to the poor," Colette said, and that got Finn to open his eyes. "He fights corrupt men, powerful men."

"Do you have it?"

"Probably," she said. It was a story that went over well with the miners, for obvious reasons. She stood and started going through the stacks of books all over the room.

"You don't have to—"

"Hush," she said, absently. He might be asleep by the time she located it. But she was happy to have something to do.

She shouldn't be surprised that he wanted a book. She'd seen the same in so many sick or injured neighbors. The stories became a comfort, a distraction, a lifeboat to get through the river of endless pain.

Colette found *Robin Hood* and took the chair once more. "'In merry England in the time of old, when good King Henry the Second ruled the land, there lived within the green glades of Sherwood Forest, near Nottingham Town, a famous outlaw whose name was Robin Hood."

Finn's eyes were closed, but he had the tiniest smile on his lips, so she went on.

He murmured every once in a while, especially when he liked a line.

"'He who jumps for the moon and gets it not, leaps higher than he who stoops for a penny in the mud,'" Colette said, and Finn hummed.

"True," he said, the word soft with medication.

Colette read through the night even after she was certain Finn was asleep. She had a feeling that if she stopped, she would fall to pieces.

Her candle burned down, the sun rose, Papa left, and still she read.

She only stopped when her voice gave out.

"I think I missed some of it, can you read it again?" Finn asked, when she finally closed the book.

Colette laughed. She laughed and laughed until Finn tried to laugh and re-split his lip and then she laughed some more. She knew the joke hadn't been all that funny, but it was the release that she craved. The exhale.

She made a show of flipping back to the beginning, and Finn reached out, his hand encircling her wrist gently. His thumb rubbed at the jut of bone there.

And she wished, oh how she wished, that life could be more like a book.

CHAPTER FOURTEEN

Millie

Missoula, Montana
1936

The week Millie had allotted to getting ready for the road trips went by impossibly fast.

One of the first things she'd done was send a telegram to the state headquarters in Helena. She trusted Katherine's assessment, but Millie also had to be thorough if she was then going to accuse one of her own staff of sabotage.

Mr. Sutter, the editor in Helena, had then arranged a telephone call with her in which he, in almost excruciating detail, walked her through the day he'd received the package from Missoula. Apparently, a good number of people in the office had watched him open the box and would gladly talk to Millie if needed.

Millie had spoken to a handful of the witnesses, all of whom had seemed believably indignant over what they assumed was disrespectful and disgraceful sloth.

Unfortunately, she believed them. As did Katherine.

Which meant Flo, Oscar, Sidney, or Professor Lyon had sabotaged their own and their colleagues' work, probably for money.

She didn't want to believe it—even of Sidney, who was at the top of her list. He'd dropped the combative act after the first day, but that made her all the more suspicious. Her presence had startled him, and now he had himself under control.

That could mean nothing, but it could mean he was feeling guilty and jumpy.

Recognizing her own bias, Millie had tried to make a case why one of the other three could have been the person to sabotage the work. And at the end of the exercise, she'd realized any of them could be the guilty party.

She'd even asked if someone else in town might have had a key, or perhaps there had been a break-in. All four of them had seemed thoughtful, but, in the end, admitted they were the only ones with access to the office and there hadn't been any signs that someone had forced their way in.

That person also would have had to know that the box was left unattended that night and was getting shipped out in the morning—which would mean one of the staff had helped the saboteur anyway.

One thing they had all agreed upon was that moving forward there would be copious amounts of copies made. Everything would go through Millie, and she would be the one personally shipping it straight to Mr. Sutter.

Now, Millie sat on the curb with the supplies she'd bought for their trip up to Glacier National Park and the one battered suitcase that had seen her through both Dallas and Washington.

When Sidney's sleek, olive-green mountain climber rounded the corner, a cloud of dust kicked up in its wake. She sighed and hoped that she wouldn't be in for a month's worth of clutching at the passenger-side door.

He braked to a stop right in front of her, but beeped the horn seemingly for the hell of it. She rolled her eyes and stood, checking out the back seat of the car. Oscar Dalton stared up at her beneath the brim of his ever-present fedora, his typewriter in a case beside him, and Flo gave Millie a weak salute, her eyes hidden behind a large pair of sunnies.

Millie couldn't help but smile at how tired and grumpy they both looked—like children forced to attend a family gathering.

Sidney finished tying her luggage to the top of theirs, and then rounded the vehicle. "Are you waiting for an invitation?"

She huffed out an annoyed breath, but got into the car. The mountain climber was old, but in good shape. It added to her impression that Sidney Walker had come from wealth, despite the fact that he would have had to take the pauper's oath just like the rest of them to get on the relief rolls.

Plenty of people had gone from the highest highs to the lowest lows on that Black Tuesday, though.

The tip of Oscar's shoe nudged her elbow, and she glanced back to find him holding out a thermos for her.

The unexpected kindness surprised her. Although, maybe it wasn't kindness, she reminded herself. Maybe he was simply trying to get on her good side so she wouldn't suspect him of anything.

Maybe she was already exhausted from maybe-ing her way through every conversation as if it were a minefield.

"Thank you," Millie said. Oscar simply ducked his head, his hat covering any expression she might have been able to read.

"Wake me when we get there," he said.

And with that, he was out like a light. She gawked at him in amazement for a second—it took her no less than a half hour any given night to fall asleep.

She glanced at Flo to share her disbelief, only to find her softly snoring, her head against the window.

Millie couldn't help it. She giggled.

Sidney looked back, and then shook his head, a fond smile tugging at the corners of his mouth. It was the softest she'd ever seen him.

"They will both sleep about ninety percent of the driving time if past experience holds true," he informed her.

"That hardly seems fair," Millie pointed out.

"Oh, no one drives my baby besides me," Sidney said, patting the dash with a possessive hand. "If I was in a horrific accident and the only way we could get back to Missoula was for one of you to drive, I'd rather we all be stranded until I bled out. Then I wouldn't have to witness the horrors."

"Please, I bet I'm better at it than you are," Millie said. "I was driving out to pastures when I still had to sit on a stack of Yellow Pages to reach the pedals."

"You've never driven on Montana's roads, darling."

"You've never driven Texas's, *sugar*," Millie drawled.

"Touché," he said, tossing her a grin.

For an older man, he was handsome when he wasn't scowling, and again she wondered what had happened with him and Alice Monroe.

Alice had to be only a handful of years younger than him—if Millie had pegged her right at early thirties—so it would make sense they might have courted once upon a time. Maybe their relationship had been as tragic as it had been romantic, à la Romeo and Juliet. It was interesting, too, that neither of them had married. Alice must be considered a spinster and even Sidney would be looked at askance sometime soon for remaining unwed.

"How does this work?" she asked, changing the topic. "With you as the photographer. Did the writers show you their sections and you picked the pictures to go along? Or did you just find the best ones?"

His eyes narrowed. "You want my opinion on the material the staff submitted to Helena."

Millie wrinkled her nose, annoyed that she'd been so obvious. "Well, yes. I am the editor taking over, it would be nice knowing what to expect."

"The writing was top-notch," Sidney said, lifting a shoulder. "Someone in Helena made a mistake and refuses to own up to it."

"Hmm," Millie hummed. Everyone was in lockstep on that reasoning. She wondered who'd been the first to suggest it. She also wondered if she was wrong to only be looking for one person at the heart of the sabotage. "You didn't actually answer my question."

"I picked my favorites." Sidney shrugged. "But the writers covered so much ground that the photographs fit anyway."

Millie thought about those towns he suggested skipping, but she didn't want to show her cards too early with him. Instead, she walked into the idea sideways.

"Is the itinerary any different this time?" she asked, as if she didn't remember.

"Yes." Sidney glanced over at her. She was surprised he was telling the truth until he added, "Last time, we spent a bit of time on the Flathead Reservation. It's a big part of life up in these areas."

That seemed like something they shouldn't skip. In fact, Mr. Alsberg had been explicit in his desire for the editors to include content about the native people in every volume. He'd even warned editors to be on the lookout for writers who had biases against the tribes.

"Too often writers on Indian life color the writing with a personal point of view. Sometimes this point of view is sentimental, sometimes it interprets tribal customs in such a way as to make the reader think of the Indian as superstitious, occasionally it is downright dishonest

and relegates the Indian to a savagery that exists only in the writer's imagination."

He hadn't been standing on a moral soapbox, but rather preaching that the lure of the native people could draw tourists' interest. Still, she wouldn't quibble with the motive when it would likely serve as a good reminder to everyone.

"I don't see the reservations on our current itinerary," Millie said, scanning it again, even though she had it memorized.

"I took over the interviews and subsequent writing on that particular section," he said, and she thought she could detect a layer of anger or bitterness beneath the words. "I was still working on them when the other material was submitted."

Millie blinked at him. "What?"

He glanced at her, eyes narrowed as if he was replaying what he'd just said, searching for a misstep. "I have the most knowledge on the tribes, so I took over that section. No one else fought me on it."

Millie nodded, but her mind took off to the races.

The interviews done on the reservations hadn't been included in the boxes shipped to Helena.

They had been saved.

Because Sidney had taken over that section of the guides.

She thought back to what he'd whispered in her ear that first day. *You might want to look around and consider just what was here before "the entirety of this country's existence."*

Sidney cared about the people who'd been displaced by settlers. He cared about them deeply.

And their interviews had been the only work that hadn't been sabotaged.

She tried to steady her breathing. This didn't prove anything.

"Who lives there?" she asked. "On the reservations. Which tribes?"

"There are two in this part of the state, the Flathead and the Blackfeet reservations," Sidney offered. "The former is home to the Salish, Upper Pend d'Oreille, and Kootenai tribes."

"And the latter?"

"Blackfeet Nation."

"Well, I'm glad we didn't lose all your work with them," Millie said, watching him closely.

Sidney drummed his fingers on the wheel. "I'm worried they won't be represented well in the guides. I wanted to take my time with the material."

That concern was valid, she had to admit. Mr. Alsberg wouldn't have gone through such pains to make sure the editors watched out for biases if he didn't suspect it would be a major problem. Even with those staff-wide memos, there were going to be writers who glorified the tribes, ones who vilified them. It would happen with the former slaves they interviewed, as well. And it would happen to the women and the Italians and the Catholics and the Chinese.

The fact that there would be someone at the top who got to decide what American stories were worth telling—or what stories were even considered *American*—was a fundamental flaw in the program. It was a fundamental flaw in their country, too.

The fact that the excuse was valid didn't make Millie any less suspicious of Sidney.

"Well we can do our best to make sure their section is compelling as hell," Millie said. "Why is telling their story so important to you?"

He laughed, but it wasn't amused. "Aren't you the one who has been preaching for the past week about the importance of all Americans' stories?"

"You didn't ever seem to be listening," Millie said, though felt chastened. She hadn't meant to imply that their stories weren't important, just that he seemed to care more than the average American did about the reservations.

"I could do your propaganda speeches by heart," Sidney said, though it came out resigned rather than cruel. "I served with a few brave men, from the Osage Nation in Oklahoma. They volunteered in the war, even after all this country had done to their people."

Millie wished in that moment she could add something intelligent, but she had to confess, just to herself, to her own ignorance. Growing up in Texas, she'd learned far more about the fight for independence and events like the Alamo revolution than she had about other history.

"The army used the men as scouts, which was one of the most dangerous positions any man could hold over there." Sidney blew out a breath, and she could read a thousand emotions in his face, all tinged with sorrow. "You know, the Osage men were worried—we were *all* worried—that we would come home and have to face a world that called us heroes. Instead, they weren't called anything at all."

When they next stopped to fill up the tank, Flo woke up to go use the washroom and Sidney lounged against the car, chatting with the man at the pump.

Oscar leaned forward from the back seat.

"You're being too obvious," he said.

Millie whirled on him, and he sat back gesturing to her. "See?"

"I'm not being obvious," Millie said, swallowing an instinctive, childish, *You're being obvious.* There were some things that stuck after being raised with so many cousins.

"It was a good line of questioning, though," Oscar said, without bothering to argue with her. He put his fedora over his face once more.

"What was?" Millie asked. She wasn't sure if it was relief, irritation, or embarrassment—or some mixture of all three—that made her snappish.

"Wondering why Sidney didn't send the work he'd done with the tribes to the Helena office," Oscar said. "Because I'm pretty sure he couldn't bear the thought of ruining it."

CHAPTER FIFTEEN

Alice

Missoula, Montana
1924

Sidney Walker was a man who got what he wanted.

That had always been obvious, but now that Alice was reaping the benefits of it, she could see his power even more clearly.

Exactly two weeks after Julia Walker had launched her campaign against the Boxcar Library, she waved the white flag. In fact, she even held a book drive with her most exclusive circle of friends, pulling in three pristine *Pride and Prejudice*s and a battered copy of the *Saturday Evening Post* that was six months old.

Mac hadn't liked the turnabout. She'd never thought of him as suspicious, but he'd spent the days following Julia's surrender watching Alice too closely.

"Why did she give up?" he finally asked one night.

They were on the porch, she licking the remnants of her orange from her fingertips, he leaning against one of the posts staring out at the moon.

"I don't know," Alice lied, guilt twinging deep in her belly. In a perfect world, she'd be able to share her secrets with Mac, but they didn't exist in that world. They existed in the one where Mac might tell her father that she'd snuck out to have a private conversation with a man well known for his womanizing ways in a town full of gamblers and whores.

When Mac gripped the railing, part of her wondered if he suspected she'd gone to Sidney. Part of her wondered if he was jealous.

But that was just silly fantasy.

"I'm leaving in the morning," he said, letting the topic go.

"Oh." She had hoped he would help with the process of hiring a librarian. He'd had complete faith in her ability to win over Julia and had sent off listings to newspapers and magazines. Alice had already received a handful of letters from interested parties and expected a few more to come in the next several days.

"I'm headed to the border ranch," he continued, still not looking at her. The border ranch was what they called the property her father owned just south of Canada. Her uncle ran the thing to give it a semblance of respectability, but she knew it was a crucial cog in her father's bootlegging operations.

Mac oversaw the biggest, most important runs, and one of these days she feared he would get a chest full of bullets for his trouble.

"Should I say 'be careful'?" she asked lightly.

His mouth twitched. "Nothing to be careful about."

She sighed. In a perfect world, she'd be the keeper of his secrets, as well. In this one, they peeked in through each other's curtains hoping to spot the truth.

"Miss Monroe?" Mac said, sounding far too serious all of a sudden.

"Murdoch MacTavish?" she said, to tease him out of it.

He took a fortifying breath. "When I return, may I talk to you?"

Alice stilled. "You're talking with me now."

Mac shook his head, his jaw set. "It's about something important; I don't want to rush it."

"You're making me nervous," she said, laughing again, but not finding anything funny in the moment. This was what she had wanted, wasn't it?

For some reason, she couldn't help but think back to that night in Sidney's Packard as they drove home and the world spun and sparkled and the mountains watched over them.

"Please, don't be," he said. "I only wish to . . ."

He trailed off and Alice didn't push him. She felt pinned like a moth, excited and hopeful but also terrified and now dreading his return.

What silly things emotions were. Alice crossed to him and put her hands on his impossibly wide shoulders. Rising to her tiptoes, she brushed her lips across his cheekbone.

"Just make sure you make it back," she whispered, before ending the torture for both of them. "Good night."

In the morning, he was gone.

Alice told herself not to think about anything he might want to *talk* about. Instead, she threw all her focus into the Boxcar Library.

The day after Julia Walker had conceded, Mr. Rutherford contacted her, acting for all the world as if the week he'd avoided Alice hadn't happened at all. They spoke about the construction of the boxcar, what would be needed—down to the number of shelves she wanted—and the timeline. He promised it wouldn't be long and she would be able to count on the inaugural journey going out before the first snowfall.

The editor of the *Missoulian* also had started to meet her eyes again, and had even let her write a small editorial about what she was hoping to accomplish. That had garnered far more donations than Julia's paltry efforts.

"A cookbook from my grandmother," one of Alice's neighbors said, handing over a clearly beloved journal. "It was written with hard times in mind. Recipes without many ingredients, that sort of thing. I think wives in the places the library is going might need it more than I."

The Darcy sisters brought their late father's collection of dime novels, full of romance and adventure and secondhand thrills.

Mrs. Marner, and her daughter Sarah, dropped off a new copy of *Little Women*. Alice wasn't sure it would be a hit with the men in the camps, but Mrs. Marner leaned in, winking. "We had to buy copies for the two boys when Sarah wouldn't share. They'll pretend not to like it, but both of mine cried buckets."

Alice pressed a smile away and thanked them for their generosity.

The next man in line, Professor Fournier, had grown up the son of fur trappers, as so many did in the Western territories. He ran the English department at the University of Montana now that he was well into his seventies. But he'd had an adventurous life in between. Along the way he'd collected plenty of novels, and he made sure to tell Alice she was doing him a favor by helping him clean some of them out.

In his box, he had George Bernard Shaw and Edith Wharton, Poe and Keats, even a signed edition of *Tarzan of the Apes* by Edgar Rice Burroughs.

But the treasure trove was his complete collection of everything that had been published by Zane Grey.

Critics called the author's depictions of the West glamorized and unrealistic, but every person Alice knew who lived out here loved them.

Maybe because life needed a little romanticizing to survive it.

"'I need this wild life, this freedom,'" Professor Fournier quoted as he handed them over.

"'The great thing is to see life, to understand, to feel, to work, to fight, to endure,'" Alice murmured back. Both Grey quotes might as well be written in permanent ink on the heart of each Montanan.

The books poured in, her community showing her why she loved it so much. The novels she'd ordered with Sidney's generous donation also started to show up in heavy packages that delighted her with each delivery.

All that was left was to find a librarian.

When all was said and done, there had been ten applicants for the boxcar librarian post.

Some of them hadn't understood what the position entailed. The concept of bookmobiles wasn't completely new—Alice didn't give herself credit for inventing the wheel. They were actually gaining in popularity across the states, especially in rural areas where traveling to a library would have been impossible for a good number of residents. But she had yet to hear one based out of a train, and, apparently, neither had her applicants.

Alice called in Mrs. Joseph and Missoula's other librarian, Mrs. Bonner, to help her whittle down the rest to three for in-person interviews.

Two were from within Missoula city limits and one was from just over the border in Idaho.

The first, Mr. Zalinski, was a professor at the University of Montana. Something about him rubbed Alice wrong from the start, but since it was nothing obvious, she tried to approach the conversation with an open mind. He acquitted himself fine under their combined scrutiny, though she wondered if he was being honest with himself about how much travel would be involved, and sometimes in the dead of winter at that.

As her final question, Alice asked him, "What would you suggest to a man who hadn't read anything since he was a boy, but wanted to try out the library?"

This question, to her, represented the entire goal of the project. Alice wasn't naive, she had been dealing with stubborn Montanan pride for years now. She suspected at least some, if not most, of the men would be hesitant to check out a book, so it would be a crucial part of the job for the librarian to be able to guide them in the right direction.

The professor thought about it for a long minute. "*War and Peace*, of course."

Alice tried to imagine handing over a Russian tome of more than a thousand pages to a first-time reader. "Why is that?"

He stared her down as if she were doubting Tolstoy himself. Or as if he were questioning if she'd ever read it at all. But she hadn't asked him to name the most prestigious book he could think of, and so she needed his answer.

"Well, it's the height of literature, is it not?" Mr. Zalinski asked.

Alice thanked him profusely for coming in and then saw him to the door.

Mrs. Bonner was waiting for her when she came back. Alice thought that out of the three of them, she would be the most receptive to Mr. Zalinski's answer, but all she said was, "Not all book lovers are meant to be librarians."

And that was that.

The other applicant from Missoula was clever and kind, but balked at the small stipend the position offered. Alice didn't even get to ask him her dealbreaker questions—he'd already had one of his own locked and loaded.

The man from Idaho intrigued Alice. He was rugged and well-read, the exact combination she was looking for. Joseph Cantor was also young enough for her to believe that he could survive the long winter on the train. He answered their initial questions with flying colors.

"What would you suggest to a man who hadn't read anything since he was a boy, but wanted to try out the library?" Alice finally asked, almost as a formality.

"Perhaps start them with a children's book," he suggested, and she could tell by the tilt of his smile that he was proud of the answer.

Alice stood to see him out.

When she came back it was to find Mrs. Joseph eyeing her kindly. "We could have given him a chance."

"We could also set fire to the boxcar and write the whole thing off as a loss," Alice said, grumpy because they knew as well as she that the men who these books were intended for would never come back if a librarian offered them an elementary school primer.

"He would have gotten his teeth knocked out at the first stop," Mrs. Bonner said, and Alice sent her a grateful smile, remembering why she'd always liked the woman despite her fussy ways.

It didn't take long for Alice's fondness to fizzle out into despair. There would be more applicants, any job posting these days drew attention. The rest of the country might be riding high on the postwar euphoria, but in Montana, people were desperate. Still, the rest of the project had been going so well after they'd moved past Julia Walker's objections that Alice couldn't help but wallow.

Alice watched the two other women close up the library, and then waved them off when they waited for her to join them at the door.

"I'm going to sulk in the pages for a bit," Alice said.

"Jane?" Mrs. Joseph asked.

"Who else in these trying times?" Alice asked, sighing dramatically. She was in the perfect mood for a reread of *Emma*.

"Don't stay too late," Mrs. Joseph warned. "I don't like when Mac's not here to see you about."

Alice frowned, but then smoothed out her expression. Just because she didn't think she needed a minder, didn't mean Mrs. Joseph didn't have a point. She was a young woman alone after all. Even though none of the locals would ever harm a strand of hair on her head, there were enough outlaws and other ne'er-do-wells who passed through Missoula that walking by herself at night posed an actual danger.

"I promise," Alice said, mostly to appease the women. Once they finally left, Alice turned to head toward the stacks—and Miss Austen—but paused when the front door opened once more.

"Did you forget something?" Alice called out, but was greeted with only silence.

Alice swung back around to find a stranger standing there instead of Mrs. Joseph. Her hand flew to her throat as she wondered just how fast she could run.

Before she could gather a scream, the stranger stepped into the light. That didn't exactly help matters, considering they had a shotgun slung over their back. But then they held their hands up, palms out in the universal gesture that they meant no harm. "Pardon me, I didn't mean to scare you. I'm here to inquire about the librarian post."

"Oh," Alice breathed out, her shoulders dropping as the tension fled her body. She studied the stranger more closely, but couldn't get a read on them. With their hat on, and the setting sun creating harsh shadows, Alice could only tell that they dressed as if coming off the plains after a long cattle drive.

That boded well.

"Please come in, come in," Alice said, retaking her seat from earlier.

The stranger did, keeping his head ducked and his hat on. Either shy or cautious. She couldn't fault him for either, not in these parts where being too friendly to the wrong person could get you killed.

Alice thought about the time she'd wasted interviewing the other three applicants when one question would have sufficed, and blurted out, "What would you suggest to a man who hadn't read anything since he was a boy, but wanted to try out the library?"

She blushed a little. She hadn't even asked for the man's name or if he knew what the position entailed. But the day had been a long one and she was tired of wasting time.

The stranger seemed thoughtful instead of insulted, anyway. "From an unlimited collection?"

He was the first candidate to ask that, already an improvement.

"Yes."

"*The Thirty-Nine Steps*," he said without a moment of further hesitation. "By John Buchan."

The novel—a thrilling adventure of an ordinary man on the run solving a mystery—had burst onto the scene about ten years ago.

It was exactly what Alice would have answered if she'd been given the question. But she wanted to hear the reasoning anyway. "Why?"

"It's fun," he said. "It's an adventure story but one for grown men. The protagonist is a common man caught up in extraordinary circumstances, which is the ideal reading material for anyone who wants to daydream about escaping their own lives sometimes. As a bonus, he was also a mining engineer before the story starts."

"I had forgotten that detail," Alice murmured, charmed.

"The critics noted that the men in the trenches found the book highly enjoyable," he continued. "I know mining and working in the lumber camps doesn't compare to war, but I think the desire to find some escape is similar."

"That's true—" Alice started. The man held up a hand to stop her.

"But the main reason I would suggest *Thirty-Nine Steps* is that there are several books in the series," he said. "Our hypothetical patron would be hooked. They wouldn't want to stop until they read the whole series, and each trip to the library increases the chance that they'll return even after they finish that run."

Alice finally let herself smile.

She had found her boxcar librarian.

"I'm so sorry, I've been unconscientiously rude," Alice said, almost giddy now. "My name is Alice Monroe."

The stranger finally took off their hat, and Alice realized the mistake she had made.

"I am Colette," the woman said, a hint of French coming out in her voice. "Colette Durand."

CHAPTER SIXTEEN

Colette

Hell Raisin' Gulch, Montana
1921

Three years after Colette began her apprenticeship, Hell Raisin' Gulch's librarian died.

Mr. Tate had turned ninety-eight the previous month, so, while she of course mourned, she also privately celebrated the promotion. Tastefully, with a few shots of bootlegged moonshine.

Papa joined her out on the porch, and she didn't even bother to hide her contraband. He laughed and held out his own glass for a pour. They sat on rocking chairs they'd sat on thousands of times and stared at stars they'd stared at thousands of times.

When they finished their first drink, Papa poured them another one and clinked their glasses together. "I'm proud of you, little bird."

Colette ducked her head, but couldn't smother her pleased smile. Other fathers might be frustrated that, at twenty-one, Colette was unmarried and childless and pursuing a vocation rather than a husband.

She thought of Finn. It had been nearly a year since she'd nursed him back to health after that Pinkerton detective had decided to rearrange all the bones in his face. He hadn't stayed out of Butte or the Company's business since then. In fact, he seemed to have doubled his efforts. Whereas he used to come through Gulch every few weeks, now they were lucky if they saw him every other month simply because he was so busy in other places.

Colette would be lying if she said she hadn't thought of him wistfully, of the way he made her laugh and of that moment the morning after she'd read *Robin Hood* to him where he'd held her wrist so gently in his hand. But she wasn't a daydreamer, never had been.

He was a *maybe* that she would never bank on.

"In another life, would you have become a librarian?" Colette asked, knowing Papa wouldn't take offense.

He rolled his glass in his hands as he considered. "I can be anything? In this life you suggest."

"Anything at all."

"Then no. It's always been you who's been a tender of stories," Papa said. His work boots were propped up on the rail, his eyes locked on the horizon he couldn't actually see.

Colette straightened, indignant. "I keep the stories because *you* tell them."

Papa grinned. "Precisely, little bird. If I could be anything in this magical life you've imagined, I'd be an actor."

She slumped back against the rocking chair. Of course he would. A Shakespearean one, without a doubt.

"You would be a good actor," she admitted.

"I would be a great actor," he corrected. They didn't live some magical life, they lived this one, where he'd become as close to an actor as could be.

"'All the world's a stage,'" she murmured, and he lifted his glass in acknowledgment.

"'And this our life, exempt from public haunt, finds tongues in trees, books in the running brooks, sermons in stones and good in everything. I would not change it,'" he quoted from the same play.

As You Like It.

He looked at her, and repeated, "'And this our life . . . I would not change it.'"

Colette blinked back a sudden rush of emotion. Because if he had not had her, perhaps he could have escaped it all with some traveling troupe of Shakespearean actors. He could have joined a medicine show, even, and become part of the entertainment that brightened up the days of simple townspeople like themselves.

"Well, what are you waiting for?" Colette asked. Her voice came out shaky but she covered it with a teasing smile. "Give us your best audition."

Papa narrowed his eyes but then after only a second's more hesitation jumped to his feet. He flawlessly delivered the monologue from *Hamlet* first, as she'd known he would. And then Mark Antony's from *Julius Caesar*.

"More," she cried when he finished, a long way from a few years ago when she begged for a break from Shakespeare. As an adult, she saw now what her younger self missed—the way Papa *became* the words he recited. Papa didn't simply enjoy Shakespeare, just like he didn't simply love Colette and the workers he spent his life trying to protect.

They were, all three, a *part* of his story.

And it was Colette's job to tend to it.

So when he finished Macbeth's and then Romeo's, Colette drank up both the moonshine and the sight of her father against the star-laden Montana sky.

She thought, *And this our life . . . I would not change it.*

A WEEK LATER, the two of them were sitting on the porch again, this time sans moonshine and monologues. Colette was simply telling Papa about her first days fully in charge of Gulch's library.

He was being quiet, more so than usual, and she could tell he had something on his mind.

"What's wrong?" she finally just asked.

Papa shook his head. "Nothing, little bird. Go on."

"Is it something with the union?" Colette pressed, refusing to let it go.

Again, Papa shook his head. But then he stopped himself and turned to her.

"You remember what I said? Last week." His voice was urgent all of a sudden.

Colette tried to think back, but all she came up with was his performances. "What do you mean?"

"'I would not change it,'" he said, leaning forward now. "Do you remember that?"

"Oh. Yes," Colette said slowly, confused by the change in his demeanor. He was watching her as if his life depended on her answer. "*As You Like It.*"

He sighed, almost sounding relieved, and then slumped back in his rocker. "Remember that, Colette."

"All right," Colette said, mostly just to appease him.

"Just, if anything happens—"

"What do you mean, 'happens'?" Colette asked.

"It's nothing to worry about," Papa said, and then slid her a glance. "Not yet. I'm looking into—"

This time, he cut himself off, straightening and cocking his head.

"Go inside, Colette," Papa said, his voice steady but deadly serious.

She did immediately as she was told, because if there was one thing she'd learned out here it was that survival could be jeopardized by questioning direct commands.

Papa didn't keep a gun, even though she'd begged him plenty

of times to get one. Colette crept toward the kitchen to grab the cast-iron pan that hung from a hook on the wall. She had to lift it with both hands, but once she had it down, she held it against her chest. Then she pressed her back to the wooden boards just beside the door.

She closed her eyes trying to picture Papa. He would be standing on the edge of the steps, staring out into the darkness, waiting for the men who had inevitably come to beat him senseless. Colette was already thinking about running to the butcher in the morning for a slab of cold meat for the bruises that would be left behind.

"Give it over, old man," a man drawled, loud enough for Colette to hear. They weren't trying to be quiet. She didn't think that was a good sign.

"I don't know what you're talking about," Papa said, and she could hear the lie even hiding in the shadows. The men easily could, as well.

"Don't play games with us." A second voice, this one was softer. Where the first had been taunting, like he wanted violence, the second man seemed to want Papa to be reasonable. "Please. For your sake, for your daughter's sake."

"Stay away from my daughter," Papa warned, and Colette gripped the cast iron tighter.

"Give us what you found," the second man said. "And we'll leave."

"No, you won't," Papa said slowly. "Because I'll know anyway. Even if you take the proof, I'll still know. Which means . . ."

One of the men sighed. "I wish you wouldn't have said that."

Colette shifted, ready to step out onto the porch to help fight off these men. These pigs who took Company money to intimidate good men.

But before she could, Papa yelled, "Colette run."

Then there was a crack, like the thunder that followed dry lightning in the hottest stretch of summer.

A cry, a thud.

Her hands went numb and the cast iron clattered to the ground.

"Christ, I'm not going to shoot a girl," one of the men said. She could no longer distinguish between the two. "We'll come back later to search the place."

Boots pounded against dirt.

Colette stumbled toward the door, knowing exactly what she'd find.

Papa lying in a pool of his own blood, the air smelling of copper and gun smoke.

Her knees gave way, and she landed on the wooden boards beside him where only a week ago he'd trodden over them like a stage.

She pressed her quivering lips together to stop the sob as she searched for the wound. Her skirt had gone heavy with blood by the time she found it.

The bullet must have missed his heart, but not by much. She could see the weakening pumps, right there in the torn flesh.

"Papa," she whispered. The word sliced her throat open, but she tried again, grasping his cold hands to her chest. "Papa."

He coughed and she gasped. His lashes fluttered.

"Papa," she pleaded. "Papa, I love you, don't leave me. Papa."

"Colette," he managed, not with sound, though. She saw her name on his mouth and she tried to stop crying long enough to squeeze his hands.

"Yes, I'm here, I love you, stay with me," Colette babbled, knowing her promises, her demands, were pointless. Even these last seconds were a miracle that she wasn't about to waste.

"'I would not change it,'" he said, and she could tell it was with his last breath. How perfect for it to be the Bard's words.

"'I would not change it,'" she repeated desperately, as if it was a promise. "'I would not change it.'"

As soon as the words were out, Papa closed his eyes, his body relaxing into the darkness.

Colette sat back on her heels, a shudder running through her, as if he'd taken part of her soul with him.

CHAPTER SEVENTEEN

Colette

Hell Raisin' Gulch, Montana
1921

Colette saw the silhouette first, bathed in the light of the dawn.

One of the men, coming back to finish her off.

She had sat on the porch all night, Papa right beside her. Her muscles were stiff, her body ached, her eyes were rubbed raw with sandpaper. But she forced herself to move, to go for the cast iron she'd dropped hours earlier.

"Colette." It wasn't one of the men. "Goddamn it. Colette. Are you injured?"

Something about knowing Finn was there let her finally collapse back against the wall.

She had been guarding Papa, she realized. But now she didn't have to anymore.

There were hands on her then, shaking her.

But the darkness called.

And she finally let it take her.

"Here we go."

That voice again, soft hands directing her into a tub full of warm water.

She was naked. Finn must have stripped her blood-soaked

dress from her body. He must have had to peel it from her skin in the places it had dried.

The washcloth was gentle against her arm, but she wanted him to scrub instead. Scrub and scrub and scrub until everything was gone. Her bones. Her organs. Her mind.

Scrub it all away.

"I've got you."

LIGHT SPILLED INTO the room, forcing her eyes open. Colette breathed in, concentrating on the way her ribcage lifted and fell so that she didn't have to think about anything.

The sheets were cool and smelled of lavender.

Her bed.

Finn had put her in her bed.

She tried to remember the last time she'd seen him. It had been weeks, but he'd bought her dinner and then rehashed some old argument about her leaving Gulch to explore the big, wide world.

Thank God she hadn't left Gulch when Finn had said she should. Papa would have died alone.

Pain sliced through her, a knife with serrated edges.

Colette thought about her ribcage. Breathed in, breathed out.

And then succumbed once more to the blessed abyss.

The next time she woke, Finn was sitting on the side of the bed, his hand on her shoulder.

"I'm sorry, Colette, the sheriff is here," he said. "I've put him off as long as possible."

She nodded, because this was worth fighting the darkness for. "I'll be down in ten minutes."

"Take your time."

Colette pulled on a white cotton housedress, slipped on a pair of flat shoes, and braided her hair into a simple plait.

Sheriff MacComber was a broad man with a bushy black mustache that hid his mouth. She could never tell if he was smiling or scowling and that remained true today.

He had also hated Claude Durand, had viewed him as a troublemaker. Odds were good he was in the Company's pocket. But even if he wasn't he'd want to stay on their good side. His was an elected position, after all.

She wasn't even surprised when he blamed the murder on drifters looking for money.

Finn had watched the exchange quietly, knowing he wouldn't be able to affect the outcome any more than her firsthand testimony had. Later, he gathered her into his chest, rocking her back and forth.

So many boundaries broken down between them by one tragic act. It felt both right and strange.

"He deserves justice," Finn said, his voice full of emotion. He had admired Papa more than almost anyone he'd met in his travels. He'd told both her and Papa that together and separately. And she could usually suss out when someone was blowing smoke—it never seemed like he was.

Finn had never been around as much as she might have liked, but when he was he'd made it count. He'd schemed with Papa over moonshine on the porch, ate dinner with them when he was in town, he'd even had Colette read to him. Not often and only by candlelight when he wouldn't have to let her see his face when he asked for the small favor that she enjoyed so much.

She knew now that he felt what he said deep in his soul—Papa deserved justice.

"He'll get it," she promised.

There were three things in life that had been important to Papa: Colette, stories, and the union.

She was certain he'd given his life for the union—those men had been from the Company, she would bet her very last penny on it.

But he'd also given his life, the entirety of it, to the workers.

She had known her father was loved and respected, but she hadn't realized to what extent until his funeral.

They held the service exactly one week after Papa had been killed. The tiny church in Hell Raisin' Gulch wasn't big enough to accommodate everyone who showed up—some from Butte and even farther afield than that—so it was held outside.

Colette knew she had to deliver the eulogy, but she worried she wouldn't be able to get a single word out. When she stepped out onto the stairs that were serving as a makeshift stage, she knew she wouldn't be able to.

Finn squeezed her hand, and then shifted back, trusting her.

A hundred faces stared up at her, all watching her with a respect that she hadn't earned, watching her that way because she was Claude Durand's daughter. And all she could see was the way his body had slumped to the porch after his last breath.

I would not change it.

The silence was suffocating, even outside, even in the fresh morning air, Colette couldn't breathe. Her head went light and she realized she was clutching at the collar of her dress, desperate. The polite anticipation from the crowd had soured into concern, at least in the front rows where they could tell she was a strong breeze away from collapsing to the ground in front of them.

A single violin note cut through the buzzing in her head, a long, drawn-out wail in perfect tune.

She didn't know who started the song, but she did know that every man joined in immediately. It was about the daughter of a miner, talking about a battle that still needed to be won against the company her father had died working for.

Colette laughed in relief, in joy, in memory. Papa had sung this union song so many times, when pulling in the sheets from the lines, when riding through meadows on the way to their fishing spot, when walking toward meetings that could only be held in the basements of ranch houses on the outskirts of town. It had become a lullaby for her, one she could turn to when she needed comfort because she could hear his voice singing it.

Tears streamed down Colette's face as the men shouted the chorus, asking the listener whose side they were on—the miners' or the bosses'.

There was nothing traditional about the eulogy, but Papa would have loved it.

Following the service, everyone came by the house to pay their respects to her, to eat the dozen or so casseroles baked by the wives of Gulch—the women who had spanked her and coddled her, scolded her and celebrated her nearly as much as Papa.

The day blurred, with Finn helping bear the condolences and hosting duties alike. She was grateful for him, and in the quiet moments in between mourners she let him bear the weight of her body, as well.

He followed her up the stairs that night, both of them exhausted. He had taken to following her to her room, making sure she was all right.

They stopped short when they entered the bedroom, knocked out of their daze.

There, resting by her nightstand, was a brand-new Browning shotgun.

"Can anyone make them pay for this?" Colette asked three

nights later. They were sitting in the porch rockers as the evening closed in around them. Finn was scheduled to leave in the morning, and she already ached with his absence. It was amazing that just a few weeks earlier she had been thinking she barely knew the man.

His thumb gently rubbed at her wrist bone, an absent gesture that she'd first come to love that night he showed up at their place with his face broken.

"Do you have any idea what they were looking for? That might help us find them."

Colette had gone over what they'd said a thousand times, in her head and out loud. None of it had made sense.

Give us what you found.

"No," Colette said, even though he didn't need it answered. They had already had this conversation. "It has to be something to do with the Company, right?"

Finn hummed. "But they can cover up murder and get away with it. What could Claude have found that was more damning than that?"

And that was where they kept getting derailed.

"Who else could it have been if not the Company?" Colette asked, knowing Finn would just shake his head.

"I'll try," Finn promised. "I'll follow the money, all right? Someone hired them, they'll have bragged about the income."

The West wasn't quite as lawless as she knew it was made to seem, but it was rough-and-tumble. There had to be hundreds of men out here bragging about kills for hire.

Finn would try, maybe he'd even catch a rumor or two. But he hadn't grown up in Montana. He was an outsider, no matter how much he fought to help them.

It would take someone who knew this place to find Papa's killers.

Her eyes slipped to the shotgun she had resting against her leg. She never went anywhere without it now.

"No," Finn said. "Colette. You let me take care of this, all right? You won't be doing anything foolish."

"Of course not," Colette promised.

They both knew she was lying.

CHAPTER EIGHTEEN

Alice

Missoula, Montana
1924

Alice hadn't wanted to hire a woman.

That wasn't because she'd thought a woman couldn't handle the position, but she had been worried about safety issues.

Wasn't that what she chafed against in her own life, though?

Wouldn't it have been better for her father to teach her how to swim instead of banning her from walking near the river? Wouldn't it have been better if he'd shown her how to recognize when a blizzard was sweeping in from the mountains instead of just locking her in her room for the duration of the storm? Wouldn't she better be able to navigate the world if she'd been given skills to survive it rather than trust that if she just didn't do anything bad she'd be safe?

How could she limit another woman who seemed plenty capable of taking care of herself?

On someone else, the shotgun Colette wore slung over her shoulder might have just been for show. But Colette handled it with the same confidence with which she'd answered Alice's questions about books.

"Are you worried about being alone out there with the men?" Alice asked point-blank.

"No," Colette answered, and then didn't expand on it.

She was young, but not that young, maybe four or five years older than Alice's nineteen. She was certainly old enough for Alice to take her word.

So, Alice did.

"Then welcome to the Boxcar Library," Alice said, holding out her hand. Colette took it.

Her palm was calloused, tough.

Alice smiled, sure this was exactly who they needed for this endeavor to succeed.

She let Colette get settled in, helping her find a boarding room for the two or so weeks it would take for the boxcar to be finished.

They had plenty to do in that time, so Alice was pleasantly surprised to realize Colette rose at dawn every morning.

"How far along are you?" Colette asked as they walked toward the library the morning after Alice hired her.

"We've acquired about seven hundred books," Alice said, and beamed when Colette whistled, impressed. "I would like to have about double that amount eventually, but I'm happy sending the boxcar on its inaugural journey with that collection."

"You brought in that amount in under a month?"

"I bought plenty of them." Partly with her own savings, partly with the money Sidney had given her. She didn't mention that part. "Many were donated from the community, though. Folks here really want to help the men."

Colette's mouth twitched. Not a grimace, not a smile. "Do they."

It wasn't a question.

Even though Colette hadn't actually said anything negative, Alice felt defensive of her neighbors. "We wouldn't be able to launch this before the winter without them."

Colette nodded. "What do we have left to do?"

Alice had the irrational urge to continue an argument Colette wasn't even having. She shook it off. She had probably misread the woman's tone. "All the books are piled in one room right now. Here."

They had made it to the library, and Alice unlocked the doors, leading Colette back to where they were keeping the books.

She turned the light on and was greeted by several small mountains that hadn't seemed all that overwhelming until just right now.

Alice grimaced, but when she shifted it was to see Colette blinking quickly, a sheen in her eyes that could only mean she was holding back tears.

"My father loved books," Colette said after a moment. "His room looked like this more often than not."

Alice waited, sensing there was more to it.

"He started his own private lending library for his fellow miners," Colette said. "But what they all loved best was his ability to recite them, almost word for word. Especially the plays."

Alice had read her favorites enough to remember special quotes, but she couldn't imagine trying to retell an entire novel.

"Have you heard of the shanachie?" Alice asked. Colette shook her head, so Alice continued, "They were Gaelic storytellers who were revered second only to royalty. They were the keepers of Ireland's mythology and history, and they would go town to town recounting tales and news and gossip."

"Like a bard," Colette murmured.

"Yes," Alice said. "A bard, and a historian, a keeper of a culture. They were the ones who ensured that it was passed down, generation to generation. It's fascinating how we can see them in every culture, in every civilization, maybe called different things. Pingshu in China; kobzar in Ukraine; griot in West Af-

rica; minstrel in Medieval Europe. But they all ex
purpose. We want to be told stories."

"It's human nature," Colette agreed. "You knov
about the topic."

"I've always been interested in it," Alice said with a
few years ago, I started correspondence with a librarian
homa who is writing a book on the subject. She keeps m
in reading materials."

"And what have you learned about why we tell each o
stories?" Colette asked. It had been a while since anyone
listened to Alice talk about this with anything more than pol
indulgence.

"They serve all kinds of purposes," Alice said. "Of course, entertainment is one. But stories are more than that. They offer explanation and comfort—especially back in the day, when less was known about the natural world. They're a way of easily teaching social norms and mores; as well as simply teaching history so that victories can be repeated and mistakes avoided."

"All very practical," Colette said.

"Oh dear, I do sound very dry, don't I?" Alice laughed at herself, and then thought about the deeper reasons humans loved stories. "They also tell us so much about ourselves. What we value, what we care about, what we fear most. And because of that, when you read or listen to stories written by people different than you, you can learn who they are down to their bones. You learn what they value and care about and fear."

"You think that's a good thing," Colette said neutrally.

"I think it's the very best thing," Alice said with a sigh, thinking of Sidney now. *In Flanders fields the poppies blow* . . . "So much of the evil and hatred in this world could be countered by understanding that in every culture we name our storytellers. We

e our children, we tend to our elderly, we find joy in a sunrise
l a warm piece of bread. We all name our storytellers." She
ushed and fiddled with the book in her hands. "You must find
e very naive."

"No," Colette said. "My father felt the same way."

"What were your father's favorite stories to tell?" Alice asked, and was rewarded with a small smile.

"Shakespeare," Colette answered without hesitation.

"The Bard," Alice said, Colette's earlier words taking on a new meaning. "Did he like the comedies or tragedies best? Or the histories?"

"It depended on the mood," Colette said. "He did love a good comedy. But his favorite of them all was *Hamlet*."

"'The croaking raven doth bellow for revenge,'" Alice quoted. She had never particularly liked that play, but she did respect the way it ripped apart and exposed so many human emotions and flaws. "There's something entirely compelling about a quest for vengeance, isn't there?"

"Yet what did revenge do for that particular cast of characters?" Colette asked.

"Nothing good." Alice eyed her. "Are you one of those terribly saintly people who rises above it all?"

Something flickered behind Colette's expression, too quick to catch.

"No," Colette said. "No, I'm not like that at all."

"WELL, BUT WE have to stock Freeman Wills Crofts," Colette said as the two of them huddled over a book catalog later that evening. They had spent most of the day separating books into categories. The next week would be devoted to adding card pockets and call numbers. Just because they were running this

library out of a boxcar didn't mean that they could let the len
system devolve into chaos.

They would still need to track the books that were taken o

Around dinnertime, though, Alice decided to shift their a
tention to the exciting part of the position—selecting novels to
order with the dwindling funds.

"Freeman Wills Crofts," Alice said, pretending at hesitancy. She enjoyed prodding Colette, who had otherwise been so contained all day. "Do we really have to?"

Colette's outrage was clear on her face. "They get hooked on Sherlock Holmes and then what? We let them fall off a cliff. No, we give them one of Crofts's books—which they'll like more because half of them involve railroads. Right there, you've created a reader for life."

She snapped to make her point, but then her eyes narrowed. "Which you know."

Alice laughed and gave up the game.

"Imagine if we could get his new one." Alice wistfully touched the title, *Inspector French's Greatest Case*. It sounded perfect for the camps. "Maybe I'll try to see how quickly we can get it shipped."

"I'm sure you can grease those wheels," Colette said a little slyly.

Alice blushed at the reminder of her family's fortune even if she didn't have free access to it. "I do have some pin money I've squirreled away."

Colette wiggled the catalog in her face. "It's worth it, admit it."

"All right, all right," Alice said, making a note to buy a copy.

When she looked up, Colette had a curious expression on her face. "Can we go see the boxcar?"

Alice's brows shot up, not sure why she was surprised when it was a perfectly reasonable request. It was evening, but the sun stayed up late these days. They would have enough light. "Yes, let's."

They weren't far from the train station, only a few blocks. And the air was refreshing after being locked up in that small room with hundreds of books. Alice loved nothing more than that most days, but it was always nice to get out, as well.

"Did you prioritize any one genre over others?" Colette asked. "When building the collection."

"For the donations, I took what I could get," Alice said. Colette had gone through enough of the stacks today to realize their haul had been eclectic. "For the ones I bought? Yes. I tried to take what I've learned from delivering books to the nearby camps—"

Colette turned sharply. "What?"

"I take books to the nearby camps," Alice said slowly, only then realizing she hadn't mentioned her pet project to Colette. "To be fair, it's mostly the women and children who borrow the books, but I've had more than one wife ask me to secretly get a book her husband would enjoy."

"That's . . . kind," Colette said, the compliment sounding rusty for some reason.

"Part of the job."

"It's not," Colette said quietly. "They probably appreciated that more than they could say."

"Nothing different than what your father did."

Colette's shoulders stiffened. "Yes."

"Well, I worked off that experience," Alice said, trying to right the conversational ship from where it had just clearly wobbled. "I also talked to some men in Mr. Rutherford's office who used to work in the camps, and they suggested nonfiction books that would help the loggers and miners further their education."

"That could backfire," Colette pointed out. She was clearly

Montanan, and her father had been a miner. She must know exactly how much pride these men had. Foisting "educational" books onto them could make them head for the hills, insulted at the insinuation that their lives needed to be *bettered*.

Alice nudged her ribs with an elbow. "Which is why I wanted the exact right librarian for the post."

That actually got a half smile out of Colette. "I did have an apprenticeship. With a library. It's not simply that I like books."

"I could tell," Alice said gently, though she knew she should have asked for certain. Because this was the first major project she'd ever attempted to launch, she was going to grant herself some grace when it came to making mistakes. There were always things to learn for next time without tearing out your hair for every misstep.

"The books are good," Colette said, in that succinct way Alice was beginning to appreciate. "You did good."

Alice tucked the compliment in the space beside her heart, and then had no more time for conversation as she focused on leading Colette through the rails toward where the boxcar lived.

"We'll need a sign," Colette said, looking up at the plain wooden exterior. It would blend in perfectly with the rest of the cars when it was hooked up to a train.

"And emphasize that it is free," Alice said in agreement as she climbed the rickety steps up to open the door.

She pushed it open and stepped inside.

There wasn't much in place yet . . . except the shelves. And that was really all they needed to get the sense that this was their library, the one that would carry Colette through all the small mining towns and logging camps between Missoula and Butte and back again.

"The living quarters will take the longest," Alice said, waving toward the far end of the boxcar, where a wall was being put in to separate the library and the tiny room where Colette would sleep. "There will be a dining car and several passenger cars where you can take your meals and use the facilities, but, honestly, you'll never have to go more than a few hours at a time between the camps. If you want company, though, I'm sure you'd be able to find it there."

"I don't need company."

That wasn't exactly a surprise considering Colette looked like she'd survived a hard couple of years on the road by herself.

"We'll make sure you are introduced to the conductor. You'll be able to go to him for anything you need," Alice said, watching as Colette slowly spun in the fading light of the day.

She'd removed her hat when they'd entered, and it allowed Alice to study her face.

There was nothing to be found in the harsh slant of her cheekbones, the cut of her jaw. She was a mystery, and Alice was simply banking on the fact that she wasn't the type of mystery to derail this project.

"Why aren't you taking this position?" Colette asked when she'd taken it all in. "This is clearly something that's dear to your heart."

Alice pressed her lips together, staring at the shelves and imagining all the books she'd collected filling them up.

And she yearned. "I can't. My father wouldn't allow it."

"But you're grown," Colette said, sounding confused, though she shouldn't. Even in Montana, it was more unusual to live like Colette than Alice.

"He's very . . . protective," Alice said, trying not to bristle.

"Don't you want to see how this all turns out?" Colette asked. "This is just the beginning. Don't you want to see this place full of the people you want to help?"

"Of course I would. But my father would drag me back by the hair at the very first camp," Alice said.

"You're right," Colette said, wandering toward the large window in the back. Alice was glad there was one, and Colette wouldn't have to ride by the light of a lamp. "I'm sure there's no way you'd be able to figure out a way around him."

"I could if I wanted to," Alice said, annoyed even though she knew she was being baited.

Colette looked up. "Then why not do it?"

"Why do you care?" Alice asked a bit peevishly.

Colette sat back in her seat and Alice wondered if she was going to change the topic to avoid revealing anything too personal.

"I grew up in a mining town," Colette said. "My father was a miner, my brother was a miner. All my friends and neighbors were, too. And we all knew what life was like. We knew the Company's collar was on our neck and that no one except for us cared we were all dying because of it."

Alice practically felt the waves of anger and anguish rolling off Colette.

"I think it would be good for you to see the difference your boxcar will make," Colette said. "But I don't really care about you all that much."

Alice laughed at the bald-faced honestly and Colette shot her a grin.

"What's more important to me is that those miners out there, the young ones especially, might see someone caring about *them*," she said. "And it might give them just enough hope to keep on fighting."

"For what?" Alice whispered.

"The right to live."

CHAPTER NINETEEN

Colette

Hell Raisin' Gulch, Montana
1921

Papa had been killed for no reason.

Or at least no reason Colette could find. It took her two months to pack up the house in Gulch—selling or donating most of Papa's possessions—and in all that time she hadn't found a single scrap of evidence that would have warranted a visit from hired guns.

Colette would have to get the answer from the men who'd shot him.

Once she found them.

At the end of those two months, she was left with an empty house where once a home had been. The only things she'd kept were some of Papa's papers, and, of course, his beloved books.

She hadn't been able to force herself to part with those.

Colette had gone through his papers carefully, but everything in there had been related to union business. She'd handed them over to his longtime confidant Sherman Lowe for a second opinion, and he'd agreed. There hadn't been anything in there to kill someone over.

Sherman hadn't had any room for Papa's extensive library, but as a last favor to the family, he'd taken over the task of finding somewhere to store the books.

Colette sold the one piece of jewelry that had been left to

her by her mother to buy three steamer trunks to hold most of them. She donated any that didn't fit to the Gulch Library, in part to ease her guilt over leaving the place high and dry without a librarian.

Before she departed, Sherman patted her on the shoulder and told her Papa would be proud while he knuckled a tear out of his eye.

Papa wouldn't be proud. He had never been one for violence. He'd likely be horrified by the shotgun she now carried with her everywhere.

But Papa was dead.

He was dead because all Colette had been able to find in the house was a cast-iron pan that hadn't been of any use when it mattered.

She wouldn't make that mistake again.

Colette caught the train to Butte and then walked to the Hennessy Building on the corner of Main Street and Granite.

The Hennessy department store occupied the ground floor of the sophisticated building that everyone fawned over.

And the Anaconda Copper Mining Company took up the top.

The location had become so synonymous with the Company that mentioning the "Sixth Floor" in Montana was enough for anyone to understand you were talking about power.

From that perch, the Company had the perfect view of Finlander Hall, where the union members met, along with the boardinghouses where the Wobblies were known to stay when visiting town.

Someone bumped into Colette and she flinched back. Then she laughed at herself. She was jumpy.

Colette found a boardinghouse a few streets over that had a vacant room, and then she headed down to Finlander Hall.

"I need to talk to someone from the Company," she said when

Bert Collins came out to greet her. He was one of the oldest members of the mining union in Butte, and she'd always thought him the smartest man she knew besides Papa.

"Now, Colette," Bert said, pulling on her arm until they were out of the main hall. Bert had a tiny office off to the right of it, and he closed the door behind them. "I won't have you doing anything foolish."

"Bert, you know it was them," Colette said, refusing to take the seat across from him even as he settled into his chair.

He stroked his long, unruly beard. "Of course it was them. You think that matters?"

"Yes," Colette said, her teeth clenching around the word. "Because they can't simply murder people and get away with it."

"They can. You know they can," Bert said. "We all do. And if you go charging on up to the Sixth Floor, you're going to be next."

Colette inhaled, exhaled, trying to get control of herself. "I need to talk to someone. I'm going to do it with or without your help."

"What are you going to say that will make you feel any better?"

"I want them to see my face," Colette said, and it came out broken. "I want them to see me."

Bert blew out a breath, still stroking his beard. He studied her. The past few weeks were living heavy in the lines by her eyes, by her mouth.

She didn't draw back, didn't try to pretend or put up a mask. She let him in on her grief, her rage, her helplessness.

"You're not going to get onto the Sixth Floor," he said, and then held up a hand. "At least three or four of them go to the M&M Cigar Store every day sometime after five."

Papa had talked about that place. The M&M Cigar Store was one of those former saloons that had to reimagine their business when the state's Prohibition laws were enacted. They served lunch, soft drinks, and, of course, cigars. In the back room, there were gaming tables where participants could have their choice of fine liquor.

"Thank you," Colette said.

Bert shook his head. "Don't thank me. Claude would take my head off if he knew I was helping you with this."

"Claude's dead," Colette said, and then left without waiting for Bert's response.

Colette wanted to go storm the Hennessy Building no matter what Bert said, but logic won out. He was right—there was no way she'd get past the Sixth Floor's lobby.

So, instead she found the M&M Cigar Store and a seat at its lunch counter. She ordered just enough food over the next several hours to not be hustled out of the swinging steel doors.

People filtered in throughout the late afternoon—men in suits, women, and even children. But none of them garnered the reaction the Company men did when they entered.

Everyone in the shop tensed at the sight of the four of them, all wearing the most expensive clothes Colette had seen all day. They were polished and sophisticated and they moved like the rest of the world should get out of their way.

Two of the men settled into leather armchairs, but two of them continued on toward the hallway.

Colette stood and tossed a few coins on the counter.

They were headed toward the poker table.

A burly man with an ill-concealed revolver tried to stop her from entering. "Invite only."

"Looks like they need another player," Colette said, pitching her voice so that it could pass as a man as long as the guard didn't look too closely. Subtly she flashed him a wad of money—he didn't need to know that it was all she had in this world.

The guard shrugged and allowed her to pass.

The Company men barely glanced at her when she took her seat at the table. The taller man was slender with sandy, thinning hair and the kind of frame that probably never filled out no matter how much he ate. He wore spectacles and a tie that looked like it cost more than her house.

The other was short and wide with a belly that spilled over his waistband. His cue ball–bald head caught the low light. The dealer greeted him as Smith, the other as Gallagher.

"Durand," Colette introduced herself, because that was her name, and she wasn't about to let these Company men steal the one last thing that she had from Papa, the one last thing she held dear.

It didn't matter anyway. Neither of the men looked up from their cards.

Maybe this was a fool's errand, maybe these men weren't high enough in the chain to be privy to the list of men the Company paid to have killed.

Or maybe they were so callous they hadn't bothered to memorize it.

There were three others at the table, and Colette didn't even look at them let alone remember their names.

Colette did well enough to not draw attention. She grew up in a mining town, she knew poker, even if she didn't love it like some of the men did.

Gallagher and Smith talked quietly between themselves, Smith getting progressively deeper into his contraband liquor. Gallagher didn't once touch his glass.

The game wore on. She won some, she lost some. She built up a nice stack of money in front of her.

And then she got lucky.

"All in," Colette said when it was her turn.

Smith folded as did two of the players whose names she hadn't caught.

The third went all in, though he had substantially less in front of him than both Colette and Gallagher.

Gallagher was looking at Colette now for the first time.

He was seeing her face.

The bet wasn't anything that he couldn't lose. But it was enough to make it sting if he didn't have the better hand.

And he didn't. He couldn't.

"Call," he said, because he didn't know who he was playing against. And she'd bluffed him a few times already.

"Cards," the dealer said. When he saw what Gallagher was holding he said, "Full house."

It had been smart for him to go all in.

Colette, though, Colette had been smarter.

"Four of a kind," the dealer announced.

Colette stared Gallagher down as she collected the pot. Then she stood, shoving it all into her bag.

"You can't leave now," Smith slurred. "You gotta give us a chance to win it back."

"Good day, gentlemen," Colette said, tipping her hat.

She walked out, half expecting the man at the door to stop her.

He didn't, and neither did anyone else.

A minute later, she was out on the street, breathing as if she'd just run up a hill.

Fingers curled painfully around her upper arm and she grinned.

Gallagher dragged her into the nearest alleyway, throwing her up against the wall. He might be slender, but there was a quiet strength lurking beneath his fine suit.

"Who are you?"

"I told you my name," Colette said, tipping her face up. Her hat had fallen to the ground as he'd manhandled her, and she could see the moment he realized she was a woman.

"Durand is not a name," Gallagher said, his voice dripping with contempt. All because she was dusty and dressed in worn clothes. There was no other reason for him to look at her like that—like a bug he was annoyed was going to make his shoe dirty when he crushed it.

"Colette Durand. My father was Claude Durand and you killed him."

He rolled his eyes.

He rolled his eyes.

He rolled—

A red mist crept into her vision and she could feel her heartbeat in every soft spot of her body, the soles of her feet, her pelvis, the dip beneath her arms.

"You killed him."

"Have you talked to the superintendent of your mine?" Gallagher said, already eyeing the street, like he was now regretting the decision to follow her out.

Colette slumped against the brick wall. "Tell me why you killed him."

"I obviously did not," Gallagher said, wiping nonexistent dust from his lapels. "I assume he died in some tragic accident."

"Some tragic accident," Colette said, with a disbelieving laugh. "Yeah, he accidentally stepped in front of a bullet that was aimed at his chest."

Gallagher's face went blank, but he actually did meet her eyes at that. She could almost see the calculations going on behind the facade. "Are you accusing the Anaconda Copper Mining Company of assassinating . . . I'm sorry, what was his name?"

He remembered. He was too smart not to.

She stared at him, refusing to play this game.

"Well . . . whoever he was, he wasn't worth a single thought from anyone on the Sixth Floor," Gallagher said. "Let alone anything as dire as you're suggesting."

"You're lying." She had no doubt of that. Of course he wouldn't admit to knowing who her father was. She hadn't really expected him to, if she was being honest with herself.

But now they would know that she knew.

"I'm going to prove it," she said.

He laughed. "You do that."

She would have to find the man who actually pulled the trigger. It wasn't a guarantee that a judge would listen to a desperate hired gun, but they could at least try to make a case. And hope others would come out of the woodwork. One person couldn't destroy the Company, but the first domino that fell never seemed important until all the rest fell down.

Gallagher patted her on the shoulder. "You know, I followed you out because I had been sure you were cheating. But you keep that money, little lady. Consider it a sympathy gift from the Anaconda Copper Mining Company for your father's years of service."

Colette could hardly breathe through her fury.

Gallagher smirked, straightened his lapels, and turned and walked away.

All Colette could do was try to stop shaking.

On the way out of town, she detoured to the union hall, and stuffed all the money she'd won in the poker game in an envelope that she slipped under Bert's door.

Then she caught a train heading west.

Staying in Butte wasn't going to get her anywhere. Not when the Company could watch her every move from the Sixth Floor.

In the dark of the boxcar she'd jumped on, she rubbed her thumb against the edge of the card she'd kept up her sleeve during the poker game.

She used to think she was a good person, that she would never cheat to get her way.

But if the other side played with a deck full of aces, all bets were off when it came to winning.

CHAPTER TWENTY

Millie

Wild Horse Island, Montana
1936

Flo was always able to find someone to talk to and people, in turn, gravitated toward her like sunflowers to the sun.

Right now, she was sidled up next to the man ferrying their little group across Flathead Lake to Wild Horse Island, which hosted one of the area's many, many dude ranches.

As the editor of the Missoula field office, Millie was impressed with Flo's natural ability.

As a journalist in training, Millie wanted to study all her tricks.

But as a lonely child and lonelier adult, Millie couldn't help the twinge of envy she felt watching her.

She thought about the girls at the boardinghouse who had excluded her so that they could have someone to talk about. She thought about her family, where she'd become more of the substitute nanny than a beloved niece.

She even thought about two particularly cruel people in the Dallas field office who had made snide comments about manure every time she walked by.

How lovely would it be? To be the sun to just one other person's sunflower.

The boat bumped into the surprisingly white sand of Wild

Horse Island's beach, and Millie finally released the death grip she'd had on the rail for the entire ride over from the mainland.

Oscar chuckled behind her and she turned to glare—an act that was lost on him because his ever-present fedora was tipped to protect his face from the sun. He was sprawled on the deck of the powerboat, looking like he'd stepped out from a bygone era where lounging on a yacht was a rich boy's entire agenda for the day.

Sidney turned from where he'd been balanced near the bow, his camera in hand. He'd been taking pictures on the short crossing and while she didn't think they would turn out technically well, the idea of movement and sky and water and trees might make compelling art.

She was curious about how good a photographer Sidney was. She hadn't been able to see any samples of his work back in Missoula, but she wasn't worried in terms of the guides. They weren't looking for anything comparable to Ansel Adams. All they wanted were landscapes and basic portraits.

Even a man who'd clearly grown up the son of a wealthy businessman should be able to handle that.

But a part of Millie wondered if there was a soul of an artist beneath all those walls he put up.

Now he jumped over the side, landing with a slight grunt. The "pier" could only loosely be called that considering it was made up of a thick ladder laid horizontally alongside the boat.

Flo stared at the makeshift dock and simply shook her head. "No."

Sidney laughed and reached up for her, easily lifting her down onto the shore. It was only then that she realized the two of them moved with an easy familiarity of longtime . . . friends? Probably not, given the fact that Flo was about Millie's age. But maybe

Missoula was so small they all considered each other as such even if they were simply neighbors.

Or were they coconspirators?

Millie sighed at herself. And the situation.

When Sidney held his arms up for her, Millie shot him a look and then hauled herself over the side of the boat.

Her boots were immediately soaked through when she landed in the water, but she shrugged off the discomfort and took in their hotel for the night.

Hiawatha Lodge was only a stone's throw from the lake. The two-story, rustic dude ranch wasn't anything fancy, but that didn't matter. Apparently, there were a dozen or so similar places between Missoula and Glacier National Park, all looking to sell an authentic "Western" experience to eager tourists.

But Hiawatha's location put them a step above all the rest. The dude ranch was on an island that not only had a spectacular view of the Mission Range as a backdrop, but came with its very own population of wild horses.

"Welcome," a big bear of a man boomed at Sidney, pulling him into a hug. He had a thick beard and a barrel chest, and Millie couldn't help but smile back when he turned his kind, friendly face in her direction.

A moment later she was engulfed by his musty, tobacco-laden scent, his chest hair scratchy against her cheek from where it peeked out of his work-rough shirt. "Lewis Penwell, the proprietor of Hiawatha Lodge."

"Howdy," Millie drawled, grinning up at him. He looked nothing like her uncle, and yet reminded her of him anyway. Both her aunt and uncle had been loving people—they had just had too much on their plate to include her in their affections. "The FWP thanks you for your hospitality."

"I expect my service medal will be in the mail any day now, eh?" Lewis said, with a wink. Then he knocked his fist against her shoulder, laughing. "Let's get you all inside."

As they all followed Lewis, Oscar leaned in to whisper, "The last owner drowned when he went out during a storm to try to save his boats. The wife vowed never to return to the island."

"Does the lake get that ferocious during storms?"

"Either that or he hit the sauce too hard and simply fell in." Oscar shrugged. "Lewis wants to turn the island into a big game hunting park."

He finally removed his fedora when they stepped into the lodge, his golden hair catching in the light of the rustic chandeliers.

"Sheep, Mr. Dalton, sheep," Lewis hollered back. "Big game and sheep. That's where the money is."

The last bit trailed off right before he greeted an older couple seated at a table in the lobby, drinking coffee.

The lodge was busy with several younger couples loitering about in horse-riding gear, a gaggle of older women just outside on the porch, and a family of four bustling through on their way to some planned activity.

When Millie had first heard of the guides, she had wondered if anyone would actually use them. Millie had barely had a few extra pennies to splurge on lipstick, let alone a cross-country trip.

But Katherine had informed everyone at headquarters that travel was actually increasing, especially road trips. It was interesting to see it in practice.

"Now, Mr. Calloway will take you to your rooms," Lewis called out. "Then you come right back down for supper. We eat family style here, and you best not be late."

The men were shown to their shared room, while Millie and Flo were taken to theirs.

"I thought I was done with this for a bit." Flo sighed and dropped her bag on one of the chairs. "At least, now I'll have company."

Millie was no stranger to sharing her space, but she was a bit to sharing her company. She wasn't really sure what she could offer. She wasn't the sun like Flo.

"Did you uncover anything damning yet?" Flo asked, in that way of hers. She was so casually blunt that Millie couldn't help but want to answer honestly. Like everyone who talked to her probably.

She didn't, but she wanted to. "I'm not looking for anything damning."

Flo rolled her eyes. "You would get more out of all of us if you drop the act, you know."

Millie leaped on that. "So, you're saying there's something to get?"

"Oh, brother, I'm not made for cloak-and-daggers," Flo said, pulling at the collar of her dress to reveal more of her generous bosom. "Let's talk about far more interesting things. Like Mr. Dalton and his pretty eyes. I wouldn't have minded him lifting me down today instead of Sid. That's not a knock on Sidney, you hear. He's just . . . old."

Millie giggled. Sidney really wasn't that old in the scheme of things, but anyone over thirty felt that way.

"You seem to know him well," Millie tried. If she actually did want to be a journalist, she would have to learn this art.

Flo paused, her mouth still pursed from reapplying her Elizabeth Arden lipstick. "He's one of our old families in Missoula. Everyone knows him."

"How is he to work with?" Millie pressed. "You said he was a good-for-nothing rascal, I believe."

"I was only teasing," Flo said, back to studying herself in

the mirror so she wouldn't have to meet Millie's eyes probably. "He cares. He cares about this work even if he doesn't always show it."

"I'll have to take your word for it," Millie murmured, though she thought about his impassioned defense of the tribes and the reservations. There *were* things he cared about, she just wasn't sure it was the essays and interviews he didn't bother saving.

At dinner, Millie found herself seated next to Lewis Penwell near the head of a long communal table filled with steaming casseroles and baskets of crusty bread loaves. The feast would have been unimaginable even a year or two ago, and Millie was going to take advantage of it.

"How did you end up on this island, Mr. Penwell?" Millie asked, after the dishes had been passed around.

"I took the boat just like you did, gal," Lewis said, and Millie laughed because she was supposed to, which just set Lewis off more. "No, no, it's a rather boring tale, I'm afraid. Believe it or not, I'm in the Montana legislature."

She made a show of studying him. "I believe it."

He boomed out another laugh, because he was good at this, as well. "I was out of my mind with jealousy that I didn't own a ranch. I had to upstage my colleagues and buy a whole island."

Millie discreetly pulled out her journal and pencil. After six months in Washington, she'd gotten a feel for what made a good politician. Someone as charismatic as Lewis likely thrived in the cigar rooms that acted as the engine *and* oil to lawmaking. "Would you mind telling me about what it's like to be a lawmaker here?"

"First thing to know is we're a state full of good, hardworking people," Lewis said.

"As are all of them," Millie pointed out, and Lewis lounged back in his chair.

"I'm allowed to be biased, I'm a representative," he said. "And we've had it hard here. Fifteen years ago, we were going through the same thing the rest of the country just weathered, and it wasn't pretty. We didn't have President Roosevelt opening up the bank vaults for us. But we made it through that crisis and then this one, and we'll make it through the next whenever that comes."

"Hopefully, there's a bit of a respite before then."

"But we'll be ready if it comes sooner."

He was exactly what she would have guessed a Montana politician looked and talked like. She wanted to prod him a little, get him to let his guard down and reveal something of substance.

"Speaking of the president, is he popular around these parts?"

"Sure is. Helena is full of Roosevelt supporters these days," Lewis said. "Hard not to be. One out of four of our residents are on relief rolls."

"That doesn't mean they like other people getting help." Millie had met her fair share of people who were resentful of the New Deal even as they accepted the aid themselves when it was offered. Millie didn't blame them for the latter bit, but she didn't understand how they could work to sever a lifeline for others that had first been used to save them.

Lewis gave her a shrewd look. "Aren't you clever?"

"I try to be," she shot back.

"That will get you into trouble."

She thought about Foxwood Hastings, about the man who'd deemed her a *hellcat* in Dallas. She thought about the fact that she was sitting here at a communal dinner table at a dude ranch in Montana. "I'm aware."

He laughed again. "None of that matters in Montana, though. What you need to know, the only thing you need to know, is it's all run by the Company."

Millie leaned forward, the topic piquing her interest in the same manner as Sidney's admission that he'd held on to the tribes' interviews.

First Katherine had warned her about the Copper Kings, then Alice had, and now Lewis was bringing them up.

It was worth digging into, at least.

"Even you?" she asked.

"What did I say about being too clever?" Lewis asked, but his tone was light. "I haven't let them line my pockets, I'm proud to say, but I haven't run afoul of them, either. And that's because I've done my best to avoid stepping even close to their toes. So, yes, even me. If you want to be a lawmaker in this state, you play by their rules."

"It seems like everyone hates them, but no one's done anything about it," Millie said, and for the first time Lewis's expression changed to one of pity.

"Not everyone hates them," he said simply. "Plenty of folks out there that think they understand the wolf, that it won't bite them. Some even think they can slip a leash around its neck. But the wolf only allows you to live at its leisure."

"I understand but I don't," Millie confessed. How had one company gained so much power? Even the millionaires in the East who had made their riches off railroads and oil didn't run entire states. Not like this. But Millie believed both Alice Monroe and Lewis when they talked about the Company.

"Do you know what aspen is?"

"A . . . tree?" Millie guessed, and Lewis nodded.

"You look at woods full of aspen, and you think they're like any other tree. You cut enough down and you clear the woods. But the aspen, they're all connected to a root system. You can't kill the thing by cutting one down, you have to pull the colony out by the roots," Lewis said, and met her eyes. "The Company's roots are so deep in Montana's soil it would ruin the state to yank them out."

Millie's pencil had dropped to the table. "Then what can you do to stop them?"

"Times are changing," Lewis said. "We have an open seat in the legislature right now that could mean the difference between charging the Company the taxes they owe or not. Some rat-bastard scab is the front-runner, of course, but the other candidate is gaining ground. A lot of people are paying close attention to that race."

"And if the underdog doesn't win?"

"Then we've lived to fight another day," Lewis said. "Ask someone in Galatia what would come first, the sun burning out or the fall of Rome."

Lewis toasted the air and finished the rest of his wine. "All empires seem inevitable right up until they're not."

CHAPTER TWENTY-ONE

Colette

Just south of Glacier National Park, Montana
1922

It turned out Colette was good at riding the rails. She was a fast enough runner to jump on the freights easily, and she was small enough to hide behind cargo when the bulls were out in force looking for hobos in the boxcars. It wasn't her preferred method of travel but it worked.

After leaving Butte, she headed north toward the border, where she heard there might be some work if she could get in with the right bootleggers.

On her third day walking the area around Kalispell, she found an abandoned Chevrolet pickup truck. No tires, no gasoline, an engine that look busted to her inexperienced eye. Likely, it had been left there by a homesteader tired of the drought and dust that Montana had offered up instead of the gold fields he'd been promised.

She trudged back to Kalispell and found the mechanic in town. He made the repairs and she handed over the rest of her money.

Then she went searching for rumors.

Not about the men she was hunting, but about the bootleggers. More than one pointed her north to Glacier National Park, where a woman named Josephine Doody lived.

The mythology of the woman grew by the day. She'd been a dance hall girl who'd become addicted to opium before her future husband kidnapped her from the place, tied her to a mule, and brought her back to his cabin in the woods. She was reported to have killed a man before any of that happened, and she was also so well known that when a train pulled into the closest stop, the engineer would simply blow the whistle for the number of cases of hooch the workers wanted.

"Why would I cut you in on the profit?" Josephine asked when Colette found her.

The woman didn't look like an infamous bootlegger. She was dressed in a plain housedress and wore her hair tied back in a severe braid. The opium had likely caused the sag in her skin, but her eyes were still sharp.

"I can expand your horizons," Colette said, going for smart and sophisticated even if she was neither.

Josephine studied her, and Colette tried not to think about the newspapers she'd stuffed in her shoes to protect her feet from the holes just in case that desperation could be read on her face.

"Where you stayin', girl?" Josephine asked.

In the truck, Colette thought but knew better than to say.

Josephine had probably guessed anyway. "One week. If you don't bring in any money, you're gone."

"Deal," Colette rushed to say.

It was the start of a partnership that got Colette through the worst of the winter. Josephine maintained her business, ferrying moonshine across Flathead River in her rickety boat and supplying her primary customer—the trains. But Colette took over deliveries into town, and then farther afield. She struck gold in logging camps that were just a little too far for the workers to easily get into Kalispell.

She brought in just enough for Josephine to tolerate her presence on a bedroll in the front room of her cabin. And in the meantime, she kept her ear to the ground.

It turned out the cooks at the logging camps had a surplus of information.

"One of the boys said he knows the rat who did it," said Bertha Madden, a robust woman with a dark mustache and a swing in her step that had all the miners watching her wherever she went. She had met Colette only twenty yards from the superintendent's house, but apparently the man's wife liked a good time every once in a while so he studiously looked away from the contraband arriving at his camp.

Colette paused, a heavy crate in her hands. Bertha tried to pull it away, but Colette gripped it tight. "What do you mean?"

"He's new, sweet kid, not even a single callus on his hands." Bertha tugged the crate again and this time Colette let it go. "But I put it out there, like you asked, if anyone knew anything about that killing down near Butte. Most fellas said they didn't, even when I mentioned the reward. But this kid, he just got here from Priest River, all the way over in Idaho. Said he passed through a town closer to the border and this rat was running his mouth at a poker table."

The air seemed to have gone thin. "Is he telling stories?"

"Seems earnest," Bertha said, taking matters into her own hands now to unload the liquor. "Didn't know the rat's name, and just shrugged when I said it might affect the reward. Didn't try to make one up or nothing."

Colette nodded, because she'd also found that was an easy way to root out the liars.

"Was there anything he could tell you?" Colette asked, hardly daring to hope.

Bertha grinned, revealing a couple gaps in her teeth. At gunpoint, Colette wouldn't be able to explain the woman's appeal, but even she found herself charmed and mesmerized all the same.

"He's got a birthmark, a distinctive one at that," Bertha said, clearly pleased with her reveal. "Big and splotchy and covering a good portion of his neck. And he's real pale, too, so it stands out."

Colette sank to the ground. This was the first piece of good information she'd gotten in the six months since she'd started all this.

Bertha patted her cheek. "Now, if you wanted to reward that young man anyway I'm sure he wouldn't be turning anything away."

"Right," Colette murmured, still dazed. But when Bertha handed over payment, Colette made sure to return a few coins. "For you, too. Thank you."

Bertha stared down at them. "Was that your father? The man he was bragging about killing?"

"Yes," Colette said quietly.

"Then you'll need this to catch him," Bertha said, and she pressed half the reward back into Colette's hands. "On the house, this time."

Colette blinked back tears, not because it mattered much either way in terms of the money, but because this stranger had become an ally so quickly.

Later that night, she and Josephine stood in the kitchen, bottling up the next batch.

"You found what you were looking for," Josephine commented idly, not even looking at Colette.

She'd learned not to be surprised by Josephine's penchant for perceptive observations. "Yes."

"You'll be leaving." It wasn't a question.

"Don't want to abandon you," Colette said.

"You've been better company than I expected over the winter."

It had been nice, having someone to talk to when the nights stretched out so long; to have a fire to come back to when she could no longer feel her hands or feet.

Before Colette could offer any excuses, Josephine spoke again. "But spring is coming."

Colette chewed on her lip, not sure she dared to ask the next question. She was leaving, though.

"I heard you killed a man."

Josephine cackled as she shoved a cork into the bottle she'd been filling. "There's lots of stories about me. The Bootleg Lady of Glacier Park."

Stories. Colette's lot in life, it seemed, was collecting other people's stories.

"I think most of them are true," Colette ventured.

Josephine dipped her head. "I was born in Georgia, though you wouldn't know it. I hammered the song of those hills out of my voice long ago."

Colette stopped working to turn her full attention on the woman.

"Followed a man from Georgia to Colorado," Josephine continued. "He was not a kind man."

"He hurt you?" Colette asked, knowing the answer.

"Would have killed me," Josephine said. "But dead men can't pull triggers."

Colette swallowed hard. "Did it change you?"

Josephine's busy fingers paused and she looked up for the first time all night, studying Colette.

"You planning on finding that out for yourself?"

"Maybe so."

Josephine nodded and went back to the still. "That's not the right question anyway."

"What's the right question?"

"It's not whether it will change you, of course it will change you," Josephine said. "The question is, will it do what you want?"

Colette shook her head. She didn't understand.

"Some people, when they kill a man, their problems go away," Josephine said, waving to herself. "You're trying to kill a man to bring your father back. Nothing can do that."

"I'm seeking justice," Colette said, "not trying to get my father back."

Josephine lifted her eyebrows in clear disbelief. "You think justice is killing those hired guns who killed your father?"

Colette hadn't realized how much she must have let slip about her situation over the past few months. That was what happened when you lived with one other person in the woods in the dead of a Montana winter, she supposed. "It's a start."

"And what about the men who paid them?" Josephine asked. "How many men's lives will it take to repay this debt you seek to collect?"

Before Colette could answer, Josephine cut her off. "No, that's not the right question. Again."

"What is?"

"This won't just cost their lives, it will cost yours," Josephine said. "Is that what your father would want?"

Colette inhaled sharply. "You don't know anything about my father."

"I know you," Josephine said. "And that seems like enough to know he wouldn't have wanted you to pay for his life with your soul."

"How can you talk? You live out here like a hermit, shelling out hooch to people who only talk to you because you have something they want," Colette snapped.

Josephine turned to stare, those watery blue eyes of hers cold and assessing. "And where is it that you live?"

Colette opened her mouth, shut it. And then feeling all of twelve years old, she said, "Not here."

Stopping only long enough to collect her travel bag, Colette stormed out of the small cabin.

When she climbed into her battered pickup truck, she rested her forehead against the wheel and, for the first time since Papa's funeral, wept.

CHAPTER TWENTY-TWO

Alice

Missoula, Montana
1924

The finished Boxcar Library was not quite a thing of beauty, but she would do the job.

Alice stood in the middle of it so she could direct Mr. Rutherford's men as they unloaded apple crates full of books from the back of her Ford.

"Such a curious experiment," Mr. Rutherford mused when he came to a stop beside her. "I do still find it difficult to believe any of those men will read these books, my dear."

"Why so pessimistic?" Alice asked, though she didn't much care. Mr. Rutherford had set no goals for this project. He'd wanted the headlines and he'd gotten them. The price he was paying beyond that—the stipend for Colette Durand—was barely a passing afterthought.

"They're a rough sort out there, aren't they, my dear," Mr. Rutherford said. "I've found they mostly prefer boxing matches and card games as a way to fill any free time they may have."

Alice wasn't as naive as some thought her. She knew men in logging and mining camps brawled—probably as a way to relieve some of the tension of dealing with harsh conditions, brutal work, and close quarters that offered little in the way of privacy.

But that was the entire point of the Boxcar Library. Bloody

knuckles and ripped flesh weren't the only ways to counter anger, irritation, and frustration. Simply disappearing into another life for an hour or two could do the trick, as well—even if men were too often taught that they could only turn toward pain to feel anything at all.

"Don't you think the library will also help them pass the time?" she asked.

"Yes, yes, of course, dear," Mr. Rutherford said, all but patting Alice on the head, as if she were a child with foolish ideas.

Just as Alice clenched her jaw around an ugly rebuke, Colette Durand sauntered up to them. "Shall we place a wager, Mr. Rutherford?"

Colette was an odd bird in general, one Alice liked but couldn't quite get a handle on. They had been working closely over the two weeks to get the Boxcar Library ready for launch, but Alice didn't feel like she knew her at all beyond some surface-level observations. Colette could be sly and funny at times, but at others, she was reserved, all emotion flattened into nothing. She was quick and clever and knew books as if she'd been working in libraries for fifty years. She didn't have a temper, per se, but there was something angry about her, as if the world had done her wrong. Perhaps it had.

They could spend hours in deep conversation about almost any book, but Colette immediately clammed up when pushed for personal information. She only briefly mentioned her father if one of his favorite authors came up in their stacks.

Sometimes, it was easy to look at Colette and know what he must have been like. Smart and tough and probably a little soft for his daughter.

Sometimes, Alice wondered if she was making up stories for Colette because she offered so few of her own.

Mr. Rutherford squinted at Colette now, never one to pass

up a chance to make money. Alice had worried that Mr. Rutherford would put up a fuss when she introduced Colette as the new librarian for his logging camps. Maybe it was Colette's quiet confidence, or even the way she dressed as a tough frontierswoman, never far away from her shotgun, but Mr. Rutherford hadn't even blinked at the news.

"Ten dollars that no more than, hmm, twenty books will be checked out in the first month," Mr. Rutherford said, holding out his palm.

Colette slapped hers into it. "Bet."

"Witness," Alice murmured, and they both glanced at her as if they'd forgotten she'd existed.

"You want in?" Colette asked.

"I'll let you handle the business side of things," Alice said, amused and pleased at how everything had worked out.

"Well, ladies, the press awaits," Mr. Rutherford said with a tip of his cap before wandering toward the gaggle of journalists who had shown up.

Tomorrow was the Boxcar Library's inaugural journey, but the train would depart at an ungodly hour. So the newspapers had turned up this afternoon to get a photograph of the thing.

"And so do the books," Colette murmured. "At this pace, we'll never get the crates unloaded."

Colette headed toward the door and presumably the Ford and Mr. Rutherford's men.

That left Alice alone in the boxcar for a moment.

She grinned and spun in a slow circle, hardly able to believe what she'd accomplished.

Everything had been kept basic and practical—as all things had to be on both ships and trains.

The bookshelves they'd seen in the early stages two weeks before lined the walls, of course. A long, beautiful wooden table—

made special by Missoula's apprentice carpenter—was bolted to the floor surrounded by heavy chairs. A small stove dominated the far corner and next to it sat a donated Victrola along with a boxful of records.

A compartment for Colette had been built into the other end of the car, blocked off by a wall with a cutout that acted as a checkout desk. She had a door that would lock, as well.

Alice pressed her hands to her cheeks, hardly able to contain her smile. They had done it. They had pulled this off. All that was left was for them to show Mr. Rutherford and Julia Walker and everyone who doubted them that the men would love this as much as she expected them to.

A light popped behind her and she whirled to find the *Missoulian*'s photographer grinning at her a bit sheepishly.

"Sorry, Miz Monroe," Mark Woodrow said. He was a pockmarked boy with a big nose and even bigger ears and everyone in town adored him and his good humor.

"Oh, don't apologize, please," she said. "Let me get out of your way."

"Erm." He shifted nervously. "We'd actually like to get a picture of you and the librarian, if it wouldn't be too much of a bother."

She glanced up just in time to find Colette frozen at the steps, her eyes darting back toward the Ford like she was about to make a dash for it.

"I just sent her to town for something I'd forgotten," Alice said, which was both vague and demonstrably a lie considering Mark had probably just seen Colette outside. But Alice had learned that something about her face—and about who she was as a person in this town—could stave off a lot of debate even when she was in the wrong.

And Mark was a sweet boy who wouldn't point out her fib.

"Surely, Mr. Rutherford should be in the picture," Alice said, before she stuck her head out of the door and called for the man. Colette was nowhere to be seen.

Mr. Rutherford was pleased as punch to take another photograph, as expected.

After they were done with that, Alice went in search of Colette. She was perched on the metal couplers that held the boxcars together, tucked so deeply into shadows that Alice walked by her three times before finally spotting a flash of movement.

"Thank you," Colette said.

Alice studied her face but, frustratingly, found none of the answers she sought. And Colette was set to leave at dawn the next day. If all went well, she'd be riding the rails for the foreseeable future, stopping in Missoula only long enough to restock or fix damaged books.

There was only one last chance to pry some secrets out of her. "Will you come to the gala tonight?"

Alice would be hosting one at her house as a way to not only thank the community for its support but also raise some more funds while interest was at its peak. Just because they were going to successfully launch this project didn't mean they wouldn't need more money in the future—either for a wider array of books, extra perks like the Victrola, or even a second boxcar.

Colette hesitated. "If you want me to, I will."

Alice sighed. Colette didn't want to go—in fact, if what Alice had observed over the past month was accurate it would be Colette's version of torture. She was quite skillful at talking to patrons one-on-one, but anytime there was a large gathering, Colette started eyeing exits. Alice had tried to trot her out at one of her fundraising teas and by the end of it, she could tell Colette was contemplating walking into the mountains never to return.

"No," Alice said. "Enjoy your quiet while I put on an uncomfortable dress and make nice with Julia Walker."

Colette flashed her a grin, having been informed of the drama that had unfolded before she'd arrived. She never missed a moment to goad Alice into bad-mouthing the woman. Alice cut her off at the pass. "An impossible task, I'm aware."

There was nothing left to do here. Alice brushed her palms against her skirt and tried to think of anything to delay the inevitable. But her work was done. Now her little library, and Colette, would have to fly or fall on its own.

"Thank you," Alice said, holding out her hand to shake Colette's. "For taking this position. I know you will be perfect."

Colette stared at Alice's hand, but didn't take it. She was silent for so long, Alice dropped her arm feeling awkward.

That got Colette to look up. "You have to come with me."

Alice shifted back, away from the intensity in her eyes. Colette had suggested Alice ride on the inaugural journey a few times over the past two weeks, but never so forcefully.

"You know I can't."

"Just for a few stops," Colette said. "Your guard dog isn't even around to stop you."

"Not fair," Alice snapped, feeling that creeping unease she always did when she thought of Mac these days. She missed him, Lord she missed him. His quiet sense of humor, his steadiness, his listening ear, his friendship. But despite the fact that she'd thought herself in love with him for half her life, she couldn't quite get excited about his return. Or whatever he wanted to talk to her about that had turned him so serious before he'd left.

Perhaps Mac, like everything in her life, had been a safe option. Loving him would never be dangerous—or rewarding—because she knew it to be an impossibility. Loving him would never leave her destroyed.

But was that really love? Or was that just another cage she'd locked herself into?

"You're right," Colette said, but didn't apologize. "You should come. Stop being so scared of everything."

"No, I . . . ," Alice said, twisting her fingers together. She wanted to refute that accusation, but she couldn't. "No, I can't. Not now."

"Not ever," Colette said, still watching Alice carefully through half-lidded eyes. No one else pushed Alice like this—except maybe Sidney Walker, who'd gone back to ignoring her completely after that night in Lolo.

It turned out she liked being challenged.

"No," Alice repeated. "Not now. Maybe next time."

Colette didn't say anything, but she stared at Alice with pity that was so easy to read she mustn't even be trying to hide it. For Colette, a fearless bird who flew into the storm, could not possibly understand what it was like in a comfortable cage.

Alice flushed. "I'll see you off in the morning."

Colette gave her a two-fingered salute. "Go make us some more money."

"It's what I do best," Alice murmured, worried, for the first time, that that was the truth.

Alice was only able to get Colette's words out of her head when she stopped to study herself in the mirror before her guests arrived.

She'd pulled out her fanciest dress for the gala, a slinky green number with pretty beading all over it. The fabric slouched and pinched in all the right places to give her a hint of a shape—an illusion she'd gladly take.

The maid had done something fancy with Alice's hair, pinning it back and to the side and dressing it up with gold flower pieces that somehow teased out the mahogany highlights that remained stubbornly hidden whenever she tried such a feat.

Notes from a Strauss waltz drifted up through the floorboards, reminding her that guests would be there soon.

She took a deep breath, stepped out of her room, and ran straight into her father.

He smiled at her—not exactly pleased with the project, but generally proud of his daughter, she thought.

"You look just like your mother," Clark said, holding her by the shoulders. "The spitting image."

"Am I like her?" Alice asked, Colette's offer rushing back in. Mary Monroe had moved west to be with her husband, at a time when that must have been a terrifying prospect. All she'd ever known was comfort in Boston, the best transportation, the best education, the best society had to offer. And she'd left that behind for love. Alice couldn't even imagine being that brave. "In other ways, am I like her?"

Her father dropped his hands, and he studied her like he'd never considered the question. Perhaps someone else would find that odd, given that he'd raised her on his own since Mary had died, but her father rarely concerned himself with anything but the logistic details of her care. He wasn't curious about who she was as a person, her hopes and dreams, her strengths and flaws.

That used to bother her, but now she realized it allowed her a certain kind of freedom that she lacked elsewhere.

"No," Clark said, without seeming to realize how much of a slap that was. "She had a taste for the wild, my Mary. You wouldn't have thought it given the way she was raised. But one look at the open skies and she wanted nothing more than to explore them and the mountains they covered."

Alice hadn't ever pictured her mother that way, and she wondered how much she was missing simply because Clark was usually too grief-stricken to talk about her.

"You're like me, my dear," Clark barged on, careless. "You like the softer things in life. That's why I work so hard to provide them for you."

Before she could say anything to that, their housekeeper cleared her throat. "Your guests."

The interruption was a welcome one. If Clark had kept talking, Alice might have ruined the makeup she'd so tastefully applied.

"Right, of course," Alice murmured, hoping her voice didn't betray her emotions.

Alice had no wild in her.

An hour into the gala, she had greeted her guests, as she'd been taught to do from a young age, collected several large donations, and delivered a clever but subtle remark about Julia Walker's gossipy nature, and Alice still felt on the verge of tears.

She was enduring a particularly tedious conversation with the owner of Missoula's most popular bakery when a hand pressed into the small of her back.

"Excuse us, Anthony," Sidney Walker said. "I believe Miss Monroe has promised me the next dance."

Alice inhaled at the brush of his thumb across her ribcage. She hated that his mere presence next to her made her lightheaded.

"Of course, of course." Anthony Carlo waved at them. "Go, young ones. Make merry."

There was no choice, then, but to join Sidney Walker on the dance floor.

"You're welcome," he murmured, right before they launched into the first step of a waltz.

"I didn't ask you to save me," Alice said, the words landing between them much heavier than she'd ever meant them to be.

"Maybe that's not what I'm saying 'you're welcome' for." Sidney directed her in a long, swooping line. He smelled of evergreens after the first snow with just a hint of tobacco layered in on top and she hated the way she wanted to sink into him, bury her face in the hollow beneath his shoulder.

"The Boxcar Library," she realized. "*That*, I will thank you for."

He inclined his head as if, now that he'd goaded her, he had to acknowledge he hadn't actually wanted her thanks.

"Have you met the librarian?" Alice asked.

"Colette Durand," Sidney drawled, somewhat dismissively. "No, but I've gotten an earful from my mother about her."

Alice nodded, because that hardly surprised her. "Colette asked me to go with her."

Sidney assessed her, his eyes at half-mast. "What did you say?"

"That I couldn't."

"Hmmm." This time when he pressed on her back it was to direct her away from the crowds, toward the open French doors that led out onto their wraparound porch.

"What?" she demanded as they both stepped outside.

"You want to go peddle books to lonely men for the rest of the winter?" Sidney asked, making it sound so terrible in his lazy voice.

"I want to make a difference in their lives," she corrected.

"Then why don't you?"

Alice stared at the sliver of moon and gripped the railing, half wishing she could be like Wendy in *Peter Pan* and fly away into the sky. "I'm scared."

She had no idea why she'd admitted that to this man, who did nothing but goad and tease and frustrate her in the few times they'd ever interacted. "That's the start and end of it. I can't ride the rails, I'm not built for that life."

"Maybe not," Sidney agreed, and she gaped at him. She had wanted him to defend her to herself, and of course he hadn't.

"You think I should go?" Alice asked.

He pulled a cigarette out, rolling it along his knuckles in a hypnotizing pattern instead of lighting it. "I think you shouldn't care what I think."

But I do, Alice was smart enough not to say. Instead, she decided to ask something she'd wanted to know more about from the moment he'd admitted it. "You said once upon a time you needed books. When was that?"

Sidney rolled his eyes. "When do you think?"

"In the trenches."

"Gold star for you," he said in the meanest voice he had. She was starting to tell the difference between the jagged edges he deployed when she got too close to his scars and the humor that, while sharp, was mostly harmless.

In the past, a comment like that would have had her rolling her eyes and plotting the quickest way to get away from him.

Something stopped her this time.

"Then tell me about it," Alice said, wanting to tug at the inky threads of pain she could all but see running beneath his skin more than she wanted to escape.

He paled at the request. Or maybe he simply shifted beneath the sliver of moonlight. Either way, Alice felt him withdraw almost completely.

"Do what you want, Alice," Sidney said, exasperated now. "Stay here, be comfortable and safe, that's actually a fine thing to crave, believe it or not. You'll have made a difference, even if you don't see it yourself." He paused, meeting her eyes. "Or go and for once in your life, live it."

Alice waited, breath caught in her throat, because he wasn't done. Not yet.

"But don't stand here and beg to be convinced not to go," he said. "It's tedious for both of us."

It came like the slap it was meant to be.

He was right, though. Here she was again, just like that night in Lolo, asking for restraints. Because she *wanted* to be the kind of person who fought against them. Instead, she just pulled at them as weakly as possible to make sure they would stay in place. She used the people around her to convince herself she was brave and independent and held back by circumstances rather than choice.

In the war, men were shot dead by their own comrades for refusing to go over the trenches, into battle, into no-man's-land. What must it feel like for Sidney to stand here and even have this conversation?

How did he stand to have *most* conversations?

"Miss Monroe," a maid called from the doorway. "The mayor is looking for you."

"Of course, thank you," Alice said, without taking her eyes off Sidney. When she spoke, she hoped he understood exactly what she meant when she said, "I'm sorry, Mr. Walker. I suppose I have to go."

CHAPTER TWENTY-THREE

Millie

Kalispell, Montana
1936

The house looked like so many others Millie had seen in the past seven years—in need of repair, covered in a thick layer of dust because there was just never enough water to scrub it clean over and over again.

But the bones were good. Sturdy.

Sidney had taken a sharp left just as they'd put Flathead Lake behind them, and then had driven them down this long, empty dirt road without saying anything. The stop wasn't on their itinerary, but that was the point of this adventure—to explore places other than the well-traveled path.

So, Millie hadn't questioned the decision. She had wondered, though.

For the past quarter mile, a young boy had ridden beside them on a dark horse. The mare's ribcage was visible, but her coat and hair were beautiful and maintained. Whoever this family was, they didn't have much, but they cared for their animals as well as they could, and that was enough to put them in Millie's good books.

When they parked, the boy trotted off to the barn, and Sidney climbed out of the car, his camera slung over his shoulder.

Millie got out of the car, but leaned against the door, watching and waiting. Flo bumped against her arm.

"Did you stop here before?"

Flo shook her head. "No."

There was something considering in her voice, in her expression. This was the first time she could see doubt creeping in.

Doubt about Sidney. Strangely, it made Millie feel better. She didn't want any of them to be guilty, but what she would hate most was if they were all working together.

A woman emerged from the house and held her arms out for Sidney. He walked into them without a moment's pause, and they hugged for longer than expected for anyone other than a dear friend or family member.

Even when the two finally broke apart, the woman pressed her palms to Sidney's face, taking him in.

"Just as handsome as ever," she said, and Millie was fairly certain Sidney blushed even if she was too far away to actually confirm that guess.

"Just as beautiful," he tossed back.

The woman slapped his shoulder, finally stepping back. "You know that slick talk rolls off my back like water on a duck."

Sidney laughed, and Millie thought it might be the first time she heard him truly do so.

He shifted then, and Millie came face-to-face with the woman. She was short and slim, and Millie guessed she was around forty. She wore a bandanna over her hair, and a serviceable dress—practically the uniform of Western farmwives. Her smile was kind, if muted, and her eyes were curious.

"Sofia Rossi, this is Miss Millicent Lang, Miss Florence Marner, and Mr. Oscar Dalton, all of the Writers' Project," Sidney said with an introductory wave.

"Pleasure," Sofia said and glanced behind her. Four faces were pressed up against the smudged glass. She rolled her eyes as she turned back to Millie and Oscar. "Those are the boys.

There are five of them around there, just in case you trip over one of them, make sure to keep watching your step. The next one won't be far behind."

Millie smiled against the pang of homesickness the warning brought. She hadn't been back to her aunt and uncle's ranch since she'd left for Dallas and the FWP job there. Before that, she had barely known a minute without one of her cousins by her side, irritating the hell out of her but also just being there. Tripping over one to find another right behind.

She was the last person who needed to be sold on the idea of the American Guide Series, but in moments like this she would have been. Here was a woman who lived a stone's throw away from the Canadian border, in a state that Millie knew nothing about, in a landscape nearly completely foreign to her, and yet she looked and sounded so much like *home* that Millie had to fight the urge not to hug her.

"Come, come," Sofia said, beckoning them inside. The boys all scattered the second they stepped into the small house. "Sidney, the room is yours."

Sidney smiled his thanks and ducked down the hallway, without any further explanation.

"He didn't tell you why he stopped here?" Sofia guessed at Millie's curiosity. More than curiosity, if she were being honest. She had all but convinced herself Sidney Walker was responsible for the sabotage, and now she needed to figure out why he had done it. Anything out of the ordinary, anything that deviated from the plan, was notable.

Perhaps this quiet woman who was clearly close with Sidney held the key.

"No," Millie said, trying to take in the place without being too obvious about her interest.

The inside of the house looked no bigger than the outside,

though everything was clean and tidy. The couch sagged and there were scuff marks and water rings on the coffee table, but, again, Millie was struck by the fact that Sofia was a woman who took pride in making do with what she had.

"My—" Sofia broke off, looking away, her fingers fiddling with her wedding ring. "We have a dark room, for developing photographs. Sidney uses it sometimes when he's up this way."

Millie considered that. Sidney had access to a dark room in Missoula. And the editor in Helena would want the raw film for the guides, so she doubted he was rushing to develop anything he'd taken on their trip so far.

This was personal, and he hadn't wanted anyone in Missoula to see what he was working on.

She and Flo locked eyes across the room. Millie raised her brows and Flo looked away. She didn't want Sidney's behavior to be suspicious.

They both knew it was.

Millie wasn't going to find anything else out from Sofia, but she could do her job, the one she was actually getting paid to do. Millie pulled out an informant intake form and showed it to Sofia. "Do you know what the Writers' Project does?"

When Sofia shook her head, Millie explained before asking, "Would you answer a few questions?"

Sofia hesitated, her eyes sliding to a framed photograph perched on the mantel. It was of a man, who had to be no older than eighteen, wearing a military uniform, grinning ear to ear.

Was this the husband?

"Of course," Sofia said, but then gestured toward the hallway. "I'm making some elk stew. Would you mind joining me there?"

Oscar pushed away from the doorway where he'd been lounging, watching, and assessing. His natural condition. "Elk, you say?"

Sofia grinned, obviously used to boys and their stomachs. "A rare treat. My oldest, Nico, was able to shoot his second ever the other week and we'll be feasting on it for a while now."

"Congratulations to him," Oscar said, sounding sincere, and it made her wonder if he had been raised in Missoula or farther out where he'd had to hunt for elk, as well.

They all settled into a kitchen that must be familiar to a million others across the country, the aroma of spices and meat saturating the air, the warmth of the stove making it just a little uncomfortable for this time of year.

Sofia tied her discarded apron back around her waist and took a spot in front of the biggest pot, where she could shield herself from their questions if she needed to.

There were a few sections at the top that Millie filled in on the form every FWP writer used. Name, state, date. Address. She guessed a little on that last one, though she didn't think it would matter overmuch.

Then to start, Millie asked what she hoped was a gentle question: "Were you born here?"

Still, Sofia's shoulders went tight.

They had all been warned that they should be careful about identifying themselves as government workers. That even now, a full term into Roosevelt's presidency, many Americans didn't trust that their politicians were on their side, that they were here to help. Instead, they viewed anyone from the agencies with distrust, in many cases rightly so. President Hoover had ruptured any goodwill Americans had toward their government.

Millie couldn't tell if that was where Sofia's hesitancy stemmed from, but it could be a factor. Maybe if they'd come without Sidney—who had clearly gained her trust—she would have turned them away without even inviting them in.

Or maybe she had deep bruises that they could trample on even with the most sensitive of interviews.

"No," Sofia finally said. "I grew up in New York. My parents were from Italy."

"That was brave of them," Millie said, earning herself a startled, but pleased, look over Sofia's shoulder.

"Yes," she agreed. "I found work at a camera shop. The owner was friendly to Italians. Not everyone was."

Millie nodded as she jotted down notes. She had never been exposed to prejudice, mostly because her tiny town was filled with white Christians. Of course, they'd had Catholic and Mexican and Black ranch hands, but as long as they did work that everyone else considered below them, they had been treated fine.

"Arthur, my husband, was a war photographer," Sofia continued. "He came into the shop two days before he was supposed to ship out. We fell in love the second our eyes met."

The smile was evident in her voice even if Millie couldn't see it. Millie wasn't one to believe in that kind of instantaneous connection—love, to her, was all about work and compromise and time. But she would cut her tongue out before she made one disparaging remark to Sofia about it. She shot Oscar a glance to cut off any mocking reply at the pass, but he simply stared back, as if insulted she'd had to check in with him.

"We wrote to each other over the course of the war," Sofia said. "That's where he met Sidney."

"Oh." Of course. "And you moved to Montana with Arthur?"

"Ah, the stew is ready," Sofia said, turning again.

"We should leave you to your dinner," Millie said. When Sofia frowned, she added, "We don't want to impose."

"I've yet to have to turn a friend away from my table, and I'm not about to start today," Sofia said firmly. "Mr. Dalton, would you mind calling in the children from the porch. Miss Lang, if you could fetch Sidney. The room is just around the corner. It's a glorified closet, so don't get too excited."

Sofia wasn't exaggerating.

Millie rapped on the door, and opened it carefully when Sidney called out for her to join. She had to pass through a strange antechamber—there, she assumed, to keep out the light—and then she was in the dark room. Squished nearly shoulder to shoulder with Sidney.

"Dinner is—"

Millie cut herself off. Sidney hadn't stopped working when she'd walked in, even though his shoulders had tensed. Perhaps he couldn't stop the process now that he'd started.

He took the sheet he'd been holding and slid it into a tray of what looked like water but was probably not. With practiced hands he slid the container back and forth until splotches and shadows emerged from nowhere on the piece of paper. Her eyes adjusted enough to make out a face, though none of the features had sharpened yet.

Using tongs, Sidney shifted the paper out of developing liquid into a second tray, and after only a handful of seconds he then moved it into a final container.

"It's like magic," she murmured.

She caught the amused twitch of Sidney's lips. "Ta-da."

With that, Sidney pulled the photograph free from the liquid, and Millie gasped.

Alice Monroe stared at her, in black and white. She was younger, but it was unmistakably her.

The background's perspective was skewed, as if she were elevated.

Like she was on top of a mound . . . or . . .

Millie caught sight of the smokestacks behind her, but even then it took her a moment to realize what she was looking at.

In the picture, Alice Monroe was sitting on top of a boxcar.

She wasn't laughing, but the corners of her eyes were crinkled as if she were trying not to. She had her arms wrapped loosely around her knees and she stared directly into the lens. There was so much emotion written onto her face that Millie had to look away.

This was an intimate glimpse of the woman—her love as obvious as if she'd been captured making the declaration itself.

And Millie was even more certain that the photographer had been in love with Alice in return. Because how else could he have drawn that expression out of her, how could he have captured her very essence, an essence Millie didn't even claim to know apart from seeing it here in black and white.

"Dinner is?" Sidney prompted now as if he hadn't ripped open his chest and shown her a piece of his battered heart.

"Ready," she whispered, her voice rough. She cleared her throat. "Elk stew."

"Sofia is so generous."

"Why?" Millie asked softly, knowing she wouldn't get a straight answer out of him, but wishing she could. Why hold back the interviews with the tribes? Why sabotage the work in the first place? Why hold on to film that must be a decade old? Why let Millie see if it was so important to hide?

Why.

"Art deserves to see the light," was what he said, before shrugging out of his heavy apron.

THEY ATE THEIR dinner of hearty stew and warm bread with Sofia and her five children. Both Sidney and Oscar tried complimenting Nico on his hunt, but the boy remained silent throughout the meal.

The rest of the children made up for it, all babbling so much and so loudly that Millie only needed to smile and nod her way through the meal, which was delicious. It never ceased to amaze her how women had found a way to make filling and nutritious and tasty food during these hard years.

"A fire?" Sofia posited to Sidney when they were all done.

That was all it took for them to head outside, the cool air a welcome relief from the stuffy house.

Nico brought out a fiddle and one of his brothers brought out a banjo.

Millie took a seat—a tree stump—next to Sofia, who held her youngest in her lap as she watched Nico form his impromptu band.

The first notes cut through the air, shocking and expected at once. There were songs they all knew, and Millie sang along when she could. So did Sofia, whose voice had been made for the stage.

Millie straightened when Nico paused for a moment, looked at the ground, and then took a deep breath. When he brought the fiddle back to his shoulder, he drew out a note that Millie felt in her chest.

Sofia made some gutted sound when she realized what song it was, and Millie wanted to rip the instrument out of the boy's hand just to protect Sofia from the pain of it.

For the first time that night, Nico raised his voice to the sky, blanketed with stars as it was. He sang a song about heaven, about how there was no depression there; he sang a song about a man who wanted to leave the harshness of the world behind for the relief of a land free from care.

For better or worse, Sofia stuck it out. And then when the final, shivering note disappeared into the air, she gently nudged her baby off her lap and slipped away from the fire.

Sofia might be a stranger, but that didn't stop Millie from following her right to the tree line. She found the woman there, pacing and swiping at damp cheeks.

"I found him," Sofia said when she realized Millie had joined her. "I found him after he'd done it."

Millie nodded. It didn't take much to figure out what had happened here. A picture of a plucky young ensign. The fact that his widow was still here, raising their five boys in a depression.

"He was never well, after he came back," Sofia continued. "He saw too much during the war. And they wanted him to take pictures, you know? They wanted him to document the dead."

The ghosts that must have followed him after that would have been vocal and persuasive. No one could have gone through that unscathed.

Sofia grabbed for Millie's hands, pulled her close. "Don't make this pretty."

"What?" Millie asked, confused by the urgency in the plea and the strength in Sofia's grip.

"Don't make all of this look dignified or virtuous," Sofia said. "This life isn't noble. This life is hard. It's backbreaking and soul-crushing and even with help and relief I can barely give my children enough food to eat. There's nothing about this kind of life that's beautiful."

"Your children—"

Sofia shook her head. "Would be much better if their mother wasn't working herself to death. If they had soft things and opportunity and—"

She broke off, took a shaky inhale. "Sidney sees the beauty in suffering, so did my husband. Photographers, that's what they do."

So did writers. They saw the extremes in life as appealing—terror and courage, fear and strength, love and hate. They were what made humans *human*. But Millie didn't think of herself as a writer. She thought of herself as a journalist. She was there to tell other people's stories.

And this was Sofia's.

A woman who'd carried on with calluses on her hands and bruises on her soul.

When you know someone's story, it's harder to hate them. It was Katherine's mantra. And maybe no one would look at Sofia now and hate her or fear her. But they had her parents. They did now with Chinese workers and socialists and Jews and . . . and . . . and . . .

Everyone had a story, and most people were just trying to get by. They didn't deserve to become empty vessels to hold other people's anger and insecurities.

They deserved to be seen. Even for their flaws.

"Tell me about it," Millie said. "Tell me what this life's actually like."

Sofia stared at her and Millie could see all the years in that moment of silence, the years of suffering and pain and joy that couldn't be shared with someone she loved because she had to be strong for her family. She saw late nights trying to stretch a penny into something far grander than it was, trying to figure out a way to make sure her children wouldn't start shouldering burdens beyond their age.

Maybe none of what Sofia said next would make it into the Montana guide, but that didn't matter. It mattered that Millie was able to listen.

CHAPTER TWENTY-FOUR

Alice

Missoula, Montana
1924

Alice couldn't simply disappear into the night. Her father would hire the entire Pinkerton staff to hunt her down, and she'd be found within the hour.

What she needed was a plausible excuse to be called out of town on short notice, without any thought to planning for her safety.

The only two things to warrant that kind of rush that Alice could think of were death or a health-related emergency.

While Alice didn't exactly have a wide range of out-of-town acquaintances, she did frequently correspond with a fair number of librarians around the state. One of them *could* have a debilitating injury in which they needed her help, not only with the recovery but to cover their work while they recuperated.

The scenario wasn't exactly likely, but her father wouldn't think too deeply about it as long as it sounded logical enough.

Alice waited until Clark went to bed following the gala before sneaking into his office to leave her note. She held her breath the entire way down the stairs, to his desk, and then out the front door, sure she was going to be stopped and then locked in her room for the rest of her life.

When no one raised an alarm, she started running, as if her reins had been let down. Cold air kissed her aching cheeks and she realized she was laughing, breathless and exhilarated and free. Alice spun in a circle, her bag flying out in a wide arc.

She tripped and righted herself and laughed some more, thankful no one was watching her behave like a five-year-old on too much penny candy.

Still, she made it to the train station with plenty of time to spare.

Alice hesitated at the door—if Colette were asleep, she would likely reach for that ever-present shotgun of hers when Alice came into the boxcar at four in the morning. But then she heard shuffling inside and her decision was made.

When Alice threw open the door to the library, Colette stood there, books in hand, grinning at her.

"We said goodbye yesterday," Colette said.

"I'm not coming to say goodbye."

"Well then, I'll have to figure out how to put you to work," Colette said, her smile only growing. "No one rides for free."

Alice laughed and laughed and then couldn't stop laughing, her breath coming too short. Her head went light and she bent at the waist to keep herself from fainting right then and there.

"This is so embarrassing," she managed to get out when she'd found her air again.

Colette placed a strong hand on the small of her back. "You'll do fine, kid."

Alice straightened enough to roll her eyes at Colette who had to be only a few years older than her, and Colette smirked.

"There you are," she said, and then nudged a tin cup into Alice's hand. "Here, have the rest of my coffee. I couldn't sleep so I made plenty to get me through the day."

As she drank, Alice shifted toward the living compartment. "Oh."

"What?" Colette asked. She'd moved on to reshelving the books in her hand.

"The living quarters," Alice said, all the nerves and excitement slipping out of her like air from a balloon. "There's not enough room for me."

Of course, of course, the one time she actually did something with her life and she was about to be thwarted by logistics.

Colette squinted into the distance, and then checked the clock. "I'll be right back."

Alice paced as she waited, her eyes flying to the door each time she heard a sound, expecting Clark to be there ready to haul her back to the house. But the next person who came through it was a boy hauling a mattress up the steps.

It ended up being a tight fit, but it worked.

"That'll do," Colette said, a smug, satisfied air about her.

"You're not going to be so happy about this when I'm practically lying on top of you," Alice said.

"I've slept in far worse situations," Colette said, and went back to looking over the books even though Alice knew them to be in perfect order. "I think we're set until the first camp, but I can't help but keep checking."

"I know," Alice said, crossing to the section that had been built into the wall for newspapers and magazines. Mrs. Herbert Hoover, the chairwoman of the Women's National Law Enforcement Committee, stared back at her from the cover of an issue of *Time*. It was from April, but it wasn't yet so dated as to be boring or misleading.

The first camp would be a good test for how ready they were. It was the closest one to Missoula and stretched for miles along the Blackfoot. They would arrive that afternoon and stay for a full three days. Even that might be too short of a time to make sure everyone who wanted a book would be able to check one out.

All the books had been cataloged, with library pockets and cards added to most of them along with classification tags. They'd created lists upon lists of predictions about how many books would be taken out at each stop, and considered how they could maintain their collection while still being generous with lending policies.

It would be a test, but it would be one they passed. "We are ready."

The whistle blew, and Alice thought about that first night, the one where she'd come up with this idea while staring at the river and listening for the train. That seemed like a lifetime ago now, and also like a second.

"We are ready," Colette echoed, and then went to close the door.

Clark Monroe hadn't stormed in. He hadn't dragged her away. Alice would be able to see the fruits of her labor, would be able to escape into the unknown.

She laughed as the boxcar jerked into motion and then crossed to the large window cut into the side of the car. She lifted it to catch the cool morning air and to wave to some of the workers and lookie-loos who were watching the departure.

Tears gathered in her eyes once more and she blamed the breeze.

"How does it feel?" Colette asked from behind her.

Alice couldn't easily describe the emotions cascading through her. There was even a bit of sadness she didn't quite understand, but thought might be tied into the loss of her youth, of her protected life.

"A bit like I'm a bank robber on the run from the law," Alice settled on. Missoula's skyline was blurring and fading away now as the train picked up speed, heading east.

When Colette laughed, Alice finally turned away from the window to join her at the table.

"What were you planning to read if I hadn't come along?" Alice asked.

Colette didn't answer for a long minute. Then she shook her head. "I knew you would come."

"You can't have," Alice said. "I didn't know myself until only a few hours ago."

"You don't do something like this"—Colette waved to the shelves—"without intending to see it through. I knew you would come."

"You can't have," Alice said again, not sure why she was arguing this. "You didn't even have the extra mattress in here."

"But I knew how to get one in about the span of three minutes, didn't I?" Colette asked. "I did start to worry there that fear had won out in the end. You cut it pretty close."

"Well, you were right," Alice said, with a happy sigh.

"How long will you stay?" Colette asked.

As long as she was allowed was Alice's initial thought. But that wasn't true. Even if she had no one to answer to, she didn't want to live this way forever. She wanted a taste of it, but she would miss Missoula too much. Her work, her neighbors, the part she played in the community there.

"A month," Alice tossed out. By then they would have gotten to the end of the line and would be heading back to town. Mac would probably catch up with her before she made it all the way back to Missoula, but that would be enough to scratch this itch. "How long do you plan on holding this position?"

Alice wasn't dumb. Not everyone could ride the rails forever, even the ones who liked the nomadic life. She was sure she would have to replace Colette eventually, but she also hoped that would be in the far future.

One side of Colette's mouth lifted. "I'm going to try to get past the first day, at least."

The answer was classic Colette. She forever had a one-line deflection at the ready, a dry and sardonic or even self-deprecating reply that never quite addressed the question.

That wasn't unusual in a place like Montana. People came out here to shed their pasts and get a fresh start. Alice respected that, she did.

But sometimes she wished she knew more about this enigmatic woman who she would now be spending a month with in tight quarters.

All those doubts must have shown on her face—or Colette just had a knack for reading her expressions.

"I'm not about to abandon you just when I've started," Colette said. "I won't promise forever, but I won't suddenly disappear at the next stop."

Mostly joking, Alice held her hand out like she was making Colette swear to her words. "Deal?"

Colette hesitated, but then smiled and slapped her palm into Alice's. "Deal."

Alice sat back and studied Colette, who bore the scrutiny with amused patience.

Part of Alice knew she should be wary of this stranger who kept herself wrapped in mile-high barbed wire. There were secrets in her past, a reason she was alone out here, taking a job that some would look at as rough at best. Alice didn't know how or why Colette had ended up in Missoula, or how or why she'd ended up in Alice's library.

But she'd started to get a feel for Colette's favorite books. They tended to focus on themes of justice and fairness and good guys triumphing over evil. For now, Alice felt like that was enough to quiet the worrying voice in the back of her head that sounded too much like Mac.

Instead, she focused on the idea that she and Colette might

become friends after all this. Alice hadn't had many of those in her life. Class boundaries might be more relaxed in the West, but there still weren't many children in town who hadn't started at least helping out with their parents' work at a fairly young age.

The one or two that might have been interested in being friends were scared away by the fact that she wasn't allowed to do *anything* beyond play with dolls in the parlor.

As a young adult, the same restrictions kept her from engaging in the social activities the young people relished. Racing cars up and down the dirt lanes outside of town, picnicking along one of the rivers, even just taking strolls up Mount Jumbo without a single thought to the wildfire smoke.

Alice truly believed that books provided incredible connections to other people. But she wondered now if she'd been using them as a crutch, as a way to avoid making connections with people in real life. Beyond helping them pick out a novel from her shelves.

That didn't mean she had to abandon reading in search of constant companionship. But it might not hurt to at least try to create a relationship out of this forced proximity with Colette.

As Mark Twain once said, *"Good friends, good books, and a sleepy conscience: this is the ideal life."*

She shifted to look out the window once more. The landscape blurred as they raced east.

Maybe Alice hadn't had what Mr. Twain had deemed an ideal life before, but she felt like now she was finally headed in the right direction.

CHAPTER TWENTY-FIVE

Millie

Whitefish, Montana
1936

I thought Montana was supposed to have mountains," Millie said, groggy and irritable. They'd arrived in Whitefish the night before, following their stay with Sofia.

Now, they were headed into Glacier National Park at a most undignified time of the morning. Both Oscar and Flo were sleeping in the back, and even Sidney, who never tired, looked a little heavy around the eyes.

But apparently the sunrise over the mythical mountains could not be missed.

Sidney pressed his thermos of coffee into Millie's hands. "You're going to feel very foolish in about ten minutes."

Millie hummed, because of course she knew she would. They were driving through flat land covered in lush pine trees, but the morning mist blocking the sight of the mountains would break eventually. She had just wanted to complain for complaining's sake.

"How did you end up with the writers' program?" Millie asked, nodding toward his equipment stowed on the seat beside Oscar.

"How does anyone?" Sidney asked. "It's a relief roll, isn't it?"

Millie ran her hand over the supple leather between them. "You could have sold this."

His fingers drummed on the steering wheel. "It's the one thing I have left from my mother."

"Ah."

His mouth twisted, but for once it wasn't in amused disdain. "We had our disagreements. But she loved this car. When she died, I couldn't bring myself to sell it."

That had turned out to be fortuitous for Millie.

"That's not what I meant, though," Millie said. "When I asked how you ended up with FWP."

He made a questioning sound.

"Not to state the obvious, but you're not a writer," she pointed out.

"There weren't any other options in Missoula, and I can't leave," he said, and she wondered if that had to do with Alice Monroe.

"You made it seem like you have no respect for the Writers' Project," Millie said, likely because she was tired and her guard was down. "That first day I came to town. Why?"

He huffed out a breath. "I didn't like that they'd sent someone in to clean up a mess that wasn't even a mess to begin with. I shouldn't have taken it out on you, I apologize."

"Thank you," Millie murmured. "But I'm not trying to slap your hand or fish for apologies."

"Then what are you trying to do?"

"I'm trying to say that you should apply to the Resettlement Administration."

His brow wrinkled. "What would I do for them?"

"They have a photography unit," Millie said, not sure how much of this was common knowledge so far away from Washington, DC. "You've heard of Dorothea Lange?"

"Of course."

The female photographer was making a name for herself across the country with her work documenting the lives of Okies and other desperate migrants who had poured into California with hopes of survival. Her picture "Migrant Mother" had resonated deeply with those who recognized the woman as themselves, old beyond her years with three children resting their weight on her dust bowl–thin body.

"She's employed by the Resettlement Administration," Millie said. "Some might call her work propaganda, or talk about it just like you talked about the guides that first day. But her pictures are telling a story, one that future generations will want to listen to and study."

"All right, you already made me feel terrible, no need to pile on," Sidney scolded.

"There she is," Oscar said quietly from behind them. Sidney's hand tightened on the wheel briefly in a surprise that Millie shared with him.

They could never actually count on Oscar being asleep. He was ducked down enough to stare out the front window, something close to wonder replacing his usually cynical expression. She followed his gaze.

The sunrise had thrown the peaks into sharp relief, the sky pink and purple and gold behind the jutting rock. Millie cranked the window down, the icy morning rushing in to greet them.

None of them cared.

She had never smelled air so fresh before, clean and crisp and rejuvenating, rolling off the range. An elk bellowed in the distance as the fog started to clear, revealing dewy pastures that ended at the feet of giants. They had driven into a postcard, only this was real life.

They arrived at the gates before the attendants so they were able to drive through without stopping. The road then led them into a green tunnel of trees, before opening up onto an enormous lake.

"Oh, can we stop?" Millie asked. She had never seen anything like this.

Sidney pulled to the side of the road and Millie could barely wait before she was out, heading toward the banks. A small beach full of red and blue and gray pebbles greeted her, and she reminded herself not to roll an ankle. When she got to the water's edge, she threw her hands out wide, tipping her face up.

She felt weightless and cold and beautiful.

A *click* sounded behind her, and when she glanced over her shoulder, grinning impossibly wide, another *click* came before Sidney lowered his camera.

Millie wondered what that developed photograph would look like, her face split by joy, the best of nature, wild and free behind her. The contrast—with her travel clothes and hat, her shoes that weren't quite nice but weren't made for hiking either—would be interesting.

He would have caught more than that, too. He would have caught the childlike wonder of seeing something impossibly beautiful for the first time; the hint of fear that they all should feel when their smallness was put in context of the earth. And then a hundred emotions in between.

"Should I get a picture of you?" she asked.

"No," Sidney said, straight-faced. "Never."

Flo had emerged from the car, and she and Oscar leaned against the door, everyone watching Millie.

Millie blushed at her own earnestness. It would have earned her a snide remark if these had been her colleagues from Dallas or DC, because wonder was viewed as embarrassing. They would talk about how she was just a naive ranch girl who had never seen anything beyond her own swimming hole, and how sad was that? How pitiful?

None of the three here and now looked at her with anything other than fond patience even though they were used to this view.

She hated that she had to be suspicious of any of them. She hated that chatting with Sidney that morning had been the closest she'd felt to having a friend in a long time, matched only with how she felt when teasing Oscar or having Flo call her some silly endearment.

Oscar clapped his hands. "Enough playtime. We have work to do."

But he was smiling when he said it.

Millie basked in the beauty from the front seat until they got about halfway up Going-to-the-Sun Road, the engineering marvel that connected the west and east side of Glacier.

"Open your eyes, Millie," Oscar said from the back, and she shook her head as the tires of the car skittered on the crushed rock that lined the road. If she opened her eyes now, she would see how perilously close they were to the low stone-wall barrier that was the one thing standing between them and death.

"Sidney," she managed, though it unfortunately did come out as an undignified screech.

Both Sidney and Oscar laughed, and if Millie wasn't holding on to pieces of the car—as if that would do any good as they tumbled down thousands of feet—she would have smacked them.

"Oh, you two are beasts," Flo said. "As if you didn't need a new pair of trousers the first time you drove this."

Millie laughed, opening her eyes in time to catch Flo's wink.

The men blustered on about their manliness, but Millie tuned them out. She knew now why they'd wanted her to look.

A deep, lush valley spread out beneath them, the yellow and orange of the autumn trees cradled by the harsh but striking peaks. In front of them, a waterfall cascaded into the road and wildflowers of every color bloomed along the banks.

Millie knuckled at the corner of her eye where tears gathered.

"Haystack Butte," Sidney murmured, pointing at the triangle where they were headed. "And the Garden Wall."

"Very important information," Millie gritted out. "But I think it's more important to have your hands on the wheel at all times."

Sidney grinned, but he complied.

"Naturalists run hikes and guided sessions from here," Sidney said when they finally pulled into the modest parking lot at Logan Pass. One of those long, red buses that hauled tourists up the road when they didn't want to drive themselves was parked in front of the building but there weren't many other cars.

Their naturalist turned out to be a man named Theodore Cooke. He had a long but neatly combed beard and thick brows that drooped over still-sharp eyes. He took them walking behind the visitors' center, pointing out flowers and plants and rocks that Millie would never have noticed otherwise.

"Have you always lived in Montana?" Flo asked. She never took notes while she chatted with people, she said it scared them off. Millie didn't try to change her mind—she had seen Flo's interview forms and they were always impeccable.

"No, ma'am. My daddy was a hotelier outside of Yosemite," Mr. Cooke said, drawing out the word "hotelier." "Government did something right, there, protecting that land."

"Oh, I've always wanted to go to California," Flo said, a little dreamily. "How did you end up in Montana?"

"Did you ever hear what Mr. Abraham Lincoln said of this

fine place?" Mr. Cooke asked. "'My favorite state has not yet been invented. It will be called Montana and it will be perfect.'"

"Are you making up tales?" Flo asked, eyeing him skeptically.

Mr. Cooke put his hand on his heart. "He said it when he signed the legislation that made Montana a part of the Union. And he was right. It is perfect."

"But what brought you to Montana?" Flo pressed.

He eyed her, like he was surprised she simply hadn't taken his pretty words as an answer without noticing he hadn't actually said anything. "There are three things that bring anyone to Montana, Miss Marner. Copper. Hooch. And women."

"You were in love," Flo guessed.

"With a mistress named whiskey," Mr. Cooke hooted. "I got drunk as a skunk in California and ended up three days later in Billings, challenging a man to race in an automobile. He hit a child, broke the girl's back. That night he ate his gun, and I swore over his dead body I'd never drink again."

And here was the beauty of Flo on display. She hadn't settled for a postcard when there had been a novel lying in wait beneath.

"These mountains saved me," Mr. Cooke said. "Anytime I got the hankering after that, I walked into the woods until it passed. No hooch to tempt me. Then one time I just stayed. Turns out you can make a living out here."

"And that was probably the best way to learn about what berries not to eat, huh?" Flo asked, redirecting them to the informative part of their walk, which they'd be able to include in the guides.

Mr. Cooke treated them like friends rather than government workers from that moment on.

"There," he said, about ten minutes later. Sidney already had his camera raised, and Millie followed where they were both looking.

She went still, swallowing her instinctual scream for the fourth or fifth time that day as an enormous bear ambled out from behind a copse of trees. His nose was on the ground snuffling along in front of paws that had to be bigger than her head.

"Do we run?" Millie asked, barely moving her lips, the bear close enough that he could probably hear even that whisper. Were they like dogs? Could they pick up sounds humans couldn't?

"Nah, he'd get you quick if you did," Mr. Cooke said. "That there is a grizzly, he'd kill you with one swipe."

"I assume most bears would," Millie said, trying not to let the hysteria slip into her voice. The bear had hardly glanced their way, intent on whatever scent he'd picked up on the ground.

"Black bears are scaredy-cats, you just yell and get big and they run off," Mr. Cooke said. "For grizzlies, you act like you're dead. You hear me? But then if he starts snacking on you, fight back. You won't have a good chance, but maybe you'll get lucky."

"If a bear gets peckish, I shouldn't just let him have at it. Noted," Millie said, and Mr. Cooke laughed. "This is all very reassuring."

"You want to know the advice for polar bears?"

"As I have no plans to ever travel to the Arctic, I don't believe I do, no."

It was Sidney who answered, "You bend over and kiss your—"

"All right," Millie cut him off. "Got it."

"Haven't had a bear death on my watch yet," Mr. Cooke said, and from the humor in the words, she guessed this was a fairly frequent occurrence in Glacier.

On the way back to the visitors' center, Mr. Cooke talked about the various lodges, hotels, and motor camps in the park. And he told them about all the CCC had done in the handful of years they'd been deployed there, including laying telephone cable up over Logan Pass. It was the first of its kind in the country.

Then he pointed them in the direction of the Going-to-the-Sun Chalets where they would be staying. "You take the boat across the lake. There's only one road between here and there, and the dock will be on your right. Can't miss it."

When they boarded, Sidney wandered off to find the best angle to take a picture of the chalets upon their arrival, Flo found yet another person to talk to, and Millie decided to take a risk. She hadn't been able to stop thinking about the photograph of Alice Monroe since that day at Sofia's.

Sidney didn't seem to be the type to take money from a greedy mining company just to protect their reputation. The way he talked about the tribes, the war, and the aftermath gave her the impression that he had a strong sense of fairness, justice, and moral fortitude.

She couldn't see him destroying months' worth of work for a quick payout from what seemed like a truly evil, soulless company.

What she could see was him doing so to protect someone he loved.

Was that someone Alice Monroe?

Was Millie jumping to all kinds of conclusions again?

Her attention shifted to Oscar who was steadily watching her, waiting.

She didn't have a strong sense of his character yet, either. Not enough to say he didn't seem the type to take a bribe from the Company. If he was desperate enough to write as many books as he did in addition to his government job, that meant he could use the money.

Was it a gambling debt he was paying off? If the Company had offered to take care of it, why wouldn't he swap a few boxes of paperwork? No harm, no foul and Oscar walks away from whatever problem that had plagued him.

But if she kept all that in mind, she could run her theory by him anyway. How he reacted would give her more information about both Oscar *and* Sidney.

"You said that it was a smart line of questioning. Wondering about Sidney sabotaging your work," Millie said quickly and quietly to Oscar. "Why do you think he would do that?"

Oscar didn't seem surprised by the question even though she'd been steadfastly pretending the exchange hadn't happened. "I still haven't figured that part out."

"Have you tried? Have you asked him anything?" When they stayed in hotels and motels or even small cabins, the two men paired up.

"He's a vault," Oscar said, sounding more curious than anything. "Sticking to the line about the Helena editor."

"Where'd that come from?" Millie asked.

"We had a meeting right after we got told off about everything," Oscar said. "Professor Lyon was the unofficial head of the office at that time. Maybe it was him, maybe it was Flo, I don't remember. At the end of the meeting we all seemed to agree that was what must have happened."

"But you don't think that's what happened."

Oscar shook his head. "No, it didn't make any sense. But I couldn't just go around accusing people."

"Accusing Sidney," Millie said.

"No, I didn't suspect him at first. But then he disappeared a few days right after," Oscar said, lifting one shoulder. "And when Flo asked him where he'd gone, he said it was a fishing trip. But I've never seen him fish a day in his life."

Millie chewed on her lower lip. It wasn't exactly damning, but combined with the rest of it, she felt they were onto something.

The only other thing to figure out was if Sidney had been acting alone. "Do you think anyone else in the office might have helped him?"

"I can't see it," Oscar said. "Professor Lyon hasn't met a rule he wouldn't follow straight into hell. And she has a good heart, but Flo would have told someone else by now."

"And you?" Millie asked, curious what he would say if directly challenged.

His brows rose, but he looked mildly impressed at her gumption. "I don't like my time being wasted. I have deadlines that are getting blown out of the water because we have to redo all this work. You don't have to trust that's enough of a reason, but believe me, it is."

Millie actually did. It was the biggest reason she suspected Sidney—he'd saved the interviews he hadn't wanted destroyed. The same logic could apply in reverse, as well.

Oscar could still be guilty, he could be manipulating her, but she didn't think he was.

His eyes roved over her face. "So, have you decided I'm not the saboteur? Is that why you're asking these questions now?"

Millie laughed helplessly, both exasperated and glad that she'd been stuck on this trip with a mystery writer. His perceptiveness would be helpful now that she'd chosen to make him an ally, but she didn't like when he applied it to her own behavior.

"You're not quite crossed off the list, yet," she admitted, and he grinned.

"I think trying to get myself off it entirely would actually backfire," he said.

Again, with the perceptiveness. "You're right."

"So why are you sharing all this?" he pressed.

"We made that stop at Sofia's because Sidney wanted to use the dark room there," she said. "He was developing film."

"He wanted to do it somewhere other than Missoula," Oscar said, arriving at the same conclusion she had. "I wonder why."

"It was also . . . old," Millie said slowly. "Maybe ten years or so. Why would he hold on to something like that only to develop it now?"

"He didn't have it in his possession until recently," Oscar said, and once he did, it sounded obvious.

The boat blew its horn before the engine kicked on, and they drifted away from the dock at a snail's pace. Millie didn't mind. They were surrounded by mountains that looked like picture-book renderings of the Swiss Alps. She wasn't sure she could ever get tired of this view.

"Did you see any of the pictures?"

"Only one," Millie said. "It was of Alice Monroe."

Oscar's eyes darted to where Sidney stood and then back to her face. She couldn't quite read his expression but something was clicking into place.

"Well," he finally drawled. "That answers that."

CHAPTER TWENTY-SIX

Alice

Rutherford Lumberjack Camp One, Montana
1924

Alice watched Montana go by in a blur.

They followed the tracks up the Blackfoot, and Alice soon discovered she liked the train best when sitting by the window. She'd offered the place of honor to Colette, but had been met with a book cover as the woman sank deeper into her own chair and the latest Zane Grey novel, *Wanderer of the Wasteland.*

Alice considered reading—she would as days went by, she was sure. But, for now, she was enjoying the freedom of the flight out of town too much.

It didn't take long into the afternoon for them to pull to a stop at the first Rutherford Lumberjack Camp. Colette put her book down when the brakes squealed and Alice stood up to nervously pace, a task made slightly difficult by the swaying boxcar.

"What if they don't come?" Alice asked, her fingers twisting into the fabric of her trousers. "What if we just sit here for two days alone?"

"More time for reading." She was so calm about it all, but that made sense. For Colette this was just one more job, one that she was well suited for at that.

For Alice, the stakes felt sky high.

She pictured Julia Walker's disdain over the past month that she'd never tried to hide, as well as all the ways the woman would celebrate Alice's downfall. She pictured Sidney on the balcony—*stay here, be comfortable and safe*—and knew he'd be disappointed if she returned to Missoula with her tail tucked between her legs. She pictured Mac, driving her home that day, so sure that she would come up with a way to bring these books to more people.

"I can hear you thinking from over here," Colette said mildly. "Make yourself useful and open the door?"

Alice let out a nervous laugh, but was glad to be given a task.

It was then that she closed her eyes and let herself bask in the moment. She had done this, starting with a foolish hope and now she was standing here surrounded by the reality she'd made from that vision.

This would be good. It had to be.

Alice exhaled and opened the door.

Nothing happened.

And then nothing happened for quite a bit of time.

Colette finally snapped at her to go get them lunch from the dining car. When Alice hopped down from the library, she could see tents and makeshift houses stretching as far as the eye could see. Men had even swarmed the train—but they were busy doing whatever needed to be done with the logs. Alice wasn't quite sure of all the logistics, but it all looked very impressive and like none of them would have time to come check out any books anytime soon.

The conductor, an older man with kind eyes named Seamus Kelly, was already in the dining car, eating with a tall bull called Moose. Alice had laughed at the idea that he was a bull Moose, but the man hadn't cracked a smile. Perhaps humor wasn't allowed for those policing the train for criminals.

Both of the men dipped their heads in greeting when Alice

took a seat at their four top. A boy who acted as waiter and all-around helper swung by immediately.

"I'll have two of whatever is for lunch," Alice said.

"Pot pie," Seamus informed her, and then waited until the boy had retreated to the kitchen car before asking, "No takers on the books?"

Alice sighed. "I have faith."

"As you should, lass," Seamus said. "Those boys will be wanting to turn off their minds once the day is done."

"Is that what reading does?" Alice asked, amused.

"Aye," Seamus said. "And I'll be stopping by later, so you'll have at least one patron."

Warmth welled up in Alice. "Thank you. What do you like? I can put something aside."

"I like a good Dublin boy, myself," Seamus said. "Is there any chance you have *An Ideal Husband* by Mr. Wilde?"

Alice had long trained herself not to judge a reader by their cover, but she was truly delighted to be shocked by the request. "'It takes a great deal of courage to see the world in all its tainted glory, and still to love it.'"

Seamus smiled. "You are a fellow admirer of Mr. Wilde?"

And just like that a thread stretched between them, one that would always be there. It never ceased to amaze her that simply liking the same book as another person could bridge a gap with a stranger that would have otherwise seemed insurmountable.

"I do adore him, but what's more is I worship that play," Alice admitted. She must have read it more than a dozen times. His wit and observations on the human condition were second perhaps only to Shakespeare himself. "But I am sad to report, we do not have it in our catalog."

"Well, it seems like I would do well taking any recommendation you have, then," Seamus said.

The boy chose that moment to deliver Alice her pot pies in round tins that would be perfect to take back to the library.

"I will think of nothing else until I come up with a good one," Alice promised while standing, already considering offering up *Emma*.

She made a quick detour to the toilet—she and Colette had a chamber pot that Alice hoped to only use on the rarest of occasions—then returned to the library where Colette confirmed that not a single person had stopped by in the time she'd been gone.

Colette dug into her pot pie with a gusto that Alice couldn't muster up, despite the fare being tastier than she would have ever guessed.

When they finished their lunch, Alice started pacing once more.

"It's not quitting time yet," Colette said for the fourth or fifth time. Alice had lost track.

"For some of them it is," Alice pointed out. There were men in this camp who would be out there since dawn's first light.

"They don't know about us yet," Colette said, not looking up from her book. *Scaramouche*.

"Excuse me?"

The voice was hesitant, but it caught Alice's attention immediately. She looked up to find a young man hovering in the doorway, his cap in his hands, his sandy mop falling over his forehead.

"Is this the library?"

Everything in Alice relaxed at that question.

"Yes," Alice said, waving the young man inside. They might be in a boxcar in the middle of nowhere, but this was familiar territory.

Just as all libraries were.

The young man's name was Jonah. He was passionate about

theater and planned to go to college once he'd earned some money working as a lumberjack. He was sweet and polite and wanted suggestions for plays so he could practice lines at night in his bunk. Silently, of course.

Colette wandered out from behind the checkout desk, sitting on the table, watching them move through the stacks.

Finally, after Jonah had dismissed a handful of Alice's suggestions, Colette offered her own. "*Pygmalion.*"

"Oh," Alice said, delighted. She only needed a moment of thought before she found the slim volume by George Bernard Shaw. "This will be perfect."

Jonah dipped his head, and took the slim play without a fight this time. Colette helped him check out, and then he was gone and the boxcar was empty once more.

Evening was drawing close and as much as Alice wanted to hold on to her optimism, she could admit it was slipping away.

Maybe Mr. Rutherford had been right.

Maybe this was a silly idea, bound to fail.

Colette was back behind her desk, feet kicked up. But she was staring at the empty doorway instead of reading.

After another hour went by without any patrons, she shifted her attention to Alice. "How well do you know *Pygmalion*?"

"Not well," Alice said, unsure if she should be embarrassed by that fact or not. In the short time she'd know Colette, she'd come to realize the woman had some sort of magical memory. She could read a passage once and then recite it perfectly without a single stutter.

"Don't we have two copies?" Colette asked, like she didn't know the answer. Except that her expression said that she did.

Still, Alice went to look and found the second one, likely a donated duplicate that was worth shelving due to the story's popularity.

Alice took it down, flipping through the pages. "What are you suggesting?"

Colette grinned. "A show."

She wouldn't expand on the answer until the end of the day after their second—and last—patron left.

"Come on, let's go," Colette said, grabbing the ring of keys that would lock everything up behind them.

Alice chewed her lip. "Where are we going?"

"You'll see," Colette promised.

They were officially deep into September, which meant they could expect snow at any time now. But they were also in the middle of a warm spell, with the air merely crisp rather than downright frigid, so Alice shrugged into a thick wool cardigan instead of a heavy jacket.

The camps were as busy as Alice would have imagined. Men came and went in rivers, not streams. They carried saws longer than Alice herself, were covered in sweat-caked dust and kept their eyes down as they trudged toward the bunks. Someone had started an impromptu baseball game, and a handful of spectators lingered at the sidelines. Machinery rumbled in the distance, and the very air smelled of pine and oil.

A main hall, which Alice knew would be the dining area, lay at the heart of the camp.

Alice and Colette's meals were provided on the train, but Colette marched into the long building without a moment's hesitation.

Hundreds of men sat around the long, communal tables that filled the room, all shoveling food in their mouths at breakneck speed. No one talked, no one looked their way.

There wouldn't be more than a handful of women in the camp. Maybe the superintendent's wife, along with some of the cooks. But beyond that, these men hadn't seen a pair of unmarried ladies in weeks, if not months.

"They're exhausted," Colette said, reading Alice's silent thoughts. "Many of them are probably getting paid by the amount of trees they cut down, rather than by the hour. It's a gamble, but if you're young and strong enough it usually works out. That means they push themselves harder than they would otherwise, though."

"Of course," Alice murmured, but Colette had gone back to searching the room.

She straightened abruptly, apparently having found whatever she was looking for. "Stay here."

Alice didn't have time to argue. She was left staring at Colette's back as she walked off toward one of the tables. Alice tracked her path and found Jonah at the end of it.

Colette shoved into the spot next to him, barely giving any attention to the burly lumberjack she'd displaced. To be fair, the burly lumberjack barely gave her any attention in return, surely used to bumping elbows and more with his neighbors.

Jonah smiled shyly and listened to whatever Colette proposed. He glanced toward Alice, grimaced, and then slowly nodded.

Deal sealed, Colette grinned as she stood.

"What are you up to?" Alice asked as Colette came to recollect her.

"I just got us our Eliza Doolittle."

The plan was simple: put on a three-man show of *Pygmalion* as a way to advertise the library's presence in the camp. The play was already fun and fast and entertaining, a perfect selection for what they were trying to do. But Colette wanted to amplify the impact by having Jonah play Eliza and Alice read for Henry

Higgins. Colette would cover the rest of the characters with her impressive memory.

"How did you convince him?" Alice asked, her belly a mess of knots. She peeked around the curtain that had been hastily hung up to create the backdrop for their dramatic reading—there would be no acting, she'd been assured.

"Hmm, I might have hinted that your dying wish was to see this library succeed."

Alice spun on her. "Colette!"

Colette, clearly unrepentant, simply winked. "There are no rules in the West, darling."

Alice spared a moment to wonder if Colette had suggested *Pygmalion* to Jonah for this purpose even before Alice realized that no one would be coming to their grand opening. In some ways it seemed like she was playing a chess game with life and Alice was wearing a blindfold trying to keep up.

She turned back to the curtain and the dozen or so men beyond it. They were gathered around the fire, some sitting on half-cut logs, some standing in the back as if they were prepared to flee in case this went even a little bit sideways.

Colette nudged her forward. "Ready or not, my dear Henry Higgins, it's time."

When they stepped out onto the "stage," they received some good-natured hoots, which only intensified when Colette waved for Jonah to join them. He emerged from the shadows with a mop on his head and a borrowed apron tied around his waist. If Alice hadn't met him earlier, she would have sworn it was a different person. Not because of his costume, but because of his confidence. With a few ridiculous props he had become Eliza Doolittle, sass and all.

The men roared their approval as Jonah sashayed past them—familiar shenanigans they were likely used to from either the war or camp life. They dropped silent, though, as soon as Colette signaled for it.

"'The English have no respect for their language, and will not teach their children to speak it,'" Colette said to a few snorts.

And they were off.

It was far from smooth. This was Jonah's first pass through—ever—and Colette, brilliant as she was, still had to borrow Alice's volume half the time to hit her lines.

Alice stumbled over her words, and probably should have been booed off the stage for all her dramatic abilities.

But . . . there was something infectious and lovely about what they were doing.

Jonah shined even with the challenge of sight-reading Cockney, and Alice understood why he wanted to study theater. Colette delivered everything with a hint of humor beneath her voice like she understood how ridiculous this all was and found it delightful that they were in on the joke together.

Meanwhile, the men were far from silent spectators. They laughed and hissed and catcalled and policed each other when the participation veered on distracting. They wanted to hear the story.

Alice couldn't remember the last time she'd enjoyed herself so much. Reading books curled up in a comfortable chair by a rainy window was hard to beat, but this? This was language and story and characters coming alive in a way that connected Alice and Colette and Jonah to their audience and them to each other and to Mr. George Bernard Shaw who probably hadn't ever imagined his story would be told around a campfire in Montana with a lumberjack playing Eliza and an audience full of men who had, until today, not known what Cockney was.

On the way back to the boxcar, she was practically vibrating out of her skin.

"I think we'll get so many patrons tomorrow," Alice said.

"Let's not get ahead of ourselves," Colette said. Alice could hear the smile even though the night was too dark to actually see her face. "Maybe one or two more."

"One or two," Alice repeated, appalled. "Now, you sound like Mr. Rutherford."

"Never say so."

Alice spun in a circle, arms held wide out like a child. "I'm so glad I came."

"I told you you would be," Colette said, smug.

"Yes, yes, the brilliant Colette Durand knows all, including the minor characters' lines in *Pygmalion*," Alice teased, happy to have someone in her life who she could act like this with. She'd always wanted a sister, and while she wasn't delusional enough to think she was that close to Colette, they were starting to form a relationship, at least.

Colette laughed, and it was a rusty sound. "I had to read at least half of them."

"That's still half more than I know," Alice said with a happy sigh as they let themselves back into the boxcar.

They traded their favorite parts of the night while they got ready for bed.

"Thank you," Alice whispered when she was half certain Colette had fallen asleep.

Of course she hadn't. "I think I should be saying that to you."

Alice shook her head even though Colette wouldn't be able to see. "You saved the library today."

"That's giving me a bit too much credit, I think."

"Maybe," Alice said, but she was too giddy to be rational. "I just . . . I want this to succeed. And I can't believe I found the most perfect librarian for it."

There was a long beat of silence after that and Alice wondered what she'd said wrong.

"I'm far from perfect," Colette finally said.

"Perfect in life and perfect for the library are two different things." That seemed obvious to her.

"Oh, yeah? Then what makes me perfect for the library?"

"You know books," Alice said, ticking that off on her finger. "You know people. You knew exactly how to break the ice today and get the word out that we exist. You knew Jonah would flourish in that role and hold his own. And you don't have any fear. The men won't send you into vapors, or anything silly like that. It was as if you were tailor-made to be my boxcar librarian."

Alice dropped her hand with another happy sigh. Her eyes drifted closed as her body crashed from the highs and lows of the day.

As she succumbed to sleep, Alice almost didn't hear Colette's response.

"It's funny how that worked out, isn't it?" Colette murmured.

CHAPTER TWENTY-SEVEN

Colette

Somewhere in Montana
1923

Colette chased the man with the birthmark from the border of Idaho all the way across Montana and back again. She sold the Ford and rode the rails to save money on gasoline.

Work was scarce these days, the drought killing towns and hope right alongside crops, so men were always on the move.

That ended up helping Colette in the long run.

The birthmark had been the key to everything. Even though she hadn't seen it yet in person, she knew now that it was memorable, especially in mining and logging communities.

The man she was chasing wasn't well liked, which was a lucky break. He'd made plenty of enemies who were willing to cough up information without even the hint of a bribe to get them going.

He didn't have a name, not one that he stuck with. He seemed to use Petey, though, more than any other, so she called him that in her head. He was short, built like a boxer. He talked like a Montanan but acted like a weasel.

She was building a picture of who he was, and feeling more sure by the day that he deserved the justice she was bringing his way.

Colette had taken to dressing like a man more days than not. The trend of big hats, long coats, and loose pants helped immensely, as did the fact that people tended to see what they wanted to.

She picked up spare jobs in the wake of the man she was hunting—maybe even his exact jobs—and she seemed to be about two steps behind him. Sometimes she lost the scent, took a wrong turn, ended up in a logging or mining camp or ranch where they looked at her funny for asking about strangers they'd never met.

But just like a hunting dog, she was able to narrow back in on the right path.

She laughed at what she imagined Papa's expression would be if he heard her refer to herself as a hunting dog.

Colette missed him like a limb. Everyone had told her the grief would fade, and yet here she was on the second anniversary of his death and she still felt like she was bleeding out. Just very slowly.

She stared up into the sky now, one full of the same stars that had watched over her as she'd held Papa's body. She was sleeping rough that night, in a little meadow she'd found off the main road. Colette tried not to stay in the woods too much, not with so many roving bands of desperate men around. But necessity called for it sometimes.

And where do you live?

It had been more than a year since she'd left Josephine's, and that question haunted her still. Colette couldn't ignore the pang of guilt she got whenever she thought back on her time with the woman. She'd sent her an envelope stuffed with some cash after she'd sold the car, but she hadn't left an address for Josephine to write her back.

She couldn't ignore that question, though, not on the nights that were especially cold and long and lonely.

And where do you live? Josephine hadn't meant the cabin itself. She'd meant Colette was becoming just like her—someone who had no family, no friends, no one left to talk to at all. She lived in the past, with only a ghost to keep her company.

Sometimes Colette wondered if that was why Papa's death still hurt so much. She wasn't letting herself find solace in others, wasn't letting herself mourn and then move on.

Even thinking that felt like a betrayal to Papa's memory, though. She didn't deserve solace, not when his killers still roamed free. She didn't deserve to move on, not when she'd failed him so catastrophically.

So she took that grief and let it become hard, impenetrable anger. She let it help her survive.

Before Papa had died, she hadn't realized how protected she'd been. It hadn't only been Papa who had shielded her, but the whole of Hell Raisin' Gulch.

In the big, wide world, though, there was just her and her shotgun. Hobos she rode beside tried to take liberties, hotel owners tried to use their spare keys to get into her rooms, farmers told her she could sleep in their barns and then visited in the middle of the night.

So far, she'd emerged unscathed. But she constantly worried about the time when there would be too many for her to threaten.

When she heard rustling from the brush beside her, she gripped her weapon.

Always vigilant. Always alert.

But it was only the wind.

When was the last time she'd slept through the night? She couldn't remember.

She managed a few hours and then packed up her makeshift camp at dawn. The railroad tracks weren't far—she never strayed too much from the arteries that ran through this state—and it only took her ten minutes before she heard a whistle.

Colette hated this part. Riding the rails was inherently dangerous for many reasons, but getting on the train itself was the worst part. Bulls were aggressive at the stations, so no one could sneak on when the things were stopped. You had to run to catch it, and Colette had now heard one too many stories of men who'd lost their legs and even their lives to the callous wheels.

But trains were the best place to chase whispers, and they got her to where she needed to go.

The locomotive was about to pull out of a one-horse town when she caught sight of it. The timing was perfect and so was the runway. Flat ground as far as the eye could see, no edges to break an ankle over.

Colette made sure her bag and gun were tied securely on her back, and then she started to run in the direction the train would be headed. Movement was crucial.

She got another lucky break—she was pretty sure she was stringing them together to make a life—because a hand reached out to help her jump into an open boxcar.

With a little skip-and-hop move that she was starting to perfect, she let herself be hauled off the ground.

She and the other passenger both tumbled to the floor of the boxcar in an ungraceful heap that was as much a part of the process as any other.

Colette laughed a little as she straightened herself and checked for her bag and gun. Then she eyed the man who'd stuck out his hand for a stranger.

He was a large, hulking shadow that might have set her on edge if not for his sweet smile and bashful demeanor.

"Ma'am," he said before settling back against a pile of crates. If he was even sixteen, she'd be surprised.

"Thank you," she said, brushing off some of the dust she'd picked up. She found her own square of wall to sit against, and decided to let him set the tone. She was the one who'd crashed into his boxcar after all. It was only polite.

"Haven't had much trouble with the bulls on this train," he said, in a gentle voice at odds with his Paul Bunyan frame.

"Have you had trouble with them on others?" Colette asked, with a strange and immediate maternal anger. She nearly waved off the question, the instinct was so shocking. She was only a handful of years older than him, and she rarely felt anything toward her fellow travelers other than the vague sense of kinship that came from people living in similar fashions.

He lifted his shoulder, let it drop. She imagined that he hadn't had an easy time hiding when the bulls started searching the cars for trespassers. And it wouldn't have just been the bulls giving him trouble, either. Men, she'd found, inevitably wanted to challenge someone who was built like this boy. They saw his ham hock hands and wide shoulders and thought that if they beat him up no one else would mess with them.

Colette tensed when he reached into his bag—just because she had a good feeling about him didn't mean she'd let down her guard—but all he did was take out a book.

The sight of it pulled a loose string taut in her chest. No one had books out here. They all traveled with one bag on their back. Something as frivolous as a novel was viewed as unnecessary weight.

The boy must have felt her eyes on him, because he glanced up, lifting his brows when he saw what must be longing on her face.

"Do you want me to read from it?" he asked, holding up the copy of *O Pioneers!* by Willa Cather. Without any prompting he added, "I can read. Mama was a schoolteacher."

Colette nodded as acknowledgment and as an answer, because she didn't trust herself to speak.

The boy flipped back to the beginning—she guessed he'd read the thing plenty of times so she didn't feel bad about it.

In his soft, gentle voice he began to tell the story of Alexandra Bergson and her struggle to keep her farm afloat even when many families gave up hope. The tale certainly rang true to their current troubles even though it was set at the turn of the century and written a decade ago.

Colette was also pleasantly surprised that this boy had picked a book with a female protagonist written by a female author.

But then he got to a particular passage and she realized why he might have connected to it so strongly.

"'. . . there are thousands of rolling stones like me. We are all alike; we have no ties, we know nobody, we own nothing. When one of us dies, they scarcely know where to bury him,'" he said, then paused, cleared his throat. By the time he got to the end of the paragraph about loneliness in cities, the tears were evident in his voice. "'We have no house, no place, no people of our own.'"

The moment came as an exchange between Alexandra and Carl, a family friend. They were debating life's hardships in the cities versus the country, but the passage might as well describe anyone who rode the rails in the West.

The boy took a shuddering breath and then closed the novel.

"My brother died in the war," he offered without any prompting. "Mama died trying to give my stepfather a son. My father left long before that trying to get work. He never came back."

No people of our own.

"Do you know what I love about books?" Colette asked. "You might think you have no people of your own, but Willa Cather is one of your people now."

The boy's forehead wrinkled. "What?"

"She wrote something that you felt in your soul," Colette said, hoping the sentiment wouldn't put him off. He didn't come across as one of those boys who feared emotion, but that was just a guess. "You keep her close to your heart. She is one of your people, you are one of hers."

"I don't know her," he said, but it came out like a plea. Like he wanted Colette to convince him. "She doesn't know me."

"You don't know the people who read that book before you, you don't know the ones who will read it after you," Colette said, nodding to where it was still cradled in his giant hands. "There are people in the world reading it right now and some of them are stopping just where you stopped and feeling just how you felt. How does that not make them your people?"

He chewed on his lip, but didn't agree.

"I can be one of your people, too," Colette hurried to say. "My brother died, not in the war but in a mine. My father was killed in a different kind of battle. I never knew my mama, but I've lost plenty of others I cared about. I haven't met someone I could call a friend in more than a year. And"—she paused, grinned—"Willa Cather is one of my favorite writers."

The boy was quiet for a moment. "I don't know you."

Colette hesitated for the first time. She didn't like to throw out her name to strangers, few people did out here. But she held out her hand. "Colette Durand."

The boy's palm met hers. "Bobby Bryant."

She offered him a crooked smile. "Now, we're practically friends."

When they broke apart, he stared down at the novel for a long moment before holding it out. "Here."

Colette pulled back. "Oh no, I couldn't, it's yours."

"It's all of ours, isn't it?" Bobby asked. "Everyone who has read it."

She could hardly preach at him about how books connected people and then reject the sweet offer. So Colette took it, and silently promised to cherish it.

For now, though, she simply opened to the page where he'd stopped and took over the reading.

When they parted ways a hundred miles later, Colette tucked the novel into her jacket, right against her ribcage.

And she wondered, for just a brief moment, if she gave up this hunt she could have her own people who lived outside of books.

Then she pushed the thought away, and headed down the road chasing the next rumor.

CHAPTER TWENTY-EIGHT

Alice

Rutherford Lumberjack Camp One
1924

The afternoon after the *Pygmalion* performance, the Boxcar Library got its first rush of patrons. The morning had been slow, but by the afternoon neither Alice nor Colette had a moment to breathe.

It was one of the best days of Alice's life.

Her favorite moment came when a middle-aged lumberjack blushed a deep red above his beard as he stammered out a request for *Maid of the Forest*, a romance set during the Northwest Indian War.

"The wife recommended it," he said, his voice gruff, but his hands eager as they took the novel. Alice didn't laugh or even smile, simply gently recommended *Emma*, which she thought would both amuse and delight someone with romantic sensibilities hidden beneath a hard exterior shell.

She found herself in that position over and over again. She had expected some uncertainty from the men, but most came in already knowing what they wanted. Then if the library didn't have it, they were eager to take suggestions.

In one of the few moments of quiet, Alice looked up to see a woman hovering in the doorway.

"Can we help you?" Alice asked softly, so as not to scare her away. She was a slight thing, not what Alice would have expected out here in the camps. Her skin was pulled tight around her bones, through birth rather than lifestyle, though, Alice guessed. She was tall and willowy, as well, and had red-chapped hands.

Likely someone who worked in the kitchens, then.

Her mouth opened and then shut, no words coming out.

"Would you like to look around?" Alice asked. There were a few men browsing the shelves, a few more pulled up at the table reading magazines. One more still sat by the Victrola, a strings record setting the atmosphere for the whole boxcar. No one seemed to mind, including Alice, who preferred a lively library over a quiet one.

Alice edged closer to the woman, who looked ready to bolt. The light shifted and Alice noticed the faint purple and yellow of a fading bruise around her neck. When the woman caught her looking she turned her head in a practiced move that threw a shadow over her clavicle.

"I . . . ," the woman started, then stopped, her voice coming out as only a whisper.

Alice chewed on her lower lip, desperately scared of spooking her. "I'm Alice. What's your name?"

After a long, terrible moment, the woman whispered, "Claire."

"A pretty name," Alice said, her first and genuine reaction. Claire smiled, weak though it was.

"I heard you have . . . I heard you're loaning out . . . books," Claire said, tentative despite the fact that they were so clearly a library.

"We are," Alice agreed. She had several wives in Missoula who she kept an eye out for. None had bruises so obvious as Claire's, but there were signs. The hesitation, the shyness. There wasn't much Alice could do to help, but she wasn't new to this, either. "Do you have anything in mind? If you don't, I'd be happy to recommend something."

Claire stared at her, as if the choice itself was overwhelming. So Alice took it out of her hands.

"I think I have something perfect," Alice said, making her way toward the middle shelves. She ran a fingertip along the spines of the books until she found Ibsen, Henrik.

Alice made sure to keep *A Doll's House* on hand, even though this particular copy she'd had to purchase and "donate" herself. The play contained a passage that she'd memorized long ago when she'd read it and her understanding of men and women had shifted.

Helmer: Before all else you are a wife and a mother.

Nora: That I no longer believe. I think that before all else I am a human being, just as much as you are—or at least I will try to become one.

Alice didn't expect books to save anyone. They were powerful but so was the world. Men had heavy fists and lightning-quick tempers. But sometimes just knowing you weren't alone in what you were feeling could make all the difference in the world.

"I don't have to pay for it?" Claire asked as she took the play.

"No," Alice reassured her. "You'll have to bring it back when we return, but that won't be for a few weeks."

Claire nodded, her eyes still on the cover. "I'll take good care of it."

Alice's breath hitched in her throat. "I know you will."

While Claire was one of the more memorable patrons, she wasn't the only woman who came into the library. The superintendent's wife, a fussy middle-aged woman with perfectly coiffed hair and shiny black shoes, arrived just as dinner was about to be served in camp.

She had a Julia Walker air about her, which immediately put Alice on the defense.

"Can we help you?" Colette asked.

The woman ignored her and started perusing the shelves.

Alice imagined her pausing at *Main Street* by Sinclair Lewis. "*We're tired of drudging and sleeping and dying . . .*"

And then *Oliver Twist*. "*To do a great right you may do a little wrong; and you may take any means which the end to be attained will justify.*"

And then *Les Misérables*. "*Not being heard is no reason for silence.*"

She pictured the performance last night, the rowdy men.

She remembered handing over *A Doll's House* to a woman who might not know how to navigate the freedom it inspired her to grasp.

This was a powder keg.

This was a powder keg and a spark.

This was . . .

The woman spun on them, her pale blue eyes eerie in the fading evening light. Colette crossed her arms, leaning against the shelves, her face impassive. Alice wished she could move through life with such nonchalance.

"This boxcar's entire catalog should be set on fire," the woman finally said, her voice calm and cold. "It's a den of depravity."

Colette straightened, but Alice held out her hand. She'd already faced this dragon. She'd survived.

"Can I interest you in a book?" Alice asked, as if the woman hadn't spoken at all. "It seems like you could use some education in your life."

The woman's face burned red, and Colette snorted.

"You could use the Bible in yours," the woman shot back.

"The same Bible that says, 'An intelligent heart acquires

knowledge,' Proverbs 18:15?" Alice asked sweetly. "Or that 'Fools despise wisdom,' Proverbs 1:7."

"Are you calling me a fool?"

"I think you're doing that yourself, ma'am," Alice said.

The woman's eyes narrowed. "I'll be writing to Mr. Rutherford about this."

With that threat she sailed out of the boxcar.

Colette winked at Alice. "Good. It'll make him complacent about the bet."

Alice laughed and shrugged off the unpleasant interaction. She'd met plenty of people like that woman, who wanted everyone to think the exact same way they did for reasons Alice never understood. Wasn't the world better when it was made up of people with a variety of beliefs and values and backgrounds? But the people who wanted to control what books others read tended to be scared, small-minded, and angry. There was only so much energy Alice could waste on them.

She'd much rather spend her time thinking about what books would be helpful for the rest of her patrons.

One of their last of the day was a loud fellow with a cheeky grin. He flirted with Alice and then with Colette and then with Alice again when he was rebuffed. Their rejections did nothing to diminish his smile.

"Come read to us again?" he asked, in the charming manner of those gifted with it from birth. "By the fire."

"We can't do all the work," Colette said.

The young man sobered for the first time since entering the car. "Some men won't come. They won't come here. Because they can't read or don't think it's useful or are scared or prideful. But they'll come to the fire, because that's what men do. They go to the fire. And if you happen to be there . . ."

Alice couldn't fault his request, of course, even if she wished it wasn't necessary.

"Of course," she murmured, and began plotting what book they should bring that evening.

They didn't go to the dining hall that night, but rather obtained a thermos of soup and a loaf of crusty bread from the kitchen on the train. Seamus had been eating with Moose again, so Alice dropped off *The Confessions of a Young Man* by George Moore. Moore, an Irishman, of course, had been friendly with Mr. Oscar Wilde when they'd been young, which was a connection Alice thought Seamus would approve of. The book was about the scandalous vie de bohème and was set in the Parisian art scene. If Seamus had enjoyed the interpersonal drama of *An Ideal Husband*, she was sure he would like this one.

She waved off his offer to join him, and retreated back to the library. As she did, she passed dozens of men loading timber onto the train's cargo cars. A few she recognized from the night before nodded their greetings.

"Come on," Colette said when she returned with their bounty. Colette jerked her head toward the ladder attached to the side of their library. Alice rubbed sweaty palms against her trousers as she watched Colette easily hoist herself up onto the roof of the car while still carrying their dinner.

She took a deep breath and gripped the metal.

Alice was trembling by the time she made it up, but when she realized the roof was flat, she relaxed enough to scooch the rest of the way. Colette was busy trying not to laugh at her fear.

"Hush up," Alice muttered, busying herself with breaking the bread into manageable chunks.

"Is it just because you grew up wealthy?" Colette asked, pouring out a serving of the soup into the thermos's lid.

"Is *what* because of my upbringing?"

"You aren't like other girls I know around here," Colette said. "You're scared of getting in trouble, of climbing up ladders, of men."

Alice figured all of those things were reasonable to be scared about, but she knew what Colette was really asking.

"I don't know how to not be," Alice admitted. "My father thinks—"

"Your father," Colette cut her off, "seems like a handy excuse."

Alice swallowed hard, the accusation layering on top of the one Sidney had thrown at her. Both of them layering on top of her own realization that maybe she had used her restrictions as a crutch her entire life.

"It's not just my father," Alice said. "His right-hand man watches me and reports back. He won't let me do anything too dangerous."

Colette took a sip of the soup. "He's a right-hand man who also won't let you out of his sight?"

That was a good point. Sometimes Alice felt like Mac was her shadow, but he often left to do her father's bidding. Hell, the fact that she was sitting on top of a railcar overlooking a sprawling lumber camp beside a woman who wore a shotgun slung over her shoulder most of the time proved that Mac wasn't quite as much of her jailer as she'd thought.

"I got used to it, I suppose," Alice finally admitted. Her eyes tracked over the giant logs stacked up waiting to be loaded, the makeshift dormitories and tents, the dining hall, and landed on the trees in the distance, bathed in the golden rays of the setting sun. She breathed in the crisp air, the wildfire smoke mostly gone now as they headed more deeply into fall.

"But here you are," Colette murmured, something soft and fond in her voice that Alice realized she'd never heard there before. She glanced at Colette, who was watching the horizon wearing a small smile.

"How are you so brave?" Alice asked. "To be living out here on your own?"

Colette's expression shifted into something neutral. It took a long time before she answered, so long that Alice didn't think she would.

"Why anyone does anything brave out here," she finally said, shrugging one shoulder in feigned carelessness. "Necessity."

Alice was so giddy after they pulled out of their first stop she couldn't even concentrate enough to read. She stared out the window for the entirety of the trip to the next camp, her mind flitting from one thought to the next without ever properly landing on anything.

Because of that, she saw the horses start to keep pace with the train long before a man kicked open the door of the boxcar.

Even though she had realized *something* was about to happen to them, she hadn't expected this. She yelped and leaped from her chair.

A man stood in the doorway dressed in all black, a bandanna tied around the lower part of his face, a cowboy hat shading the rest. He pointed a pistol at Alice.

"In the corner," came the gruff demand.

The directive was simple enough, some part of Alice realized. But the rest of her refused to move. Not because she wanted to make a martyr of herself during a train robbery but because she'd lost function of her legs and arms.

When she didn't immediately scurry to get out of the way of the outlaw, he turned fully toward her.

"Get. In. The. Corner," he said, enunciating every word this time.

"See, I want to very much, sir," Alice said on a rush, her hands flying into the air to show she wouldn't resist. "But I don't seem to be able to move at the moment."

"Lady, don't test me today," he said, taking a step closer. "I don't want to shoot you."

"Yes, I would rather you didn't shoot me either," Alice said, the edge of hysteria clear in her voice. Her heart was loud in her ears, so loud she wasn't sure she would be able to hear any more directions he tossed her way. "Sir, we only have books, not money."

"We're not looking for money," he muttered, and for some reason that was what broke her spell.

She dropped her arms. "What?"

He shook his head and then in the blink of an eye advanced on her. Alice squealed, backing up until the bookcase pressed into her spine.

"I'm sorry, I'm sorry, I'm sorry," she babbled, not really knowing what she was apologizing for.

But the barrel of the gun was already pressed up against the soft spot beneath her chin.

A tear slipped out as she thought about her father, about how he would feel when he realized Montana had finally killed her.

"I'm someone's daughter," she breathed out. A last-ditch plea.

"So am I," came Colette's voice, a clarion bell that cut through the cotton in Alice's mind. It was followed by the cocking of a shotgun.

Alice blinked the world—and Colette—into focus. She was standing behind the bandit, her weapon pressed into the base of his skull.

"I'm feeling generous," Colette said, in the same tone she might talk about the weather. "So, I'm going to let you jump off this train in the next five seconds." When the man didn't move,

Colette jammed the gun in harder. "The other option is I paint the inside of this car with your blood."

The bandit paused, clearly weighing his options. While he could likely overpower them, he was outnumbered and they had a bigger gun.

The man's eyes narrowed, but then in an impossibly smooth move he withdrew his pistol from Alice's jaw and pointed it at the ceiling in surrender.

Colette backed off enough to let him rush the open train door.

By the time Alice realized what he intended to do he'd already thrown himself through the opening. She refused to go check to see if he was anything more than a speck on the ground behind them. With any luck, he'd simply grabbed on to some piece of metal and swung himself onto the next car.

Meanwhile, Colette just sighed and headed back toward the space behind her checkout desk. "I'm surprised that hadn't happened yet."

"We're on a mining train, not a mail train," Alice pointed out. Roving bands of robbers weren't exactly uncommon out here, but she had never known them to attack targets that didn't guarantee a large payout. "What on earth did they think they would find?"

Not money. Then what?

Books?

That couldn't possibly be the case.

Alice's legs trembled and she let herself sink to the floor. "How are you so calm?"

"You ever come across a snake?" Colette asked. "Making all sorts of noise at you? But you know it doesn't want to bite?"

"Yes," Alice said, mostly because she didn't want Colette to think worse of her. She had come across exactly one snake in her life, and Mac had killed it on sight, two bullets to the head.

"All bluster, no bite," Colette continued, shaking her head as she resettled into her chair. She picked up the book she'd been reading—*The Secret Garden* of all things—as if nothing exciting had happened at all. "You live out here long enough you learn to suss out the vipers from the garden snakes."

"Have you met many vipers?" Alice dared asking, knowing they weren't talking about creatures any longer.

"More than my fair share." Colette nudged her shotgun. "But I know how to handle them."

"What do you think he wanted?" Alice didn't know why her mind had latched on to that momentary slip. Probably it was the panic receding, taking rational thought along with it. All that was left was irrational musings.

"Books are valuable," Colette said, sounding completely disinterested in the topic. Alice would believe the act if she hadn't just spent the past week riding the rails with the woman.

"You think he was planning on selling them?" Alice couldn't believe that would be profitable enough for anyone to break into a boxcar and terrorize the women he found there.

"Could be."

That was one of the most preposterous things Alice had ever heard—how did he plan on making off with enough books to justify the risk of robbing the train?

"Well, count me lucky I have a snake-handler on board, I suppose," Alice said, pushing herself to her feet. Her legs weren't quite steady, yet, but she was starting to feel silly and vulnerable on the floor.

Colette's mouth twitched into a half smile.

Alice crossed to the window and finally let herself look back. There was nothing but track behind them.

"There were other bandits beside him," Alice said, thinking

of the horses she'd spotted running alongside the train. "Do you think they'll come for us?"

"Don't know," Colette said, sounding completely unbothered. "But if they do we'll be ready."

"You're truly unconcerned?" Alice asked, a little annoyed now at her nonchalance. Something must have slipped into her voice, because Colette pressed the open book to her chest and looked up.

"Do you know what makes me scared?" Colette asked.

"No, but please tell me, because from where I'm standing it seems like nothing," Alice said, knowing she still sounded exasperated.

"It's not lowlifes like that bandit," Colette said. "He's easy to understand, and rarely cares about anything more than his life. Show him a gun, show him you're ready to shoot it, and he'll run away."

"I'm not sure he would have believed I would shoot him even if I was in the midst of pulling the trigger," Alice muttered.

Colette laughed. "Fair. But you understand?"

Alice jerked her head in agreement.

"What scares me are the men who want power more than anything," Colette said. "The greedy men, the ones who care more about money than their lives or the lives of thousands of other men."

"Like the Company owners," Alice said.

"Yes, ma'am," Colette said. "You hold a gun up to one of those men, they won't run. They'll take your gun and then your family and then everything you've ever loved."

There was that anger again, and while Alice knew it wasn't directed at her, she took a half step back anyway, her body already feeling like prey.

"It's not bandits on trains that scare me," Colette said, picking up her book once more as if she hadn't just ripped her chest open. "It's the ones in suits."

The next two weeks passed in a blur. Word had begun to spread about who they were and where they were headed. Alice had even agreed to carry letters to workers' friends in camps along the way—letters that hopefully vouched for the respectability of the Boxcar Library.

They hadn't had to prove themselves once since that first night—which led her to believe that not only did miners and lumberjacks move from camp to camp with some speed and frequency, but as they did they gossiped fiercely along the way.

She was also starting to get used to the rhythms of both train and camp life. She and Seamus had become fast friends—they both hit the kitchen car in the early hours of the day to get thermoses of coffee. She'd brought him two more books and he'd regaled her with tales of the Irish rails. Sometimes she could even get him to gossip about the train workers who all lived together in the caboose and got into domestic spats more nights than not.

At some point, the Boxcar Library would be unhitched from Seamus's train and picked up by another, but until that happened, Alice would look forward to the few minutes they spent every morning chatting as the sun rose.

Bull Moose joined them occasionally. He had apologized profusely for the bandits, even though they weren't his fault, and then had never spoken again. Alice found his presence comforting.

Those mornings made the hours stuck in the boxcar traveling between camps more bearable. Colette was hardly a lively conversationalist, and they spent most of their rail time reading. But Alice appreciated having somewhere to go and people to talk to who weren't a surly librarian with a penchant for ignoring questions she didn't want to answer.

It was a minor miracle the two of them hadn't killed each other yet. The living quarters had been designed with one person in mind. Sleeping wasn't terrible, especially when they were moving. The gentle rocking tended to send Alice into the abyss no matter how uncomfortable she might be in the car that had trapped all of the heat from the day.

Getting ready each morning was nearly impossible, though.

After four days of jamming elbows into soft places, they'd established a routine. If they were near a creek, Colette would wander off to splash some water on herself while Alice got ready. The next day they would alternate.

They had also gotten to the point where they could politely ignore the other one making use of the chamber pot.

For the first time in her life, Alice was uncomfortable *most* of the time.

And she loved it.

She loved the dirt crusted in her elbows, and the way she couldn't stand her own scent sometimes when the wind went still; she loved being so hungry she could eat through an entire loaf of bread because of how busy the day had been; she loved her tired-restless legs at the end of the night and the way she could drop into sleep the minute she closed her eyes.

Most of all, she loved how many people she'd gotten to meet over the past two weeks. They were bold and shy, curious and stubborn, flirtatious and subdued. And Alice got to ask them about their lives under the guise of trying to find them the perfect book. Did they need escape? Were they trying to learn something? Did they want to impress a girl they were hoping to court? Alice would never not be amazed at what you could learn about a person from what they wanted to check out from the library.

Exactly two weeks after they'd chugged out of Missoula, they pulled into their first real mining camp. Unlike the temporary logging towns, this one had a more permanent feel to it. There was a depot with a hotel attached, one that probably carried the most up-to-date newspapers that even the library didn't have in stock. There were a couple permanent buildings—likely the Company store, a barber, and a laundry service.

Since this place had more to offer its permanent residents, Alice did wonder if they would have the same number of patrons as they got at their other stops.

Alice was just about to share her thoughts with Colette when something caught her eye.

Her stomach clenched, and what was left of her nerves sparked back to life.

She let her eyes slip from the front of the ostentatious, out-of-place Packard toward the driver's side door, where a man stood, casual as anything, his eyes on the train as it rolled to a stop.

It was too far to actually lock eyes with him, but she swore she did.

"Goddamn it," she said out loud.

And that's when Sidney Walker grinned and gave her a lazy, sly salute hello.

CHAPTER TWENTY-NINE

Millie

Going-to-the-Sun Chalets
1936

The Going-to-the-Sun Chalets sat atop the cliffs, looking as dramatic and romantic as possible. Following their arrival, Millie, Flo, Sidney, and Oscar had taken dinner and compared logistics notes they'd gathered from the day. After, Millie decided to take her journal out to the porch.

She sat in one of the dozens of rocking chairs that lined the rail and let the magnificent sunset inspire her.

Millie hadn't written much prose on this trip, keeping most of her notes to half-jotted thoughts and lists of facts. But her current view all but demanded prose.

The park is a wild mountainous area with an unusually wide range of appeal. To a rider the peak of appreciation may come as he dangles a leg over a thousand vertical feet of space; to a fisherman when, knee deep in a rushing stream, he brings to net a fighting rainbow; to the hiker when he meets a bear or mountain goat on some high trail; to the picture hunter when he catches a bull moose wallowing along the edge of a marsh. Some will find the greatest lure in the loneliness of a summit.

"Poetic," came a voice behind her, and Millie's hand flew to the hollow of her throat where her heart pounded against thin skin.

"Christ," she said softly as Oscar dropped into the open rocking chair beside her. His hat rested in his lap, the setting sun softening his features for once.

Oscar wasn't handsome by most standards, but he was interesting to look at.

"That'll go in," Oscar said, with a jerk of his head toward her journal as if to assure her he hadn't been employing sarcasm just then.

Millie closed the journal anyway. Writing felt like a vulnerable thing to her, as if the words she chose could reveal her underbelly to attack even when the subject was as impersonal as a national park.

"What did you mean on the boat?" Millie asked. "About Alice Monroe."

"A dog with a bone," Oscar muttered, but he didn't sound peeved about it. He wanted the mystery solved, as well. "Do you know why I became a writer?"

Millie glanced over, surprised at the change of topic. But he just stared back, patiently willing her to go along with it. She also couldn't deny her natural curiosity, that desire to get to know this man better. "Why?"

"I grew up in a mining town outside Missoula," he said, and it was only then she realized how little she knew about Oscar. "My mother had a bushel of kids and I was the oldest. I helped raise most of my sisters."

"That sounds familiar," Millie murmured, as another piece of the puzzle fell into place. Not with the mystery of the sabotage but with the mystery of why she'd trusted this man so much and so quickly. Like recognizing like.

"Back in the day, Miss Monroe used to bring library books out to our camps," he continued. "I hadn't realized how special that was until we moved on to somewhere new."

Millie wasn't surprised at all. She barely knew the woman, but could tell just after that one encounter what type of librarian she was.

"She gave me the very first book I ever owned," he said. "*Treasure Island.* She'd heard we were leaving and just . . . let me keep it. I'm sure she replaced it with her own money."

His Adam's apple bobbed with emotion. "I thought I would end up in the mines, like everyone in my family had. Like everyone in my life had. But she gave me that book. She got me to fall in love with reading. Turned out, I wasn't too bad at the writing thing when I tried my hand at it."

The enormity of that stole Millie's breath. One book. That's all it had taken to change an entire life.

"I published my first novel at seventeen," he continued, with a laugh. "I barely made back the postage it took to send the thing off to New York."

"It's wonderful you found a publisher," she said. "Someone who would take on an author so young."

He shot her a look. "No one would have published me as some young kid. I made up a persona, a name, too."

"Oscar is a nom de plume?" She didn't know why, but she didn't like the fact that she didn't know his real name.

"It's my name now," he said. "But I was born Nathaniel. Nathaniel Davey. No one calls me that anymore, though."

"Not even your mother?"

"Not even my mother," he said. "I lied about how old I was when I sent my first manuscript out. And Oscar Dalton fit my genre better than Nathaniel Davey."

"That would have been perfect if you were writing novels set in Kentucky or Tennessee," Millie said, and Oscar laughed.

"Precisely."

"That's very brave," Millie said softly. "To bet on yourself like that. To open yourself up to rejection. And then to have such incredible success so young? What an accomplishment."

She thought he might have blushed at that, but couldn't be quite sure.

"I send all the money I make with the books to my family. They . . . they respect what I've become as Oscar." He slid her a look. Assessing. "I joke about my books. But I'm proud of them. I'm proud that they provide people the same entertainment that I got as a child through the books Miss Monroe brought."

"She must have been so thrilled when you came back to Missoula," Millie said, and Oscar shook his head.

"I never told her who I was."

"What?" Millie was appalled. "Why?"

"She wouldn't have remembered me," Oscar said, and Millie gaped at him. "Or cared."

"I met that woman for ten minutes and she cared more about me than most people I've met in my life," Millie said. "She would love to hear about all that you've done."

He lifted a shoulder, and in that one gesture she saw the stubborn boy he must have been. "There's a reason I'm telling you all this."

It took Millie a moment to remember they were in the middle of an investigation. They, because she'd fully taken him on as an ally. "Right."

Oscar's eyes slid to her but then away again. "My mother didn't want me to stop reading after we moved. And I was so upset over leaving, that I might have just given up because I was so angry at the world. So my mother, she found newspaper articles about this Boxcar Library that Miss Monroe launched only a few months after we moved. My mother told me I was the one who'd inspired the whole project. I believed her because I wanted to."

"You might have." What could she say? She was a romantic at heart.

He shrugged as if it didn't matter, even though he wouldn't have mentioned it if it hadn't. "Alice Monroe outfitted a whole train car as a library just to bring books to mining and lumberjack families across the state. I had never had an outsider care about us as much as she did."

"Did you move to Missoula because of her?"

"No. My family settled in the area, and I wanted to be close to them," he said. "But . . . it's been nice knowing she's there."

"Do you know what happened with her and Sidney?" Millie asked.

"No," he said. "But the gossip around town is that they've been at odds forever. I'm surprised he even had a photograph of her."

They were in love, Millie thought, but didn't say. "The photograph. She was sitting on top of a train."

"Well, I know she hired someone as the librarian; she didn't take the position herself," Oscar said, sounding lost in history. "Maybe she had just been giving him a tour?"

"The landscape behind her wasn't Missoula."

He quirked a brow at her. "Oh, are you an expert now?"

She shook her head, smiling. "No. But the landscape was . . . remarkably different."

"Hmm," Oscar hummed. "Maybe she went along on one of the trips."

"Why would Sidney have gone with her?" Millie asked. *Of course he'd followed her* was what her heart said.

There must have been more to it than that. And why hadn't he had the photograph until now?

"What if something happened?" she asked slowly.

"Like what?" Oscar asked, sounding intrigued.

"Something serious enough that it caused a falling-out between the two of them," Millie said. "Something serious enough that they would have to hide any evidence that it occurred."

"By destroying all that work?" Oscar asked, clearly following her logic.

"The three towns Sidney mentioned, the ones he wanted to avoid," Millie continued. "What if he found something in one of them? Something that would give away what happened ten years ago."

"You're creating quite a story for yourself," Oscar chided gently.

Millie deflated. "I know. I just can't help but wonder if this is all connected somehow."

"It makes more sense than Flo being in the pocket of the Company or any other theory the FWP headquarters came up with," Oscar said.

"It's hard to simply trust names on a paper," Millie said, wanting to defend Katherine. She had been the one who'd believed in *most* of the staff, after all. "I wonder if we could find that librarian, the one Alice had hired. Maybe they would know what happened."

But Oscar shook his head.

"You don't remember who it was?" Millie asked.

"No, it's not that. Like I said, my mother was fascinated by the whole thing; she cut out all the articles about it," Oscar said. "The first boxcar librarian was named Colette Durand."

"Then why can't we find her?" Millie asked before she thought through what he said.

Was.

He nodded at her little mew of realization.

"She died more than ten years ago."

CHAPTER THIRTY

Colette

Miles City, Montana
1923

The last place Colette expected to see Finn Benson was at a tiny union meeting in Miles City, Montana, on a Tuesday night in February, two years after her father was shot.

Colette went to gatherings like these when she could, even if she was one of three participants. Papa had given his life over to the union, and carrying on his legacy meant more than just hunting down the men who'd killed him.

She had been debating going to the one in Miles City. The night was frigid, the temperature dipping well below zero, and that wasn't even accounting for the wind. But all she would have done otherwise was stare at the bunk above her in the boarding-house. At least the union meeting had tea.

There was a good turnout, perhaps for the same reasons Colette had dragged herself to the thing. Being around other people made you feel warmer even if you weren't actually hud-dling together.

She poured herself a mug of the oolong and then turned toward the podium. The crowd shifted and she almost dropped the tin cup in her hand.

Finn Benson—looking handsome and passionate—took the stage, holding the dozen or so workers' attention with an ease she admired. His eyes landed on her and then continued on, clearly not registering who she was.

Colette wondered then how different she looked. She rarely had access to a mirror, but whenever she caught sight of her reflection she barely recognized herself. Every minute of the two years living rough now lived on her face.

Finn's eyes flicked back to her a moment later, his brows lifting in shock. He didn't pause or stutter in his address, because he was the ultimate professional, but she saw the corners of his mouth twitch into an almost smile a handful of times.

The moment he was done, he bounded off the stage toward her. Without letting herself think too deeply about it, she fell into his open arms and relished the way he held her tight against his beating heart.

She moved around too much to get mail, and so even if they'd wanted to write, it would have been difficult. But she would never forget the way he'd acted after he'd found her with Papa's body on the porch.

The love with which he'd treated her.

"You're alive," he said now, when he pulled back. There was a hint of criticism in his voice—he hadn't wanted her to embark on this revenge mission—but also relief. Happiness.

No people of our own.

Colette wouldn't be so bold as to call Finn hers, but she thought maybe he could fit the bill sometimes. They were the kind of friends to move in and out of each other's lives without missing a beat.

"I'm alive," she repeated, without addressing the disapproval.

A dozen or so handshakes later and they found themselves in the local saloon that called itself a drugstore. The piano man was playing a lively rendition of some Bach classic, and girls were dancing on the stage, revealing glimpses of their knickers. The alcohol flowed as freely as the laughter and chatter.

Finn rubbed a hand over his face. "How long has it been?"

"Twenty-two months," Colette said, because she'd last seen him a week or so after Papa's funeral. And she knew that date down to the minute.

"Give or take," he murmured, his eyes searching her face and again she felt self-conscious.

Any softness, any femininity, any *beauty* had been stamped out of her by the life she'd been leading over the past two years. She slept outside a good number of nights, which meant her face was chapped and rough. A permanent layer of dust had seemed to settle into her skin, and she couldn't remember the last time she'd worn something other than a man's work shirt and trousers. There was never any money for makeup or dresses. Even her vocabulary had taken a turn for the vulgar. When she did speak, it was usually within the company of rough men.

If Finn Benson had ever wanted her, those times were surely long gone now.

She wouldn't ever regret the years and hardship she wore on her body, though. She was proud of what she'd survived, and what she was doing.

"How's Chicago?" she asked, because that was where he'd last called home, even if he was on the road more time out of the year than not.

"A little more murder there than to my liking," he said, with a half smile. "I guess that's everywhere out here, though."

"Yes," Colette huffed. "Story of my life."

He was back to studying her. "Are you all right, Colette?"

At some point, he'd taken her hand in his. His thumb rubbed absent, soothing circles over her wrist bone like he'd always done.

In that moment, she felt the entire weight of the past years. The nights she hadn't dared close her eyes in case someone found her vulnerable and alone; the days she'd toiled beneath the hot sun, wearing men's clothes and thus being expected to produce as a man would; the heartbeats she'd counted hiding from bulls on the trains she'd hopped, terrified they'd toss her off while they were crossing a ravine without a second thought.

"No," she finally whispered.

When he tugged her into a hug, she let him. When he led her up the stairs to his hotel room, she followed. When he stripped her to her bare skin, she relished the touch of kind hands against her body.

He directed her to the tub and then climbed in behind her, his knees cradling her hips, his lips soft against the nape of her neck.

She tipped her head back, so that she rested against his shoulder, and let him work her skin with his mouth and teeth and tongue.

His hands cupped her modest breasts, his thumbs brushing over the nipples before moving on. As if he was mapping out her body to live in his memory.

It didn't take long for the water to cool, and when it did he helped her out of the tub, drying her with the same care as he had after Papa had died.

Then he laid her down in a bed that felt too soft, too warm, too comfortable and kissed her for the first time.

He held her face, his eyes locked on hers, as he pushed into her. Her legs came up around his waist, holding him close.

No people of our own.

Maybe she barely knew this man beyond some of the worst moments in her life. But for right now, he was hers. She was his. They were each other's.

It wasn't her first time. After living on the road for so long, she'd had several opportunities—with both men and women—ones she hadn't turned down.

But this felt different.

After, when they were lying sweaty and exhausted in each other's arms, she tried to figure out why that was. Her younger self would have expected fireworks here, and there hadn't been. Everything had been soft and sweet and intimate, rather than hot and fast and passionate.

They had been seeking comfort, not pleasure, though the latter came as an inevitability.

Maybe it was simply the culmination of what had started the day he'd found her on the porch.

Maybe this was the one other person in the world who knew what she was going through right now and she had found immense relief in having that.

"Have you had any luck?" he asked, softly enough that he wouldn't have woken her had she already fallen asleep.

"Some." She pushed up on her elbow. "I've been chasing a man who goes by Peter, or Petey, some of the time. He has a birthmark on his neck and was bragging about killing a union man near Butte right after Papa died."

Finn's eyes went wide. "You found him?"

The shock was clear in his voice, and she didn't blame him. She was just a girl, and Montana was a big place. But the web of workers who traveled between logging and mining towns was smaller than she'd ever realized.

"He's a tumbleweed," she admitted. "I feel like I'm forever a few steps behind him. But he has a habit of making enemies wherever he goes. He cheats at cards, picks fights with bigger men, tries to get out of work half the time because of laziness and half the time because he drank too much the night before. There have been plenty of people who have pointed me in his direction."

"Well, shit," Finn said, drawing out the cuss until it sounded like *sheet.* He sat up, his back against the headboard, and ran a hand through his hair. "You found out a lot more than I did."

"You were busy," Colette said, trying not to draw too much attention to the fact that this was what she did now. Finn was trying to save the workers of the world, whereas her world had narrowed down to one man.

"Did he say anything about why he did it?" Finn asked, swinging his legs over the side of the bed as if he was about to charge out into the night to find the bastard. He fumbled for his pants, tripping as he pulled them on.

"Finn, you'll freeze your balls off if you go hunting him now," Colette said, laughing. She couldn't remember the last time she'd done that.

The language got Finn to turn around, hands paused at his waistband, eyebrows raised. "That's quite the mouth you've got on you now."

"You weren't complaining twenty minutes ago," she reminded him bluntly, and loved the flush of pink spreading across his chest.

"Come on," Colette said, lifting the blanket for him. "We'll make plans tomorrow. But let's sleep for now."

He slid into the space she'd left open and she pressed against him, her body humming with the pleasure of someone else's touch. They drifted asleep and then made love again when they both woke.

This time when Finn dressed it was with reluctance. "I have to get back to Chicago for a meeting, or I would stay longer."

Colette shook her head. Last night had been lovely, but after so long by herself she wasn't even sure she would enjoy his company much longer. "Would you like me to write you? With updates?"

"Yes," Finn said, shoving his feet in his boots as he did. "Now that you've uncovered this detail, I might be able to get more information, as well. Just let me know when you'll be in one place long enough to receive mail."

"Or a telegram," she pointed out. "I will."

Finn paused from where he was collecting the rest of his possessions scattered around the room. He crossed to her in three strides, leaning his weight on his palm just beside her head. He pressed his lips to hers in a kiss that felt more like a promise than a goodbye.

She didn't want to think like that—if she got attached, she might forget what she was doing here in the first place. So she pulled back first.

He didn't move, but his lips quirked into a sad, knowing smile. "I hope you find what you're looking for, Colette."

This time, there was no quiet confidence to give warmth to the words. Instead, it was cool and a little bitter, as if she'd rejected him.

Before he left the room, he paused and, without turning, whispered, "I just don't think you ever will."

His words stayed with her long after the memory of that kiss faded.

CHAPTER THIRTY-ONE

Alice

Rutherford Mining Camp Three
1924

It wasn't absurd for Sidney Walker to visit Rutherford Mining Camp Three.

His father was an investor in the company, after all.

But Alice's hackles rose at the sight of him, resentful with the too-familiar feeling of someone watching over her shoulder her entire life.

She loved Mac, but she hadn't realized just how frustrated she'd become with his hovering until she'd broken free from under his watchful eye.

Alice had thought Sidney was different.

He'd taken her to Lolo. He'd pushed her to go on this adventure.

Now, he showed up like a safety net she'd never asked for, even though this particular tightrope wasn't even high enough to warrant one.

"You look angrier now than you did with a pistol in your face," Colette murmured, joining Alice at the window. When she spotted Sidney, she laughed. "Ah." She paused. "You want my shotgun?"

Alice thought about saying yes for the sheer pleasure of shoving the barrel of the weapon into Sidney's belly. But knowing her luck her finger would get twitchy all of a sudden and he'd end up with a hole in his stomach.

And . . . she still thought about that dark stretch of empty road on the way to Lolo. Still thought about the way his hands had shaken as he told her he could hurt her if she wasn't careful.

He'd had too many guns pointed at him in this lifetime.

"I'd like to say yes," Alice said on a sigh. "I suppose I should be mature about this, though."

"Why?"

Because she liked Sidney. She also owed him. But that sounded silly, so she just asked, "Will you be all right for now?"

"Go," Colette said, even as two men lingered below their window, hands in their pockets, eyes darting toward the library sign on the boxcar. That had been happening at every stop they'd pulled into since the first, and Alice delighted in the sight.

Alice wove through the crowd that had gathered to greet the train at the station. This was one of the bigger stops, and the platform was built up, a hotel standing right along the edge. Patrons hung out the upper windows to call to the group below and plenty of people hollered back everything from hellos to obscenities.

Sidney smirked at her as she approached, so disdainfully amused by life. By her.

"If you've come to collect me like luggage, you can get right back in your car," Alice said, already with a full head of steam as she marched up to him.

"Well hello to you, too, Miss Monroe," Sidney drawled, all indolence.

"I'm serious, I'm not going home with you," she said.

"Not a phrase I usually hear, I have to admit," he said, and Alice flushed hot with mortification.

And something else.

"Do you take anything seriously?" she asked, frustrated and envious and irritated that she was either. She wished she could just be nonchalant for once in her life.

Sidney's face tightened, the lazy good humor melting out of it. "Yes."

The clipped answer was more devastating than had he lectured her for twenty minutes. How had she so quickly ended up on the side of the conversation where she had to apologize? "I'm sorry."

He looked away. "As beautiful as you may be, you're not the sun, Alice."

Alice's blush deepened. "What does that mean?"

"The world does not revolve around you," he said. "I came here for a different reason."

She scoffed at that. "You're waiting for my train to come in."

"Everyone was buzzing about the library coming to town, I had to see it for myself," Sidney said. "But the timing is coincidental. Believe it or not, this is my fourth camp this week that I've visited."

That stopped her. "Why?"

"My father wanted me to see how they're run," Sidney offered easily.

She narrowed her eyes. There was the veneer of truth to that, she was sure, but it wasn't the whole story. "And you just happened to pick this time to come tour them? When you knew I would be out here?"

"I was curious," he said, with a shrug. "Can you blame me?"

Alice deflated. She supposed she couldn't—not when she'd roped him into helping her make the decision in the first place.

"And anyway," Sidney said, pushing away from the Packard. "Neither of those things is the real reason I'm here."

He held the passenger seat door open for her. Of course she climbed in. She wasn't sure there was anywhere she wouldn't go if this man goaded her into it.

"What's the real reason?" she asked, once he slid behind the wheel.

"I'm looking for a friend of mine."

"How did you misplace him?" Alice asked, teasing.

"I was careless," he said, deadly serious.

Alice swallowed. Was this a friend from the war, then? It always seemed to come back to that with Sidney. She had known the fighting had affected the men who'd gone overseas to serve, but she hadn't realized just how much it had shaped their lives even now, more than five years later.

Sidney's eyes swept over her as he changed the topic. "You're surviving your grand adventure?"

"Thriving," Alice corrected, deciding against telling him about the bandit. She no longer thought he was here to drag her home, but she didn't want to test it. "How is my father?"

"Fine and dandy," Sidney said. "He still thinks you've gone off to . . ."

"Billings," Alice filled in.

"Billings. Though he did send that knight-errant off to fetch you home," Sidney said. "I'd say you have a few more days before you'll be telling him you won't go home with him."

The double meaning—and the fact that she did now believe Mac would be interested in that—had her blushing once more. "Mac is not my knight-errant."

Sidney made some considering sound. "Fiancé, then?"

"No," Alice rushed to say. "Not. No. Mac is. No."

"So that's a no, then?"

"Mac is easy to love," Alice said, not sure where the words were coming from. But there was something about the cozy space that made her want to tell Sidney all about her life. "He could never see me as an equal, though."

"That's the case in plenty of marriages."

"Maybe, but I wouldn't want it to be the case in mine," Alice said, the distance finally allowing her to see beyond her childish infatuation. "I've spent my life being treated as a child. Mac would never be able to think of me as a woman."

"Then he doesn't know you at all," Sidney said.

"You think of me as a child," Alice countered, remembering his exasperation with her.

"No," Sidney said, shaking his head. "I just know where to cut people so they bleed. I've warned you, I'm no hero."

She didn't know what to say to that. He was right—he wasn't a hero. But she had a sneaking suspicion that he might be a good man.

He wouldn't want to hear that, though.

It didn't matter, because he pulled to a stop outside the dining hall. After the past few weeks, Alice had come to realize that the building often acted as the heartbeat of the camp. If you wanted information, you only had to hang around the dining tables for a few minutes. Inevitably, the gossip would be offered up with just a little prodding.

Sidney garnered immediate attention when he walked in and strode directly toward the card game that had drawn the biggest crowd.

Alice grabbed his sleeve before he got too far. This would go faster if they split up. "What was his name?"

"Patrick Roy. He lost an eye. And half his face. He's memorable."

Sidney ended up being right—his friend was easy to find.

Or, not him, but someone who knew him.

She asked the man to stay where he was and searched for Sidney.

When they both returned, the man had taken out a small block of wood. A whittling knife danced and twirled, unearthing the shape buried within.

"You served?" the man asked, without even glancing up at Sidney.

"Yes, sir," Sidney said. Alice knew people usually gave their rank and company in the silence that followed but Sidney didn't. He just waited.

The man nodded. "Patty hung himself three weeks back."

Sidney's expression didn't change, he didn't shift, he didn't even breathe.

Alice wanted to grab his hand, but she stopped herself. He wouldn't appreciate that now.

"You knew him?" Sidney asked.

The man tipped his head from side to side. "As much as I could. He was a quiet fella. Had the ghosts haunting him. Too many came back with those damn ghosts hanging around."

"Yes," Sidney agreed simply.

"I had a boy," the man continued. "Shot for cowardice."

Alice couldn't help the small murmur of distress that escaped, but Sidney just nodded.

"Wouldn't go over," the man said. "At least that's what someone told me. You would think they could have made up a better story for me, don't you?"

"Yes," Sidney said again. "They should have."

"Didn't tell his mama he ran away," the man continued, as if Sidney hadn't spoken. "She would have searched down the lieutenant himself."

"It—" Sidney started, stopped himself. "I knew men who

shared that same fate. And it was never cowardice that had them running away. It was love. It was . . . it was because they loved someone more than themselves. And they didn't want that person to have to suffer their death."

It was pretty and maybe a lie, but it certainly was the story the man had deserved to be told in the first place.

The man's lips twitched into a small smile. "That was a kindness I haven't earned."

"Kindness isn't something to be earned," Sidney said. "But you did anyway. Thank you for telling me what happened to Patrick."

"He was a good man. Worked hard, kept to himself but not in an unfriendly kind of way," the man said. "The nightmares kept him awake. And then down in the mine . . . well. He didn't stand a chance."

"No," Sidney said. "We're all playing against the odds."

At that, Alice did step closer until her shoulder brushed against Sidney's. He didn't acknowledge the touch, but he didn't shift away, either.

"I hope you win," the man said, finally looking up. He tucked away the knife and held up his carving. A poppy flower.

Sidney stared at it for a long time, before slowly reaching out to take it. He cradled it carefully in his palm as if it would snap. "Thank you."

After that, Sidney moved in a daze. He drove her back to the train, but didn't say a single word. When he parked, she got out, rounded the engine, and opened his door. She took the hand that had so gently held a wooden flower and tugged him out. The line to the Boxcar Library was out the door, but she knew Colette was fine. She would have to be in the coming weeks after Alice returned to Missoula, anyway.

Alice led Sidney around the next train car, so that they could get to the roof without being seen. Then she nudged him up the ladder. The view from the top wasn't anywhere close to incredible now that they were in the plains. But the sky was settling into the soft blue of evening, and the rush of people felt so far away even just a little removed from the ground.

"What was the book?" Alice asked, because when all other words failed, she could always talk about this. "What was the book you turned to the most? When you needed it."

Sidney licked his lips. He was sprawled so casually on the roof, one leg tucked up, one out. The sun kissed his upturned face and had she not known better she would say he had not a care in the world.

He'd perfected that mask of his long before the war, she realized.

"'Men are so quick to blame the gods: they say that we devise their misery. But they themselves—in their depravity—design grief greater than the griefs that fate assigns,'" Sidney quoted, and Alice had to think for only a handful of seconds before she got it.

"Homer," she said. "*The Odyssey.*"

"When we were over there, it felt like the most impossible task," Sidney said. "Getting home."

Not in a coffin was left unsaid, but Alice knew it was there.

"That's all that kept me going most nights," Sidney admitted. "The thought of getting home."

"And then you got here," Alice realized.

"And then I got here," Sidney said. "And I realized it no longer felt like home."

CHAPTER THIRTY-TWO

Alice

Rutherford Lumberjack Camp Five
1924

He's in love with you," Colette told Alice as they pulled into their next lumberjack camp.

Sidney's Packard was already there.

Alice didn't argue, not because she believed it to be true but because she knew Colette would ask for an alternative reason he had followed them there.

And Alice didn't have one.

She thought after they'd watched the sun set over the mining camp, Sidney would go back to Missoula. That hadn't been the case.

This time she didn't go out to meet him.

A knock drew her attention away from the boxcar's window.

"Eager," Colette murmured, though she couldn't hide the pleased tilt to her smile at the idea of one of the lumberjacks waiting impatiently for them.

One of their first patrons who wandered in was on the older side—a surprise, considering these camps tended to draw in younger workers.

Alice let him browse first, but when he stalled out in front of the small children's shelf, she crossed over to him.

"Can I help you, sir?" Alice asked, startling him.

He casted a shifty glance toward the door as if he were about to bolt, but then he lifted his chin. "I need a book."

Alice smiled. "You came to the right place."

"Ah-yup," he said, while his nervous fingers stroked his long, unruly beard. "I'm traveling to my daughter's house next week."

"That will be nice."

He nodded, then shook his head. "My granddaughter. She's scared of me."

"Oh." Alice eyed him again. He had the large frame and thick bones of a lifelong lumberjack. His face had been weathered by years of sun and Montana winters; while his hands were gnarled from holding the saws. He . . . might very well scare small children.

"I try to get little, so as not to frighten her," he said. "But she cries every time she sees me. I don't . . . I don't want her to remember me that way."

"Oh," Alice said again, touched. So many men out here had to live their lives stoically, tough in the face of loss and love, heartbreak and joy. She believed they could have tender emotions, too, though.

The man jerked his head toward the bookshelf. "Maybe if I brought a book along . . . we could read it together."

Alice nodded, afraid that if she agreed it would come out too earnest and scare him off. "How old is she?"

They talked through the basics—her age, her interests, her personality.

"*Anne of Green Gables*," Alice said, plucking it from the shelf. She thought one of her favorite quotes from it could be painted on the library's walls: *The world calls them its singers and poets and artists and storytellers; but they are just people who have never forgotten the way to fairyland.* "The main character is a plucky, clever girl. She sounds just like your Diana."

"I'll give it a go," he said, the words thick with emotion. "Thank you, miss. Appreciate it."

Alice got him checked out, but called out before he got to the door. "Do the voices, too."

"Excuse me?"

"The voices," she repeated. "Do different voices for different characters. No one can sound scary when they're trying to be Anne."

His lips twitched and he nodded in agreement.

"That's why you wanted to do all this," Colette said from behind her. Alice whirled, surprised to find her there. She must have been lurking.

Alice didn't bother agreeing—she didn't have to. It must be written all over her face.

Sidney came by, but the library was too busy for her to stop and talk for long. Still, she asked him about the box he was carrying.

"A camera," he said. "I told my father it was why I was traveling to the camps. That I would document the conditions and report back."

She wrinkled her nose, not liking how much that sounded too close to spying.

"I'm not . . ." Sidney shook his head. "I'm not doing that. But I like taking the pictures. Capturing their faces."

He looked away and shrugged as if he'd revealed too much. To Alice, though, it seemed like only the tip of a very deep iceberg.

"Can I take pictures in here?" Sidney asked. "Perhaps the newspaper would like to show how much of a success this all is."

Alice nearly clapped her hands at the idea, but refrained. She also refrained from saying that she would pay money to see his mother's reaction to such an article. "Please go ahead."

He spent the next ten minutes on the periphery as she and Colette moved about. Some distant part of Alice noted that Colette would duck her head or shift her body if she felt the lens pointed in her direction. There was probably not one good shot of her on the entire roll.

But plenty of people were wary when a camera came out.

Sidney threw her a lazy salute before he headed for the door, off to find more faces to capture.

Another patron came through right after him. Alice stopped counting how many came in after that, but she had to believe it was the most they'd had in one stop since they'd started.

"We're going to run out of books," Colette said, eyeing the empty spaces on the shelves. There weren't many—they were well stocked and they had brought several crates along to refresh their catalog. But Colette wasn't completely wrong in her assessment.

"We're swinging back toward Missoula soon," Alice said, hardly believing she'd made it this far. She never thought she'd get to the turning point and she was almost sad with how fast it had gone.

If she were being honest, she would miss the freedom of the open road, but she wouldn't miss the lack of a good bath.

"Let's head down to the campfire tonight if they have one," Colette suggested, like she knew Alice needed to soak up every minute of the rest of the time she did have.

They had to kick their last patron out, a good-natured young man who took some heavy tome on ancient Greece that Alice had thought would never get checked out.

The calendar had just recently flipped into October, so Alice shrugged into her coat before following Colette out of the library. They ate a quick dinner, and then were directed toward the campfire.

A dozen men were there, sitting on stumps, sitting on the ground, leaning against trees, a little removed. Sidney of course circled the outside of the group, his camera still out, though she couldn't imagine he could produce any quality images with the light so low.

One of the lumberjacks who had come to the library that day stood up, holding a novel in the air. "I promised you fellas, didn't I?"

A cheer rose from the group, and Alice tried to remember what book he'd picked out.

"Now quiet down, ya hooligans," the man demanded, and, impressively, the group dropped silent. The reader cleared his throat. "'Mr. Sherlock Holmes, who was usually very late in the mornings, save upon those not infrequent occasions when he was up all night, was seated at the breakfast table.'"

The Hound of the Baskervilles. Sherlock Holmes. She was fairly certain the reader had picked it out for himself, but it was one she would have recommended for any of the men. An entertaining, easy-to-read mystery that had the added bonus of being a series? The only surprise was that they'd still had a copy left for him to check out.

She'd read the story more than once, so instead of paying close attention, she watched the faces of the audience. They were far from the polite, attentive crowd Alice was used to for such events. They hollered suggestions and criticisms for Holmes, then hazard guesses where the book was headed. Just like when Alice and Colette had done their little presentation, they made the work come alive in a way she wouldn't take for granted.

When their reader ended at a cliff-hanger, she thought the men might riot.

"Come back tomorrow," the man said, a mischievous glint in his eyes that reminded her of Puck.

"There's a card game I want in on," Colette said as she stood, her eyes focused on something over Alice's shoulder.

Alice tucked herself deeper into her coat at the thought of leaving the warmth of the fire. The cold that rushed in was almost worse because of the memory of the heat it chased away. "Of course. I'll be fine getting back to the car."

"I know," Colette said, laughing. Alice didn't understand the amusement until she felt someone nudge her shoulder.

She looked back to find Sidney standing behind her.

"Did you enjoy the reading?" Colette asked.

Sidney didn't take his attention off Alice's face. "Yes."

Colette laughed again. "I'm off to fleece some lumberjacks."

"Hmm," Sidney hummed.

"I won't be back until later," Colette said as she backed away, still looking far too amused.

That got Sidney to shoot her a glance. "Noted."

Alice stood, very much feeling like she was missing something important. "Well, good night all."

Colette guffawed off into the darkness.

"What is so funny?" Alice finally asked, but Colette was gone and Sidney just shook his head.

"I'll walk you back to the library."

"You don't have to do that." These men might be rough, but she didn't feel like she was in danger around them.

He held out his arm instead of arguing, and she sighed. It wasn't as if she didn't *want* him to walk her back.

"You must be happy," he said as they strolled toward the train.

"I am," Alice said, sending him a smile. "But why must I be?"

"That reading was everything you wanted from this adventure, wasn't it?" he asked, jerking his head in the direction of the campfire. "I don't believe they thought about the hardships of life even once."

"No one can resist a good mystery," Alice said lightly. But he was right. She would be thinking of this evening for a long time to come.

Sometimes a book could be the spark to a powder keg, setting the world on fire so that it burned the evil from it.

But sometimes all it had to be was enjoyable. Most of the men who'd sat around the campfire hadn't come into the library that day. Maybe tomorrow they would. Or maybe they would simply clamor for more chapters from *Hound*, properly hooked and reeled in. Either way, they would walk away from today with connections that hadn't been there yesterday.

"Speaking of mysteries," Alice said, feeling brave for no other reason than the night had closed in around them. "Why are you here?"

"Photographs," Sidney said easily.

She pinched his arm, and he huffed out a breath.

"Do you remember you gave me a book before I left," Sidney said.

Alice did. She had been very young and very impressed with how brave Sidney was, leaving the comfort of his life to go fight for all of them. "I gave you *The Red Badge of Courage*."

Even as she said the words, she realized how foolish she had been as a girl. Why had she ever thought it a good idea to give a departing soldier a novel about cowardice in war?

But Sidney laughed at her obvious distress. "'At times he regarded the wounded soldiers in an envious way. He conceived persons with torn bodies to be peculiarly happy. He wished that he, too, had a wound, a red badge of courage.'"

She inhaled at that, at the realization that Sidney had come back whole, at least in body.

"I lost my entire platoon during the Meuse-Argonne Offensive," Sidney said, his voice devoid of any emotion. "I was the only one to survive."

In Flanders fields the poppies blow
Between the crosses, row on row . . .

Alice almost retched. "I shouldn't have given you that."

"No," Sidney said, not like he was agreeing but like she didn't understand. He shook his head, and then nudged her forward. They were at the boxcar now, but instead of going into the relative warmth, they, through some unspoken agreement, started up the ladder. When they got to the roof, Sidney sat down, spreading his legs. He tugged at her hand. "Here."

Alice resisted for only a heartbeat before she let herself be arranged into the V of his legs, the insides of his thighs pressing against her hips, her back against his solid chest. Everything in her burned just as bright as the campfire.

He rested his chin against her shoulder, his voice soft against her ear. "I woke up in a hospital, uninjured. That first night there, I found a pistol, put it in my mouth. I pulled the trigger."

Her hands came up, tangled with his until they were palm to palm. She rubbed her jaw against his and gave silent thanks that it hadn't worked.

"The chamber was empty," he said. "There was nothing to do. I was in a ward with soldiers who had their bodies blown apart, who were missing half their faces or their ears or their tongues. I was in a ward with men whose nightmares were beyond what the devil could have dreamed up for hell. And I had not a thing wrong with me."

Alice wanted to protest that not all wounds were physical. But he must know that by now. He was living that truth.

"I remembered the book," he continued. "I'd read it on the ship over and thought of you. A slip of a girl with big eyes who gave me a war book about cowardice while everyone else promised I would die with courage."

She couldn't think of anything to say. Her words, her quotes, they failed her.

"It kept me sane to realize I wasn't the only one with such thoughts," he continued, not needing her to prompt him now. "It saved my life, knowing that. Seeing my deepest shame on the page. Because I knew at least one other person on earth shared this burden I hadn't believed I could carry alone."

"Then you came home," Alice said, her eyes slipping closed. "And I thought the war hadn't affected you at all."

He hummed. "It was . . . hard."

"Yes," Alice agreed. She couldn't imagine going through what he'd survived and then coming home to a town that was preoccupied with the spring dance or the fall festival. People in Missoula did have real problems, their state was struggling even as the rest of the country prospered. But it wasn't the hell that Sidney had walked through. Especially for people like his parents. Like her. "You must resent us all."

"No," he said quickly. "No. Life is not a competition of who has suffered the most."

"But it was difficult to talk to us," Alice guessed. She could see so clearly now how his behavior had let him build a wall around himself and a moat and a drawbridge that he almost never let down.

Except, for some reason, right now he had.

He didn't respond, and Alice shifted, a sudden move that put her face-to-face with him, her legs now pressed against his hips, the rest of her snug against his body. She went hot everywhere, but ignored the pulsing need she barely understood.

"You're not a hero," she said, watching his eyes closely. "You're not a monster, either. You're just a man."

Sidney exhaled at that, as if she'd relieved a weight he hadn't realized he'd been carrying.

"You're just a man," she said, cupping his cheeks with both hands. She pressed her lips ever so gently against his cheekbone and then his forehead. His eyes drifted closed and she kissed each lid, gently; his hands gripped the outsides of her thighs, pulling her impossibly closer. "You're just a man," she breathed. "And that's enough."

CHAPTER THIRTY-THREE

Millie

Outside Condon, Montana
1936

There were plenty of ways Millie would describe Sidney Walker, but volatile wasn't one of them.

Until now.

Millie, Flo, and Oscar stood on the side of the road staring at the mountain climber and its two flat front tires.

Sidney, meanwhile, kicked at one of them, cursing an impressive blue streak. Oscar stood, arms crossed, watching him with that enigmatic expression that made her suspect he was somehow responsible for their current predicament. After all, they were just outside one of the three towns Sidney had gotten scratched from their itinerary.

She jumped back when Sidney slammed his fist into the hood. He gritted his teeth, clearly holding back a yelp, and shook out his hand.

"I don't think damaging the thing further is going to help us," Flo offered mildly.

There had been a road sign for Condon, but she couldn't remember how far they'd come since then. Millie didn't think they'd have to walk more than a few miles, but she hoped Oscar had timed it so they wouldn't have to find somewhere to camp along the way.

Millie glanced over at Oscar, who met her eyes. If Sidney's reaction was anything to go by, they'd struck gold on their first try.

Flo caught the exchange, her own eyes narrowing in suspicion. Millie just shook her head, a tiny move that Flo seemed to accept.

For now.

Millie was fairly certain she would be grilled as soon as they were alone.

In the next minute, a hunter-green Chevrolet pickup truck came motoring down the road behind them, headed in the direction of Condon.

The young woman driving it slowed to a stop, and called out a friendly greeting. "Need help?"

"Think we need an auto mechanic," Millie said, shielding her face with a flat hand to get a better look at the girl. She had a sweet round face with a generous sprinkling of freckles and wore her long mouse-brown hair in twin braids.

"I'll take you to George, he's my uncle," the girl said. "Boys, you can hop in the back with the chickens."

Sidney hesitated. "Where's George's shop?"

"Oh, come now, beggars can't be choosers," Millie said brightly as Oscar swung himself into the flatbed.

"Condon," the girl answered anyway, and Millie all but saw the tension curl tighter in Sidney's body.

Millie held out a hand as she scooted into the middle seat to leave room for Flo, who hopped up gracefully behind her. "Millie Lang. This is Flo. And that's Sidney and Oscar in the back. We're with the Federal Writers' Project stationed in Missoula."

The girl's eyes went impossibly wider. "You're a writer?"

"An editor," Millie corrected without withdrawing her hand.

The girl stared at it and then gripped it with an endearing ferocity. She pumped it up and down like she was trying to get water out of a dry well.

"Beth Franklin," the girl said. "Everyone calls me Cookie, though."

Beth cringed as if she hadn't meant to offer that particular tidbit. The nickname was likely a holdover from childhood.

"Pleasure to meet you, Beth," Millie said, and the girl beamed. "Thank you for stopping."

"You're not from around here," Beth said, a smug smile in her voice. "We don't need any gratitude for stopping."

"Oh, she understands," Flo said, and Millie pressed a smile away.

"I'm from Texas," Millie offered.

"Golly," Beth said, sounding so young it was almost painful. Millie wasn't exactly old at twenty-four—and she very much remembered a time not long ago when she'd been as amazed by the idea of a state all the way across the country—but the innocent wonder still made her feel the handful of years separating them. "I want to go there. Well, I want to go everywhere."

"Is that right?"

Beth nodded. "Everywhere. Even Mount Kilimanjaro."

"Where?" Flo asked, laughing.

"Haven't you heard of 'The Snows of Kilimanjaro'?" Beth asked, sliding them a look. "Hemingway published the story in *Esquire* just last month."

"Oh, *Esquire*," Millie drew out, teasing. "I must have missed that volume."

Beth's pale skin pinked up. "My mother was a model in New York City before she married my father. Artists used to draw her for their pretty ads. My father made sure she got the latest magazines, even when we barely had money for food."

"Now, that's a love for the ages," Flo said on a sigh.

Millie snuck a hand in her pocket, groping for her journal so she could take notes. "What brought them to Montana?"

"Oh, you know, my father was a restless soul," Beth said, lifting one shoulder. "He thought he'd get rich out here, and Mama didn't have much of a choice, what with me tagging along in her belly."

"They must have found something that was worth sticking around for," Millie prompted.

"Got here just as the war work dried up along with the land." Beth sighed, now sounding much older and wiser. "But when everyone left for California, Papa was able to squat long enough in an abandoned ranch to grow roots and make it his own."

"Does your mother miss New York?"

"Only after a bit too much 'shine. She pulls out some of those old drawings and tells the same stories she's been telling all my life." Beth sent them a sly smile. "She was a foxy lady."

Millie laughed, wishing she could talk to the mother, as well. Something about that tiny detail—the husband still buying his wife fancy magazines even in the worst times—made Millie want to write their whole story.

"Here we are," Beth announced, and Millie was startled to realize they'd arrived in town.

Condon wasn't much of anything beyond a main street. But Beth had pulled to a stop by a shop with several different automobiles parked in front of it. George clearly had a stranglehold on the mechanic business in the area.

Sidney had already hopped out and was striding toward the building.

"Where would you go right now, if you could go anywhere?" Millie asked.

Millie expected some fashionable city as the answer.

Beth shook her head. "It's not about the where, it's about getting there."

And wasn't that exactly what the guides were all about? Sure, they were writing about destinations, but more so they were writing about everything along the way.

There was probably a lesson about life buried in that, but Millie wasn't feeling particularly introspective.

She *was* feeling incredibly fond of Beth Franklin, though. "Well, if you make it to Missoula, look me up. I'll make sure you get a copy of the travel guide we're working on."

"Nah," Beth said, with all the impishness of youth. "A guide would take all the fun out of it."

Millie laughed and followed Flo out of the truck, waving as Beth pulled off, not expecting anything in return for her help.

You're not from around here, Beth had said when Millie had first thanked her for stopping. She used to think like that, too. Like her little town in Texas was the only place in the world with a strong community of people who would go out of their way to help each other. But through traveling, Millie was starting to understand how much the impulse was simply human. Even in the hardest times, people—in Washington, DC, and Chicago or the middle-of-nowhere Montana—wanted to reach out a helping hand if they could.

Flo immediately whirled on her and Oscar. "You two plotted something, and you are absolute beasts for not telling me, too."

"You're giving me too much credit," Millie muttered. She glanced at Oscar. "What did you use?"

His eyes were locked on the shop. "A hatpin."

A few miles before the tires had given up the ghost, Oscar had begged Sidney to pull off to the side to take care of some business. Millie had been on the road with the two gentlemen for two weeks now, and so she hadn't blushed at the request. Still, they all liked to give each other privacy when they could.

Now, she realized Oscar had done that so they would be forced to stop here.

"You think it was Sidney who sent those blank pages to Helena?" Flo asked, not as if she hadn't followed along, but that she thought it so absurd she had to say it out loud.

Millie could dance around this, but she was tired of that approach. "Did you?"

Flo rocked back. "Of course not."

Millie didn't let up. "Did Professor Lyon?"

Flo pursed her lips. "Of course not."

"Did Oscar?"

Flo didn't say anything, and Oscar tore his attention from the shop, his brows lifted.

"No," Flo finally said.

"Did Sidney?" Millie asked. This was why Katherine had sent her to Montana, she realized. She didn't pull her punches, even when it would be easier to.

"He's a good man," Flo said, serious, for once.

"I didn't say he wasn't." Katherine had thought whoever sabotaged the guide was in the pocket of someone influential—a Copper King or a politician most likely.

Millie wasn't so sure anymore.

"Don't look at this like we're getting Sidney in trouble," Oscar added. "Look at this like we're helping him even if he doesn't realize it."

"You all said I was here to hand out pink slips, but that was never what I was told to do," Millie said, honestly. "All I have to do to save all of us is get our materials for part of the guide to Helena by the next deadline."

"Why would you protect Sidney?" Flo asked, and it sounded like she was asking, *Why would you protect any of us?*

Because you let me spin for joy beside a lake didn't sound like reason enough.

"My fate is tied to yours," Millie said. "Save the staff here, save myself."

Flo didn't say anything for a moment, though she seemed disappointed. She probably would have preferred to hear Millie simply liked them all, but Millie wasn't used to those kinds of declarations.

Finally, Flo crossed her arms and huffed out a breath. "What can I do?"

"I think we have to retrace whatever you did last time," Millie said. "Can either of you remember anything about this stop?"

"There's a hotel with a restaurant attached," Oscar said. "A saloon and a general store. We talked to people at each."

"Anyone in particular?"

"The piano player at the saloon," Oscar said slowly. "The professor talked to him for about an hour. That was the longest interview we did here."

"Didn't he mention a bookmobile project?" Flo asked. "I didn't pay much attention at the time, but he said it was around here, didn't he?"

Millie gaped at her. The professor had mentioned that in passing back on her first day. He even said he'd managed to get a photograph of the librarian from a local resident to include in the essay he'd been planning to write about statewide efforts.

Millie grabbed Flo and kissed her cheeks. "You are a genius."

Flo giggled and her cheeks went a delightful pink.

The door to the mechanic shop opened and Sidney stormed out.

"Three days," he said when he stopped in front of them. His

expression remained neutral but his voice was tight with annoyance. "If all goes well."

His anger could be easily attributed to the delay and the fact that his beloved mountain climber was broken down on the side of some road. And everything else that made her suspect him could be explained.

Maybe he'd uncovered the old film right before they'd left on their trip, in an old box in his closet. Maybe he'd been telling the truth about why the interviews with the tribes hadn't been included in the packages that were shipped to Helena.

But all she could see right now was a man trying desperately to hide a secret.

Trying desperately and knowing he was going to fail.

"What do you think he's hiding?" Millie asked softly later as she and Oscar watched Sidney come down the stairs from the hotel. The two of them had already nabbed a table in the tiny dining room.

"Murder, betrayal, scandal?" Oscar offered.

"This isn't one of your books."

Oscar chuckled. "If it was, I'd have written myself as the main character."

"You're not?" Millie asked, lifting her brows.

He gave her a look. "Clearly Sidney Walker is."

Millie sighed. Of course Sidney was. "Which do you think it is? Murder, betrayal, or scandal?"

"All three," Oscar murmured just before Sidney pulled out his chair to join them.

"All three what?" Sidney asked, not nearly as grouchy as he had been coming out of the mechanic shop.

"Rest, water, and a darkened room," Millie said, standing.

The men scrambled to their feet and she waved them back down. "I was telling Oscar here that my poor head is throbbing. You boys have dinner without me, I'll have some soup sent up."

Oscar watched her with fake concern, while Sidney's expression shifted to suspicious. But there wasn't much he could do without confronting her directly.

Millie walked away before Sidney could come up with some excuse to leave dinner, as well. What she needed was Oscar to make sure he stayed there for at least a few courses.

She went up the stairs only to run into Flo as the woman was coming down, looking far fresher and polished than she had a right to.

Flo's eyes narrowed immediately. "You're up to something."

Millie glanced back. "I'm going to the saloon to find the piano player."

"Oh, can I come?" Flo asked.

"I think it might be better for you to keep Sidney occupied at the table," Millie said, though she saw the benefits of both.

Flo nodded in agreement. "I'll buy you at least an hour."

"Thank you," Millie whispered, squeezing Flo's arm before continuing on to find a way back out into the alley behind the hotel. From there it was only a short walk to the saloon.

It was housed in what looked like the owner's large shed, though it was lit with lanterns to turn it into something quaint and romantic instead of shabby and scary.

The bar was a glorified drink cart, but the piano was beautiful, glossy and dark and larger than she would have expected for such a place.

She ordered something pretty and fizzy from the bartender because it was polite, and then made her way over to the piano player.

He had dark hair, a wide smile, and the sparkling eyes of someone who viewed the world with good humor and amusement. He was tickling away at that popular tune that everyone sang these days. "The Way You Look Tonight." A crowd-pleaser even when there wasn't a crowd to please.

Millie couldn't help herself. She leaned against the top of the piano, and waited for the right moment.

"Someday, when I'm awfully low," she began. She wasn't a singer who would draw a crowd, but she could hold a note. The piano player smiled up at her, and they made it through the whole song without incident.

The three other patrons in the saloon clapped politely when Millie reached the finale, but the quickness with which they turned back to their pints hinted at their relief that it was over.

"Passable," the piano player said with a cheeky grin, and Millie laughed.

"Millie," she said, introducing herself while she grabbed a chair to pull up next to him.

"Red Fox," he said, before going back to noodling the keys. Not a particular melody, just notes to keep the music flowing.

"I'm wondering if you could help me solve a mystery," Millie said.

He sent her a considering look. "Why would you think I could help?"

"Did you talk to a professor a few months ago?" Millie asked. "He was with the Federal Writers' Project, working on a travel guide series."

Red Fox hummed. "I remember."

Millie's heartbeat ticked up. "Could you tell me what you spoke about?"

"Why don't you ask him?"

"I won't see him for a while," she said, which was mostly true.

Red Fox's fingers flew over the keys, the resulting tune fast and happy. But his expression remained somber. "I don't snitch."

"It's not . . ." She trailed off. "I'm not trying to get anyone into trouble. I think . . . I think I'm trying to help."

That didn't feel like a lie. Whatever she'd thought about Sidney during that first meeting had been replaced over the past weeks. He was a thoughtful, intelligent man who cared about people and had probably had a rough go of it after the war. He saw beauty in the trees and mountains and lakes and beauty in people. He had inspired deep friendship in Sofia Rossi, and, from what she could tell, had the type of personality men would follow into battle.

She didn't think he was hiding the fact that he was in the Company's pocket.

Red Fox stared at her for a long time, his fingers never once faltering. But finally, he lifted his hands and turned toward her fully.

"We got to talking about libraries," Red Fox said. "And I told him about a woman who used to live here. She had a large collection of books, and loaned them out whenever she came into town."

Of course. Flo had been right.

"What was her name?"

He squinted at her, but then shrugged. "Colette Durand."

She rubbed her suddenly sweaty palms against her trousers as she heard Oscar's voice. "How long ago was this?"

"Two, three years ago?" Red Fox said with a shrug.

She died more than ten years ago.

Her pulse kicked up. "Did she leave for somewhere else?"

His eyes went soft. "No, dear. I'm sorry to say, she died. The flu."

"Are you . . ." Millie wanted to ask, *Are you sure?* But of course he must be.

She shook her head and she must have looked distraught because Red Fox patted her shoulder. And then he tapped out a pretty melody that sounded like birdsong. "She was a nice lady."

Millie nodded her thanks, before she walked, a bit mindlessly, back out onto the street.

She leaned against the outer wall of the saloon thinking about her puzzle pieces. She felt like she had them all but couldn't make them fit together.

Colette Durand had died twice.

Sidney Walker had gone out of his way to make sure they didn't stop in the town where she'd last lived.

Colette Durand had been the librarian for Alice Monroe's pet project.

Sidney Walker had recently developed a photograph of Alice sitting on top of the train where Colette had worked before she died.

All Millie knew for certain was that all roads kept coming back to that damn Boxcar Library.

CHAPTER THIRTY-FOUR

Colette

Shelby, Montana
1923

Posters advertising the heavyweight fight between Jack Dempsey and Tommy Gibbons were plastered on every available brick surface in Shelby, Montana.

Young, shoeless boys in tattered pants tried to sell Colette tickets but she had already bought hers. She wasn't about to miss this event.

It had been the talk of the summer leading up to July fourth. Jack Dempsey was a crowd-pleaser, for both the boys and the girls. His opponent might be a no-name, but the Shelby organizers were banking on the idea that Dempsey would turn their floundering town into a tourist stop.

Colette didn't think they'd be successful. Shelby was too far north to draw casual tourists, and anyone who came this far would simply travel on to Glacier National Park. It probably wouldn't be anything more than a pit stop on the way to something else.

But this wasn't her circus or her monkeys. She had one reason to be in Shelby and it wasn't for the fight.

"Mister, best seats in the house."

"Sir, sir, sir, I've got tickets right on the ropes."

"You'll taste the blood."

Colette grinned. She wanted to taste blood, but not Dempsey's or Gibbons's.

Thousands of people streamed toward the barn where the organizers had set up the boxing ring, but she was only looking for one patron in particular.

It had taken two years, two years on the road, by herself, picking up as many jobs or poker games as she could, learning how to best threaten a man with a shotgun, learning how to shoot it, making allies, making enemies, making friends out of strangers, sleeping on the ground, sleeping in bunk beds beneath men who snored as loudly as they farted, sleeping in boardinghouses with matrons who barely deigned to talk to her, hiding out in whorehouses, in saloons, in caves and boxcars, losing everything she had but the clothes she wore, gaining it all right back, learning how to make moonshine, learning how to avoid the Prohibition agents, learning how to drive a Ford down a road that was more mud and rock than anything, kissing men, kissing women, bathing nude in a lake with ice already forming, two years of turning her entire body, her entire soul, into a tough callus that could withstand everything Montana threw at her.

Two years and she'd finally found her man thanks to a whore three towns over who'd sworn Petey would never miss this boxing fight.

Blood pumped through her chest and she tried to steady her breathing, her shotgun bumping against the backs of her thighs with every step.

It took an hour of careful searching, and even then, luck was on her side.

A young girl tripped in front of her, and Colette helped her get back to her feet. Her brother ran beside her, and she took off after him, crying at being left behind.

Colette grinned after them, following along until they got swallowed up by the crowd.

Swallowed up, really, by a group of men swapping bills and cigarettes.

The light shifted and so did the group to reveal a pale man built like a boxer.

A large, red and blotchy birthmark stretched over almost the entirety of his neck.

Peter "Petey" Severson, who went by a dozen other names. The man who had killed her father.

Colette exhaled, her fingers reflexively gripping the strap of her shotgun.

After all this time.

After all that sacrifice.

Here he was. Right in front of her.

It almost didn't feel real.

She found a spot far enough away that she didn't think he would be able to feel her eyes on the back of his neck, but close enough that she wouldn't lose sight of him.

Petey stayed until round four. It was a decent fight, but with nothing extraordinary happening he probably wanted to make it back to the rodeo before all the tourists got bored at the barn.

The makeshift ring wasn't far from town, and once the crowd thinned out, it was easy to follow Petey along the path back toward the rodeo grounds.

Shelby had put on her best holiday clothes for her guests. Every streetlamp and storefront was decked out in red, white, and blue. Flags blew in the breeze and children ran up and down the streets with spinners and streamers. Young ladies walked arm in arm licking ice creams, while their beaus trailed behind hoping to get their attention.

Colette ignored all of it.

She waited for just the right moment. He took a sharp turn down an alley, a shortcut that he would pay for, and she pounced.

"Petey," she called out, her shotgun already in her hands. Not pointed at him, but held at the ready.

The man turned. He had thin lips and cold eyes and he looked her up and down, likely assessing if he could rob her. "Who's asking?"

She stepped closer, he stepped back. They continued the dance until he was pressed up against the wall. The shadows closed in around them, protecting her from witnesses.

"My name is Colette Durand," she finally answered, enunciating each word. "And you killed my father. Claude Durand."

His nostrils flared, derision slipping into his expression now that he realized she was a woman. "You're crazy, lady."

"I was there," she said. "I was there when you killed my father."

Doubt flickered into his eyes. "I don't know what you're talking about."

She stepped closer, jamming the barrel of the shotgun beneath his chin. "Yes. You do."

He shook his head, but she pressed the gun harder into that soft bit of flesh and he immediately stilled.

"Claude Durand," she repeated. "He was a union man in Hell Raisin' Gulch. You shot him dead two years ago."

A muscle in his jaw ticked. "I don't always know their names."

"You bragged about this one," she said, grinding the metal into his flesh. "The Company paid you handsomely for it."

His eyes met hers. She saw realization there—and something else.

"What?" she asked.

"I'll tell ya if you get this goddamn gun out of my face."

Colette considered it. She didn't want to let up, but she did want answers.

She stepped back. Not too far. She'd heard enough about this man that she wouldn't trust him any more than she'd trust a rattler.

Petey rubbed at his chin where he bore the mark of her weapon. "It wasn't the Company."

The words didn't make sense. "What?"

"Claude Durand, he wasn't killed because of the Company." Petey licked his lips, the nervous rat he was. Cornered and ready to give up anyone to save his hide. "Sure, the Company would have wanted him dead, if he was a union man. They wanted all those men dead. But they're not the ones who paid me to do it."

That couldn't be true. Of course it had been the Company. "You're wrong."

"Sure, lady," he said. "Believe what you want."

Colette swallowed hard. He was probably playing her, probably trying to buy himself amnesty. But she'd spent the past two years getting good enough at poker to sustain her through her jobless periods. He wasn't bluffing. Or, he was and was a better actor than everyone who'd spoken about him had reported.

"Do you have a name?" she asked.

"Maybe," he said, shifting like he was going to run anyway. In the blink of an eye, she jammed the barrel of the shotgun right back beneath his chin.

"You're crazy, lady."

"You already said that," she reminded him calmly. "Do you have a name?"

"Who's to say you won't just splatter my brains against this wall if I tell ya?" he asked.

"That's a calculation I'll leave up to you to make," Colette said. "I would like the pleasure of pulling this trigger, so feel free not to tell me the name. I've spent two years dreaming of this moment. But, if you give me something, maybe I'll return the favor by letting you live."

His Adam's apple bobbed. He could read the truth in her face, and maybe even in the steadiness of her trigger finger.

"But I can't stand here all day," she continued. "So, I'll be generous and give you to the count of three to decide what you're going to do. A name or . . ."

"Listen—"

"One," Colette said, fairly certain he would break. She wasn't bluffing, she would shoot him. But that would feel a bit like destroying the gun instead of the man who'd loaded it.

"Hey, hey, hey."

"Two," she said, already strategizing how to get the information if he remained stubborn.

"I can't tell you, it'll get me killed," Petey protested, and Colette nearly laughed.

"Now or a month in the future, it's your choice," she said, with what she thought was a reasonable assessment of the situation. "Thr—"

"Wait," Petey yelled. "Crazy fucking cunt. Wait."

"You might not want to call me that if you don't want your head blown off," she said mildly. "A name."

Petey screamed and she let him. He was reckoning with the fact that he would likely die either now or very soon. "Fine. Fine, goddamn it. I'm blaming you when I lose all my toes to the Yukon winters."

Escaping north probably was his best option for survival. "At least you'll have toes to lose. A name."

He shook his head. "It was some rich fella over in Missoula."

"A name," she repeated once more.

"The mayor," Petey finally said. "Clark Monroe."

CHAPTER THIRTY-FIVE

Alice

Rutherford Lumberjack Camp Five
1924

Alice awoke to Colette stumbling into their tiny shared room behind the checkout desk.

It felt like she had just climbed down off the boxcar roof after her kiss with Sidney, but the tiny bit of light streaming through the window told her it was closer to dawn.

"Désolée," Colette murmured, or something like it. Considering she'd never spoken French before, Alice figured she'd misheard her.

"Did you win?" Alice asked, rubbing the grit out of her eyes.

For some reason, Colette started laughing, a startlingly free and happy sound that Alice had never heard from her before.

The force of it tipped Colette back into her narrow bed, and she simply flopped there, her body half on the mattress, staring at the ceiling and giggling every so often. "Did I win?"

She said it like it was a joke instead of a question for Alice, so Alice didn't say anything in response.

"They were liberal with the moonshine, were they?"

"Shhhhhhhh." Colette held a finger up to her lips. "Pro-hibi—Probiti—the Prohis. They'll get you."

"The *Prohibition agents*," Alice couldn't help but tease.

Even though they wouldn't. They didn't really care about lumberjack camps in northern Montana.

"You just sleep, you hear?" Alice said. She was awake now, so she pushed herself up and tucked Colette properly into her bed.

"Did I win?" Colette asked again, a smile on her lips. "Alice Monroe, I think I did."

"Sure you did," Alice said, placing a kiss on Colette's forehead.

It was too early to do anything of much except get out of Colette's hair, so Alice went outside and climbed the ladder to the roof. She sat cross-legged and stared off toward the horizon waiting for the sun to actually rise.

Alice didn't let herself think of last night. Sidney had been a gentleman, and his hands had barely wandered past her hips and thighs.

But it had felt like the start of something, and she didn't want to spook it into disappearing.

She smiled at the image of Sidney as a skittish horse and then smiled at the real Sidney as his head appeared over the edge.

"I thought I'd find you here," he said, carrying a tin cup of what she hoped was coffee.

He handed it over and then pulled the camera box that had been slung over his shoulder into his lap. He took the little machine out and then pointed it at her.

"No!" She laughed as the wind tugged at her hair. It would be light enough that the photograph would come out clear—she wouldn't be able to hide her bedhead and rumpled clothing with the shadows.

Sidney snapped the button anyway, and Alice rolled her eyes.

"Please burn that one," she said.

"You always look beautiful."

"Liar," she said, but knew if he took her picture now he'd see the blush on her cheeks.

"And I am, of course, gorgeous in the mornings," Sidney said, sprawling with a grace she knew he meant to be silly but was actually incredibly appealing.

"You've gone fishing now," Alice chastised.

"Men don't need reassurance?" he asked lightly.

She shifted, until her hip touched his shoulder. "Not just in the mornings."

When she slid him a glance, she caught him beaming off into the distance.

They didn't say much else as the camp woke up. At some point, Colette opened the library door beneath them, and Alice could hear her headache-grumbling from all the way up on the roof.

A part of Alice wished she could live in this moment forever—the anticipatory joy of her relationship with Sidney; the steady confidence she had in herself now that she'd not only survived but thrived living on the rails; the quiet calm of a morning routine that was anything but boring. They would roll out of the camp today, and Alice had become enchanted with that feeling, of loving a place and leaving it. For somewhere better, for somewhere worse, it didn't matter. It was the stripping away of expectations to start over that became a rush she could easily become accustomed to.

"Will you go back to Missoula?" she asked, pushing to her feet. She stretched toward the sky, her back protesting just enough to feel good.

"Yes. Unfortunately," Sidney said. "When are you planning on ending this brilliant adventure of yours? Or will you take to the rails for good?"

She laughed at that. "We're turning around at the next camp. I'll disembark back in Missoula if I can."

Even as she said the words, she saw a kick of dust in the distance. An automobile, moving at top speeds.

Her stomach clenched. There was no reason to assume that

the person was coming for her, but she had been waiting for this shoe to drop for too long for her mind not to go there.

Sidney followed her gaze as he moved to stand beside her. His jaw tightened. "Mac?"

"Maybe," she said, but thought, *Yes.*

They both followed the dust until it materialized into a car, a Ford, to be specific. Thousands of Montanans had that same make and model, but Alice would recognize it anywhere.

"It was nice while it lasted." She sighed.

Sidney grabbed her arm. "You don't have to go with him. If you don't want to."

She stared at his hand until he released her. But she hadn't taken umbrage at his touch. Instead, she was lost in search of an answer. What did she want?

Alice had just assumed she would go with Mac when he inevitably found her. But what if she simply said no? Colette had a shotgun—not that Alice would ever let her actually threaten Mac with it. Sidney was still here, and enough lumberjacks would show up to the library that if she needed a barrier she could create one.

But this was Mac. Not some Prohis chasing her down.

"It had to end sometime," she said. A muscle in Sidney's jaw ticked at that response, but he quickly turned away.

"Of course," he said. "We wouldn't want to put Mac out at all."

"That's not—" she started, but Sidney was already over the edge, heading down the ladder.

Alice sighed and followed him at a slower pace.

When she got down to the ground, she went into the library, knowing Mac would be pointed in her direction.

To her surprise, Sidney had gone in there to browse the stacks instead of storming off. This early, they only had a few patrons, and they were all taking care of themselves.

Colette looked between Alice and Sidney and wriggled her brows. Alice shook her head. It was too complicated to get into.

None of them said anything as the three patrons eventually found books and checked them out.

A handful of minutes later, Mac's large frame filled the doorway. He didn't even bother with pleasantries or questions.

"Miss Monroe," he said, breathing hard. "You have to come with me."

Even though Alice had been planning to go without a fight, this demand put her back up.

"Hello, Mac," Alice said as calmly as she could. "How nice to see you. How have you been?"

He blinked at her, and then scowled. "Miss Monroe—"

"I have been wonderful," Alice cut in over him. "And you can tell my father—"

But it was his turn to interrupt. "Miss Monroe."

His serious tone stopped her, and the realization started to creep in. The cloud of dust coming from an automobile moving far too fast. His labored breathing. The way he hadn't even looked around the boxcar, but had gone straight for her.

"It's my father," she said, not a question.

He answered anyway. "A heart episode. The doctor . . . he doesn't know if the mayor will survive it."

Her knees trembled and she fought to keep her balance as the room swayed around her.

Mac was at her side immediately, his big hands cupping her shoulders.

"Was it my fault?" she whispered, staring into the eyes of the man who would lie to protect her in a heartbeat.

"No," he said, proving her right.

She closed her own.

"We have to go." His voice was low, urgent.

This time, she nodded and stepped away from him, certain she was on steadier ground now.

But when she turned it was to find herself face-to-face with the business end of a shotgun she knew too well.

"I'm sorry to say," Colette said, "that no one is going anywhere."

CHAPTER THIRTY-SIX

Colette

Rutherford Lumberjack Camp Five
1924

Alice Monroe stared at Colette with those devastatingly big eyes of hers, her mouth pursing into a little moue of confusion.

Colette immediately shifted the shotgun from Alice to Murdoch MacTavish, one of the men who had brought her to Missoula.

Clark Monroe's gun of choice.

"What?" Alice managed to get out before Sidney Walker crossed the room in three aggressive strides and pushed her behind him.

"Now's not the time to act the hero," Colette said, without taking her eyes off MacTavish.

"Who are you?" Sidney asked, voice tight. He had been a soldier, but Colette guessed that he hadn't actually seen action. Not with how wealthy he was. Those types paid for their cowardice in poor men's bodies.

"My name is Colette Durand," Colette said, mostly for MacTavish's sake. She hadn't lied—it hadn't been necessary. After only a few weeks' observation, she'd realized Clark Monroe didn't pay a single ounce of attention to Alice's life. He would never have asked for the name of the librarian Alice had hired for her pet project.

Recognition flashed into MacTavish's eyes. If there had been any doubt he'd been involved, it was put to rest in that moment.

"Colette," Alice said, peeking around Sidney, who kept trying to shove her back. "Colette, there must be some mistake. Let's put the gun down and clear this all up."

Colette didn't take her eyes off the man in front of her. "Is there a mistake, Mr. MacTavish?"

"How do you know his name?" Alice asked, desperation creeping into her voice. She wasn't dumb—she knew that it wasn't a good sign.

"Is there a mistake, Mr. MacTavish?" Colette asked again.

His eyes darted to Alice, before returning to Colette's face. She saw in that instinctual glance the way he felt about Alice Monroe.

Alice, meanwhile, was staring hard at Mac in return, pleading him with her silence to deny that he knew anything about what was happening.

Colette liked Alice, but, in this moment, she remembered how much of a pampered princess the girl was. Alice would have died long ago if she'd tried to survive the years Colette had just made it through. Her naivete rankled now, especially considering that she either knew about her father's crimes and looked away, enjoying wealth built on the bones of dead men, or she had never cared enough to find out.

"Mac?" Alice asked, because she was holding on to hope.

"It's not a mistake," MacTavish finally said. Colette didn't blink, but it took everything in her to cover her surprise. She hadn't expected him to admit to it so easily. Not when he had been the one to pull the trigger.

"What's not a mistake?" Alice asked.

"He killed my father," Colette said bluntly. There was no use in talking around it, and the fewer interruptions from Alice, the better.

Alice gasped, but Colette ignored her. "Now, Mr. MacTavish,

I have a few questions for you, and how you answer them will determine how the rest of this morning unfolds."

MacTavish watched her through narrowed eyes. "I didn't kill him."

That threw Colette off her stride. "What?"

"You said I killed your father. I didn't. I was there, yes," he said. "But I didn't shoot him."

Of course he would say that. Petey Severson had as well. Only, Petey had been in extreme pain after Colette had shot him in the kneecap. He'd thought Colette was going to finish him off, as well. She'd found that men in that kind of situation were more honest than others.

"Why would I believe you?" Colette asked. "Your associate pleaded not guilty, as well."

He made a low, irritated sound, one she'd come to expect any time she mentioned Petey Severson. "He's a liar, a cheat, and a no-good sonofabitch."

"And yet you kept company with him," Colette pointed out. "What kind of man does that make you?"

MacTavish flushed red and once again glanced at Alice. He didn't want her to hear all this, to think poorly of him. Colette enjoyed having that particular card to play if she needed to.

"I've never killed anyone."

"You just let it happen," Colette said, even though she wasn't sure she believed him.

Colette remembered every second of that night, at least before Papa was killed. Afterward, that was a blur. But the confrontation before that was written on her soul.

Don't play games with us. Please. For your sake, for you daughter's sake.

That had been the second man. He'd had a soft voice, and she'd thought it had come across as pleading instead of taunting.

That fit better with the MacTavish who stood in front of her now than with Petey Severson, who probably hadn't been gentle a day in his life.

Shit.

What that meant for her plans, she didn't know.

Colette hadn't killed Petey—though she hoped someone had caught up with him by now. There were enough people who wanted to put a bullet in the back of his skull that surely it would happen soon.

She had wanted to kill him. She had thought she could.

And then he'd given her an excuse not to. It had been Murdoch MacTavish, Clark Monroe's right-hand man, who had actually killed Claude. She now realized she had seized that information with both hands because it let her send Petey on his way, injured but still breathing.

She thought of Josephine back in her cabin just outside Glacier, toiling away as a bootlegger.

He wouldn't have wanted you to pay for his life with your soul.

Colette had thought of herself as calloused until she'd had to stare into a man's eyes and pull a trigger.

She'd believed him because she'd wanted to.

Now she believed MacTavish because she believed he was actually telling the truth.

But if she let anyone in this boxcar know that, she'd lose all her leverage. What she needed to do was continue to convince them she was serious. So she pulled her shoulders back, bringing attention to the shotgun in her hands once more. It hadn't wavered at all. She was strong, she'd practiced holding it like this for long stretches of time, knowing this was a moment she couldn't afford to falter.

"Why were you sent to him in the first place?" Colette asked. "You told him to give you something. What was it?"

He sighed. "I don't know. We were told he would know what we were asking for."

That she believed. From what she'd been able to gather, Clark Monroe was no stranger to the dark side of life. He would have been smart enough to know that he shouldn't give information to a hired gun who could then take it to the next highest bidder.

"Why did he care?" Alice asked, stepping around Sidney. She looked at Colette. "Your father, he was a miner? Just outside Butte?"

"Yes."

"I've never heard him mention Butte other than in passing in my life," Alice said, sounding genuinely baffled. "Did he have connections with the companies there?"

"No," MacTavish said slowly. "Not even Anaconda. He's deeply invested in Rutherford Mining, so he viewed them as a competitor."

He waved to the boxcar as if he needed to offer proof.

"I didn't know Petey was going to kill him," MacTavish said. "I swear, Miss Monroe, you have to believe me."

Alice had pressed a hand to her mouth. "I don't—"

A knock sounded on the boxcar's door.

She had a guess of who it was, but she couldn't be certain. If she was wrong, and it was some innocent library patron, she didn't want them caught up in this mess.

"Over there," she said to MacTavish, directing him into the far corner of the library, away from the window.

"You two, don't do anything foolish," Colette warned Sidney and Alice. "I would prefer not to shoot either of you, but I don't feel strongly about it either way."

It was a lie, of course. One thing she would never admit out loud was that she actually liked Alice Monroe, pampered princess though she might be. It had been nice to have a friend after so long alone.

"Oh, good to know," Alice muttered.

"Isn't it?" Colette kept her back to the wall and her gun on MacTavish as she edged toward the door.

"We're closed," she called out, and it only took one quick look at Alice to see the woman was contemplating yelling for help.

Sidney put a hand on her wrist to stop the thought before it gained any traction, though.

Smart man.

"It's me."

Colette let out a quiet breath before unlocking the door.

Finn Benson stepped inside quickly, pulling a pistol from his jacket holster as he did.

His eyes slid over her, checking to make sure she was all right. She would never get used to this man caring about her, but she couldn't deny the pleasure that came with the realization every time. The memory of that warm bath following Papa's death, the one in his hotel room. The bed they'd shared only once, his arms wrapped around her.

Every experience they had together was *warm*. The rest of Colette's life in the past three years had been so cold.

"Hello," she breathed. She'd seen him recently—when she'd arrived in Missoula, she'd carefully watched the Monroe family. Once she'd determined that it was likely Petey had been telling the truth, she'd written to Finn.

Even though she'd hunted Petey Severson for two years, she hadn't had much of a plan when she'd confronted him. That had been a mistake Colette had learned from.

She hadn't just wanted to put a bullet in Clark Monroe's brain. She'd wanted to ruin him.

And for that, she'd needed help from the one person she'd been able to call *hers* since Papa had died.

"You were right, it was a good idea for me to stay in town," he said with a crooked smile. He hadn't wanted to—waiting around was not his forte. But she was glad they'd established that he would keep his eyes on Monroe while she took care of Alice. "Monroe's at death's door."

Alice made a pained sound that she pressed back behind tight lips. Colette didn't enjoy the glassy sheen of tears in the woman's eyes, but she couldn't care about that now. If she had learned nothing from *Hamlet*—if she'd learned nothing from the past three years on the road chasing vengeance—it was that a quest for revenge destroyed everyone including the person seeking it.

She had gone into this hunt knowing she would come out as ash. That had been the price she'd decided she was willing to pay.

Colette thought of Josephine, and that sweet boy on the train whose name she couldn't even remember now, and the hundreds of people whose paths she'd crossed along the way. There were plenty who had approved of her quest for vengeance, but more often than not the ones who had stuck with her were the ones who'd warned her away from it.

They were too close for her to alter her plans now, though.

Finn hadn't simply spent his time in Missoula waiting.

Colette had been clear—she didn't just want to kill Clark Monroe, she wanted to burn his empire to the ground. Finn had been working on the financial side of it all while Colette had targeted Alice.

When she'd started this hunt, she would have never imagined it would be so easy to walk away with the daughter of the most powerful man in Missoula.

They had caught a lucky break with the library, though. It was almost poetic, if she let herself be whimsical about the turn of events. Papa had loved books, and they were what would help her bring the sword down on his killer's neck.

Colette had never planned to kill Alice. She wasn't heartless. But she had wanted Clark Monroe to think that, to blame himself, to hit rock bottom in the last moments before she sent him to hell.

Now, he lay dying, not knowing where his daughter was, with his financial empire crashing down around him along with his reputation—if Finn had executed his part of the plan.

She waited for the righteous satisfaction to hit her.

She waited.

She waited.

And it never came.

Clark Monroe was a stranger. A name that she'd been able to give the endless well of hopelessness she'd been stuck in since Papa had died.

Tears streamed down Alice's face, and Colette realized that she was doing to her what Clark had done to Colette.

And this woman, who was barely out of girlhood, had done nothing but befriend her, offer her a job that she'd actually enjoyed for the first time in years. She'd tucked Colette into bed and listened to her and tried to be brave for her.

No people of our own.

Alice wasn't Colette's, but she could have been. If Colette had simply taken the librarian position, if she'd given up this single-minded chase. If she'd let the books and Alice and the lumberjacks and miners and the tracks and the taste of freedom even while having a soft bed to sleep on, if she'd let all that fill the space that she'd kept so purposely empty for the past three years.

But that hadn't been the choice she'd made. This was, and there was only one way forward.

She looked at Finn. "They don't know why they were sent to kill Papa."

"You believe them?" Finn asked, for her ears only, though the boxcar was too small to keep anything just between them.

Colette nodded. "If Clark is really on his deathbed, we should try to make it back to Missoula to get answers. It's our only hope."

"We can try," Finn said, though he sounded as resigned as she felt. "But first, do you want to do the honors?"

She stared at him, not understanding. When she didn't say anything, he jerked his pistol toward MacTavish. "Have you forgotten? He killed Claude."

Alice gasped again, and tried to shift toward MacTavish. "No."

Sidney grabbed her wrist, yanking her back.

"He didn't kill Papa," Colette said, and Finn shot her an incredulous look.

She understood it. He hadn't been the one chasing this revenge. The murder was still fresh, because he so rarely thought about it. His well of anger was full because it was untapped.

Finn had devoted the past few weeks to this hunt, and so he felt entitled to see it through.

Still, Colette lowered her gun.

"He didn't kill Papa," she said again. This time when Finn looked at her, it was with pity.

He thought she was weak, that she couldn't do it.

But in that moment, she realized *this* was strength. Offering up mercy instead of a devastating fire of hatred was what would save her soul.

"Oh, Colette. This is why you have me," Finn said. And then before any of them could realize what he was about to do, he aimed his pistol at MacTavish's chest and pulled the trigger.

CHAPTER THIRTY-SEVEN

Alice

Rutherford Lumberjack Camp Five
1924

Alice reached out a hand as if she could stop the bullet before it slammed into Mac's chest.

She couldn't. Nothing could stop what was about to happen. Alice screamed even as Mac crumpled to the ground like a puppet whose strings had been cut.

"No," she cried, dropping to her knees. She pulled him into her lap, rocking him. "No, no. No."

Something warm seeped into her skirts, and her hands came away bloody when she tried to reposition him. She swallowed against fear and bile and looked down at the wound in his chest that had been made at such close range. The clothes and flesh were torn away and then seared together. She could *see* his pulse in the way his life spilled out of him.

Yet she didn't want to stanch the bleeding in case she made it worse.

"I'm sorry, I'm sorry," she whispered as Sidney dropped down beside her. He'd stripped his own shirt off and pressed it to the hole in Mac's chest.

Mac shivered and coughed, his eyes blinking open to desperately find hers. "Alice."

It was the first time he'd ever said her name and it pierced her like nothing else would have. Hot tears splashed from her cheeks onto his as she bent to press her lips to his forehead.

Before she could say anything in response, his eyes drifted closed and his body went limp.

Dead weight.

Alice choked on her inhale.

"Goddamn it," Sidney swore, and leaped to his feet. He took two strides toward Finn, before Alice desperately grasped for his pant leg.

"No, Sidney," she pleaded.

Her entire world had just collapsed beneath her feet. Her father was dying in a place she could never get to in time, her best friend had just died in her arms. The woman she had trusted had betrayed her to devastatingly cruel lengths.

And the worst of it was that this was all her fault.

If Sidney were hurt, if he were hurt because he was in this goddamn boxcar with her, she would have nothing left.

"I don't want to shoot you," the man said. He was so calm but his hand was steady and so was the promise in his voice. He may not want to shoot Sidney, but he would.

Sidney's entire body was coiled, but he didn't move. "He was just a kid following orders from a man who saved his life."

"He was a man when he showed up at Claude Durand's door," the man corrected. "And he faced the consequences any man should."

Colette made a sound that Alice couldn't decipher. She was staring at Mac's body, the color completely gone from her face.

"He was following orders, Finn," she said, echoing Sidney. It came out hollow. As did the accusation that followed. "You killed him."

"I did what you've been trying to do for years. All that work, all that sacrifice, all that time. You were just going to throw it all away." Finn sounded confused. "Colette, I knew it would be difficult for you to actually follow through. That's why I came out here behind him."

"I . . ." Colette trailed off, shaking her head, her eyes still locked on Mac and Alice.

Her shotgun had dropped to the floor at some point.

A knock on the door interrupted them once more. This time Alice yelled out before anyone else could. "Help, help us."

Finn glared at her, but she didn't care. She wasn't sure she would even care if he shot her point-blank right there. Everything ached, and it would be a relief if the pain just faded into black.

Whoever was on the other side of the door tried the handle and failed. He started pounding.

"This is the camp's superintendent. Open up," he said, voice booming through the thin wood. "We heard a gunshot."

Colette stumbled back into the wall, seemingly unable to do much more.

Finn, however, crossed the room in three quick strides.

"I'm glad you're here," he said to the superintendent as he ushered the man inside. Finn gestured toward Mac's body, before pulling Colette into his side. "I had to shoot him, he was going to attack my partner here. I had to protect her."

"That's not true," Alice said, her voice sounding unstable even to her. "Mac didn't even have a weapon. Here, check him."

Sidney groaned, even before the superintendent flipped open Mac's jacket to reveal a Smith & Wesson revolver.

"I think we better get the sheriff out here," the superintendent said. "None of you are going anywhere until we sort this out."

"That man killed this woman's father," Finn said. "And he was going to go after her next."

"Is that true?" the superintendent asked. He was thin and

seemed frail, but his eyes were hard. He ran a large logging camp full of rough men. He wouldn't be easily intimidated.

Colette opened her mouth, closed it. Her eyes were still on Mac.

"She's distraught over all this, sir," Finn said, his arm tight around Colette's waist.

"They're lying," Alice said, though she knew she had hurt her case by insisting Mac wasn't dangerous. With his size, and that weapon on his person, no one would believe her protestations that he would never have harmed any of them.

Could she really even swear to that? Clearly, she hadn't been aware of what he was capable of in the name of serving her father's interests.

Finn ignored her. After a second of assessment, so did the superintendent.

"Well, we'll get this sorted," he said. "I'm calling the sheriff out, he shouldn't be long."

The superintendent stepped outside the boxcar, but didn't go far. He called for a boy running by to go summon the sheriff.

"Get me out of here," Alice whispered when Sidney came to kneel by her. She clawed at the collar of her dress. "I can't breathe. I can't breathe."

"All right," Sidney murmured. "All right."

He hauled her to her feet and immediately wrapped an arm around her to keep her steady.

Alice didn't want to leave Mac's body with his killers, but she thought if she didn't get out of the boxcar that very moment she would be sick all over him anyway.

"She needs air," Sidney told the superintendent when he tried to stop them. "Come on. She just witnessed her friend die."

He studied them, but then nodded once. "Stand over there."

Alice found the closest patch of shadows and then all but fell into Sidney's arms. He held her tight, his cheek resting against the top of her head, his palm spread wide at the base of her spine.

"I have to try to get to my father," she mumbled against his shirt.

"They won't let us leave until the sheriff comes," Sidney said. "But then we can take the Packard. We might be able to make it."

"A sheriff who's not going to do anything," Alice said. "That man is going to get away with killing Mac."

Her voice broke on his name. She tried to picture him on a summer day driving her along the Blackfoot, the sun in his hair, a gentle smile on his face, but when she closed her eyes all she could see was his shocked expression as the bullet slammed into his chest.

"I'll try to talk to him first," Sidney said, but it came out hesitant. He realized how this was going to go. Alice didn't know this Finn person from Adam, but he was a slick talker. And sheriffs out here were often perfectly happy to go along with the story presented to them.

Sidney stiffened, and Alice pulled away to see what had caught his attention.

Colette was standing there, sans her shotgun. Without it, she looked smaller somehow. Like a lost girl.

"I wasn't going to shoot him," Colette said, and Alice snapped.

Before she could think about what she was going to do, she'd already crossed to Colette. With all the strength in her small body, she slapped Colette across the face. Her palm stung and her blood sang.

Tears sprung to Colette's eyes, eyes that had been dry as she'd watched Mac die.

"I don't care if you weren't going to shoot him," Alice screamed in a guttural unleashing of anger that felt too close to guilt. "You started this, you brought that man here. You wanted Mac to die. Don't talk to me about what you weren't going to do. You did it. You killed him the day you walked into my library."

Colette exhaled. "You're right."

"And you know the worst thing?" Alice said, her voice steadier now. She straightened her spine so she wouldn't appear weak in front of this woman. "You thought Mac deserved to pay, you thought my father deserved to pay. But it was me you made complicit in their deaths. It was me you made pay for your father's death."

Colette looked away. "I can't cry that one of my father's killers is dead. I *am* sorry that you lost your friend."

Alice's palm tingled with the desire to slap her again, but she stopped herself this time. She thought about the anger she'd seen in Colette's expression sometimes, when she didn't realize it was seeping through. Alice thought about how she herself felt now, what she wanted to do to Finn and Colette and the sheriff who would no doubt write Mac's death off as brought on by his own actions.

She thought about every book she'd read about the search for vengeance. It was never a balm, it was only ever a poison. "'The croaking raven doth bellow for revenge.'"

"Yet what did revenge do for that particular cast of characters?" Colette asked.

Alice's eyes drifted back to the Boxcar Library she had been so proud of, that she had loved so much, that had represented the freedom she had been denied for so long.

All she saw now was Mac's coffin.

"Nothing good."

CHAPTER THIRTY-EIGHT

Colette

Rutherford Lumberjack Camp Five
1924

Colette watched the Packard kick up dust as it sped away from the logging camp, the Boxcar Library, and everything that was inside.

Maybe Alice Monroe would reach her father in time, but it didn't seem likely. It had taken three hours for the sheriff to arrive and sort everything out. Colette had confirmed that Murdoch MacTavish, the dead man, had been at the scene of her father's murder. Once that was established as fact, the sheriff didn't seem inclined to dig any deeper than Finn's account of what had happened despite both Sidney's and Alice's protestations.

She wasn't sure how she felt about it all. Finn had skewed the facts so that both of them walked away clean, and she couldn't blame him for that. But the guilt was hard to ignore, as was the fact that Finn had shot the man in the first place.

In all the years she'd known him, she hadn't ever seen him violent. Passionate, of course. Fiery, without a doubt. But even when workers clamored for arms, Finn was usually the one to direct them toward more peaceful protests.

Knuckles brushed against her wrist, and she flinched.

Finn stood there, his brows raised, hurt flickering into his expression before he smoothed it away.

She closed her eyes and shook her head. "I'm sorry, you surprised me."

He inhaled. "We should get out of here."

"I can't leave," she said, gesturing toward the boxcar.

"What?" he asked, rocking back on his heels. "You can't be serious. You only took that position to get closer to Monroe's daughter."

"What will they do with the books?" Colette asked, knowing she wasn't quite making sense. But she couldn't focus on anything else.

"Sweetheart, it doesn't matter," Finn said. "Why do you care?"

Colette stared at him, not seeing the warm, gentle man she knew in front of her but a stranger who didn't understand her at all. "They're books."

"You got rid of your father's books," he said, confusion evident in the deep V of his brows.

"No, I didn't," Colette said, surprised that he could even think that. "I would never do that."

"Where are they then?" he asked.

She didn't know, which was something that ate at her now. She had handed them over to her father's friend who had promised to find a safe place for them. So, she shook her head, it didn't matter anyway.

"She'll send someone," Colette said, heading toward the boxcar's door now. "I just have to stay with the library until Alice sends someone."

"She won't," Finn said, at her heels.

They both stopped and stared at the bloodstain on the wood. Colette would have to clean it.

"You shouldn't have to look at that," Finn said, but he didn't tug her out of the boxcar. He didn't move at all.

She exhaled. "Yes. Yes, I should."

Finn found her on the boxcar's roof at dawn. He had tried to pull her into the bed with him sometime last night, but she couldn't sleep. All she could do was stare at the place Mac's body had been.

Now she flinched when Finn's shoulder brushed hers and this time she couldn't blame surprise. He had made plenty of noise on the ladder getting up there.

"I don't know why you're treating me like the villain," he said quietly. He mirrored her position, one leg pulled up to his chest, the other stretched out in front of him. The sky was pink and purple, not yet golden, and they both watched the horizon for the first glimpse of the sun.

Colette couldn't explain it herself, so she didn't try. "It should have been Petey Severson instead."

"If MacTavish was telling the truth, he still would have done it had Petey not," Finn pointed out gently. "They were there to kill Claude. Just because MacTavish didn't pull the trigger doesn't mean he wouldn't have."

"You can't punish people for crimes they might have committed," Colette said. "You can only hold them responsible for the things they've done."

He was quiet for a long moment then. Finally, he said, "I thought I was doing what you would want."

She understood that even if he thought she didn't. And she admitted the one thing that had been haunting her since she'd launched this plan. "Perhaps the problem is that I should not have gotten what I wanted."

Colette scrubbed at the wooden floor of the boxcar until her hands were rubbed raw. The stain was gone, but she couldn't quite get herself to stop.

Out damned spot, she thought, amused for the first time in days. Papa would have enjoyed the *Macbeth* reference.

The train whistle blew and she finally sat back on her heels. Finn had tried to convince her a few more times to abandon the Boxcar Library, but she hadn't been able to. He didn't think Alice would send anyone, he thought she would just let it sit until the train returned to Missoula.

But Colette knew better. Alice Monroe cared about books more than almost anything in the world.

So Colette went through the motions at the camps. She did her best, especially if someone came in completely lost about what they wanted, but a fog had descended over her mind.

It was over.

The planning, the hunt, the lying and manipulating.

It was over.

Colette tried to read her way into feeling something. She tried Shakespeare, and then when that failed, Austen and Thoreau and Tolstoy and Twain and Dickens. In a fit of desperation, she tried *O Pioneers!* again, and yet all she could think about was how disappointed that boy would have been had he known what she would go on to do.

For the first time in her life, books were simply a collection of words on a page.

Two weeks after Alice Monroe had sped away from the library, she sent a replacement for Colette.

The man was old but had a cheerful disposition. He'd simply shrugged at the tiny living quarters and threadbare mattress. "I've slept on worse."

Colette stayed on for two more days to teach him about their checkout system and catalog, but she could only linger so long.

The thought of heading back to Hell Raisin' Gulch made her skin crawl. Without Papa there, it was no longer home.

She would have to find a new one, and once she did, she could go back for Papa's things.

At dawn on the third day, she sat on the rooftop of a boxcar she hadn't realized she'd come to love and thought about the places that meant anything to her.

They were few and far between. She had been to plenty over the past three years, but Colette had never let any of them stick in her heart.

The only thing that came to mind was that pond by Seeley Lake, where she and Papa would go in the summers to fish.

The idea settled into her chest, the roots of it wrapping around her ribcage, eager now that she had unleashed them.

She scrambled off the roof and grabbed the bag she'd left on the ground. She'd already said goodbye to her replacement the night before and so she simply started walking.

They weren't far from the main train line, and she had plenty of practice riding in the cargo bays.

It wouldn't take her long to end up near Butte, and from there it would be easy to head north toward the pond.

She found a boardinghouse with an empty bed, and for the first time in two weeks fell asleep easily.

At midnight, she woke to a knife at her throat.

CHAPTER THIRTY-NINE

Millie

Missoula, Montana
1936

Flo was waiting for Millie when she returned to the hotel after talking to Red Fox.

"Golly," Millie breathed out, her hand flying to press against her racing heart. She had turned on the light to find Flo sitting in one of the chairs, a shadow come to life. "What are you doing besides trying to send me to an early grave?"

Flo grinned, clearly pleased with her own theatrics. "What did you learn?"

Millie slipped out of her shoes and crossed the room in her stockings to accept the flask Flo held out in a silent invitation. After she took a decent size swallow, she plopped on the bed and filled her in on what Red Fox had said.

"And Oscar says Colette Durand died ten years ago?" Flo asked.

Millie sagged a little in disappointment. She had been hoping Flo could confirm that.

"Yes, though he was still very young," Millie said, grasping for anything. "Perhaps he got the years confused."

He hadn't seemed like he'd gotten the years confused, though.

"The Woman Who Died Twice," Flo said, and then made a face. "That would be a delicious title for a play."

"You should write it," Millie said, sidetracked for a moment.

The shadows shifted over Flo's face. "Please, I don't have

enough brains in my head to do anything but recite other people's words."

"That's not true at all," Millie said, indignant because by the change in Flo's voice it was obvious that she was repeating something she'd been told.

"That's kind of you to say, peaches," Flo said. "But we all know what women like me are good for."

Millie remembered the way Flo had handled every person's story with care and interest and curiosity. The writing itself could be taught, but Flo had the hard part down already.

"Well, when you're ready for an editor, you send it to me," Millie said, deciding to ignore Flo's pessimism.

It seemed like the right tack considering the way Flo lit up. Of course, being her, she had to bluster a bit. "If you're still around when you're eighty."

"Even then," Millie promised. "So, the Woman Who Died Twice."

"I do feel like I just saw this in a film," Flo said, staring off into the distance. "Maybe Colette Durand, the original, really did die in the twenties and someone simply took her name. They moved here and died a few years ago."

"Why take her name, though?" Millie asked.

Flo tipped her head. "Good question. Maybe the first death was simply reported in error. And Colette Durand, the first boxcar librarian, lived long enough to die out here in the middle-of-nowhere Montana."

"Sad either way," Millie murmured, allowing herself a moment to grieve a woman she'd never met. "But I think it's the latter."

"You do, do you?"

"Sidney so clearly wanted us to skip this town," Millie said. "Why would he care about a woman who had simply stolen Colette's name."

"Why would he care about Colette in the first place?" Flo countered, and Millie shook her head.

Millie couldn't help but think it must have something to do with Alice Monroe.

She wasn't about to say that to Flo, who had spoken highly of Alice back in Missoula. And she didn't want to start a rumor when she didn't exactly have any proof of anything.

"Probably something we're not going to figure out tonight," Millie said. And then she tried something she'd always dreamed about doing. She gossiped with a girlfriend. "Now, put me out of my misery—which of these fine men has actually caught your eye? Because I could have sworn it was the professor, but you did mention Oscar . . ."

Flo squealed and covered her face with the hand still holding her flask. The question somehow kicked off several hours' worth of conversation that went deep into the night and veered off the tracks more often than not.

And though Flo could tease with the ease of breathing, she never veered toward mean-spirited about any of Millie's—admittedly mild—confessions. She held them with the same care as she did anyone she ever talked to.

When they were finally too tipsy to do more than giggle at each other, they got ready for bed.

As Millie closed her eyes, she thought about Flo's question from earlier wondering why Millie would protect them.

She thought maybe now Flo would believe her when she said it was simply because that was what friends did.

George the mechanic ended up getting them back on the road by the next afternoon, and the rest of their trip went smoothly, with Sidney considerably more relaxed than he'd been before they'd stopped in Condon.

"You're back," Professor Lyon said, already looking behind Millie for Flo as they all tromped into the too-cold FWP office in Missoula for the first time in weeks.

Millie smiled as she thought about Flo confessing that she was waiting for Professor Lyon—*Tommy*, as she called him—to finally ask her on a date. But that she wasn't holding her breath for him to get up the courage, either.

"Yes, how did everything go here?" Millie asked, feeling like she was coming home even though that made no sense. Out of all the places she'd lived, her shortest stint had been in Missoula.

And yet, still . . .

"I've rewritten much of the historical sections," Professor Lyon said, looking pleased. Office work clearly suited him.

"That's wonderful."

"Oh, and a telegram came for you, just this morning, actually," he told Millie, though his eyes were locked on Flo. "From Washington."

"Professor," Millie said quietly as she took the paper. "She'll say yes."

She winked as he blushed and then she stepped away to read the telegram. On the first pass, the words didn't make sense so she read it two more times through.

The note was simple, but it still didn't make sense. Katherine wanted her to send everything they submitted straight to Montana state senator Walsh's office instead of the FWP editor in Helena. But Katherine had been insistent from the jump that they couldn't trust politicians.

"Do we know Senator Walsh?" Millie asked.

Flo wrinkled her nose. "Unfortunately. He was famously a scab when he was younger, and has spent his entire time in office introducing anti-union legislation like he was getting paid by the word."

A scab . . .

That rang a bell. Millie thought back through the past few weeks and landed on Lewis Penwell, the owner of the dude ranch on Wild Horse Island. What had he said?

We have an open seat in the legislature right now. . . . Some rat-bastard scab is the front-runner, of course, but the other candidate is gaining ground. A lot of people are paying close attention to that race.

But this was a sitting senator, not someone trying to get into office.

Professor Lyon interrupted her thoughts. "Why do you ask?"

Millie stared at the message again. She needed to talk directly to Katherine.

"The post office has a telephone, yes?" she asked, already grabbing her coat.

"Sure does, peaches," Flo said. "But you're just going to leave us curious?"

"I'll explain more when I can," Millie offered to their restrained grumblings.

It didn't take more than a minute to get Katherine Kellock on the telephone. Upon answering, she said, "You got my telegram."

"I had to make sure it was coming from you," Millie said, not needing to remind the woman of her own orders.

Katherine's sigh traveled the length of the country. "It came from above my head, with the assurances that you could keep copies of the work to make sure nothing was altered."

"How can they even justify asking that of us?" Millie asked, still trying to make sense of it all.

"Millie, you know not everyone believes in our program," Katherine said, sounding far more weary than she had only weeks earlier. "There's this committee."

"Oh, brother," Millie muttered, because Congress did love their committees and they were usually pointless at best, program-ruining at worst.

"The McCormack-Dickstein Committee," Katherine said, "and you can imagine the fun we're having with that name."

Millie snorted out a laugh. "Are they deserving?"

"The most deserving. And they've got a bee in their bonnet to put it mildly," Katherine said. "They're going after anything they view as anti-American."

"These guides are hardly anti-American," Millie protested.

"Aren't they?" Katherine asked softly.

"No," Millie said. "Not if you define the word as the people who make up the country and not the government that rules over them."

"Ah, but that's not how people here define it," Katherine said sadly. "The copy just came in for the Massachusetts guidebook. It has one—*one*—mention of the 1912 textile strike and now I can't get to my door in the morning, what with the congressmen camped on my stoop. Even a mention of something that makes the government or officials look bad is going to receive scrutiny."

"They want us to just write up pretty paragraphs about mountains and lakes and not mention any of the warts?" Millie was incensed. The dark parts of a country's history were just as important—if not more so—than the good parts. How else could they move in a better direction if they didn't know how bad it had gone before? "That's not right or fair to the people who are paying us to do this. Actual Americans."

"I'm not giving up the fight, Millie," Katherine said. "We just have to be careful, give a little when we can so we can maintain control of the ultimate product. It's either that or they shut us down completely."

"Senator Walsh's request," Millie realized.

"It seems harmless, since you'll be retaining copies of the work," Katherine said, the shrug obvious in her voice.

"But the reason you sent me out—"

"Millie," Katherine cut her off, not in frustration but in warning. "I know why I sent you out there."

The interruption came as a slap. There was an operator listening in after all. "I understand."

Katherine was silent for a long moment. "Make copies. The senator's office will be in charge of sending the work on to Helena, so you can't leave anything out. But you can request to see the final versions to compare the two."

Millie chewed on her lip. "What does this mean for the future of this office? I know you said we had until the next deadline. . . . Does this change that?"

"That depends," Katherine said. "What will be turned in at the next deadline?"

"Good work," Millie said on a rush. "This office is filled with capable, dedicated people who care about giving a voice to the people of this state."

"Then it sounds like we should keep everyone on," Katherine said. "Including you."

Millie exhaled, relief flooding in. There were bigger things to think about, but right now all she could do was be happy that her staff was safe from pink slips.

"Thank you," Millie whispered before returning the receiver to the holder.

She waved to the postman who was busy scowling at her for no reason that she could figure and then she stepped outside.

Millie stood there, her hands shoved into her coat, wondering if she'd simply gotten everything wrong. But no. Sidney's behavior couldn't be shrugged off, not when he so clearly wanted to hide the fact that Colette Durand might have been alive long after she was supposed to have died.

Millie thought back to her puzzle pieces.

The Boxcar Library that was started by Alice Monroe.

The mysterious librarian who never returned to Missoula . . . who had been hired by Alice Monroe and had died not once but twice.

The photograph of none other than Alice Monroe.

Millie could just see the corner of the Missoula Library over the tops of the trees.

She started in its direction.

It was time to get some answers from the woman at the center of it all.

CHAPTER FORTY

Alice

Missoula, Montana
1925

The dew-laden grass made quick work of Alice's dress, but she didn't rise off her knees.

The cemetery was peaceful this early in the morning and she had no interest in leaving yet. The wet earth became a tether to her father, to Mac.

It was the latter's whose grave she knelt before now. It had been a year since he'd died, and she still missed him every day. Could still hear the way he'd said her name as his last words. The soft gasp, the surrender to the darkness.

Alice stayed there as the sun fully rose in the sky.

This was one of the few places she felt safe these days.

She didn't understand her affliction, the terror of leaving her house for anywhere other than the library, where she still worked.

There was nothing stopping her from visiting the lumber and mining camps, even though Mac was no longer there to drive her. But the one time she'd tried, she'd ended up curled up in the back seat of the Ford, her heart racing so fast she'd thought she was dying.

Her only thought at the time had been *Good*.

The doctors had tried prescribing her laudanum after that,

but wandering as a ghost through her own home had been worse than the nerves.

So she got by. A local boy was in charge of doing her shopping and she ordered any clothes she might need. For some reason, being surrounded by books at the library kept her calm in a way nothing else did, so she had no trouble interacting with patrons there.

Her life, which she'd believed to be small, had shrunk to almost nothing.

Except she spent her free time reading, which meant her life would always be big.

Because once upon a time, I needed books, too, Sidney had said. He'd understood the way they could reach through the grief and fear and fog and pull a person to safety. Even if it was fabricated safety.

She pushed thoughts of him out of her mind.

Of course Alice didn't blame him for the events that had occurred, but she'd found that every time she looked at him, all she could see was a bullet smashing into Mac's chest. All she could see was her father's lifeless eyes, dead an hour before she returned home.

Or go and for once in your life, live it, Sidney had said to her when convincing her to take the one step that had irrevocably and devastatingly ruined her entire life.

Of course Alice didn't blame Sidney.

She blamed herself.

And yet every time she looked at him, all she could feel was a seething rage that felt like fire in her blood and tasted like rotten meat on her tongue.

"You have to forgive yourself," Sidney said from behind her now, because of course he had shown up. He watched for her sometimes when she came to the cemetery, like he knew she, too badly, wanted to be swallowed up by the earth beneath her.

He would be there to grab her hand if she tried to let it.

"I have," she lied. She had flown free of her cage once in her life, and this was what she'd gotten in return. A dead friend, a dead father. A fear of being outside more often than not. A man who she loved and couldn't even stand the sight of.

"Liar," he said, because he'd never pulled a punch where she was concerned. She'd always adored that about him even when she hadn't thought she liked him at all.

He was the man who had taken her to Lolo. He was the man who never let her wallow in her own pity. He was the man who was trying now to save her from herself.

I'm not a hero, he'd said, and she hadn't believed him.

Now she did. Because a hero might be able to save her, but he certainly couldn't.

"You're just never going to talk to me again?"

"I'm talking to you now," Alice said, staring at the dates on Mac's grave instead of Sidney's face.

"Sure you are," Sidney said easily, calling her a liar once again with his tone.

She didn't hear his footsteps retreating, not with the way the grass absorbed his departure, but she knew he had left.

Alice didn't stand to follow until her knees ached and her feet tingled.

As she stretched toward the sky she caught sight of something resting on the grave behind her.

A book.

She stared, the same tight feeling in her chest she would get if she were facing down a viper.

But she forced herself to cross to it.

The cover of *Les Misérables* stared back at her.

She flipped to the title page and saw Sidney's swoopy writing.

Because once upon a time, I needed books, too.

Alice let out a trembling breath and turned to the page he'd bookmarked, terrified and yet unwilling to throw the gift aside.

She had made it through the epic twice before, and she knew it was littered with quotes about love. But that wasn't what she found.

Her tears dropped onto the page as she read and reread the passage.

"If the soul is left in darkness, sins will be committed. The guilty one is not he who commits the sin, but the one who causes the darkness."

CHAPTER FORTY-ONE

Colette

Reno, Nevada
1926

The whorehouse was the best place to hide.

Colette had thought she was done running after Clark Monroe had died. But that had just been the start, it turned out.

Two years ago, she'd woken up in an unfamiliar boarding-house with a knife at her neck. It had been pure luck that the man sleeping above her had swung his legs over the bed at just that moment, knocking her attacker back for long enough that Colette could scramble out the other side.

She had written it off as just another thwarted robbery—an inevitability anyone living the kind of life she did had to face when traveling in the West.

But then the man with the gun had jumped on the train she had been riding in.

He didn't try to go after any of the men who were in there. Colette had been the target.

A week later, in Butte, she'd stopped at a speakeasy and had found herself dodging out the back when a hired gun in an over-large Stetson had started asking around about her loud enough for her to hear.

That had been enough to convince her there was a price on her head.

It was a good thing she had so many years of practice disappearing—just one more desperate worker in a long line of them. She already knew how to find a spot in the woods to sleep, how to fish for her breakfast, and build a fire to cook it. She knew the best cities to lose a tail in. She knew how to change her appearance just enough so that no one she left behind would be able to point anyone in the right direction.

What she learned was that the closer she got to Butte, the more dangerous her life became. Whereas she could go several months in Idaho without a hint of someone following her, if she got even in sniffing distance of the city, she would have no less than three men to shake off.

She was still trying to throw a hired gun who'd nearly caught her on her last attempt to go home. Reno was one of the best places to lose a man, and a whorehouse in Reno couldn't be beat.

There were two or three famous brothels in the city, and Colette *did* avoid those just on the off chance the man pursuing her was interested in patronizing the establishments himself. The closest calls she'd had in the past two years had been coincidence instead of smarts on the hired gun's part.

So instead, she found one that was the next rung down. There were still waitresses who would bring her a drink, but it wasn't the highest quality of liquor available.

"Here, baby doll," one of the girls said, setting a glass down in front of Colette. She winked. "You let me know if you want *anything else*."

The emphasis was just in case Colette had all of a sudden forgotten where she was.

Colette tipped her hat, which she had worn inside for the cover it gave her. The whores clocked her as a woman, but she didn't think any of the men had.

After finishing her drink, she wandered over to a poker table where she let three inebriated cowboys take most of her available cash.

"You hear anything about a bounty?" she asked the closest one after she'd "lost" a big pot. He was riding high on whiskey and winning and the promise of a friendly woman when he was done.

"You're gonna have to narrow it down, my friend," the man said, the words slurring around his grin.

"A woman, on her own," Colette said, and the man reared back.

"Not many take those." That proved a theory she'd been developing. The men who'd shown up in the towns she'd tried to lose herself in had been bottom of the barrel.

Just like that man from the Boxcar Library who'd stuck a gun in Alice Monroe's face as if he was robbing the train.

She had thought the incident strange at the time.

Now she wondered if it had been the start of all this.

Most of the time, she thought Alice Monroe or Sidney Walker was behind this manhunt. But the memory of that man always stopped her. He had jumped on the train long before Alice had found out what Colette was planning.

After she dismissed them as the ones who were hiring these guns, though, she was left with nothing. Except . . . except maybe someone thought she had whatever Papa had "found." Clark Monroe had paid MacTavish and Petey Severson to take out Papa, but that didn't mean he was the only one with a vested interest in the matter.

There was someone else out there who wanted to make sure whatever evidence Claude Durand had managed to dig up never saw the light of day. Colette only wished she knew what it was.

"A person would have to be pretty desperate to go after a lady.

But"—the man at the poker table swung his goofy smile in her direction—"the West is full of nothing if not desperate men."

"Don't I know it," Colette muttered. She was getting so tired of running, of looking over her shoulder every time she stopped to take a breath. She missed Montana like she would a limb. She missed her father's library. She missed pillows that she recognized and a bed that knew the shape of her body.

She needed to figure out who had put a price on her head, or she would never be allowed to go home again.

A throat cleared behind her. A man in a dust-covered, floor-length coat watched her from beneath a beat-up Stetson. "I've heard tell about that contract you mentioned."

Colette swiveled around to study him. His face showed signs of outside living, just as hers must. The sun and wind left their deep marks on all of them. Judging by the state of his clothes and his boots, he seemed like he worked for a living—rather than making his money from poker tables and bank safes—but that he could use another quarter in his pocket.

He held out his palm. "Roarke O'Callahan."

"Co—" she cut herself off. She hated that she wasn't able to use her name, but this man could easily be the one looking for her. "Colleen. Colleen Banzhaff."

"Let's get ourselves a table?" Roarke offered.

"Why would I want to do that?" Colette asked.

"So your marks there don't seize the day," Roarke said dryly, and Colette glanced over her shoulder to find everyone at the table watching her hungrily.

Information could be currency out here, especially when it came to that information leading to actual currency.

"Thanks, boys," she said, standing. "I guess I need some better luck next time."

"You could have taken them all for every penny," Roarke murmured as he found them a table in the back. It was a Monday night in August, but that didn't mean anything to this crowd. No one lived on a business schedule in Reno, certainly not the bootleggers or the drug lords or the madams. No one even had to try to hide the bad behavior, not here, where the mayor had declared he wanted to place a barrel of whiskey on every corner and spotting a Chicago gangster in hiding was just as likely as seeing a horse on the street.

Colette didn't like or dislike the city. It served a purpose and that was enough for her.

The waitress from earlier circled back, dropping down into Roarke's lap.

"I'm up for a crowd," she purred, her eyes on Colette even as she played with the ends of Roarke's hair.

Colette smirked, amused at the boldness.

"In another life," Colette said. "I'd make you an offer you couldn't refuse."

The waitress laughed. "In another life, I wouldn't be here to accept it."

She winked, but was professional enough to know when not to linger. She brought them drinks and then went in search of better opportunities.

"What will this cost me?" Colette asked. Her coffers weren't barren, nor did they overflow. Probably like Roarke's.

"Nothing," he said.

"Nothing's free." Anyone who'd spent even a minute out here knew that.

"This one time it is," Roarke said. "The man you're looking for, he worked for the Anaconda Company."

That wasn't surprising, necessarily, though she didn't know why they would be wasting money hunting her down. Petey Severson might have been a rotten liar, but he'd told the truth about Clark Monroe being at the heart of it all. "Do you have a name?"

Roarke glanced around, then lowered his voice as if the noise level in the place wouldn't cover them even if they were shouting at each other.

"Finn Benson."

The answer punched the wind out of her lungs.

A warm bath, a warm bed, warm hands.

A still-smoking pistol. A dead body.

"I'm sorry, I think I misheard you."

Roarke watched her face carefully. "Finn Benson."

A high-pitched whistle sounded in her ears, and she shook her head. "No. No you're wrong. He didn't work for the Company."

Her heart pounded against her ribcage. A warm bath, a warm bed . . . a warm body still bleeding out on the boxcar floor.

"He's been on their payroll for almost ten years," Roarke said. "But . . ."

She glanced up and it was only then she realized that she'd doubled over as if she'd been attacked. "But what?"

The words came out desperate even though she knew there was nothing he could say that would make this better.

"He pretends not to be," Roarke said.

"A union spy?" she breathed out. She remembered the first time she'd ever seen him, chasing a man through the street. Colette had helped him catch the traitor. All she could manage was a weak, "No."

"I'm sorry," Roarke said and sounded genuine. "I've been tracking him for a while now. There's no doubt, he infiltrated most of the union network in western Montana. But he collects a paycheck from the Anaconda Copper Mining Company."

It didn't make any sense, except that it did. Every man, woman, and child in Butte and its surrounding areas had been lectured plenty about the prevalence of spies trying to disrupt and inform upon their union meetings. Of course a man as charismatic and appealing as Finn Benson would be the perfect candidate to do that dirty work.

I don't know why you're treating me like the villain.

Colette swallowed hard against the acidic bile rising in her throat. He had said it so sincerely, as if he'd been wounded by her distaste that he'd killed a man.

A man she'd thought he'd killed *for* her.

"How do you know all this?" she finally asked.

"My brother was killed because of one of them," Roarke said, the disgust clear in his voice. "That's why this one's free. I listen for any rumors now, for anything that's related to union espionage." He paused. "And I pick up the contracts when I can."

The words took a second to make it through, but when they did, she reached for the knife she kept strapped to her thigh.

He held his palms up. "I wanted to see who had him hot under the collar."

Colette didn't let go of the handle of her weapon as she thought about every exit route possible. Of course it hadn't been coincidence that some man at a brothel in Reno knew the name of the person hunting her.

Knew Finn Benson and his history.

"He'll figure out I'm not interested in killing a lady. But in the meanwhile, I bought you some time," he said, standing and dropping some coins on the table. "I'll buy you as much as I can."

Right before he turned away, he said, "Don't waste it."

CHAPTER FORTY-TWO

Alice

Missoula, Montana
1926

Sidney didn't stop bringing Alice books.

Even when she ignored him. Even when she stopped going to the cemetery. She would find them on the porch, a page bookmarked that he thought would speak to her.

The first ones had been about grief and pain, often through the lens of the war.

The Return of the Soldier by Rebecca West showed up wrapped in brown paper with her name on the front.

I understand had been written on the title page by a hand she was now beginning to recognize.

She had curled up behind one of the stacks to read the bookmarked passage.

"Grief is not the clear melancholy the young believe it. It is like a siege in a tropical city. . . . Water and wine taste warm in the mouth, and food is of the substance of the sand; one snarls at one's company; thoughts prick one through sleep like mosquitoes."

Alice had read the entire book that night when otherwise she would have stared at the ceiling thinking about all the things she'd done wrong to lead to the deaths of the two people most important to her.

The novels weren't all about death and despair, though.

Dracula had shown up on her porch swing.

Could always be worse had been on the title page. It was the first time Alice had laughed since that day on the train.

There had been no bookmarked passages, but Alice had sat on her swing and read the entire novel that afternoon.

The sun had felt warm against her skin, and she took a moment to appreciate it before it set completely.

Alice realized the gifts weren't all about her when the housekeeper handed over Alexandre Dumas's *The Three Musketeers* one morning during breakfast.

One of my favorite reads.

She flipped to the bookmarked page.

"*The merit of all things lies in their difficulty.*"

The eggs went cold on her plate as she read from there on. She knew the plot well, as it was also one of her favorite stories.

On the second anniversary of Mac's death, she paused while searching through a book catalog for the library. *The Invisible Man* by H. G. Wells stared back at her.

Sidney would find it an interesting read, she thought, and then added it to her order.

When it arrived, she read it over the course of three evenings, returning to one page in particular.

She underlined the passage: "*I never blame anyone. It's quite out of fashion.*"

Alice used a dried flower as a bookmark and then she placed the book in her bedside drawer, knowing she would never send it to him.

ALICE HAD HER routine. Being outside no longer terrified her, but she still didn't like going to crowded stores or having to talk to too many people outside of work. She couldn't remember the last time she'd been somewhere other than the library or church.

That tended to mean she let her guard down when she was treading the familiar path to work.

One moment, she was wondering when Sidney would stop leaving her books, and the next she was being shoved into the passenger seat of a Ford.

The door slammed behind her before she could scream.

As her absconder rounded the engine, Alice grappled for the handle, but her fingers wouldn't listen.

She froze as the driver's door was yanked open.

And there was the one person she'd thought she'd never see again.

Colette Durand.

"I'm not here to hurt you," Colette said before Alice could get anything out.

"That's so reassuring as you kidnap me," Alice said. "What do you want?"

"I just want to talk," Colette said, swerving into the road. "Where's Sidney?"

"How should I know?"

That earned Alice her first real look from Colette. "I would have thought you'd have married by now."

Alice recoiled. "No."

Silence greeted that. "Is there someplace we can go where no one will see us?"

She almost said the cemetery, just to punish Colette. "Rattlesnake Creek, head north. It's popular with the fly fishermen, but it's late enough in the day they'll have come and gone by now."

"It's only nine in the morning," Colette said, but took the next left.

"Exactly."

They didn't speak again until they hit the bumpy road that ran alongside the creek.

"Anywhere," Alice said, and Colette immediately pulled into the grass.

As soon as the Ford stopped, Alice was out, heading toward the creek. It soothed something in her to be able to establish control over herself once more. She had never liked being manhandled, and she'd found it almost paralyzing in the last two years.

"You look like horseshit," Alice said when Colette joined her on the banks. The water was high with snowmelt as it always was in August, the rush of it almost loud enough to drown out the words.

Colette laughed. "Well then I look the way I feel. And when did you get a mouth on you?"

Alice hadn't, but she was angry. She didn't like being shoved into cars by women who had destroyed her life.

"What do you want, Colette?" Alice asked again, exhausted all of a sudden.

"Finn Benson," Colette said. "The man who shot MacTavish—"

"Yes, I remember," Alice snapped.

"Right. He put a price on my head," Colette said. For the first time since they'd met, there was a crack in Colette's mask and Alice could see the emotions simmering beneath. "I've been running for two years now."

That didn't make any sense. The two had been working together. "Why?"

"He was paid by the Anaconda Copper Mining Company to spy on union organizers, including my father," Colette said, that visible frustration also bleeding into her voice. "And I know it. That information could get him killed. In Butte especially." She added under her breath, "Which is why he never lets me get close to the city."

"Is that why he killed Mac?" Alice asked, trying to piece everything together. "Because he knew?"

"I believe so," Colette said, lifting one careless shoulder as if they weren't talking about the murder of a man. "I don't know why your father would have cared enough to involve himself in the matter, though."

Alice had been sorting through her father's things ever since he'd died. And while she would never have wished the heart failure upon him—and she continued to blame herself for it—he had not been a good man.

Claude Durand's death had been the least of his sins.

She had been spending the past two years trying to distribute her inherited wealth to the families he'd affected the most, but the list was never ending.

"He picked politicians," Alice said. "Ones who would be favorable to his interests. Then he would get them elected, usually working in tandem with the Company."

That hadn't been the most damning thing she'd found in his hidden safe, but it seemed to be the thing that had the most far-reaching impact. Clark Monroe had his fingerprints all over a dozen state legislators' seats and nearly a hundred other positions—including on judges' benches—across the state. People said the Company had influence, but so had Clark Monroe. "He must have picked Finn Benson as someone to invest in. With how charming he is, he could run for the federal Senate seat even. And who knows after that."

"And my father must have found evidence he was a spy for the Company," Colette said slowly. "What's one poor man's death in comparison to national office?"

Alice had spent two years uncovering the misdeeds of her father. At this point she was almost numb to them. "My father made sure they owed him. That was the tactic he liked to use.

Find young boys, bring them into the fold. If your father found evidence that could have destroyed Finn back then, my father would have gladly sent Mac—and some low-level hired gun—to take care of it. Then Finn could never say no to him."

It was both brilliant and sick, and Alice could feel the grime on her skin every day, just from having grown up in his household.

"What do you want, Colette?" Alice asked a third time. She was tired of being haunted by the brief slice of her life where she'd made every bad decision she could.

"I need you to find a way to spread rumors of my death," Colette said, without beating around the bush any longer.

Alice raised her brows. "Faked death, I presume."

"I hope, at least," Colette said somewhat wryly, and Alice could hear her own exhaustion echoed in Colette's voice. "I don't know if it will work, but it's the only thing I can think to try. Or killing him, but that might not be in my nature, believe it or not."

"You could move," Alice suggested. "To Maine, to South Carolina. To Texas."

"I've tried plenty of places, he keeps finding me," Colette said. "I'm a threat to him. And apparently his political aspirations."

"Why would Finn Benson believe any rumors about your death if he doesn't have proof?" Alice asked, because she didn't want to help Colette in any way. She didn't want to feel sorry for her, she didn't want to *think* about her.

Colette gave her a knowing look. "Because you hate me, there's no reason you would lie to protect me."

"I don't hate you," Alice said, surprising both of them. She hadn't thought enough about Colette to put a name to the emotion there, but she knew hate would be far off the mark.

"Any reasonable person would think you did," Colette said. But she was eyeing Alice now, curious but probably knowing she shouldn't push her luck. "Run an updated article about the Boxcar Library, mention my tragic passing, perhaps due to some natural illness so it's more believable."

That would probably work, Alice realized. If Finn Benson was keeping an ear to the ground for any news on Colette Durand, that would reach him. But it wouldn't be so obvious that he would be suspicious of the source.

"Why do you think I'll help you?" Alice asked.

Colette laughed and then broke it off when Alice remained stony in the face of her incredulity.

"Alice Monroe," Colette said. "You are a good person. You help people, it's what you do."

Instinctively, Alice stepped back. "I'm not a good person."

Colette rolled her eyes and then waved that off. "I'm not one for good or bad anyway. What am I? Certainly not good, but maybe my motives were. I'm not bad, I've never killed a person. But my actions led to the death of someone. Anyway, we are all far more complicated than good or bad, don't you think?"

Alice just waited, refusing to indulge her with a philosophical debate about the human condition as if they were in some Shakespearean play.

"You created a Boxcar Library for miners and lumberjacks," Colette said, as if she was making a point instead of stating a fact. "You weren't raised in a community like that, but we have a long tradition of taking care of each other. We know there's no help coming from the outside. Except, with you, there was."

"It's just books," Alice said. "I'm no hero."

"No, you're not," Colette agreed easily. "And I'll never call you one. But you are someone who cares about other people. It's probably your biggest weakness."

Alice laughed, a surprised huff of air. "You shouldn't be insulting me when you're convincing me to do you a favor."

Colette's mouth lifted in a half smile. "The fact that you haven't shot me dead in this remote location where you could dump my body in the river? That proves my point."

At that, Alice rolled her eyes. "No one thinks like that."

This time it was Colette who laughed. "Everyone thinks like that. Except you. Which is why you'll help the woman who ruined your life because otherwise she'll end up in some river sometime soon."

Of course Alice would help, that had never been in doubt. Colette had been at the center of a plan that had wrought incredible devastation on Alice's life. But she hadn't killed Mac.

Finn Benson had.

"I'll help, though I can't promise it will work," Alice finally said, and couldn't even be annoyed by Colette's smile. "Where will you go?"

Colette turned so she was looking toward the mountains in the distance. "Home."

CHAPTER FORTY-THREE

Millie

Missoula, Montana
1936

"You sabotaged the guidebook," Millie said.

Alice Monroe stared back at Millie, wearing a serene expression. "Why would you think I'd ever do a thing like that?"

"Because you did," Millie said, more confident this time. Alice hadn't denied it.

"Shall we walk?" Alice asked, rounding the checkout desk.

Millie was a head-and-a-half taller than Alice and outweighed her by probably a good forty pounds. She wasn't worried the woman would take her somewhere and attack her, but she did wonder if Sidney would be lying in wait for them.

Still, Millie wanted answers, so she followed Alice out the door.

"I panicked," Alice admitted, once they were on the sidewalk where Millie couldn't study her face. "I'm not proud of it."

Millie closed her eyes and exhaled. She had been right. "Does this have to do with Colette Durand?"

That obviously surprised Alice, who glanced over sharply. "The fact that you know that name means I didn't do a good enough job cleaning up this mess to begin with."

"It was a hunch," Millie admitted. "And I got there through a few wild guesses."

Alice nudged her into the town's cemetery. It was a quiet, peaceful space, with well-manicured paths. They walked in silence before they reached an elaborate grave with a sculpture of a globe sitting on top of it. Beside it was a simple headstone.

"Murdoch MacTavish," Millie read out loud.

"He was a dear friend," Alice said, wiping away a single tear that had escaped down her cheek. "Who did terrible things because he was loyal to the wrong person."

She took a deep breath then, and without once looking at Millie, explained what happened in the fall of 1924.

Millie didn't take her eyes off Alice's face during the entire recounting. Millie was getting the facts, she could tell, but there were layers upon layers of emotion beneath them all that she couldn't begin to decipher.

Alice cleared her throat after she described manipulating the newspaper editor into including a sentence about Colette's death.

"She was supposed to disappear then," Alice said. "I never heard from her after that. And then Sidney came to me one night, he said Professor Lyon had stumbled onto a local story about a woman who ran a library out of her house on the pond up by Seeley Lake. The woman's name was Colette Durand, and the professor even had a picture of her. And all of that was going to be sent straight to Helena, where—"

"Finn Benson has plenty of sway," Millie guessed.

"Yes," Alice said. "And I panicked. I can't say Sidney was thinking straight, either. We knew we couldn't simply steal the notes about Colette, because Professor Lyon would have sounded the alarm. And the dear man is a gem, but he is quite the stickler. He would have raised a fuss, and then everyone would have figured out everything we've been able to hide for over a decade.

"So, we filled the box with mostly blank interview forms and some gibberish notes," Alice continued. "Again, not our best-laid plan, but all I wanted to do was buy Colette some time."

Millie blinked at Alice. "Pardon?"

"I thought the editor in Helena would think there had just been some mix-up," Alice continued. "But instead you showed up looking to hand out the pink slips."

"I wasn't—"

"Sidney drove out to warn her—"

The conversation was running away from Millie. "Wait. Stop."

Alice shut her mouth and turned big, innocent eyes on Millie.

"You said you wanted to buy Colette time," Millie said. "But Colette Durand died a few years ago."

"Oh," Alice said, blinking quickly. Then she smiled. "Well, at least one lie stuck."

CHAPTER FORTY-FOUR

Colette

Condon, Montana
1936

Colette had grown weary of saloons during her time both hunting for her father's killers and running from Finn Benson's hired guns. So, even ten years after finding her *home* it was a rare evening that she made an appearance at the local joint in Condon.

But occasionally she craved more company than her dog and her pond.

"What's the news?" Colette asked Larry, the man behind what could only be generously called a bar. He already had a glass of her favorite gin poured.

"Government folks were in here a few nights back," Larry said.

Colette tensed. She was a Montanan through and through, and a woman with a sketchy history on top of that. She didn't like government folks on principle.

"What were they doing?" she asked. "Trying to build more roads?"

She couldn't imagine there was anywhere else to put them—the New Deal had pretty much paved over their entire state. Not that Colette minded. She was thankful her neighbors had food in their bellies and a new ability to visit loved ones who'd moved away. But she could still poke gentle fun at all the projects, as well.

"Nah." Larry poured himself a glass to match hers. "They were writers."

Colette paused, her drink halfway to her mouth, her heart loud in her ears all of a sudden. Writers, to her, meant newspapermen. But that couldn't be, they wouldn't stop in Condon for any reason. The biggest news in these parts was when Mrs. Bird's dog had its litter.

"Writers for what?"

"Couldn't make heads nor tails of it." Larry sighed. "Some travel book? But that doesn't make sense. People don't got any money for things like that."

"But it's the government you said." She could tell by Larry's sharp glance that she wasn't hiding her concern very well. "They're painting all the post offices across the country. They could very well fund some travel books."

"Suppose," Larry said. "What's it to you?"

She shook her head, not even sure why she was gripping her glass too tightly. "Did they talk to you? Ask you questions?"

"They asked me a few, I guess, but they moved on pretty quick." He grinned, revealing his missing canine. "They talked to Red Fox for near an hour."

Colette stood, dropping too much money on the bar. "Thank you."

"You need help home?" Larry asked, sounding worried.

She forced a smile, feeling stupid for the nerves running through her bloodstream. She supposed that was the residual effects of so many years running for her life. "No, no."

Red Fox glanced up when she put a hand on his shoulder. He never stopped playing—he rarely would. Usually she marveled at the skill.

"The government men who were here," she said without any preamble. "Did you talk to them?"

"Suppose I did for a bit," Red Fox said. "One of the men. He was a professor, a buttoned-up type, but he knew about the history of the land more than most."

"Did you mention me at all?" Colette knew that was an absurd question, but she had to know. She'd woken too many times to knives at her throat, she'd dodged out of too many saloons with pistols drawn behind her.

Red Fox's fingers paused, and he grimaced. "Might have."

Black crept in at the edges of her vision and she took deep steadying breaths. "Did you use my name."

"Oh, Colette." Red Fox stood, and it was one of the few times she'd seen him leave his piano. "We were talking about libraries and books. I mentioned that you bring in novels for people in town since we don't have a library. I thought it might get some money thrown our way for one."

Colette nodded, barely seeing him. She was just an offhand comment, that was all. A brief line in a long interview—no one who knew what her name meant would see it.

No one would care. Not after all this time.

"I didn't know," Red Fox murmured, clearly reading her distress. "I shouldn't have said anything."

"It's all right," she rushed to reassure him. "I didn't hide, not here. You wouldn't have known not to mention me."

She hadn't wanted to, which was a foolish, foolish thing she realized now. She'd spent years living under names that weren't her own, and when she'd finally settled in a safe place, she hadn't been able to resist.

That man back in Butte, the Company man who she'd beaten at poker, had pretended not to remember Papa's name. She realized now that he probably hadn't known it, but she had told him only moments before and still he'd been a prick about it.

Because those men, they knew that names held power. It was

harder to pretend a worker was just a machine part when they had a name, when they had a family.

When they had a story.

So, after months of checking over her shoulder and finding no one there, Colette had gotten to Condon, a town that was barely a blip on the map. She'd gotten to her cabin that was an hour's drive down a rutted, overgrown road.

And she'd thought, why not?

Her father had named her Colette because it meant "victory of the people."

It was what he had fought for all his life.

And she had been furious to think Finn Benson could steal that from her.

Red Fox nodded, but it looked hesitant and she grabbed his hands. "Please, this is my mess. But I do have a favor."

"Anything," he promised.

"If anyone else asks about me, can you tell them I've died?" she asked. "Years back. And spread the word?"

Red Fox lifted his brows but quickly agreed. "Of course."

"Thank you," she breathed, the tension melting out of her body. Even if Finn Benson or his hired guns found their way to Condon, they wouldn't be able to find their way to her.

Except, of course, they could.

Except, of course, they would.

SIDNEY WALKER LOOKED old.

He always had, but the past decade lived heavy in his face now. Colette wondered how he would look if he'd married Alice Monroe instead of letting her retreat into a shell of a person.

It wasn't Colette's problem at the moment, though.

Sidney pulled up to her cabin in a pretty—though beat-up—mountain climber three days after Colette had talked to Red

Fox. Word in town spread quickly, which meant Sidney had known exactly where to find her because the professor really had written down all her information given to him from Red Fox like a dutiful scribe.

"I already know," she called, and then walked back into her cabin, silently inviting him in.

"I didn't read the professor's notes until it was too late," Sidney said the moment he stepped over the threshold. No pleasantries despite the fact that she hadn't seen this man in over a decade. He hadn't been in Missoula when she'd begged Alice to help her fake her own death. So the last time she'd seen him had been when Murdoch MacTavish's body had still been warm, lying on the floor of that Boxcar Library.

She swallowed and looked away. That wasn't something she could worry about right now.

"Did anyone else see them?"

"A mystery writer we have on staff might have skimmed them," Sidney said, and she tried to make the sentence make sense.

"You have a mystery writer on staff?"

He waved that away, and she was glad he did. "He's a good man, but barely pays attention to his job. He writes those salacious crime novels that are all the rage now and turns one in every month. I can't imagine he cares."

"No one in Helena saw?" Colette asked. She had kept track of Finn Benson's career. He held a prominent role in Senator Walsh's office, but was now running for an open legislature seat himself. He was about to launch that political career Clark Monroe had invested in so long ago.

It was a small mercy that he hadn't had more success up to this point.

Sidney shook his head and she studied him.

"Why are you still helping me?" she asked. "After all this time. You barely even knew me then."

He lifted a shoulder. "Alice cares."

Colette laughed at that. If there was one thing she could bank on in this sorry life, it was that Alice Monroe cared. Colette didn't deserve it, but she did appreciate it.

"That reminds me," she said, crossing to a small wooden box she kept on her desk. She shifted a few things inside before she found the film. "You left this."

He caught it when she tossed it to him on sheer instinct. But then he stared at it like it held all the answers in the world. Perhaps it did.

"You kept it."

Colette shrugged. After he and Alice had torn out of that logging camp to try to make it to Clark Monroe's deathbed, Colette had found Sidney's forgotten camera and the film that had still been inside.

She wasn't sure why she'd kept it and never developed it. Except that it had been a reminder that for a very short amount of time, Colette Durand had people who were hers. Or, one person. Alice Monroe.

"Thank you," Sidney said, his voice thick with emotion.

Colette looked away, embarrassed at the evidence that she was human.

He looked hesitant now, like that one small gesture had changed his opinion of her.

"I can't guarantee someone didn't leak your name to the wrong person," Sidney said. "But now you've been warned, at least."

"Appreciate it," Colette murmured. And she did, despite her hard tone.

He stopped by the door. "We're done. I just put an entire staff of hardworking people in jeopardy of losing their positions. Finn

Benson shouldn't get what he wants, not after everything he's done. But you haven't earned anything more than what we've already gone through."

Or maybe he hadn't changed his opinion at all.

"I hear you," Colette said.

Sidney Walker nodded once and then he was gone.

Colette watched the car until it disappeared and then watched the road for a while longer.

Finn Benson shouldn't get what he wants.

She agreed, but he would because this had never been about her. What Finn Benson wanted was power and money. He wanted a state seat and then a national one and then maybe even the most important job of all.

And he'd get it. Because the Company picked out who they wanted to succeed and who they wanted to fail, just like Clark Monroe had done all those years ago.

Colette was tired of it.

She was tired of looking over her shoulder, wondering if she was safe even all these years later.

She was tired of snakes who seemed to get ahead while everyone else struggled just to survive.

She was tired of thinking of Finn Benson as a monster who couldn't be slayed.

Colette crossed to her desk and pulled out a fresh piece of paper.

The beautiful thing about having been on the run from this man for so long was that she understood him.

All she needed was one sentence. The envelope with her name and return address would do the rest of the work.

She smiled as the ink dried.

I found it.

CHAPTER FORTY-FIVE

Alice

Missoula, Montana
1936

Colette Durand is alive?" Millie Lang asked Alice.

"As of a month or so ago," Alice said. There was no way Finn Benson would have been able to find her—Alice and Sidney had made sure of that. But that snake seemed to have powers beyond what they could predict.

"Why does this politician care so much?" Millie asked.

"He's running for office," Alice said. "He wants to tie up loose ends."

Millie just stared at her, the confusion clear on her face. "Loose ends from what, though?"

Alice started to respond, but then stopped herself. She didn't even know what she was going to say. "The . . . murder?"

"But he was cleared on that," Millie said. "The sheriff cleared him. So what loose ends?"

When put like that, it did seem absurd. Alice and Sidney had both witnessed him shoot Mac, as well, and he hadn't spent fifteen years trying to silence either of them.

"He was a Company spy," Alice said slowly. "He worked for the Company and spent years gathering privileged information from meetings and organizers. That information could get him killed."

But Millie just shook her head. "One, you knew that and he

didn't come after you. And two, he's running as an anti-union scab. I've heard that from multiple people now. There's no reason for him to cover up his past, he'd more likely brag about it."

"I suppose we don't know he's still after Colette," Alice said, though she couldn't help but think about the two years Colette had been on the run from that man. By then, Finn had secured a position with a young Senator Walsh's office. There had been no need to keep hunting her.

"But we do," Millie said, reaching into her pocket. She held out a telegram. "We were just ordered to send everything through Senator Walsh's office. Benson must be behind it."

Alice stared at the terse message. "Yes, that's who he works for. I just . . . it's been so long."

Millie started to pace while clearly being respectful of the graves. "Why did your father care about Claude Durand?"

"He was a kingmaker. He picked politicians to succeed so they'd be loyal to him," Alice said, exhausted by the sins of her father.

"Right," Millie said, sounding distracted. She plucked at her lower lip, staring at the ground. "But why did your father care about Claude Durand?"

"He must have been a threat to Benson."

Millie was like a hunting dog on a scent. "How?"

"He'd found evidence that Benson was a Company spy," Alice said slowly.

"You think the Company couldn't have handled that?" Millie asked. Everything about her was tense and urgent, and Alice couldn't figure out why. "With how powerful they are? They couldn't have made sure he was safe?"

"I don't know if they would have cared enough about him." But she was starting to understand Millie's point. If Benson had realized someone had made him as a spy he would have turned to the Company, not her father, to take care of matters.

"Colette's father found something else," Millie said, on a roll now. "Something that would be devastating to Benson's political aspirations. That has to be the missing piece here."

"Something worse than murder?" Alice asked. Once Millie pointed them out, Alice could see the holes in her original theory.

"It all comes back to the Company," Millie murmured to herself, and then met Alice's eyes. "That's what everyone here says. The Company runs the state, it runs the newspapers, it runs everything."

"Yes, that's true." If Finn Benson wanted to get elected in Montana, he'd need the support of the Company. But, of course, he had it. He'd done their dirty work, he'd toiled away on the staff of a senator who'd pushed anti-union legislation for the past ten years. He was well and truly a Company man.

So why would he care about Colette?

"What could be worse than murder for them?" Millie asked.

The Company wasn't a person. The people who ran it didn't seem to follow the moral and social norms of society. Alice might rank murder as the worst crime anyone could commit, but the Company didn't see the world that way.

Good for them meant increasing profits. *Bad* for them meant losing money.

Their *saints* were people who figured out ways to cut costs; their *demons* anyone who demanded their fair share of what was earned.

For the Company, it all came back to accumulating wealth.

Which meant the very worst thing anyone could do . . .

"He stole their money," Alice said, the idea filling in all the empty spaces that she hadn't realized existed. "He skimmed, maybe? Or straight out took it. If the Company found out about something like that, they'd ruin him."

"Or kill him?" Millie asked.

"Yes. He must have confessed it all to my father," Alice said. "And my father told him not to worry about it. He deployed a hired gun and Mac to oversee it all. Like it was just another Wednesday."

Something was going on behind Millie's expression that Alice couldn't read. "You said Finn Benson stayed in Missoula to watch your father while Colette 'absconded' with you, correct?"

"Yes." Alice hated that she had to keep facing down one of the worst decisions of her life.

"Your father who was the one other person in the world who knew," Millie said, her tone leading.

Alice rocked back on her heels. "You think he killed my father?"

Millie shrugged. "Why wouldn't he? When that would mean the only two people who could ruin him were dead?"

The world shifted around Alice and then sharpened. What if . . . ?

What if she hadn't been responsible for her father's death? What if she hadn't even been responsible for Mac's? Finn would have killed them whether she'd gone with Colette in the Boxcar Library or not. He couldn't have let them live, not if they'd known what he'd done.

She inhaled a shaky breath. "There must be evidence."

"Wouldn't have Colette made it public by now?" Millie asked. "If it was enough to bring Finn Benson down?"

"She doesn't know she has it," Alice realized. "She doesn't know she has it."

"How is that possible?"

"I don't know," Alice said, sighing. "I guess we'll have to ask her."

Alice had liked Millie Lang on sight.

But she wished the woman had never come crashing into her life.

It wasn't fair to blame her for this upheaval, yet Alice didn't feel like being fair.

Over the past ten years, the paralyzing fear of those first few months had softened into something that had doctors deeming her *nervous*.

Not hysterical, at least, but not exactly brave, either.

She had started going to shops again, and even walking along the various rivers in and out of town. She had found a young man to take over her routes to the mining camps. Though she did miss interacting with the families, there was such turnover in the camps that she didn't think anyone she knew was still there.

Sidney had stopped sending her books after a few years. She'd heard he'd begun courting Christine Darcy right around that time, and Alice had cried over the copy of *Emma* that he'd gifted her.

Badly done, *Emma* had been bookmarked and underlined. But he'd also scribbled one of her favorite quotes on the title page.

"If I loved you less, I might be able to talk about it more."

Alice had never given him that copy of *The Invisible Man*.

The wedding announcement she feared never came. She began hearing rumors that he was spending too much time back in Lolo, drinking and gambling with money he no longer had.

She'd gone to Julia Walker's funeral and he hadn't even looked at her.

Alice didn't blame him. She'd never blamed him.

But she'd never been able to believe she deserved the life he could give her. Not through money, but through sunsets on a boxcar's roof.

Quiet joy and freedom was all she'd ever craved. And he would be able to give her that.

She stared at *The Invisible Man* now, the rest of her bag mostly packed. Millie Lang would be here any minute to pick her up in the FWP's Ford so they could drive out to Colette Durand's cottage on Bluebird Pond.

But Alice couldn't move.

What if Finn Benson had killer her father? And not the stress of Alice leaving Missoula?

What if . . . what if all of this really *wasn't* her fault?

What if the one time she'd seized her freedom hadn't been the downfall of everyone she loved?

A knock on the door sounded below, and Alice jolted realizing she'd picked up the novel.

She stared at it for one second, two. And then she dropped it in her bag.

"No," Alice said when Millie pulled to a stop in front of Sidney's humble lodgings.

"We should bring him," Millie said reasonably. "He's tangled up in this, too."

That was a truth Alice didn't have to like. She might be starting to thaw after a decade of being frozen to the world, but she wasn't about to cozy up to Sidney now. Not when he likely hated her for how she'd pushed him away.

Alice watched Millie head up the path toward the house, and realized that she was a striking young woman. Pretty didn't really do her justice, not with the angles of her face and the cut of her jaw. Her face would look stunning in a photograph.

Had Sidney taken one look at her and fallen hard? What had they been doing on those weeks they'd been on the road?

Alice didn't have a right to even wonder.

And yet still she did.

A few minutes later, Sidney strode out of the house, Millie trailing behind.

"Miss Monroe," he said when he climbed into the back seat.

"Mr. Walker," she murmured back.

"All right," Millie said, loud and over-cheerful. "Alice, would you like to fill Sidney in on our wild guesses?"

Alice proceeded to do so as Millie drove them out of town and up along the Blackfoot, the same route Alice and Mac had taken all those years ago. She spared a moment to think about Nathaniel. Did he even make it past childhood? Was he in the earth somewhere, digging copper out of rock? Did he still have that copy of *Treasure Island* she'd given him with the hopes of turning his day around?

"Why didn't we ever think about this?" Sidney muttered when she'd finished explaining.

"Because I tried not to," Alice said. She hadn't done much thinking about Colette at all until Sidney had come knocking on her door all those weeks ago.

When he didn't say anything, she glanced back. He lifted his brows. "You believe that?"

Alice blinked, out of practice with the way Sidney had always seemed to see what she didn't want him to. Of course she'd thought of Colette and Mac and the Boxcar Library. But she'd never let her thoughts shift into questioning. She'd told herself a story of what happened, with her as the dupe. Digging any deeper would have made her start to question other aspects of her life—like why she had voluntarily caged herself for over a decade.

Or it would have made her confide in Sidney, who must have had dozens of friends who had come back from war with similar symptoms.

Hell, Sidney had come back with his own demons, they simply wore different faces than hers.

She hadn't wanted that understanding to break down her walls.

Sidney didn't demand an answer from her—probably because he could read it on her face. He simply sat back in his seat and stared out the window, his point having been made.

Millie Lang was both watching them and trying to pretend she wasn't. "Can I ask you something?"

"Depends on what," Alice said a bit cheekily, and Millie snorted.

"Why didn't you lie? When I confronted you. You could be in trouble with the government."

"I almost immediately regretted what we had done," Alice admitted. "We shouldn't have touched the notes. It would have taken a little time for them to get shipped to Helena anyway, enough so that we could have warned Colette. But sometimes it's hard to think clearly when lives are on the line."

"So, once I figured it out . . ."

"You deserved to know the whys of it all," Alice said. "Even if that means you report back to your supervisor."

"You're not asking me to keep quiet about it?"

Alice lifted one shoulder in a careless shrug. "I would never want anyone to lie for me."

"You did it for Colette," Millie tossed back.

To Alice, it was the most obvious thing in the world. Some

lies were worth the black mark on the soul, but that was her calculation to make and she wasn't about to ask someone to skew theirs. "Yes, but those are decisions only I have to live with."

"My supervisor wanted the material redone by the first deadline, and we'll easily hit that," Millie said. "There's no reason to further litigate what happened, I don't think."

Alice knew she should be relieved, but she didn't feel much of anything. She saw Sidney and Millie share a look, and then she shifted so she could stare out the window, a passenger like she'd always been.

Watching the Blackfoot rush by with Mac, watching the mountains in the distance on that train so long ago. Watching the trees blur now as she headed back into the past.

Watching life fly by instead of taking the driver's seat herself.

They soon realized getting to Colette's cabin was easier said than done. Millie had to navigate ruts, washed-out road, and fallen trees the entire way.

Colette had found herself a nature-made fortress of sorts. No one simply looking for a nice day by the pond would dare to take this road much farther than the first half mile.

It took them an hour of careful driving before everything opened up and Alice caught sight of a cozy cottage surrounded on three sides by the forest. Even the position of the house seemed planned—Colette would have ample warning if someone was coming down the road.

There was another car parked at an angle blocking the porch and Millie pulled to a stop beside it.

She made a show of flexing her shaking fingers and Sidney gave her a golf clap from the back.

Millie laughed, shooting him a grin. "I used to think Texas roads were bad."

Alice climbed out.

Sidney joined her and they stared at the house for a long minute while Millie waited in silence behind them.

It was silly, but Alice thought Colette was better suited for that boxcar than a storybook cabin.

She shook her head. Truth be told, she'd barely known the woman at all.

Alice started forward, and that's when they all heard the gunshot.

CHAPTER FORTY-SIX

Colette

Bluebird Pond, Montana
1936

It took longer than Colette had expected for Finn Benson to come, but he was nothing if not predictable.

Colette could hear the car's engine from a quarter mile away. She had been sitting on her porch with more frequency these days, awaiting this very moment. She stood, slinging her shotgun around her back as she did.

In that moment, she was young again, hunting her father's killers, living in a Boxcar Library, hitting the road on the run from desperate men who wanted to kill her.

She hadn't had to routinely wear her shotgun in so long. There was the occasional wild animal to contend with, but, here, she'd been able to relax.

Mostly.

After today, she'd be able to exhale the whole way.

The car was as sleek as she'd expected. Finn Benson was a striver and a cockroach—he didn't die in the hard times but rather found a way to flourish. Usually, through someone else's misery.

Finn Benson was just as sleek as he'd always been, too. His hair had darkened in interesting ways, the sun catching the auburn streaks. He smiled up at the cabin, even though he probably couldn't see her standing in the shadows, and she was thrown back to that street in Butte. The first day she'd met him, when he'd likely been pinning his own crimes on a hapless bystander.

She was thrown back to that first union meeting where he'd held the room in the palm of his hand and then offered it up to Claude, as if it was the most natural thing in the world.

She was thrown back to that bath when he'd so gently scrubbed her father's dried blood from her skin.

Blood he'd paid to spill.

Her hand gripped her shotgun and she thanked God for men's arrogance. He had come, and he'd come alone.

And he'd pay for that decision with his own blood.

She shifted into the light and his eyes went immediately to her weapon. At least he wasn't dumb.

"Is that any way to greet an old lover?" Finn asked.

"When he spent years trying to kill me, yes," Colette answered.

"I never wanted to see you hurt."

Colette laughed, genuinely amused by the way he hadn't denied it. And how he seemed to think this was going to go any way but one.

"I must have been confused by all those men who held knives to my throat and pistols to my head," she said sweetly before turning and walking into the cabin.

He followed as she'd known he would.

"Are these your father's books?" Finn asked, gesturing to the shelves. She had a vague memory of him asking about them all those years ago, too. He'd thought she'd gotten rid of them.

"Why do you care about some books?" Colette asked, curious for the first time since he'd arrived.

"Making conversation." His shrug was so smooth and easy she knew it to be fake.

"While minutes away from your own death?" Colette asked, and he smirked at her.

"Where's that girl from Hell Raisin' Gulch with stars in her eyes?" he asked. "The one who quoted Shakespeare."

"'If I be waspish, best beware my sting,'" she said, a fire lighting in her blood. Up until now, she'd been coolheaded, calculated. Because she needed to be. But not anymore.

He squinted. "*Much Ado*?"

"*Shrew*," she corrected, and he rocked back on his heels with a groan. "You never were very bright, though. Maybe if you'd read more Shakespeare you wouldn't be in this position."

"What position is that?" Finn asked, not rising to the bait. He held out a hand. "Oh, right. A few minutes from my imminent demise. Of course, how could I have forgotten."

His mocking tone grated on her nerves, but she also appreciated it. It meant he wasn't taking her seriously, that he didn't have his guard all the way up.

Pure arrogance.

Men like him were used to getting what they wanted simply because they wanted it. He'd relied on the backs of powerful allies and his natural charm to get him through life, so when faced with a scenario where he actually had to go head-to-head with a real adversary he'd come up miles short.

And she was done playing with her food.

"Toss me your weapon," Colette said. "And then take a seat right there."

She swung the barrel toward a plain chair she'd placed in that exact spot for this purpose.

He heaved an overdramatic sigh and then flicked open his coat in a deliberately casual gesture. The pistol gleamed in his shoulder holster and clanged to the floor at her feet a moment later.

There would be other weapons, but not one he could grab as easily as that.

"You really think you can kill me, in cold blood?"

"Isn't that what you're planning to do to me?" Colette tossed back. "What, because I'm a woman, you don't think I can?"

"I think you're softer than you want to believe."

Colette pulled the trigger without a moment's hesitation. The bullet slammed into the wall a few inches over his right shoulder, and she grinned at the way he'd flinched.

"Crazy bitch," he spat at her, all that practiced cool gone in an instant.

"Well, now I think you're starting to get the picture," Colette said, because she was a crazy bitch.

The cabin's door slammed open.

There, standing silhouetted by the light, was a figure she'd recognize anywhere.

"Well, Alice Monroe," Colette drawled. "So nice of you to join us."

CHAPTER FORTY-SEVEN

Alice

Bluebird Pond, Montana
1936

Alice sagged against the doorjamb, hardly able to hear Colette over the pounding in her ears.

She'd thought they were going to find the woman dead, having arrived only a few minutes too late to save her. Alice should have known better.

This was Colette Durand—of course she was the one holding the shotgun.

She always had been.

Millie made a soft sound of surprise as she caught sight of the tableau in front of them.

Alice could hardly look at Finn Benson, the man at the heart of this all. She knew that if Colette had meant to kill him with that shot, he'd be dead. But some vicious, vengeful part of Alice wished Colette hadn't deliberately missed.

The thought shocked her into moving forward. Never in her life had she wished someone dead—besides herself in her worst moments. Even in that darkness, her rage had never turned outward.

Seeing Finn Benson on the business end of Colette's wicked shotgun, though, soothed some part of her she hadn't realized was still bleeding.

"Um." Millie slid forward toward Colette. She was probably

the only one in the room who didn't want to see a bullet take Finn Benson out of this world and into the next. "Shall we put the weapons down?"

"No, I don't think I will," Colette said calmly.

"All right," Millie drawled out. "Perhaps we should let Mr. Benson leave, then?"

"Perhaps Mr. Benson should stay exactly where he is," Colette countered, and though Millie made some distressed sound at Colette's stubbornness, Alice couldn't help but find her amusing. She remembered in that moment she had liked Colette, once upon a time. Had wanted to be her friend, had even wanted to be more like her.

"What are you doing here?" Colette asked.

"We think your father found evidence of Finn skimming from the Company," Alice said, and Colette absorbed that with interest.

"That would make sense," she said after a moment. "It must be fairly damning evidence, as well, for this snake to slither all the way out here just to make sure I don't find it."

"That's not—" Finn protested.

"I would be quiet if I were you," Sidney suggested. "Unless asked a direct question."

"And if I were—" This time Finn was cut off by Sidney's fist colliding with his jaw.

It wasn't as hard as it could have been, even Alice could tell that. But Finn howled anyway. Such a weak man when he couldn't hide behind a weapon or a smile.

Sidney glanced at Colette. "Apologies. Carry on."

Colette raised a brow and though she didn't smile, Alice could tell she'd enjoyed the show.

"Well, now I know what you killed my father over, I have no

further questions for you," Colette said, staring down Finn now. "Which means I have no more use for you."

"You keep saying you're going to kill me, and yet . . . ," Finn said, but there were beads of sweat at his temples now as his eyes flicked between all of them. He thought they would come to his rescue, but he'd picked the wrong crowd for that.

Alice shifted her attention to Colette, who had her shotgun up and her attention on the eyesight.

Finn might not be able to read her, but Alice could. She was about two heartbeats away from lodging a bullet through his skull.

She didn't blame the woman for wanting to kill Benson, Alice would be right behind her in that particular line. But when Alice thought about Colette it wasn't just her shotgun that came to mind. It was the careful way she'd helped those miners pick out the perfect book from their little library. It was the way she'd teased Alice for her fears and then also gently pushed her to overcome them. It was Colette reading anything and everything within sight.

The way that had made her so understanding of anyone she came across, no matter how different their circumstances were from her own.

Alice wanted Finn Benson dead, but she didn't want Colette Durand to be his executioner.

Not when it was like this, with Finn outnumbered. In cold blood.

From what Alice knew, Colette had yet to take a life in her hunt for vengeance.

Colette wouldn't be able to come back from this. Even if she couldn't see that past her rage right now.

Alice had maybe a half a second to stop her. Colette wouldn't listen to reason right now, she wouldn't even pause if Alice called her name.

So Alice did the only thing she could think of.

She stepped in front of the gun.

In front of Finn Benson.

Colette was an excellent gunwoman. Her finger came off the trigger.

"The proof is here, Colette," Alice pleaded. "I know you want justice. I know you *deserve* justice. But you don't have to kill him to get it."

"I've lived here for ten years now," Colette said, sounding like she wanted to be convinced. "I've never seen any evidence, and I've searched through my father's papers for it."

Alice didn't know why she cared so much about saving Colette from herself. She'd only known her for about two months more than ten years ago—and the woman had lied to her the whole time.

But maybe this wasn't about saving Colette.

Maybe this was about saving herself.

It hadn't just been guilt that had eaten Alice alive over the past decade, it had been anger, as well. Anger that they hadn't made Finn pay for Mac's death. Anger that power and money could cover up the murder. Anger that she'd watched her neighbors in Montana crushed beneath the boot of greed for far too long.

It had been a helpless kind of anger, one that had soured and rotted away inside her chest. Colette simply shooting Finn now would be a hollow justice. No one would know what he'd done, he wouldn't even have to live a single day in fear or grief.

Alice didn't want to save Finn Benson.

She just wanted him to actually pay for what he'd done.

"You don't want to shoot him," Alice said.

"Actually, I very much do," Colette drawled.

Alice shook her head. "You don't want to kill him."

"Wrong again."

"No," Alice said, dredging up a conversation from over a decade ago and praying it would work. "'The croaking raven doth bellow for revenge.'"

The last time she'd said those words, Mac lay dead not ten feet from her, the victim of this woman's quest for revenge. The last time she'd said those words they preceded Colette losing years of her life hunted like an animal.

Colette made a sound in her throat, and shook her head.

"'The croaking raven doth bellow for revenge,'" Alice said, refusing to back down.

Millie inhaled like she was about to ask something and Sidney jerked his head to cut her off.

Come on, Alice urged sotto voce. Because they both knew how this ended. In blood and death and an outcome that would leave the darkest mark on all their souls.

What good was reading all those Shakespeare plays if they couldn't help mere mortals like themselves avoid the human flaws and foibles that the Bard wrote about with such aptitude?

There was a reason *Hamlet* was a tragedy and not a hero's tale.

She tried one more time. "'The croaking raven doth bellow for revenge.'"

Colette's eyes flicked to hers. "Yet what did revenge do for that particular cast of characters?"

Alice exhaled and said quietly, "Nothing good."

While Colette didn't lower the shotgun, Alice could see she'd gotten through to her, even if they were the only two people in the room who realized that.

"He has chased you to the furthest corners of Montana," Alice said.

"And Nevada," Colette added.

Alice tipped her head. "Whatever Claude uncovered must be damning. You know that."

"That only matters if we can find it," Colette pointed out. "There's nothing here."

"It must be papers, right?" Alice asked. "Or perhaps a photograph?"

Millie cleared her throat and stepped forward, grimacing a little in apology when they all swiveled to her in unison. "Sorry. I'm sorry. But I can't help noticing that this room is filled with paper."

It took Alice a second, and judging by the way Colette's brows snapped together it took her one, too.

But then it hit.

The books.

Colette rocked back on her heels and looked back at Finn, who resolutely stared out the window, offering them nothing but his profile like he was making sure he didn't give anything away with his expression.

There was a moment of silence and then . . . Colette started laughing.

She laughed and laughed and laughed until her cheeks were wet with tears. When she caught her breath she swooped Alice into a one-arm hug and pressed a kiss on top of her head. "Of course. It's the books."

"Millie did figure it out," Alice felt inclined to mention.

"Oh, it's quite all right," Millie said, pink cheeked. "Happy to help."

Colette exhaled and it was shaky. She gestured toward Sidney. "You strike me as someone who knows his way around a weapon."

"Yes, ma'am," Sidney said, somehow both serious and teasing. A specialty of his.

"Come on then," Colette said, motioning for him to take the shotgun. "Do you hate him enough to kill him if need be?"

"I hate him enough to shoot him in the kneecaps if he makes one wrong move," Sidney said easily.

"Or if he makes one wrong move toward Alice?" Colette asked.

Alice's face went warm.

"Then I'll kill him," Sidney said without missing a beat.

"Good man," Colette said, slapping Sidney on the back before handing over her precious shotgun. Alice guessed she had at least a pistol—if not an entire arsenal—hidden on her person. But still, it showed some sign of trust.

Millie was already surveying the shelves that contained hundreds of books. "Divide and conquer?"

"No," Alice said, tugging Colette's attention back to her. "I'm sorry, this is indelicate. But your father, was he alive when you found him?"

"Barely," Colette said.

"Was he able to speak?" Alice asked. "Was he able to say anything at all?"

Colette shook her head, but then her brows pinched together.

"What?" Alice pressed.

"Just. . . . It was nothing," Colette said, but she sounded hesitant.

"It might be everything," Alice said.

"He quoted the Bard," Colette said, that pinch of confusion still evident in her face. "It was something he'd said to me earlier that week, to make sure I knew he was happy with our little life."

Earlier in the week before he died, when he might have already known he was in danger.

"And," Colette said, her voice gaining power, "he reminded me of it right before the gunmen showed up."

Alice's eyes flew to the bookshelf. "What was the quote?"

"'And this our life, exempt from public haunt, finds tongues in trees, books in the running brooks, sermons in stones and good in everything. I would not change it.'"

"*As You Like It*," Alice murmured, and Millie quickly crossed to the shelves.

It only took her a few moments to pull a slim volume out. She waved it in the air, and Colette snatched it from her.

She flipped through the pages. Back and forth, a few times before she shook her head. "There's nothing here."

Alice deflated. She had been so certain—

"Um." It was Millie. "Sorry again. I'm sorry. I do feel like I keep stepping into a moment but . . ." She turned to Colette. "Do you by chance have a sharp knife?"

Colette's brows went up, but she easily produced one and held it hilt out toward Millie.

"Wonderful," Millie said, taking it. She then held her hand out for the book, which Colette passed back over with some reluctance. "Now, I grew up in a household with six boy cousins and had almost no possessions of my own of which to speak. But when I did get any possessions of my own of which to speak, all six of them tried to take the thing or look at the thing or break the thing with their grubby little hands."

As she spoke she flipped *As You Like It* open to the very back page. Then she dug the tip of the knife into the paper protecting the binding. She squinted one eye and stuck out her tongue as she performed her surgery.

"I had to get creative with my hiding places," she continued. "And if all of us here got to the answer of the books so quickly, your father probably knew they were a vulnerability of his. His enemies might check his entire library looking for what he didn't want them to find. So, he got creative, too."

Finn made some kind of distressed sound behind them, but none of the women spared him a glance as Millie gently pried the thick inner paper away from the cover.

"Voilà," Millie said with a flourish, and they all bent forward.

And there were two yellowing pieces of paper nestled into the tight space Millie had revealed.

Colette made a gutted sound. "All this time."

Alice reached out for them, since Colette didn't seem able to move at the moment.

It took her a second to understand what was on the pages, but when she realized what she was looking at she gasped. "Oh you terrible, arrogant man. You could have had anything you wanted, and yet you weren't satisfied with that."

Colette shifted back to life and grabbed the papers herself.

The first was a balance sheet signed by the president of the Anaconda Copper Mining Company and Finn Benson.

The second was a doctored balance sheet for the same transaction, less five thousand dollars.

It had been signed by Finn Benson and their old friend Mr. Rutherford.

"Five thousand dollars," Millie breathed out, her eyes flying to Finn. "That's quite bold even for a greedy bastard."

"This was one transaction," Alice said. "How much did you steal from them?"

Finn just stared, jaw clenched. But the beads of sweat at his temple had begun to slide down his face.

"Goodbye, campaign money," Alice said. "Goodbye, political career."

She didn't say what they all must be thinking. The Company had killed over far less than this.

Alice started to turn back to Colette, but the screech of wood against wood stopped her.

Something hard slammed into her from behind, and in the next moment she was pulled up against Finn Benson's chest, the tip of his dagger digging into her throat.

"Goddamn it," Colette swore, and Sidney echoed her. When he did, she whirled on him. "You said you'd do it."

Sidney had gone pale. He'd probably thought he could pull the trigger if necessary. But had he held a gun since he'd been in the trenches?

He'd hesitated, and that was why Alice had fallen in love with him in the first place.

"Here's what we're going to do. You are going to hand me those papers." Finn nodded toward Colette. "Then everyone will go sit with your backs to the far wall until I leave."

Finn likely saw the calculation in Colette's expression as clearly as Alice did. "And just in case you think about getting too clever for your own good, I'll be taking Miss Monroe with me."

"No," Sidney spat out.

"You can collect her wherever I feel like dumping her off," Finn said. "No one needs to get hurt if you all comply. And we can go on with our lives just like we've been doing for the past ten years."

"Shoot him, Sidney," Colette said.

Alice pressed her lips together, because she knew Sidney wouldn't risk it.

But they couldn't simply hand over the proof that Claude Durand had paid for with his life.

That, in all truthfulness, Colette Durand had paid for with hers.

"The papers, if you please," Finn said, his voice dripping with confidence once more despite the fact that his palms were sweaty against her skin.

"Give him the papers, Colette," Sidney said, his voice harsh. "They're not worth dying over."

Maybe they weren't, but they were worth quite a bit for the people Finn Benson would continue to harm if he were given even more power. It would hurt the Nathaniels of the world, and Dawn who loved Agatha Christie, and all the men Alice had met while living on the rails for a few glorious weeks.

It would hurt the Claude Durands of the world, who only wanted to help their fellow workers so they could maintain their dignity while earning a wage to support their families.

It would hurt the Colettes of the world, who watched their loved ones work themselves to death with nothing to show for it but more debt.

There was nothing special about Finn Benson. He was the embodiment of greed and soulless ambition, while being completely devoid of a moral compass. If he died today, a dozen more just like him would take his place.

But that was the kind of helplessness the bosses wanted them to feel. They wanted the masses to simply accept that evil was inevitable instead of something that could be stopped if the rest of them all joined together to do so.

There were four people in the cabin who wanted to make sure those papers got into the right hands.

There was only one Finn Benson.

Alice met Sidney's eyes, because it wasn't Colette who needed convincing. "Yes, actually, they are."

CHAPTER FORTY-EIGHT

Millie

Bluebird Pond, Montana
1936

Until the past six months, Millie had never appreciated how much being raised along with six boy cousins had given her skills she'd never dreamed she'd need.

The right hook that had started all this had simply been the tip of the iceberg.

She'd been particularly impressed with the back cover trick, as well.

But here was something she'd learned above all else.

When you were standing in a line awaiting punishment for some wrongdoing, the best option was for everyone to take off running and hope tempers cooled by suppertime.

Only, the person who took off last usually got their neck scruffed simply because they had the poor luck to be slower on the uptake than the rest.

Millie had never been as fast as the boys, so she'd learned how to be smarter than them.

Some of them stood stock-still, waiting for the perfect moment. But then the second they moved, everyone knew to scatter, and more often than not that boy ended up getting his mouth washed with soap.

Millie had noticed, though, that if she shifted her weight, if she wiped at her nose, if she folded her arms in chagrin that the moment she was about to flee trouble would become less obvious.

The second Finn Benson lunged for Alice, Millie shifted so that she was on the very outside of his vision. He could still keep track of her, but his focus had to be on Sidney and Colette.

While Finn went on about some sort of instructions, Millie assessed the situation.

Alice wouldn't be able to do much. If she breathed wrong, the knife would slice through her throat.

Colette looked like she was making the calculation about how much Alice's life was really worth, and it didn't seem like she was going to come down on the side of letting Finn Benson escape.

Sidney had the gun, but none of the leverage, which made him both the best and worst option.

That left Millie to get them out of this situation.

So, she started to shift, a bit restlessly. She was the odd man out of the tableau and no one was really paying her attention. They were all locked on to the papers in Colette's hands. But Finn hadn't made it this far to be the type to lose track of one of his hostages.

His eyes did flick her way a few times, but the conversation between the other three kept drawing his attention back to the center of the room. By the time Millie took an actual half step, he didn't even glance over.

Now, all she needed was a plan.

She chewed on her lip as she surveyed the space.

It was filled with books, and it wasn't just the shelves. They spilled over into every space, stacked up on side tables and on chairs and even on the floor.

She thought about that magical moment of realization from Alice.

The books.

It all came back to the books.

Millie eyed the ones near her, looking for something suitably hefty.

She spotted the perfect tome, right behind Finn. She shifted again. No one looked at her.

"Give him the papers, Colette," Sidney said, his expression tight with rage and fear. If Millie had ever had a doubt about his feelings toward Alice Monroe they were put to rest in that moment. "They're not worth dying over."

"Yes, actually, they are." It wasn't Colette who said that, but Alice, looking like she was about to burn the world down to rid it of injustice.

Millie took another small step so that she was completely out of Finn's line of sight. Colette tensed but thankfully didn't glance in her direction. Smart woman.

Distract him, Millie tried to silently telegraph into Colette's mind.

"Why were you so kind to me?" Colette asked, in such a vulnerable voice that even Millie—who had been focused on inching toward the book—stopped to stare. Colette stood there in her weatherworn clothes and weatherworn body, hair cropped short and not an ounce of softness to her.

Except for that one question.

The contrast came like a punch to the gut.

This was a distraction, but maybe part of her really wanted to know the answer.

"After my father died," Colette continued, and Millie snapped out of her daze. Colette was opening herself up to cruelty from this man, so Millie had to make it count. "Did you act like you loved me simply to get into my house?"

Finn laughed meanly, as everyone in the room could have

guessed he would. "Of course. You think anyone would actually want *you*?"

With Finn's attention locked so intently on Colette—men like him would never pass up an opportunity to see how their lashes landed—Millie was able to catch Sidney's eyes.

She inclined her head toward the book at the top of the stack just behind Finn.

Sidney blinked slowly. He understood.

That was good, because Millie wasn't certain how she was going to ensure Alice made it through Finn getting whacked in the head with her throat unscathed.

Apparently, she didn't need to worry about that with two people who hadn't spoken barely at all over the past decade.

Finn continued to spew hateful insults at Colette who bore them with a grace and fortitude Millie would have admired had she taken the time to listen closely to any of it.

She watched Sidney's finger tap against the shotgun a few times, and then pause.

And then three beats. Pause.

Millie reached out for the book, gripping the sides.

Two beats. Pause.

She inhaled as quietly as possible.

One beat.

All hell broke loose.

Colette let out a bloodcurdling scream. Finn startled, but thankfully didn't jerk back.

Alice used the moment of shock to bring her arm up to his elbow and push the knife away from her throat. Not enough to escape but enough to buy Millie breathing room.

And she took it.

In one smooth movement, she brought the heavy tome up and swung the thing directly at Finn's head.

He never saw it coming. It crashed into his skull, taking him neatly to the floor.

Sidney crossed the room in three quick strides and jammed the shotgun against Finn's throat.

The gesture was intimidating, but ultimately useless, considering Finn had been knocked out cold.

Millie spun to find Alice blotting at the thin trickle of blood on her neck.

"I'm fine," she said before anyone could ask, and then beamed at them all. "I knew we could do it."

"What did you hit him with?" Colette asked, still carefully clutching the papers that would likely be this man's death sentence.

When Colette laughed until she was doubled over, Millie glanced down at the title.

The Complete Works of William Shakespeare

CHAPTER FORTY-NINE

Millie

Missoula, Montana
1937

Katherine Kellock's letter was short and sweet.

Millie read it over and over as she sat on the porch of the house she was beginning to think of as home. It was almost impossible to believe there was a time when she'd thought of Montana as a foreign land. She now rented a room with an older widow whose sons had moved out of state to try to make their fortunes. Mrs. Wheatley liked the company and had a bit of a mischievous streak, so they got on swimmingly. Eventually, Millie hoped to save up enough to buy her own little cottage on one of the quiet, tree-lined streets she so enjoyed walking down, but she was in no rush to leave.

The porch swing dipped, and Millie looked up, startled. She'd been so absorbed in her thoughts she hadn't noticed Flo even with her heavily pregnant belly.

"I don't want to hear it," Flo said, dramatic as always.

Millie laughed. "Don't want to hear what?"

"How I am positively glowing," Flo said. "How I am currently the most beautiful I have ever been in my life."

"I am guessing you got your fair share of that from Professor Lyon this morning," Millie said, amused at her friend's woes. Flo had not had a quiet pregnancy up to this point and Millie didn't expect anything to change in the final few months.

"And the baker, and Miss Darcy, and, quite ridiculously, the sheriff who barely got the compliment out before turning beet red and running, yes running, in the opposite direction," Flo said. "Now, you have distracted me long enough. What did the message say?"

Flo, of course, had been there to watch Millie receive the letter from Katherine that afternoon.

There was no point in hiding it—she handed the paper over.

> *Millie, congratulations on the upcoming publication of the Montana guide. You've exceeded all my expectations from when I sent you there, even if I truly believe I've never gotten the full story. (One day, off the record over drinks, perhaps you'll finally tell me. When I come visit?)*
>
> *The first twenty pages of the* Women of Montana *series you sent were riveting, and I believe it will be a perfect addition for our broader folklore and life program that we've launched underneath the Federal Writers' Project umbrella. Think of it as the American Guide Series without the train and hotel details. Please send along the manuscript attn: me when it's ready.*

"I knew she'd love it," Flo declared with a wide grin.

Millie ducked her head. "It means more typing."

It was a silly complaint, but she *had* written the project out longhand and she wasn't looking forward to transferring it into print as she knew she would have to.

But she also couldn't actually pretend to be grumpy about it. She was going to be published.

Millie had devoted as much time as necessary to the Montana guide to make it a success, but when she had free minutes or hours or days over the past year or so, she focused on the project that Sofia Rossi had inspired her to work on.

Don't make this pretty, Sofia had said of her life. The way she'd survived so much hardship. *Don't make all of this look dignified.*

Of course, Millie had been swept up in the strength of the women she'd met in Montana. But she had kept Sofia's plea in her mind the whole time.

"About that . . . ," Flo said, shifting to reveal a box that she'd put on the swing beside her.

"What's this?" Millie asked, taking it with shaking hands.

"That's what opening it's for, peaches."

Millie pulled the top off the box.

And there, nestled safely inside, was a stack of pages.

Her book. All typed up.

She pressed her lips together when they wobbled with some silly emotion.

"It wasn't just me," Flo said, before Millie could offer up her gratitude. "Oscar and Tommy chipped in, too. Sidney told me to tell you he thought about helping, which is monumental for him."

Millie laughed even as her eyes welled. "You didn't know she'd say yes."

"We did," Flo promised.

Millie touched her fingertip to the title page where her name was printed and then quickly swiped at a tear before it could fall and smear the ink. Once upon a time it would have been inconceivable to her that she had people in her life who would do such a thing, just to make her happy.

It hadn't just started and ended with these pages, either. Oscar had talked her through weaving the stories she'd collected together with a narrative to make the book more compelling. Sidney had written letters to the reservations vouching for her, so that she'd been able to report on *all* the women who lived in Montana. Professor Lyon had curated journals, letters, and other research material on the history of the pioneers and settlers who were the grandmothers of these women.

Flo had held her hand through it all. And she'd shared her own story, a vulnerability Millie hadn't taken for granted.

It's nothing special, Flo had said at the time, and then spoke of a girl who had a simple life and big dreams, a face too pretty for the rough-and-tumble West, a fear of never leaving and then having to choose to stay.

Maybe it wasn't unique, but that had been part of the point of the project. So many women could relate to Flo's story, they just hadn't seen it told enough to look at those feelings and say, *Ah, maybe I'm not alone in this world.*

Millie gently set the box aside so as not to disturb any of the pages. And then she reached over to hug Flo.

"We're squishing the baby," Flo teased, but she didn't pull back until Millie did.

Millie placed her hand on Flo's belly with the ease of close friendship and believed for the first time in her life, *Ah, maybe I'm not alone in this world.*

One week later, Millie got another delivery from the postman. The package was heavy enough that she had no doubt what it was.

"It's here," she cried out as she stepped into the Federal Writers' Project office.

Chairs scraped against the floor as everyone gathered around Millie's desk.

"Open it," Flo said, as if Millie wasn't already tugging at the neat wrapping.

"Patience."

"I am being patient," Flo said, her hands joining Millie's and doing more harm than good.

"All right, all right," Millie said, swatting her away. "You're ruining the moment."

"I could never ruin any moment," Flo scoffed, but she pulled back, leaning into Professor Lyon as she did. "I have impeccable timing and grace."

"Well, I can't argue with that." Unimpeded, Millie ripped the last bits of paper off, revealing a thick book with a deep blue cover.

MONTANA was stamped across it in gold, running above THE AMERICAN GUIDE SERIES.

Flo squealed and Millie thought maybe she did, too.

"Whiskey," Oscar said.

"Speech," Flo cried out, and though there were only just the four of them so it might seem a little silly, Millie agreed the occasion called for it.

She stood, and they all held their glasses at the ready. "I was given a choice before coming here: Montana or a pink slip. And I almost chose the latter.

"But I believed in what we were doing. America is nothing without its people—*all* of its people. This might be a guidebook, but at its heart, it's an introduction. An introduction to the Salish women who sell jewelry up near Flathead Lake; to the Chinese druggist in Lolo whose father built the railroads that became the lifeblood of the state but then never received any acknowledgment for doing so; to the widowed mother of four who wakes up before dawn every day to milk her starving cow. To the heiress in Missoula who used that wealth to try to make people's burdens a little easier with a boxcar and a dream. We are a country of beautiful and flawed and strong and cowardly and happy and fearful and loving people. And we will always be stronger together."

Millie took a deep breath, for a moment thrown back in time a year ago when these people had all been strangers to her. Strangers who viewed her as the enemy. *Montana or a pink slip.*

She blinked and she was in the present again.

"No matter what, we," Millie said, gesturing around to the group, "will always be stronger together."

"To our ragtag little staff," Flo cried out.

"To Millie," Professor Lyon said.

Millie blushed and shook her head. She raised her glass and the rest followed her lead.

"To Montana."

CHAPTER FIFTY

Colette

Bluebird Pond, Montana
1939

Colette dove into the water, only stopping when her fingers brushed the smooth stones on the bottom. She snagged one pebble and then pushed toward the surface.

The sun greeted her like an old friend—or she like it—because the thing had hardly been around the past few months.

But it was full into summer now and Colette would enjoy the weather while she could. She would especially enjoy the clear roads on the way to town.

There had been a time there, right after Finn Benson had come for his little visit three years ago, that Colette had thought she'd leave Condon and her little cabin in the woods.

But she'd made this her home. She'd made a life worth fighting for.

Sometimes, she pulled out that battered and tattered *O Pioneers!* and found that line that had stuck with her so much when all she'd had was her shotgun and a vendetta.

"We have no house, no place, no people of our own."

At the time, she'd thought she might die without finding any of them.

Now she had a house.

She had a place.

She had people of her own.

Colette no longer *needed* to hide in the woods, but that meant she could admit she still wanted to.

She did expand her library. Not the one in the cabin but one she'd started for the people of Condon when she'd realized they hadn't had one of their own. Now, she traveled by truck to all the nearby towns, just as Alice Monroe had done fifteen years ago.

That kept her busy enough.

She also still kept in touch with Roarke O'Callahan.

The hired gun who'd unmasked Finn Benson for her had never given up his crusade against union spies, and he spent the bulk of his time ferreting them out of organizations all over the country. He also simply helped those local chapters when he could, and through their letters Colette began to realize that she knew a lot more about organizing than she'd thought. She was able to dole out advice, both through him and when he put her in touch with local leaders, some of whom she still wrote to long after Roarke left their towns.

She wondered if he would go fight if the winds of this European war ever shifted in their direction. Colette hoped not. She'd grown fond of her would-be killer turned ally.

Roarke wasn't her only pen pal, either. She kept up a steady correspondence with Alice Monroe and Millie Lang—and even saw Millie on the rare occasions Colette traveled down to the city. Millie rented a quaint house on the outskirts of town and invited Colette over to drink wine in her candlelit garden beneath the stars on the first night of spring.

Colette already had an order placed for Millie's book.

And of course there was the mutt, who whined at her from the beach now, chin on his paws, tail wagging.

He'd come sniffing around her cabin a few years back and had decided it was a nice enough place to spend the winter. He hadn't minded the elk and deer she'd routinely brought home either.

She'd been glad to give him a roof and a soft blanket as a bed. When he'd shown up, she could count each of his ribs and he had the hungry eyes she'd seen in the mirror a time or two when she'd been on the run.

Now his coat was thick and shiny and his grin was a near constant. He followed a half step behind her everywhere she went, except into the water, which he hated. So when she went swimming he cried and begged her to come back to land.

This time, she acquiesced because she had an appointment to keep anyway. It was *not* because he turned those strange hazel eyes on her and whimpered.

She was much stronger than that.

Colette dressed quickly and plaited her hair into a simple braid.

The mutt watched her, this time from the bed.

She'd already loaded the books that morning, so all she had to do was whistle for her boy to hop into the passenger seat and then she was off, down her terribly rutted road—a blessing more than a curse because it kept idle visitors away.

At first, she'd been stubborn about going to everyone's homes to hand out the books, as she wasn't a doctor making house calls. She realized it was easier in the long run, though, and most people usually had either small gifts or gossip to offer, both of which she gladly took.

She had a special book at the ready today, and so she altered her usual route to head toward the launderer. The father enjoyed westerns, as so many men out here did—at least the ones who read. The mother asked for children's books for her whole brood, ages perpetually newborn to twelve, and Colette liked to think she delivered more often than not.

This wasn't any other day, though.

A special package had come in meant for Mary, the twelve-year-old who greeted Colette every visit with a request to tell her about an adventure she'd experienced.

As she drove through town, Colette waved to a few people who were trying to get her to stop, pretending not to hear them as she drove on.

Mary, of course, was waiting on the porch, and when she caught sight of Colette's truck, she dashed out to the sidewalk.

"Hello, Miss Durand," Mary said, bouncing on her toes. Her mother must have scolded her into politeness.

"The book came," Colette said, quickly putting Mary out of her misery early. Colette reached behind her to the top of her box, where she'd stashed *Bright Island* by Mabel L. Robinson. It starred Thankful Curtis, a young girl who loved nothing more than sailing with her grandfather. She was pressured into trying to fit what a proper girl should be, but continued to dream about the ocean in the meantime.

"*It's a man's world, Thankful, and they like to think they lead us,*" the mother tells the main character at one point. "*You would never be a good follower.*"

Colette knew she'd been lucky with Papa. He'd never wanted her to be anyone but who she was.

She worried no one in Mary's life wanted her to be exactly who she was.

But at least with this book, Mary could feel less alone about it all.

Loneliness. Colette had been thinking a lot about that all morning, and yet the rest of the day was filled with people. After Mary ran off to read her new book, Colette passed some time with Mary's mother. And then their neighbor, and then the grocer and his heavily pregnant wife. Then the baker and the gas station attendant and the schoolteacher.

By the time Colette was back on the road heading toward her cabin, she was exhausted. The mutt snoozed in the passenger seat and the sun had begun to dip down in the sky. It was July, though, so it would be a good hour before night crept in.

Impulsively, Colette took the turnoff right before her cabin, the one that led to a meadow. A few minutes later, she stood over a small stone marking. She'd kept the engraving simple.

Claude Durand. Father. Friend of the workers.

Papa wasn't buried there, but she'd wanted somewhere close by where she could sit and talk with him if needed.

She wondered what he would think about this little life of hers and she guessed the reaction would be mixed. He would have been tickled pink about her bookmobile. But he wouldn't have liked the years she'd given over to vengeance. He would have liked even less the woman she'd been when she'd held a shotgun on Finn Benson and been ready to pull the trigger.

He might have had a fiery temper, but he would never have wanted her to kill, not for him.

Colette owed Alice quite a bit for stopping her in that moment.

Papa would be quite pleased to hear about Finn's fate. It had been extremely satisfying to hand over evidence of the man's crimes to the authorities. He'd been dragged through the mud in the papers, his reputation destroyed as his victims came out of the woodwork. About six months after he'd been revealed for the snake he was, he'd been found in a roadside motel, dead of apparent suicide.

Colette didn't care who'd actually pulled the trigger, he was dead and she'd drunk a few glasses of a nice whiskey she'd been saving for the occasion that night.

Revenge might not be the answer, but sometimes it felt really, really good anyway.

The mutt barked from the passenger seat, and Colette laughed. She was late feeding him dinner.

That night, Colette stood among her books, a collection that had been much diminished by sharing them with others. These were what had created a community for her, a place, a home, full of *her people*.

It had been the books.

Colette had been called many things in life. A daughter, a friend, a gambler, a rogue, a bitch, a librarian, a wandering spirit, a recluse, a neighbor, a bad influence, a godsend.

But she thought about the name Alice Monroe had given to Papa.

Shanachie.

A keeper of stories, a teller of tales.

And she thought, out of all of them, that might be the one that fit her best.

CHAPTER FIFTY-ONE

Alice

Missoula, Montana
1936

There was a book waiting for Alice on her porch swing the morning after the events at Colette Durand's cabin.

Little Women by Louisa May Alcott.

Of course Alice had read it a dozen times and had owned at least three copies, but she smiled until her cheeks hurt at the sight of it.

She bit her lip as she nervously flipped open to the title page.

Go, and for once in your life, live it.

They were the exact words Sidney had uttered to her on her porch more than ten years prior when she'd been all but begging him to tell her to stay home, stay safe, stay protected.

With trembling fingers, she found the page he wanted her to. This time, he hadn't marked it with a piece of paper, but with a photograph.

Alice inhaled sharply. Her own face stared back at her.

Sidney had taken it when they'd sat on the roof of the Boxcar Library, and she'd never been happier before or after than she had been on that day.

She carefully removed the picture, making sure not to leave any oily fingerprints on the glossy paper. Her eyes searched for an underlined passage, one she knew it would be before she even found the words.

"Lovely weather so far; I don't know how long it will last, but I'm not afraid of storms, for I'm learning how to sail my ship."

The passage slammed into her, knocking the air out of her lungs.

She didn't know how long she stared at it, but the evening had grown cold around her by the time she forced herself to move.

Before she could overthink it, she dug in her bag for the copy of *The Invisible Man*.

Back when she'd picked it out for Sidney, she'd left the title page blank.

Now she paused, her pen a centimeter above the page. This was a man she hardly knew, or at least that was what reason told her. They had flirted at the edges of love one fall ten years ago and then hadn't really spoken since—beyond the books he'd left for her.

They were both different people now.

But maybe . . . maybe they hadn't been ready for each other back then. Maybe they had both been too scared, him of his demons, her of the world.

Would they fit, these new versions of themselves, as much as their younger selves seemed to?

Alice didn't know. But she would like to find out.

She scrawled the words, and then read them once, twice, three times as the ink dried. He would remember them, just as she had remembered his.

I'm sorry, Mr. Walker, I suppose I have to go.

Leaving wasn't as easy this time.

Alice was now the town's only librarian, and beyond that she had other duties she had to take care of before she up and disappeared.

She recruited Christine Darcy to take over for her at the

library. The woman was all nerves and excitement and Alice couldn't believe there was a time that she'd looked at her with envy simply because Sidney Walker had paid her attention.

If anything, it revealed that Sidney had a type he preferred and that was a woman who loved books.

Christine was practically in raptures at the end of every day. The past five or so years hadn't been easy for her or her sister, both living on the meager savings their parents had left them. They'd made it through the Depression, but Christine's cheeks had gone hollow around the second year and they had yet to fill out again.

It was the perfect fit.

Millie Lang threw Alice a goodbye party, which almost everyone in town attended.

Except for Sidney Walker.

"Take care of Missoula," Alice told Millie, who'd settled into the city as if it had been made for her.

"Take care of that big, wide world," Millie said, pulling Alice into a hug. "And write to us."

That night she stood over her half-packed suitcase and nearly cried in terror, as she realized she didn't know how not to be scared.

Almost blindly, she reached for *Little Women* and the photograph she kept tucked there. She slid to the floor holding both, staring at the face she barely knew as her own and telling herself she was *that* person, the one who'd hopped on a boxcar and headed west.

It was just that she'd buried her under guilt and fear and grief.

But her rebellion hadn't been what killed Mac, it hadn't even been what killed her father. Finn Benson had been responsible for both deaths, and he was going to pay for that.

Justice would be served, and maybe for the first time in forever, Alice would actually be able to breathe again.

Alice ran her fingers over the words Sidney had underlined for her. *Lovely weather* . . . until the sun splashed shadows on her bedroom floor.

It was time to go. *I'm sorry, Mr. Walker* . . .

She nodded once, decisive.

That was all it took to get her derriere off the floor.

Alice finished packing—she had a train to catch after all—and the last thing she threw on top was *Little Women*, the photograph of herself tucked neatly inside.

For courage, when she needed it.

She said goodbye to her housekeeper, who would, naturally, be keeping up the house in her absence, and then stepped outside.

Her suitcase hit the porch, her fingers numb.

Sidney Walker stood there, leaning against a battered old Ford that she'd never seen him drive before.

"What?" she asked, and realized he couldn't possibly hear her. She grabbed the handle of her suitcase and hurried toward him. "What are you doing?"

"Who doesn't need a cocaptain?" Sidney asked.

Alice swallowed, her eyes sliding to the Ford. "What happened to the mountain climber?"

"I sold it," Sidney said easily, as if it hadn't been the one reminder he had of his mother. That he had traded his past for a potential future didn't elude her. "The difference should last us, oh, about a year."

"I have funds," Alice murmured, but she couldn't deny the warmth that sparked in her chest.

"Cocaptains pay their own way," Sidney said.

She looked away. "You can't be my protector."

That wouldn't work, not now when she was finally, finally breaking out of her self-imposed cage for good.

"When have I ever?" Sidney asked, a question that had been backed up by years of evidence. He had *never* tried to protect her, not in the way that her father had. Not in the way that was stifling to who she was. Sidney had wanted to keep her safe, but he'd done so by standing next to her instead of locking her away.

"Well, if you can keep up," she teased. "I suppose you can come along."

He opened the passenger door for her. The automobile was a far cry from what the Sidney Walker of her childhood memories would have driven. But it fit him now.

"I can at least try," he said before stashing her suitcase in the back. When he climbed in behind the wheel he glanced her way. "Looks like we have lovely weather."

Alice grinned. "Sure does. But I wouldn't mind a good storm."

War came, as it always seemed to.

By the time it did, they'd spent five years on the road, often following routes suggested by the various American Guide Series that Alice had grown incredibly fond of.

They learned where to camp to save their sometimes paltry funds, and where to pick up quick work as needed. Six months in, Alice had instructed her attorney to sell her house, and that had carried them for a long time.

Out of all the things she could crave on the road, Alice missed books the most.

Sidney, of course, saw it in her expression every time they passed a display at the druggist or a library or a bookstore. And even though he kept her in dime-store novels and made sure she had at least one book with her at all times, it often felt like a bandage over a bullet hole.

Alice was used to being able to match a novel to her mood, to the setting, to the *moment*. She pointed that out to Sidney, reminding him how he'd always been able to find the perfect passages to convey exactly what he'd wanted to when that was the only way they'd spoken.

"Should we go home?" he'd ask then.

"Not yet," she'd say. Time and again.

The road became addicting, just as the train had. They left fights and bills and bad days in their rearview mirror. They drove toward the rising sun, toward fresh starts and easy mornings.

Life wasn't perfect. They were two humans with flaws and preferences that didn't match up perfectly, essentially living out of a battered Ford that gave up the ghost at the most inopportune times.

But, God, were they happy.

That was something else Alice had learned. Life didn't have to be all rainbows for it to be *good*.

They listened to the radio play-by-play of Pearl Harbor while sitting around a table with an old married couple in Kansas. The pair had graciously allowed them to sleep in their barn for the night, and had come banging on the doors on that fateful Sunday.

Sidney was old enough at that point that Alice didn't fear any kind of draft.

But she knew the man she loved well.

"I want to go over," he told her while they watched the stars come out a week after the attack. They were in Louisiana; it was cold, but they had blankets and neither ever seemed to mind the chill.

"With your camera," Alice said. He nodded.

And so Sidney left. After five years of living out of each other's pockets, Alice felt his departure like a limb being sawed off.

He wrote. He was in danger and he wasn't, not quite on the front lines, but just enough to have bombs falling on his head more often than not.

Alice tried not to think about it.

She volunteered for the Victory Book Campaign, a project that focused on collecting novels for the troops run by some of the best librarians Alice had ever met. When the VBC turned into bigger and better things, she found herself, in all places, in Atlantic City. The army had turned the hotels into war hospitals, and the whole of it was dubbed Camp Boardwalk by the nurses and soldiers alike.

It turned out that men recuperating from horrific war wounds loved books.

When she rolled her little trolley through the aisles of beds, she couldn't help but be reminded of Montana and the rough men who had also needed the relief offered in the pages of novels.

What a universal experience that was—finding comfort in stories.

Once upon a time, I needed books, too, Sidney had confessed so long ago.

Alice wasn't afraid to admit that she saw Sidney in so many of the young men who circulated through those hospital beds. She imagined him waking up at the tail end of that war they once thought would end all wars, whole and healthy in a hospital just like the one she visited every day and learning that everyone he called a brother-in-arms had been killed.

Sometimes she sat on the beach and cried for the boy she'd never really known, the one who didn't have ghosts in his eyes. And then she thanked God for the one who did. The one who'd volunteered to march into hell to capture the faces behind the numbers, the humans behind the headlines and propaganda.

He collected and told their stories just as he had when he'd been working on the American Guide Series; and just as he had while they traveled the country for five years meeting every type of person imaginable.

Just as she knew he always would.

The war ended, as they mostly did. With unimaginable death and suffering.

But there was hope, too.

So many strides had been made in those four years through necessity and desperation. Just like there had been during the Great Depression.

Sidney came home.

It was strange, this pattern of theirs. To be so close, so far, so close, so far. But Alice never felt like she'd fallen out of step with him.

She met him in New York City when he was finally discharged. He came off the ship with his camera box slung over one shoulder, looking fifteen years older than the last time she'd seen him.

And yet, he still looked like that man who'd driven her to Lolo. He still looked like that man who'd opened his scars on the roof of a boxcar in the middle of Montana. He still looked like the man who'd driven her from San Diego to San Antonio to St. Petersburg and then back again, making her laugh every mile along the way.

It took him a while to laugh.

Months, she thought.

And then she handed him a letter from Millie. Her youngest daughter was made for the stage, just like her aunt Flo, and had a personality as dramatic to fit. Millie had written them a long list of things that had set the girl off into tantrum—including that she couldn't touch a hot stove or go find a bison to pet.

Sidney had snorted in amusement and it had been like a dam cracking, crumbling and then giving way.

By the time his laughter had turned into sobs, Alice was already cradling him in her arms.

"It's time to go home," she said.

MONTANA WAS GOING to kill Alice Monroe.

She'd heard that all her life, so many times that she'd started to believe it.

Alice just hadn't realized it would be three days after her ninety-third birthday.

A blizzard raged outside, one so familiar to so many she'd lived through before.

The doctor wouldn't make it, though. And truthfully, Alice didn't mind.

She'd accomplished what she'd wanted to, and she was ready to join Sidney once more.

He had passed two years earlier and even though they had grown used to separation throughout their relationship, she was eager to see his face again.

They had never had children, something that Alice had felt a pang or two over during their years. But their lives had been so filled with love, she'd hardly noticed anything missing. Millie, who had married Oscar Dalton three years after she'd arrived in Missoula, provided them with four girls to shower with affection. Those daughters then brought home a total of ten grandchildren, all as fiery and smart and clever as their grandmother.

Alice considered them family and knew they would miss her. But that was part of life, as well. Grief, mourning, and then moving on.

It had taken her too many years to realize that last part was as important as the first two. She hoped her chosen family wouldn't be as stubborn as she had been.

She coughed, and wished it had been something other than pneumonia that would help her shuck off these mortal coils because it was such a pain in the ass. But it wouldn't last much longer.

With her last bit of strength, Alice pushed herself out of bed and crossed the room at an awkward, slow shuffle. The bookcase was stocked full, as were each of the ones in their home.

Alice squinted in the low light to find what she was looking for, and then pulled the novel out from its neighbors.

She slowly made her way toward one of the two armchairs they kept in front of the bedroom's fireplace. Sitting provoked another coughing fit that came replete with blood. But she simply dabbed it away with her handkerchief.

The book was heavy in her lap, and she opened it to the title page. There, tucked inside, was a photograph of her, on top of her Boxcar Library.

That first time she'd ever been brave.

Gently, she lifted it away from the words that it covered.

Go, and for once in your life, live it.

The wind howled outside, the snow piling up, the hail beating against the window.

Montana might kill Alice Monroe.

But, because it loved her and she it, Montana hadn't taken her before she'd gone and lived a life.

AUTHOR'S NOTE

One thing you should know is that my dad loves forts. When he came to visit me while I was staying in Montana for a few months, of course I had to take him to Fort Missoula. As fate would have it, that is where the real Lumberman's Library boxcar now lives.

I only scratched the surface of its history that day, but I did tuck the knowledge of existence away like I do with so many nuggets I find at such places.

The library continued to whisper to me over the past several years, its voice so insistent that I knew the story of it deserved its own novel. What better way to explore this brand-new (to me) era than through the lens of the power of books?

Alice Monroe—as well as all the main characters in *The Boxcar Librarian*—is fictionalized. But she was inspired by Missoula County librarian Ruth Worden, one of the two women who came up with the idea for the Lumberman's Library. (The other one is not named in any of the sources, unfortunately.) Ruth hailed from one of Missoula's founding families, and thus had a lot of pull with some of the businessmen in the area. She approached a man named Kenneth Ross, of the Anaconda Copper Mining Company, and proposed setting up a collection of books for the workers. Ross, the man in charge of the lumberjack camps, was skeptical, not because he didn't think the men wanted to read but because he worried it would sow discontent within the miners and lumberjacks. But he couldn't say no to Ruth.

Here, I took some liberties with the story and condensed the creation of the Boxcar Library; in reality, the books were first housed in a hotel for a year. At the end of that span, the books had been checked out over four thousand times. The Anaconda Copper Mining Company was thrilled that the workers were using it as an example of how good they had it, and so Mr. Ross built Ruth her boxcar. The shelves were stocked with donated books, novels from the Missoula Library, and purchases made with the $400 worth of subscriptions the lumberjacks and miners threw in themselves.

Thankfully, pictures and blueprints of the original design of the car still exist, so I tried to portray it to the best of my abilities. The Boxcar Library was wildly popular, hitting a peak of nearly ten thousand visitors in one year with nearly eight thousand books checked out in that time.

Alice's eventful journey was completely fictionalized on my part, but she is a nod to the plethora of women librarians who helped the Lumberman's Library succeed over the years.

For a while, I've also been drawn to the Federal One Project, the Works Progress Administration's answer for what to do to help the desperate creative professionals during the Great Depression. The fact that the government funded the arts to such a degree is still astounding to me even after having written a book about it. I had always known about the post office murals, but once I dove into the program for writers, and the American Guide Series, I knew it would complement the story of the Lumberman's Library perfectly. During one of the hardest stretches of time in our country's history, people recognized the need for books, art, theater, and music. And that resulted in a series that allowed people all over the country to connect with each other in ways they'd never done before.

Those involved with the American Guide Series describe it

as one of the first times that America really embraced its own identity at the same time it was discovering it.

While far from perfect—it was, of course, a product of its time—the series made an effort to include all the voices that made up America. I strongly believe one of the best ways to fight fascism, hatred, and bigotry is by getting to know the people who are scapegoated, who are different than us, who live in a different state, pray to a different God, eat different food, listen to different music, love different books. And so did the people who created and worked on the guides.

While the mystery that Millie gets caught up in is fictionalized, I tried to portray the real work that went into the guides to the best of my ability. I did, however, condense the time it would have actually taken Millie's crew to complete the guide to better serve the pacing and plot of a novel.

Apart from the fact that I found the guides ideologically appealing, I also loved them because many of the offices *were* run by fabulous, brilliant women. And it wasn't just in Western states, but all over the country. One such woman was Miss Dorris May Westall, who was brought into the Maine offices to rescue a staff that had been paralyzed by the incompetence of her male predecessor. Westall had little experience—she'd worked for her hometown newspaper and had been fired for smoking. But she whipped the staff into shape, and Maine managed to turn its guidebook in long before most of the others. While their stories are different, she served as an inspiration for Millie's character. As did one female guide writer who had been deemed a "wildcat" by the male supervisor in her Michigan office—likely because she'd turned him down—and had been transferred to Washington, where she'd then thrived.

Of course, I have to mention that the indomitable Katherine Kellock was a real person and contributed greatly to the creation of the guides. After some Red Scare gossip about her husband cut short her work as a field office supervisor, she was given a position in Washington, DC, where her talents could be appreciated. She certainly did rub her colleagues the wrong way sometimes, but she was brilliant, exacting, and devoted to bringing the guides to life.

While I drew inspiration from stories coming from all over the country, for the creation of the guide in this novel I relied on the actual source material itself.

Writers and editors in the Montana field offices actually did have to traverse high-altitude passes in mountain-climbing cars, wade through rivers, eat dinners at the dude ranches that dotted the western part of the state, hike and swim, and—most important—talk to the people who lived in that slice of the world. They had to learn their stories.

For more fun, interesting, and colorful details, please read *The Dream and the Deal* by Jerre Mangione, who worked for the Writers' Project.

Finally, Colette.

I didn't set out to write a book about unions, but the more I read about Montana I knew I couldn't *not.* While the mystery surrounding Colette, and the death of her father, was fictionalized, plenty of the sentiments and events were real. The Speculator Mine disaster occurred in June 1917 and killed 168 workers, kicking off a strike where the metalworkers were eventually betrayed by the other unions that joined them. Spies paid by the Anaconda Copper Mining Company infiltrated union meetings and offices across the state, Pinkerton agents were called in to wage an unofficial war on the miners, the Company had the state in a copper collar, and violence was thick on the ground. Frank Little, a prominent organizer, was pulled from his boardinghouse, beaten, dragged behind a car, and then hanged from a railroad trestle. A note pinned to his body read "first and last warning." It was from that environment that Colette's story was born.

With all three arcs, I wanted to think deeply about community, how our basic survival as humans is because of those strong bonds we build. How in the cold we can share each other's heat, in the dark we can stand back-to-back to fight off a lion, in the light our celebrations can turn even more joyous with the food each of us brings to the table. Books, trains, unions, rivers—they connect us and make us strong. And they hopefully connected the women in this book to you.

As always, while I've tried to portray everything accurately to the best of my ability, I'm sure I've made a mistake or two. They are mine alone, and I hope you can grant me some grace while still enjoying the story. Thank you for letting me tell it.

ACKNOWLEDGMENTS

This book wouldn't exist without Fort Missoula and its preservation work on the Lumberman's Library car. I'm so grateful for the fort, as well as anyone who puts effort into saving these slices of history. A special shout-out goes to Professor Robert G. Dundas and his piece "An Account of ACM's Rolling Reading Room," which offered the most comprehensive description of the library.

Writing about the American Guide Series and the Works Progress Administration in general wouldn't have been possible without *The Dream and the Deal* by Jerre Mangione. Sometimes it's the small details that can bring life to an era, and Mangione, who was part of the Writers' Project, helped me be able to do that with Millie.

Other resources that proved indispensable in writing this novel: *Montana: A History of Two Centuries* by Michael P. Malone, Richard B. Roeder, and William L. Lang; *Daily Life in the United States, 1920–1940: How Americans Lived Through the "Roaring Twenties" and the Great Depression* by David E. Kyvig; and *Fight Like Hell: The Untold History of American Labor* by Kim Kelly.

And, of course, the Montana American Guide itself, along with every person who worked on it.

Many thanks to my editor, the brilliant Tessa Woodward, and the entire William Morrow team.

Thank you to my incredible agent, Abby Saul, who, among so many other things, helped me sharpen Colette's journey.

To my family and friends, who are so amazingly generous with their support and love, thank you, I couldn't do it without you.

And to my readers, whether you've been here awhile or this is the first book of mine you've picked up, I appreciate you so much. Thank you.

ABOUT THE AUTHOR

BRIANNA LABUSKES is a *USA Today*, *Wall Street Journal*, and *Washington Post* bestselling author of historical fiction and psychological thrillers. Her books have been translated into more than a dozen languages. She lives in Pennsylvania with her puppy, Jinx.

Explore more captivating historical fiction
from *USA Today* bestselling author

BRIANNA LABUSKES

"*The Lost Book of Bonn* sheds light on the the youth groups of Germany who fought back against Hitler and highlights the Aryan women who protested the arrest of their Jewish husbands. Equal parts riveting and heart-wrenching, this is a story of fighting back, of doing what's right. Brianna Labuskes has done it again with another powerful book about books that historical fiction fans will adore."

—MADELINE MARTIN
New York Times bestselling author of
The Keeper of Hidden Books

"In her excellent debut novel, Brianna Labuskes writes lovingly of the power of books, libraries, and friendship to sustain us in difficult times, while also offering a stark, unmistakably relevant warning about the dangers of censorship. Fans of historical fiction featuring courageous women will savor *The Librarian of Burned Books*."

—JENNIFER CHIAVERINI,
author of *Resistance Women*